D0475476

THIS IS NO LONGER THE PROPERTY
OF THE SEATTLE PUBLIC LIBRARY.

PRAISE FOR MATTHEW FITZSIMMONS

PRAISE FOR *DEBRIS LINE*

"Matthew FitzSimmons writes the kind of thrillers I love to read: smart, character-driven, and brimming with creative action sequences. If you're not yet a fan of FitzSimmons's Gibson Vaughn series, strap in, because you soon will be. *Debris Line* is tense, twisty, and always ten steps ahead. Don't miss it."

—Chris Holm, Anthony Award–winning author of *The Killing Kind*

"Matt FitzSimmons continues his amazing literary feat of creating an ensemble cast of troubled heroes and shooting them through page-turning thrillers with his latest, *Debris Line*, continuing the fast-paced adventures of Gibson Vaughn and his crew as they battle to stay alive and find some measure of justice in this unforgiving world. The Gibson Vaughn series is on its way to being a classic franchise of thriller fiction, with a unique voice and an unusual approach that keep the stories as appealing as they are entertaining. Highly recommended."

—James Grady, author of *Six Days of the Condor*

"*Debris Line* . . . doesn't waste a word or miss a twist. It's always smart, always entertaining, and populated top to bottom with fascinating and unforgettable characters."

—Lou Berney, author of *November Road*

PRAISE FOR *COLD HARBOR*

"In FitzSimmons's action-packed third Gibson Vaughn thriller . . . fans of deep, dark government conspiracies will keep turning the pages to see how it all turns out."

—*Publishers Weekly*

"*Cold Harbor* interweaves two classic American tropes: the solitary prisoner, imprisoned for who knows what; and the American loner, determined to rectify the injustices perpetrated on him. It's a page-turner that keeps the reader wondering—and looking forward to Gibson Vaughn #4."

—Criminal Element

"There are so many layers and twists to *Cold Harbor* . . . FitzSimmons masterfully fits together the myriad pieces of Gibson Vaughn's past like a high-quality Springbok puzzle."

—*Crimespree Magazine*

PRAISE FOR *POISONFEATHER*

An Amazon Best Book of the Month: Mystery, Thriller & Suspense Category

"FitzSimmons's complicated hero leaps off the page with intensity and good intentions, while a byzantine plot hums along, ensnaring characters into a tightening web of greed, betrayal, and violent death."

—*Publishers Weekly*

"[FitzSimmons] has knocked it out of the park, as they say. The characters' layers are being peeled back further and further, allowing readers to really root for the good guys! FitzSimmons has put together a great plot that doesn't let you rest for even a minute."

—*Suspense Magazine*

PRAISE FOR *THE SHORT DROP*

"FitzSimmons has come up with a doozy of a sociopath."
—*Washington Post*

"This live-wire debut begins with a promising lead in the long-ago disappearance of the vice president's daughter, then doubles down with tangled conspiracies, duplicitous politicians, and a disgraced hacker hankering for redemption . . . Hang on and enjoy the ride."
—*People*

"Writing with swift efficiency, FitzSimmons shows why the stakes are high, the heroes suitably tarnished, and the bad guys a pleasure to foil . . ."
—*Kirkus Reviews*

"With a complex plot, layered on top of unexpected emotional depth, *The Short Drop* is a wonderful surprise on every level . . . This is much more than a solid debut, it's proof that FitzSimmons has what it takes . . ."
—Amazon.com, An Amazon Best Book of December 2015

"Beyond exceptional. Matthew FitzSimmons is the real deal."
—Andrew Peterson, author of the bestselling Nathan McBride series

"*The Short Drop* is an adrenaline-fueled thriller that has it all—political intrigue, murder, and suspense. Matthew FitzSimmons weaves a clever plot and deftly leads the reader on a rapid ride to an explosive end."
—Robert Dugoni, bestselling author of *My Sister's Grave*

ORIGAMI MAN

ALSO BY
MATTHEW FITZSIMMONS

The Short Drop
Poisonfeather
Cold Harbor
Debris Line

ORIGAMI MAN

THE **GIBSON VAUGHN** SERIES

MATTHEW FITZSIMMONS

THOMAS & MERCER

This is a work of fiction. Names, characters, organizations, places, events, and incidents are either products of the author's imagination or are used fictitiously. Any resemblance to actual persons, living or dead, or actual events is purely coincidental.

Text copyright © 2020 by Planetarium Station, Inc.
All rights reserved.

No part of this book may be reproduced, or stored in a retrieval system, or transmitted in any form or by any means, electronic, mechanical, photocopying, recording, or otherwise, without express written permission of the publisher.

Published by Thomas & Mercer, Seattle

www.apub.com

Amazon, the Amazon logo, and Thomas & Mercer are trademarks of Amazon.com, Inc., or its affiliates.

ISBN-13: 9781542091985 (hardcover)
ISBN-10: 1542091985 (hardcover)
ISBN-13: 9781542091992 (paperback)
ISBN-10: 1542091993 (paperback)

Cover design by Rex Bonomelli

Printed in the United States of America

First edition

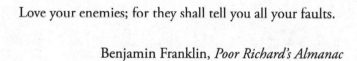

Love your enemies; for they shall tell you all your faults.

Benjamin Franklin, *Poor Richard's Almanac*

CHAPTER ONE

Tinsley's chest rose and fell. He breathed. In and out. Otherwise, he lay dormant.

Waiting.

Listening.

Five weeks now, but he felt no impatience. Time meant nothing to him. It never had. He had never known boredom. He blinked and a week passed. Blinked and a month passed. What people failed to understand was that anyone could be a time traveler. All that was required was the will to have no connection to the present.

There were toads that lived in the desert. These toads hibernated most of the year, metabolisms slowing to viscous night. Slumbering in underground burrows until the rains returned. Only then did they emerge to feed and to mate and to die.

Tinsley was waiting for the rain.

———————

A sound reached him.

He stirred, eyes flickering open.

Through the drywall, he heard the voices of men. A security team performing a final sweep to confirm that the house was empty, secure. They were professional, experienced, thorough, but they would not find him. They wouldn't think to look for him here. They were looking for men, so only looked where men would hide. Tinsley looked like a man, but he was something else. He was a desert toad.

The voices faded.

It wouldn't be long now. A day. Two at the most. The master of the house was returning. Tinsley would be waiting to greet him.

He blinked. Time passed.

Children's voices—thirteen, nine, seven. Girl, boy, girl. Excited to be back. The renovations to the villa had lasted nearly a year, and they oohed and aahed over the changes and additions. Their mother issued instructions to the household staff, directing traffic and overseeing the distribution of luggage and sundries.

Then came the voice that Tinsley was waiting to hear. He'd studied recordings—political speeches, interviews—so that he would recognize it. Even through a wall, there was no mistaking the voice of Georgi Ivov—deep and resonant and commanding.

The rain had come at last.

Tinsley passed the day listening. Learning the family's patterns. Their footfalls. The children came and went. Scampering out to the new pool or down to the beach. Three women arrived to play tennis with the lady of the house. She had been born near Varna, and her friends had missed her while the construction kept her away.

Ivov disappeared into his office all afternoon. Dinner began without him as he was detained on a business call. He arrived midway, offering apologies. His wife accepted graciously, but Tinsley could hear years of ingrained frustration etched into her voice. This was an old issue between them, but she would not let it ruin the first day of summer vacation. The children chattered excitedly. They had been taken out of school early, a perk of their father's power and position, and would be here until August. The possibilities were endless.

After dinner, the head of security arrived to review Ivov's travel plans for the following morning. The household staff retired for the evening. Tinsley listened to the children play until bedtime. The hollow pock of a Ping-Pong ball. The solid clack of pool balls. The man and woman shared a bottle of wine on the veranda, talking and laughing, the first day of summer vacation casting a hazy spell over the evening. It was well after midnight before they headed upstairs to bed.

The house grew still. Tinsley waited until all he heard was the white noise of the air-conditioning. Then he waited another hour. Sometimes the girl, thirteen, had trouble sleeping and would get up to watch television. At the family's home in Sofia, the security detail didn't use the motion detectors at night because she kept setting them off. Tinsley counted on the guards to make the same mistake here. After all, the exterior of the house was a fortress.

Tinsley detached the IV and withdrew the feeding tube that snaked down his nose to his stomach. He removed the catheter. Using a keyhole saw, he worked slowly and methodically to cut a passageway through the drywall. Given the size of the house, he didn't expect to be overheard but paused frequently to listen for any indication that he'd been discovered.

He eased out the slab of drywall and propped it against the wall. Cool air rushed in to greet him. Tinsley released the harness supporting the weight of his body and fell forward out of the wall cavity and into the pantry. He dropped to his knees and rested there, curled into a ball. After so much disuse, his arms and legs felt heavy and weak. Gradually, he increased his breathing and moved into child's pose, his atrophied calves and back screaming in protest. His body was a long way from twenty-five. Things that had once been easy now took more care and attention. From there, he moved through a sequence of yoga poses, stretching carefully, blood flowing again through his unused limbs as his body emerged from its slumber.

When he felt steady, Tinsley stood and removed his equipment from the wall. He packed up his medical waste and scrubbed down the drywall cocoon. Finally, he slipped on his Kevlar, laced up his boots, and armed himself. Then he let himself into the kitchen and went up the stairs to meet the master of the house, curious how many of the children would die before Georgi Ivov gave up what Tinsley had come for.

CHAPTER TWO

Behind the wheel of the idling vehicle, Tinsley slipped his hand under his blood-soaked shirt and probed the improvised field dressing. Pain lanced up and down his spine, out along his arms, and up to the crown of his head like forked lightning searching for ground. Not that it showed on his face, which remained as placid as a midnight lake. Only his eyes moved, distant and unfocused, as if he'd been asked to calculate a large sum in his head. In this case, the equation he was trying to solve was for x, if x were his chances of living divided by blood loss multiplied by time. At least two ribs were cracked, and though he couldn't reach it, he could feel where the small-caliber bullet had exited his back. Through and through. A stroke of luck. And his breathing remained easy and regular. The bullet hadn't pierced his lung. Fortunate again. But he would still require a doctor, and sooner rather than later.

The nearest competent physician who could handle this kind of injury lived in a small town near Istanbul. Six hours south of Varna by car. Tinsley did not relish the drive, but he required a real doctor, not some black-market pharmacist dispensing rudimentary care to those who couldn't afford to answer a hospital's questions. His man in Istanbul was a disgraced cardiac surgeon who no longer had a license to practice medicine in Turkey. Tinsley had used his services in the past and found him to be discreet and reliable. And very, very expensive. He transferred the money to the good doctor's account and reviewed the events of the past few hours.

Everything back at the villa had gone according to plan, up to and including his exit. Unusual for an operation with so many moving parts. But that was why Tinsley had gone to such lengths to talk to Ivov with his family present. Men were always more compliant around their wives and children. Even men who didn't love their wives and hardly knew their children. They all shared the hardwired belief that sacrificing themselves to protect their family was the grandest gesture a man could make. Tinsley didn't understand that at all. Wives were fungible, and it didn't take but five minutes to make another child. Or so he had read.

It wasn't until later at the exchange that Tinsley realized he'd been betrayed by his client. Payment had been contingent on securing the thumb drive that Ivov had given up to spare his family. Tinsley's client had insisted on a face-to-face meeting. Not an unreasonable request under the circumstances. Tinsley had set the terms of the meet, and the client had acquiesced to all of his conditions—time, place, the public venue. Perhaps that was why Tinsley had been slow to spot the double cross. It was unlike him, but his reflexes and instincts had been dulled by his five-week confinement. He hadn't even worn his Kevlar.

In retrospect, he recognized that had been the client's intention from the start. He had been manipulated, expertly, and that offended Tinsley far more than the chest wound that was currently killing him. He was accustomed to arranging the pieces on the board, not to being one of them. Fortunately, the client had meant to take him alive. Tinsley had seen it in the old man's eyes. That had been a mistake. If the client had simply come to kill him, then Tinsley would be dead. As it happened, luck more than anything had saved his life. When the opportunity presented itself, he would apply those hard-earned lessons.

But before that, the client would have to die. Not out of any misguided need for revenge. Vengeance was a human impulse that Tinsley would never understand no matter how many times he killed in its name. No, his client would die because loose ends clouded Tinsley's mind like a swarm of gnats on an otherwise peaceful night. Because the client would almost certainly not stop now. And because it set a bad precedent.

But to do so, he would need to learn the client's identity. Tinsley had been hired anonymously, and it would take work to pierce that veil of secrecy. Luckily, their mutual anonymity put the client at a similar disadvantage.

Tinsley turned the flash drive between his fingers. Georgi Ivov had traded it for his children's lives . . . but only under extraordinary duress. How valuable must it be? Valuable enough for the client to turn on Tinsley once he'd seen it. Perhaps it also contained a clue as to the old man's identity. But first things first—not bleeding to death.

The doctor and his assistant were standing by when Tinsley arrived in Istanbul. His car bumped to a stop against an ancient wall like a rudderless ship drifting into dock. It jarred Tinsley momentarily back to full consciousness. For the last few hours, he'd operated on bleary-eyed autopilot, chin dropping to his chest again and again. He had no memory of how he'd gotten here. Nor had he noticed until now that blood had seeped through his bandage and pooled in the seat around his thighs. The doctor helped Tinsley out of the car and down a flight of narrow stone stairs into the basement while the assistant hid the car in a barn at the back of the property.

There was no mistaking the basement for a real doctor's office, but neither was it a putrid cesspit. A single bare bulb hung above a rusted examination table. The air smelled reassuringly of industrial disinfectant. No brackish viscera clogged the drain at the center of the cracked cement floor, and the bodies of the last three customers weren't stacked like cordwood in the corner. The kind of place to make a man optimistic about his chances.

Tinsley had bled in worse places.

The doctor eased him onto the table and cut away his clothes with a pair of medical shears.

"No anesthetic," Tinsley said, even as he felt himself tipping into unconsciousness.

When he came around, Tinsley was alone. Apart from the clean bandages patching his chest and back, he lay naked on the examination table, his ruined clothes in a bloody pile on the floor. Tinsley took a deep breath, which told him the doctor had heeded his instruction. The pain was profound, but he had no time to indulge it now. Tinsley ushered it to a room at the back of his mind and locked the door behind it. Forcing himself into a sitting position, he waited for the gray static filling his head to dissipate.

From the static emerged a face. The face of the old man who had shot Tinsley after he'd slipped into his trap. It was an unsettling face. Blank, empty, worn—a cold void. Much like his own. The face of a professional killer. Tinsley had questions for the apparition, but before he could ask, the static dissolved, and the face along with it.

A gunshot snapped Tinsley from his fugue. From upstairs, the unmistakable sounds of a man begging for his life drifted down through the floorboards. Judging by the pitch and timbre of the good doctor's voice, he would not keep Tinsley's whereabouts secret for long. Tinsley had paid well, but money didn't spend where the dead went.

How had the client found him? There were only two possibilities. Either Tinsley had been trailed here from Varna, or else the client knew where he would go. If it were the latter, then the client had penetrated Tinsley's network and learned his identity. In the short term, it was irrelevant, but before plotting his next move, Tinsley would need to know exactly how compromised he really was. Assuming he escaped this basement alive. It had only one entrance and exit—the exterior stairs from the back of the house. No windows. No useable crawl spaces. Only the shadows offered any refuge.

A second gunshot told him that the good doctor's interrogation had come to an end. They would be coming now. Boots on the floor above moved toward the back of the house. He couldn't tell the number—more than one, less than a battalion—but, being naked and unarmed, he knew it was too many.

With all of his equipment stowed in the trunk of the car, Tinsley took an inventory of the basement for something to improve his odds. A row of scalpels set on a counter caught his eyes. They would be little use against a gun. Unless . . . unless . . . there was bait. In a small refrigerator, he found three bags of red-blood-cell concentrate. That gave him an idea: not bait, exactly, but chum for the sharks gliding toward him. It was almost certainly a bad idea, but since it was the only one he had, he saw no alternative but to forge ahead.

Selecting a number-twenty-two scalpel—the largest available—he climbed back onto the examination table and cut slits into the bags of blood. He held each to his neck and slopped the contents down his chest. The more of an unholy mess it made, the better. Satisfied with the effect, he tossed the empty bags into a dark corner and traced a finger across his throat.

The human neck was packed with sensitive anatomy—carotid arteries, vertebrae, larynx. So m ny ways to kill or cripple. The brain was protected by the skull, the heart by the rib cage, but this essential passage connecting head to heart was unprotected and vulnerable. It was a foolish design that had always fascinated him. Perhaps that was why he had chosen to hang so many of his targets over the years. But this would be the first time he'd taken a blade to his own.

With a steady hand, he ran the scalpel from one ear to the other. Not deep, no more than a millimeter. Enough to let his blood flow freely, mixing with the concentrate, to create a grisly tableau. Tinsley hoped it would pass a cursory examination. Then, feeling with his fingers, Tinsley located the sternocleidomastoid, a long band of muscle running from the base of the skull down to the thorax. If cut laterally, he would lose control of his head, which would loll helplessly to one side. Tinsley knew the look well. Instead, he sunk the scalpel in vertically. It went in easily, nestling between the fibers of muscle, which held the scalpel snugly in place. Then he lay back on the table, eyes open and unblinking, and let himself go dormant.

He didn't have long to wait.

Two men came down the stairs, single file, good spacing. They both wore khaki cargo pants and heavy boots—civilian versions of the combat gear preferred by ex-military. Tinsley assumed they also wore ballistic vests under their black tactical jackets. The lead man swept the right side of the room with a shotgun while the second man covered the left with a pistol.

That only two men had come downstairs told Tinsley the client hadn't trailed him from Varna. Otherwise, he would have been facing a battalion. Especially after the havoc Tinsley had caused at the exchange. No, this meant that the client had been forced to spread thin his resources. Covering as many bases as possible, hoping to get lucky. All of Tinsley's safe houses in the region were no doubt receiving similar visits. He regretted that. It had taken a decade to build a reliable network, and now he would have to start again from scratch.

The two men finished their sweep. Satisfied that they were alone, they converged on the examination table. Tinsley's scene setting must have been convincing because they lowered their weapons and looked at each other in disgust.

"Требаный трус," the Shotgun said to the Pistol.

Tinsley knew no language that expressed contempt so perfectly as Russian. The men did not think highly of Tinsley's apparent suicide. The one who appeared to be in charge holstered his pistol and radioed that the target had cut his own throat to avoid being taken alive. A gruff voice told them to search the basement for the thumb drive.

"It's a butcher shop down here. Come help us," the Pistol said irritably in Russian.

"I'm covering upstairs," the voice on the radio replied.

That meant they hadn't found the car yet. Tinsley wasn't about to allow that to happen.

The Pistol lit a cigarette and shined his flashlight on the bloody rags that had been Tinsley's clothes while his partner knelt and searched the pockets one at a time. Tinsley thought this would be a fine opportunity to make introductions. Sitting up sharply, he threw his legs over the side of the table. Covered in blood and spontaneously returning from the dead, he must have made a gruesome sight. The Pistol stared at him dumbly.

"Help me," Tinsley whispered in Russian.

Reflexively, the man leaned forward to hear what he had said. A mistake.

Tinsley plucked the scalpel from his neck and slashed the man's jugular. Not deeply enough to kill him. The blade wasn't long enough, and Tinsley didn't have the proper leverage, but people always over-reacted to wounds to their necks. The man's mouth fell open, and his cigarette dangled forgotten from his bottom lip. Tinsley had his undivided attention now. The man stumbled back, one hand trying to form a seal over the wound, the other fumbling for his pistol. Tinsley hopped off the table, set his feet, and drove the scalpel through the man's eye and into the vulnerable terrain beyond. As the man fell, Tinsley drew the pistol from the holster on the man's hip and turned on his partner, who was only now bringing the shotgun to bear. Tinsley put the barrel to the man's forehead and suggested he stop. The man agreed and set the shotgun down on the floor.

"Your clothes. Give them to me," Tinsley said in Russian but adopting a soothing, calm English accent. One that insisted that, despite all evidence to the contrary, here stood a reasonable man. For inexplicable reasons, people trusted an English accent, doing what it asked even when they knew it had to be a lie. Of course, when a blood-soaked man with a slit throat held a gun to your head, what other choice did you have but to believe the unbelievable?

"Don't kill me."

"If I meant to kill you, you would be dead."

That wasn't technically true; he just didn't want to get blood on the man's clothes.

Tinsley started the engine, killed it again, took the key from the ignition, and sat behind the wheel, contemplating where to go. As it turned out, the Russians hadn't been Russian at all but Georgians hired out of Tbilisi. They had no more idea who had hired them than did Tinsley. Before the third man died, he had confirmed Tinsley's suspicions—his network was compromised. The Georgians had been assigned to stake out the good doctor in case Tinsley came for medical help. The other elements of their team were covering Tinsley's known associates around Istanbul. More contractors had no doubt been deployed elsewhere in the region. Tinsley needed to go to ground. But where? Where could he go that they wouldn't be waiting for him? Had they compromised only his European network, or was he vulnerable worldwide?

There was no way to know. Wise to assume the worst. And the worst didn't leave him much in the way of options. He would need time to recuperate and time to strategize. Most of all, he needed technical help accessing and analyzing the contents of the thumb drive hidden inside the steering column of the car. He needed to go somewhere his client would never think to look. The last place on earth that anyone would expect him to turn for help.

A name came into his mind. If Tinsley had known how to laugh, he surely would have. On its face, the idea was absurd. Insane. But for that very reason, he knew that it was perfect. Tinsley slid the key back in the ignition and started the engine. He had a long journey ahead of him.

CHAPTER THREE

The two yachts drifted side by side in international waters some thirteen nautical miles off the easternmost tip of Grand Cayman Island. Beneath an obsidian sky, the lights from the *Topaz* and *Al Kidamm* glittered off the Caribbean Sea like a long-lost city emerging from the depths. The *Topaz* was a gorgeous vessel, sleek and luxuriously appointed. The epitome of excess, or so Gibson Vaughn had thought when they'd set sail from George Town a few hours earlier. *Al Kidamm* helped put things back in perspective: there was money, and then there was capital-*M* Money.

Sequestered belowdecks, Gibson could only gawk through a porthole as the *Topaz* tied up to the larger boat. Four hundred feet from stem to stern, *Al Kidamm* made the *Topaz* look like a dinghy. A floating cathedral to obscene wealth—helicopter pad, two swimming pools, a gym, a climate-controlled garden, a movie theater, and twenty staterooms. A conservative estimate placed *Al Kidamm*'s daily operating expenses at north of a hundred thousand dollars. The owner, a Qatari businessman by the name of Mohd Fakhroo, had a net worth of nine billion, so Gibson didn't imagine he was sweating the receipts.

"I mean, what does one person need with that much boat?" Gibson asked.

"When a man sells his soul, he wants people to see he got a good price for it," Hendricks replied. "Now quit fooling around over there, we got work to do."

Gibson rolled his chair over to Hendricks and the bank of monitors displaying live feeds of the *Topaz* and *Al Kidamm*. Hendricks tapped a finger on a central monitor—up on deck, the festivities were getting underway. At the top of the gangway, Mohd Fakhroo waited to welcome his guests aboard *Al Kidamm*. Hendricks zoomed in to get a better look at him. At only thirty-two, Fakhroo was a year younger than Gibson. A fact Gibson found profoundly depressing. He was well aware of all the ways that his life had gone off track without having it rubbed in his face by a younger man who literally had it all. "Lay off," Gibson wanted to tell the universe, "I get it already." The universe, for its part, seemed to be of the opinion that Gibson was a very slow learner.

Not a physically imposing man, Fakhroo nonetheless stood out against the nighttime sky. Even on Hendricks's monitor, he crackled with energy and good health. He wore a tailored suit of exquisite blackness that absorbed all light like a sartorial black hole. Light that he seemed to store like a battery and project out through his capped teeth. They gleamed incandescently when he smiled, as he did now at the sight of Mirella Lima—Gibson's and Hendricks's client—striding up the gangway, Fakhroo's arms flung wide in greeting. The two billionaires embraced warmly, Lima's retinue coming to an awkward halt behind her on the gangway.

At the head of Lima's retinue was Jenn Charles, who led the physical security team while George Abe stood back discreetly among the lawyers and advisers. Lima cupped Fakhroo's face affectionately in one hand as he laughed in delight. If you ignored the armed guards and squinted just right, you might confuse them for close friends. Gibson didn't, and neither did Mirella Lima, which was why the team was here. Theoretically, this summit was mere formality. A signing ceremony. The culmination of a yearlong negotiation that would add a zero to

Fakhroo's net worth and more than double Mirella Lima's considerable fortune. But that didn't mean that she trusted her new business partner.

A Brazilian industrialist, Mirella Lima was CEO and chairperson of Lima Ltda. Founded by her great-grandfather Abelardo Lima, the company had fallen on hard times due to the mismanagement by her father, a notorious drunk and playboy. But since taking over twenty-six years ago, Mirella had rebuilt Lima Ltda. into an international powerhouse. She had a reputation as a shrewd, hard-nosed businesswoman.

Mirella Lima had her own security, but due to the off-the-books nature of this meeting, she had opted to contract with an outside team unconnected to Lima Ltda. Her scheme to leverage the widening crisis in Venezuela was not, precisely speaking, legal. Not precisely illegal either. Hence the clandestine meeting in international waters, far from prying journalistic eyes or legal oversight. *Quasilegal*, as George tried diplomatically to paint it. The term made Gibson roll his eyes. When he died, they could put that on his tombstone: "Gibson Vaughn— Quasilegal." However, quasilegal was also why Mirella Lima had hired Abe Consulting Group. Not that they dared call themselves by the old name. ACG hadn't existed officially since the dark days of the Suzanne Lombard investigation, but in private, it lived on as a rallying cry among the four international fugitives.

Their first year on the run, they'd bounced from one place to another. Portugal for six months. West Africa. Argentina. Until the prospect of work had brought them to Grand Cayman Island. They'd realized quickly that the Caymans' status as an international tax haven meant there was no shortage of employment for their skill sets. They'd been on a winning streak of late, finding steady work. But staying off the grid was expensive. After bribes and payoffs, after they paid into their rainy-day fund (money set aside in case they had to run again on short notice), there wasn't a lot left over. Mirella Lima represented a huge opportunity to build more of a financial cushion. George had wooed Lima aggressively for months, and tonight was something of an audition. It was imperative that they impress. Lima was as well connected as anyone in this part of the world. Her seal of approval would make a tremendous difference to their bottom line.

Gibson and Hendricks watched Fakhroo lead his guests upstairs to the sundeck where a lavish buffet awaited—everything from lobster tails to Wagyu filets to grilled squab. Off to one side, a string quartet played Hayden's op. 74, no. 2, in F Major. Or so George claimed over their comms. The only classical music Gibson could name was "Ride of the Valkyries," but he was inclined to believe the older man.

The breadth of George's education often made Gibson self-conscious at his lack of one. Or maybe it was the complicated nature of their association that made Gibson feel insecure. George had been a presence in his life since Gibson was a boy, first as a close friend of Duke Vaughn, Gibson's father, and later, after Duke's death, as an enemy for life. Except that hadn't been the end of the story. The last few years had seen a reconciliation of sorts, with George evolving into something resembling a partner, each man relying on the other for safety. But did that make them friends? No, Gibson still wouldn't go that far.

None of their fixed cameras were high enough to see the sundeck of the taller yacht. George had vetoed the use of drones, concerned it would give the wrong impression. Instead, Hendricks relied on Jenn's and George's lapel cameras for visual surveillance of the upper decks. On the monitor, Mirella Lima took a seat at a round conference table. An assistant brought her a glass of champagne and a plate of shrimp the size of sausages.

"I could eat my weight in shrimp," Gibson said.

"Maybe we should buy ourselves a boat," Hendricks said.

That caught Gibson by surprise. "What kind of boat?"

"I don't know . . . a little one?"

"So people can see what we got for *our* souls?"

"Forget it," Hendricks said.

"No, what do you mean?"

Hendricks stared at him, gauging whether Gibson was playing him along. "Thought maybe we could buy a used boat. Run fishing and diving charters in between jobs. Diversify our portfolio."

"Was *Shawshank* on last night or something?" Gibson asked.

"Forget it."

"What do we know about boats?"

"What the hell does that have to do with it?" Hendricks demanded. "I'm only fifty-three years old. You saying I'm too old to learn something new?"

"No, man. No. Nothing like that."

"You sure that's not what you're saying?"

"Yeah, I'm sure. What are you so touchy about?"

"I said, forget it."

George's unwaveringly polite voice crackled over their headsets. "Jennifer has signaled to me . . ." Only George called Jenn and Dan by their full names, the way a parent did to reinforce their close, special relationship. ". . . that if you don't keep this channel clear, she will make you swim back to shore."

"Sorry, Jenn," Gibson mumbled, fiddling with the send button on his headset until it released.

"Daniel, how does it look out there?" George asked.

"Quiet. Real damn quiet," Hendricks replied. "Maybe Lima has this Fakhroo guy figured wrong."

Mirella Lima had hired them to determine if Fakhroo was keeping his hand out of her cookie jar. Their plan was fairly simple: present an inviting target during the meeting, sit back, and watch how Fakhroo responded. To that end, the gangway to the *Topaz* was unguarded—not a soul on deck. Just Dan and his cameras, which covered every door, hatch, and deck. But so far, no uninvited guests. Maybe Hendricks was right.

Gibson's laptop began to chime—*hold that thought*. Touching the brim of the worn Phillies baseball cap that rarely left his head, he began to type. Hendricks might not be able to see them on his monitors, but pirates were swarming over the sides of the *Topaz* in massive numbers. A blitz of cyberattacks targeting the yacht's Wi-Fi network, hunting for a way to infiltrate the servers that held Lima's financial records. Thirteen miles out to sea, there was only one place the attacks could be coming from—*Al Kidamm*. You couldn't tell from all the pageantry up on deck, but Fakhroo had covertly declared war.

Gibson would sort through the data later, but at first glance, the scale and sophistication of the attacks suggested that whomever Fakhroo had hired was good. Really good. Unfortunately for them, the pirates would be going home empty-handed. The decks of the *Topaz* weren't the only thing they'd wanted to appear vulnerable. Even before the *Topaz* left port, Gibson had isolated the servers from the network. What Fakhroo's team was attacking was a honeypot—a dummy network Gibson had set up to study and assess any attacks. His bogus network was well defended, but not too well. He had left vulnerabilities for them to exploit. He wanted them to beat him, interested only in how long it took and what tactics they employed to do it. Whatever viruses and malware the attackers installed would be dissected and studied. From that data, Gibson would project who Fakhroo had hired and how Lima should protect herself going forward.

However, patsy was not a role that suited Gibson. He preferred offense to defense. He'd grown up hacking vulnerable networks like this one. At least until he'd been caught and almost sent to prison at sixteen. Fortunately, the Marines had provided an alternative, a lifeline, and put his skills to good use. His years in the Activity, the branch of the Joint Special Operations Command tasked with providing support and actionable intelligence, had taken his raw talent and molded him into a dangerous man at a keyboard.

"Do you know how simple it would be to hack these idiots back? They're leaving themselves wide open to countermeasures."

"Gibson, no," Hendricks said as if scolding a puppy for peeing on the carpet.

"I know, I know, I'm just saying. It would be easy. Arrogant pricks."

"That is not what we're being paid to do. Study the attacks and write your report. That's it."

Gibson relented, turning the cap backward on his head. "But where's the fun in that?"

CHAPTER FOUR

The coral reef surrounding George Town meant larger boats had to drop anchor in Hog Sty Bay and tender passengers ashore. Mirella Lima had said her good-byes aboard the *Topaz*, which wouldn't be spending the night in Grand Cayman. Lima had financed a film entered at Cannes, so the *Topaz* would need to depart for France immediately. The thought filled Jenn Charles with resentment. Why could a woman like Mirella Lima come and go as she pleased, welcomed everywhere, while Jenn lived her life in the shadows? It wasn't fair.

Grow up, Jenn chided herself. *This is the real world. When did fair have anything to do with it?*

As the tender killed its engine at the dock, George settled up with Mirella Lima's number-two while Jenn, Hendricks, and Gibson offloaded their gear and carried it to the rusted-out pickup that served as the company car. Hendricks walked to the edge of the dock to light up. There had been no smoking aboard the *Topaz*, and if Dan didn't have a cigarette soon, people were going to die. Gibson called after him, suggesting nicotine gum might be a good idea in the future.

"Where am I gonna find nicotine gum on a goddamn desert island?" Hendricks demanded.

Gibson lifted his cap, finger-combed his hair thoughtfully, and refitted the cap on his head. "Amazon?"

Hendricks did not acknowledge the suggestion.

"What's this about a boat?" Jenn asked. She'd only been half listening to their conversation onboard the *Topaz*, but she could have sworn they'd been talking about boats.

"He wants to buy one," Gibson said.

"A boat?" Jenn said.

Gibson shrugged. "So he says."

"What kind of boat?"

"A little one."

Jenn thought that over, enjoying the breeze blowing off the water. When Hendricks came back from smoking, she asked him about it.

"So, you want to buy a little boat?"

"I'm thinking on it," Hendricks said, wary of an ambush.

"What do you know about boats?"

"Why you all keep asking me that? There's nothing to hit out there. I know that."

"Besides land?" Gibson suggested.

"Boy, I oughtta drop you in the harbor," said Hendricks.

Jenn laughed, not that it was particularly funny. Not unless you knew Gibson and Hendricks. Then the way they picked at each other became strangely charming. Perhaps because there'd been a time, not so long ago, that she'd have braced for one of these knuckleheads to wind up in the harbor for real. When Gibson and Hendricks first met around five years ago, they'd hated each other on sight. Hendricks, a retired forty-nine-year-old African American ex-LAPD detective, hadn't had any patience for a lippy twenty-eight-year-old white hacker. And vice versa. But the last few years had leavened that antipathy with a grudging respect and, lately, something approaching affection. It was a minor miracle, and it made Jenn smile. These were her people. God help her.

"You up for a drink?" Gibson asked Hendricks. "I'm buying."

Gibson was in good spirits tonight. Lately, that had been the rule more than the exception, which was not the Gibson Vaughn she'd met five years ago. She'd never known anyone who punished themselves more than he did. Hendricks had once joked that Gibson couldn't find happiness in a litter of puppies all named Happiness. So, while the change over the last year was nice to see, Jenn couldn't help but wonder if it was real or profound denial about their situation. Still, she allowed that her skepticism might be due to her inability to share in Gibson's newfound optimism.

"Boy, it's one in the morning," Hendricks replied.

"Okay, two drinks. I'm easy."

Hendricks thought it over. "Yeah, that'll work."

Pleased, Gibson looked over at Jenn. "You in?"

"Not tonight, I'm beat," she said, repeating her line in this well-worn script. They asked, she made an excuse—that was their unspoken arrangement. She was eighteen months sober, and hanging around in bars after a successful job was asking for trouble. Still, she appreciated that they always thought to include her and pretended to be disappointed when she said no. If she ever did say yes, she suspected they would both develop spontaneous migraines and call it an early night. That she found their protectiveness sweet rather than patronizing surprised her as much as anything. The Jenn Charles of five years ago would not have tolerated that crap, not for one damned minute.

Never accept help. It means that you're weak. That was the first of many extracurricular lessons that the CIA had beaten into her: men who asked for help were ambitious; women who needed help only proved that they couldn't cut it. So she had convinced herself that she wasn't like everyone else. She was tougher, smarter, and didn't need things other people needed. A woman apart. That was what she had wanted to believe anyway, and maybe it had even been true at twenty-five. At thirty-six, though, it had begun to sound like youthful arrogance.

With each passing year, the traits that she'd once valued as strengths seemed more and more like weakness. Sebastião had been fond of teasing her for exactly that. *"Minha garota durona,"* he called her in his native Portuguese: "My tough girl."

Jenn recoiled from the memory, pushing away his name, his smell, his taste, the brush of his stubble on her cheek, and the murmur of his voice in her ear. Sebastião Coval was not a man she had any business thinking about. Eighteen months ago, he'd asked her to marry him, and to her great surprise, she'd come within a heartbeat of saying yes. Something else she'd long ago sworn she would never do. But in the end, she'd told him no, and that was that. She had to accept that, like home, Sebastião was something else that she'd left behind forever.

George came up the dock to join them. The limp was less noticeable, and he no longer needed a cane, but Jenn could see the subtle hitch in his stride and the way he favored his right leg. It had been a long road back, his injuries at the hands of Titus Eskridge and Cold Harbor too numerous to count. He reminded Jenn of an old song about a guy who'd come out of a fight like a jigsaw puzzle with pieces missing. Except that wasn't quite right; the pieces of George were all still there, they simply didn't fit together anymore. There had been a time when she would have described George Abe as ageless, but now he looked every one of his fifty-eight years. And then some.

"What's the verdict?" Hendricks asked.

"Very positive." George held up a check made out to the holding company that laundered their earnings. Another benefit of working on Grand Cayman: no dearth of bankers willing to look the other way. For yet another fee, of course. "We'll get the other half when we deliver our report, but Ms. Lima was impressed. She said we could expect more work next month when she returns from Cannes. Nice job, everyone."

The news put a smile on everyone's face, even Hendricks's. Gibson looked delighted. It marked an important win for the recently resurrected Abe Consulting Group, but Jenn found it difficult to share in the celebration. She couldn't help but wonder what exactly they were celebrating. More and more, it pained her to work for the Mirella Limas of the world. A woman who looked at the humanitarian crisis in Venezuela and saw only a way to cash in. It was beneath them—or should have been.

God help me, I'm starting to sound like Gibson.

Traditionally, Gibson played the part of team moralist, something she'd always found infuriating and naïve. Lately, though, they had traded roles. Gibson seemed content to put his head down, not ask too many questions, and take the money. Pragmatism ahead of principle. Not that Jenn didn't appreciate the reality of their situation. Unlike Dan and George, she and Gibson remained fugitives, and staying under the US government's radar wasn't cheap. They didn't have the luxury of turning away work because the client was a scumbag. It wasn't as if the Girl Scouts were waiting in line to hire them.

Still, it bothered her.

Two years ago, they had broken into Dulles International Airport and hijacked an aircraft belonging to Cold Harbor, a private military contractor with a flexible definition of patriotism. They'd done it to rescue George Abe but, in the process, had foiled Cold Harbor's brazen theft of US intelligence. That distinction had been lost on the CIA and FBI, which took a dim view of gunmen stealing aircraft from American airports. They'd been on the run ever since.

She'd known there would be consequences. Rescuing George had been dangerous and illegal, but it had been the right thing to do. Faced with the same choice, she would do it again without hesitation. The problem was, Jenn couldn't accept that the consequence of that decision would be selling her soul, piece by piece, simply to survive another day. Was this all she had to look forward to? Scraping by? Living off the grid? Unable to ever put down roots? There had been a time when she'd been *about* something. Her father had been a Marine who had given his life in the Beirut bombing in '83. Her mother had been a pilot in the

Navy. Jenn had joined the CIA to honor their memory and to make a contribution. What exactly was she contributing now?

She sighed. *Now who's being infuriatingly naïve?*

They all squeezed into the cab of the pickup truck so Hendricks could drop George and Jenn off before hitting the town with Gibson. She listened to Gibson and Hendricks discuss the logistics of buying a boat and running charters. Gibson seemed to be warming to the idea. Never mind the fact that neither knew the first thing about diving or fishing. How hard could it be? they reasoned. George listened silently, a peaceful smile on his face.

After they dropped George off, Jenn had second thoughts about not going out, the little voice in the back of her mind whispering to her again. The one with a million ready excuses why one drink wouldn't hurt anything. So when the pickup pulled to a stop outside her bungalow, she had to force herself out of the cab.

"Run in the morning?" she asked, pulling her duffel bag out of the back of the truck.

Gibson rolled down the window. "Sounds good. Could you take ours as well? Don't want to leave them in the back of the truck. I'll grab 'em tomorrow after the run."

"Sure." Jenn invited Hendricks on the run, already knowing the answer.

"Not now, not never." Hendricks was exercise agnostic—it might exist, but that didn't mean he believed in it.

"See you in the a.m., Charles," Gibson said.

"Zero dark thirty."

"Oorah," he called out with a toothy grin and slapped the outside of the door in farewell as the pickup pulled away.

Jenn fished her house keys out of her duffel bag. For safety's sake, they all lived separately and, as a rule, avoided congregating in public during daylight hours. They were much more recognizable as a group. George had made discreet inquiries through his contacts in Washington and had been reassured that while Gibson's and Jenn's names still circulated on international-fugitive lists, they weren't a priority. No one was actively hunting them. As long as they didn't broadcast their location to the world, they were reasonably safe. *Reasonably.* That didn't mean that if some random on vacation made an ID that the FBI wouldn't have them extradited. Jenn had heard enough stories of such incidental identifications that she could never entirely relax.

Ironically, it was the prospect of never feeling safe again that preoccupied Jenn as she let herself in the front door. She wondered later, if she'd been more alert, would she have noticed the hum of the window-mounted air conditioner? The one she always turned off before leaving. Instead, a light from the kitchen caught her attention. She dropped the duffel bags by the door and walked through the living room to turn it off. It was the overhead light on her stove. She must have accidentally left it on while making coffee that morning. That wasn't like her at all.

She poured herself a glass of water and drank it, leaning against the counter while she ignored how much the water didn't taste like vodka. A reminder of why it had been the right call not to go out with Hendricks and Gibson. Besides, now she had Gibson's blow-by-blow recap to look forward to in the morning, which, if she was being honest, was much more entertaining than actually being there.

As she gazed sleepily back into the living room, the outline of a figure emerged gradually from the gloom. A man sitting comfortably in her armchair as if he were a welcomed guest. So still that she tried to convince herself it was only the shadows playing tricks. Rorschach reminding her of the terrors that haunted her. But then the man blinked, and she knew he was real. Casually, she reached for the Ruger pistol hidden behind the refrigerator.

"It's not there," the man in the chair said, pleasantly, in a posh British accent.

He was right, it wasn't, and she'd stowed her sidearm in the duffel bag before coming ashore. She had a Sig Sauer in the bedroom, though.

A baseball bat behind the bathroom door. But she'd have to go back through the living room to get to either.

Time to improvise.

She looked at the knife block.

Empty.

She realized then that the stove light had been bait to draw her back to the kitchen, where she'd have no way out except for a small window above the sink. She was cornered, and her uninvited guest had stripped the kitchen of anything that might make a weapon. To confirm her suspicion, she slid open one of the drawers. Empty as well. He hadn't left her so much as a carrot peeler.

"Your kingdom for a scalpel, am I right?" the man asked.

She didn't understand what that was supposed to mean. "Are you from Cold Harbor?"

The man chuckled mirthlessly, as if doing an impersonation of laughter. "No, decidedly not. Why don't you come and sit down so we can talk comfortably?"

"I'm good here," she said and refilled her water. Partly to show him she wasn't afraid, which was a lie; her heart was rattling like it had thrown a rod. And partly because she wanted an excuse to bring the glass with her. It could make a decent weapon if broken correctly.

"Please," the man said patiently. "I do not intend you any harm. Come have a seat."

He said it so genially that Jenn felt the temptation to believe him. It was a trap, though, the camouflage a predator wore to convince prey that it was a sheep, not a wolf. Everything he had already done in her home was a promise of harm; she wasn't about to believe otherwise simply because he sounded like he'd stepped out of a BBC studio.

"All right," she said, letting her shoulders slouch forward to signal how powerless she felt. Men had fallen for less.

"Leave the glass in the kitchen."

Suddenly the slump of her shoulders wasn't an act. She felt like a rat being run through a maze, each step a foregone conclusion. But what choice did she have? She smiled compliantly, set the glass down on the counter, and went into the living room, wondering how this didn't end with her dead.

CHAPTER FIVE

Laid out neatly on the coffee table were the firearms that Jenn had stashed throughout the house. They had been arranged so she could see at a glance that all had been unloaded. Like a cunning shopkeeper displaying his wares in some back-alley bazaar, the man swept one hand across the coffee table. "I thought this would help to clarify your odds."

She looked them over, spirits waning—he hadn't missed a single one. Her eyes drifted to the man's other hand, which held a Browning Buck Mark .22. Jenn was intimately familiar with it—a simple, reliable weapon favored by Agency wet boys of a bygone generation. Attached to the threaded barrel was a coal-black suppressor that followed her attentively like the muzzle of an attack dog aching to be let off the leash.

"Slim and none?" she offered.

"Half right. Won't you have a seat?"

Jenn didn't move. "If you're not Cold Harbor, who sent you?"

"Have a seat," he said again, his hand tightening subtly around the grip of his pistol to indicate that it was no longer a polite request.

She did as she was told, perching on the edge of the couch to keep her feet under her in case an opening presented itself.

"Thank you," he said.

Now that she was nearer, Jenn could tell that his accent was phony. "Why are you pretending to be English?"

The man shrugged. "Some find it comforting. Would this suit you better?" he asked, shifting into a gentle German purr. "Or this?" His accent developed an Afrikaans cadence. "Or this? Or this? Or this?" Transitioning smoothly from Israeli to Italian to Russian. "Or maybe a touch of home?" he asked, adopting the South Carolina lilt of her grandmother.

His casual familiarity with her past unnerved her as much or more than his presence in her bungalow. His every action calculated and premeditated, communicating to her that he held all the cards. It was intended to demoralize her, and even as she recognized his game, she could feel it working. As if death itself had come for her at last and everything else was a mere ritual.

"Have we met?" she asked.

"Not formally, no."

"Informally?"

"In passing. I have seen your work. Impressive."

"Who are you?"

"There's something I've been meaning to ask," the man said. "That night in Charlottesville. How did you find me? I've always wondered."

"Oh, fuck me . . ."

"Ah, I see you do remember."

Jenn ran her tongue over her teeth and realized how dry her mouth had become. She wasn't accustomed to being afraid. At least she wasn't accustomed to letting it overwhelm her. Fear paralyzed the mind, all but guaranteeing the worst possible outcome, and she'd been trained to control it, to keep moving forward. But her training abandoned her now, and a creeping, near-supernatural dread climbed her spine. Her suspicion that she might die tonight hardened into absolute certainty.

Death had indeed come for her or, at the very least, sent its favorite son. This was Calista Dauplaise's hired killer. In the flesh. The bogeyman who had hanged Duke Vaughn in the basement of his Charlottesville home and staged it as a suicide, leaving the body for fourteen-year-old Gibson to discover. Who had stalked Dan and Gibson and her throughout their search for Suzanne Lombard, finally snatching Gibson and dragging him back to that same basement some fourteen years later and hanging him from the same crossbeam as his father.

Gibson still bore the scar around his neck. He had grown a beard to hide it, but his fingers often sought it out in quiet moments the way a devout Catholic might pray the rosary. If Jenn and Dan hadn't arrived when they had, well, Gibson would be lying beside Duke in the family plot. Dan, an ex–homicide detective, had been so shaken by his own run-in with this man that he'd lived the last few years in a paranoid crouch, waiting for him to return and finish the job. Now it appeared the bogeyman had done exactly that. She only wished there was some way to warn them, to give her friends a fighting chance. She hated to die for nothing.

In the dark of the living room, Jenn studied him. Over the years, she had harbored doubts that Dan and Gibson could possibly have encountered the same man. Their descriptions varied too wildly. Now she saw why. An inconsequential-looking white man, he was slight of build with a dusting of fine brown hair. Not old, but at the same time there was something ancient in the deliberateness of his movements. His was a background face, as forgettable as a storefront mannequin's, with vaguely defined features that might have been molded from clay by a child. If she had to guess his profession, she would have picked a dental hygienist or a branch manager of a small Midwestern bank. An hour from now, she wasn't sure if she'd be able to describe him with any accuracy—and she'd been trained to recall faces. The only detail Dan and Gibson had agreed on was his eyes. Staring into those vacant, unwavering sockets, Jenn understood why. It was like gazing down into a dormant volcano.

"So? How did you find me that night?" the man prompted.

"A tracker sewn into Gibson's bag. We didn't find you, we found him."

"I hadn't considered that," he said with a satisfied nod, as though she'd settled a bet for him. "It was you who interrupted me—do you think you could have put me down? Had you not stopped to save your friend?"

Jenn's memory flashed back to that dark basement. Charging blindly down the stairs of Gibson's childhood home. Gibson thrashing from the end of a rope, face purple and bruised, legs bicycling frantically through the air, hunting for purchase. By the time she'd freed him, his attacker was long gone.

"Yeah," she said. "I would have."

The man thought it over. "I agree. You were always the most formidable. That's why I've come to you first."

"That's flattering, but why all the theatrics? Or is that your thing? Talking people to death?"

"Calista Dauplaise is dead. Any motivation I had to cause you harm died with her."

"Clearly," Jenn said, nodding at the gun in his hand. "So you've just stopped by to hold me hostage at gunpoint."

"No, I'm here to enlist you."

She took her time replying, intent on keeping the surprise from her voice. "Enlist me for what?"

"I require access to this," he said, holding up a thumb drive.

"What's on it?" she asked.

"I don't know, but my employer attempted to kill me for it. Twice. Unfortunately, his identity is not known to me, so I have no way to persuade him that is an unprofitable course of action."

"And you think the thumb drive will tell you who he is?"

"That or something that will lead me to him. Unfortunately, it's encrypted. I require Vaughn's assistance accessing it."

There was no hiding her surprise now. "You have to be kidding me."

"Do I seem like the sort of man who tells jokes?"

"You murdered his father."

"Twenty years ago," the man said, seemingly impatient at the notion that anyone could hold on to such a grievance for so long. "In any event, he was not in the best health. He would most likely be dead now."

It was a grotesque argument, but explaining morality to this man would be pointless. It would be like describing the sun to someone who had lived their entire life underground.

"And you thought to yourself, Gibson Vaughn is the man for that job? Gibson's good, but he's hardly the only hacker on earth."

The man grimaced. "I am being hunted. My former employer has rendered my conventional contacts unavailable to me. They would not expect me to come here."

"That's real compelling," Jenn said. "But that's not going to make a difference. God on his throne couldn't talk Gibson Vaughn into helping you."

"No," the man said, tightening his grip on the gun for a second time. "But I believe you can."

CHAPTER SIX

"He was hiding inside the wall," Georgi Ivov said, and not for the first time.

Jurnjack knelt on one knee to inspect the section of drywall that had been cut away. A tape measure confirmed his suspicion—a perfect square. But why? There was no tactical benefit. Speed should have been of the essence, especially in such a vulnerable position. It made no sense, and because it made no sense, he felt certain that it offered an insight into the man who had cut his way out.

Leaning inside the wall, Jurnjack inspected the narrow cavity with a flashlight. Not much larger than a child's coffin. How long had the man lurked inside? Renovations had been completed six weeks ago. Security had swept the villa and taken up its post at the beginning of the month. That suggested a time frame of between four and six weeks.

How was that humanly possible?

Jurnjack clicked off the flashlight and stood up gingerly, brushing sawdust from his trouser legs. He had forgotten to take the medicine for his arthritis, and his knees throbbed.

"He was hiding inside the wall," Ivov whimpered.

Whimpering. Jurnjack didn't know what else to call it. Ivov had been trailing him around the villa like a faded ghost from a Dickens novel. Thankfully, Ivov wasn't sobbing any longer, but that was only because he'd cried himself out at the funeral. It would have shocked the voters who had elected him to the Bulgarian parliament. On the campaign trail, Georgi Ivov, champion of the common man, was all fire and conviction. Now he sounded like a child awakened from a nightmare who needed Mommy to kiss it and make it all better.

But there would be no making this better. Not ever. Ivov still wore the suit he'd worn yesterday to bury his wife and eldest daughter. That had been an unwelcome development. In Jurnjack's estimation, Georgi Ivov was a soft bureaucrat, cushioned from the harsh realities of life by his money and privilege. Jurnjack had counted on him to wilt at the first threat to his family, but Ivov had shown uncharacteristic resolve, calling the killer's bluff not once but twice. That was the kind of fear that their mutual employer inspired. Better to watch your family executed than to betray Anatoly Skumin. It hadn't been until the gun had been turned on his only son that Ivov had given up the thumb drive.

Men and our precious legacies, Jurnjack thought. *What monsters we become in its name.*

He took one last look at the hole in the wall.

What monsters we unleash to protect it.

Jurnjack, in particular, regretted the daughter, a sweet girl with a voice like an angel. A true innocent in all this. The wife had known what kind of man her husband was and had accepted the risks and the many rewards. Not that Jurnjack had tears to shed on either's behalf. What was done was done, as was the way with everything in this life. He had long ago rationalized away the collateral damage that came with war. And this was most definitely a war now.

Anatoly Skumin had dispatched Jurnjack to Varna to survey the battlefield and gather any useful clues that might point them in the right direction. It had been a week, and they were no nearer to tracking down the man in the wall. Herr Skumin's network was vast, and twice he'd doubled the reward, but the man in the wall had vanished. Jurnjack needed to catch a break. He needed the man found, and found quickly. Herr Skumin was losing patience, and Jurnjack's master did not begin the day a patient man. Sooner not later, the blame would fall on him. If it hadn't already.

What Herr Skumin didn't know, and couldn't be allowed to learn, was that it had been Jurnjack himself who had started the war. Jurnjack who had hired the man in the wall to steal the thumb drive, which Skumin had foolishly entrusted to Georgi Ivov for safekeeping here in Varna. It had been a delicate matter, with Jurnjack personally overseeing the design of the security at Georgi Ivov's villa. It was a masterpiece. Impenetrable. It had had to be. Any blind spots would only point an accusing finger back to him, and he needed to be above suspicion if his plan had any hope of succeeding. That's why he had hired a contractor with a reputation for the impossible.

The Origami Man.

Jurnjack had scoffed at the ridiculousness of the name, but men he respected, men who feared nothing and no one, spoke it with hushed reverence. Frankly, some of the stories surrounding this so-called Origami Man had sounded exaggerated to the point of absurdity, no doubt inventions of the contractor himself to enhance his myth and raise his asking price. Now Jurnjack wasn't so certain. The Origami Man, blank as paper, only folded into the shape of a man. Or into a wall for six weeks. The villa's security had been designed to repel an army. Jurnjack hadn't considered the possibility that the army might already be inside. How could he? It was inconceivable.

The frustrating part was that the Origami Man should already be dead. Improbably, he had evaded not one but two attempts on his life. During the second, he'd put down a squad of former Spetsnaz in Istanbul, all while nursing a gunshot wound to the chest. Jurnjack should know; he'd been the one who'd taken the shot. Since then, the man had gone to ground, wisely avoiding all of his expected haunts. Jurnjack wondered if he would get another opportunity. How did you find a man who could spend a month sealed inside a wall? Twenty years ago, the question would have excited him, but now it only made him tired.

"He was hiding inside the walls," Ivov said again.

Jurnjack understood the need to restate the obvious. When something felt incomprehensible, the only way to make it real was to put words to it.

"What if there are others?" Ivov asked.

"Others?"

"Have you searched the walls?" Ivov cast a panicked look around the pantry, as if killers might burst out at any moment.

Jurnjack had seen it before, of course. The swelling hysteria when death came for the wealthy. When they saw that all their money had only bought the illusion of safety. One thing was certain—Georgi Ivov would never set foot in this house again after today.

"I'll see to it personally once you and your children are secure. I would suggest your house in Borovets. Up in the mountains. It is far more defensible. Your family will be protected. You have my word."

"Protected? This is your fault," Ivov said with a bitter laugh. "Protected? It was your job to protect my wife and daughter in the first place. What use is your word? Maybe Skumin is right. Maybe you're too old for this."

Jurnjack ignored the implied threat. It had been a bad week, and he expected the days ahead to be much, much worse. From here, he would fly to Saint Petersburg to brief Herr Skumin on the lack of progress. Jurnjack did not relish the prospect. Whether or not Skumin suspected that he had anything to do with the theft, Jurnjack could be killed outright if Skumin was in one of his dark moods. Georgi Ivov was right about one thing: at seventy-one, Jurnjack was too old. Too old to give up simply because things hadn't gone as planned. When had they ever?

"So what did he take?" Jurnjack asked despite knowing full well. But since Ivov would report back directly to Herr Skumin, it would raise suspicion if Jurnjack didn't at least ask the question.

"Skumin didn't tell you?"

"No."

Skumin hadn't told Jurnjack about the thumb drive. But Skumin rarely confided in him anymore. They had known each other for more than fifty years, but it had never been what one might call a close relationship. Jurnjack despised his master, and Anatoly Skumin knew it. But because Jurnjack had proven himself to be a dependable asset, Skumin had always chosen to overlook that fact. Over the past decade, though, Skumin had included Jurnjack less and less in his thinking, gradually cutting Jurnjack out of the business until he had been reduced to little more than an errand boy with no grasp of the big picture.

Or so Skumin believed.

Jurnjack had his own ways of keeping himself in the loop, and to be honest, how little Herr Skumin took Jurnjack into his confidence would prove beneficial in the coming days. It offered him the cover to play dumb. Cover that might mean the difference between life and death when they met in Saint Petersburg.

"Then how do you know something was taken?" Ivov said.

Jurnjack gave him a withering look. "Because you are alive. If this man didn't come to kill you, then he came for something else. Come now, what did he take? Or would you prefer to tell Herr Skumin yourself?"

Ivov had been through hell, but his face still blanched at the prospect. He clearly accepted the logic but hesitated nonetheless. Jurnjack understood. The thumb drive represented five years of work and tens of millions of euros. All of which paled beside the billions that Skumin stood to make if the operation were a success.

"You must ask Skumin. It is not my place to say."

Jurnjack made a show of fuming at the lack of transparency. "How am I supposed to do my job if I don't know what I'm looking for?"

"Ask Skumin. But you must tell him that I had no other choice. He killed Diana and Emilia. I had no choice." Ivov dissolved into tears at the enormity of his loss.

Jurnjack doubted that it would be any consolation, but it would all be over soon enough. Ivov and his family were liabilities now; in time, Jurnjack would be sent to finish what the Origami Man had begun.

"I will tell him," Jurnjack said. "But I don't know that it will matter."

"Why? What would he expect me to have done?"

"Herr Ivov, you still had two children left."

CHAPTER SEVEN

"Jenn?" Gibson called, pounding on her front door a second time. "Let's go already."

He cupped his hand to the frosted glass panes beside the door and peered inside, but the house was dark and still. The prospect that Jenn Charles—high priestess of punctuality—might actually still be asleep put a smug smile on his face. Especially since he and Hendricks had made something of a night of it, celebrating the success of the Mirella Lima job and the promise it held for their future. Things had gotten out of hand after Gibson had told Hendricks about his plan to start putting his cut of their take in a trust for his daughter's education. She was only eleven, so if he started now, he reckoned he'd have a healthy sum set aside by the time she was ready to apply to college. Hendricks had smiled approvingly and bought a round of shots. The first of many, as it turned out. They'd stayed out so late that Gibson's body still hadn't had time to start its hangover. Yet here he was, right on time. They would write epic poems dedicated to the amount of crap he would give Jenn during their run.

Buoyed at the prospect, he knocked again but still got no answer. Calling wasn't an option—his phone was at home, charging on the bedside table. Unsure what else to do, he tried the door. It opened. That

Gibson had not expected, and he felt a pang of alarm. Jenn sleeping in *and* leaving her front door unlocked? What were the odds? He put one foot inside her entry hall and listened. Their duffel bags sat undisturbed against the wall. Nothing looked amiss, but they had so many enemies. They'd been fools to think they were safe here.

He called up the stairs.

From the direction of the kitchen, Jenn answered, "I'm back here."

Gibson huffed a sigh of relief, chuckling at how quickly he'd leapt to the worst possible scenario. He found her sitting alone at her small kitchen table, both hands around a coffee mug. It took him a moment to realize that she wasn't dressed for a run. In fact, she was still wearing her clothes from the night before.

"Are you okay?" he asked, coming to an abrupt halt.

"I'm fine. I need a favor."

"Name it."

"Thing is, though, I need you not to ask any questions."

"That's two favors," he said, trying to coax a smile out of her. He didn't get one. His sense of unease returned and cracked its knuckles menacingly. "What's going on?"

"That's a question."

"Fine. Tell me what you need."

She slid a thumb drive across the kitchen table. "I need this opened."

He eyed it suspiciously, recognizing the manufacturer. It was high-end commercial grade, with half a terabyte of storage and built-in encryption. It was a newer model, which meant that it was too soon for any vulnerabilities in the crypto or controller chips to be common knowledge. The simplest approach would be a physical attack on the thumb drive—break it open and extract the storage chip. But he'd need a machine shop to mill it apart; otherwise, the thumb drive's tamper protections would fry whatever data it held. That only left one option, and it wasn't a good one.

"Where'd it come from?" he asked, wondering if it had something to do with last night's job. Had Jenn been running a shadow operation on the *Topaz*? It wouldn't be the first time they'd held out on each other. It wouldn't even be the tenth.

"Come on. Question."

"Right," Gibson said. "Sorry. Force of habit."

It wasn't in Gibson's nature to do anything without knowing the reason why. A quality that had not ideally suited him to military service. Of course, by the time he'd arrived on Parris Island, the Marines had already amassed more than 230 years' worth of experience breaking teenage hard cases who fancied themselves smarter than their drill instructors. The battle of wills had been short and lopsided. The Corps' lessons hadn't stuck, though, and as soon as he'd been discharged, Gibson had reverted to his old ways. Worse, probably, if he was being honest. As if six years of following orders had exhausted whatever small reserve of deference he'd been allotted at birth.

But this was Jenn asking, and she never asked. And she never looked scared, even when she ought to. He went out to the front door and fetched his duffel bag. Back in the kitchen, he plugged the thumb drive into his laptop's USB port—a simple text box popped up asking for a password of up to sixteen characters. Not awesome but about what he'd expected to see.

"How long will this take?" Jenn asked.

Gibson gave that due consideration. "Between five minutes and forever."

"That's super helpful."

He shrugged. A brute-force hack didn't require any skill. It was simply a matter of processing power and patience. The more power you had, the less patience it took. The server farms at Fort Meade would chew through this encryption in no time. His laptop, on the other hand, powerful though it might be, was only a single machine and would take 125 years to break a sixteen-digit password. Assuming that the original owner had observed strong password protocols, which Gibson did, given the high-end gear. Still, he would try hashes—tables of commonly reused passwords—in the unlikely event that the thumb drive's owner had been sloppy.

Fortunately, Gibson had more resources at his disposal than his laptop. Over the last year, he had hacked a number of private networks and cobbled together a server cluster that boosted his processing power exponentially. He fed multiple cloned images of the thumb drive to his cluster now and let it go to work on the thumb drive. That done, there wasn't much for him to do but let his server cluster cycle through every combination until it hit on the right one. A process that made accurate estimates virtually impossible.

"Want to go for that run while we wait?" Gibson suggested. Waiting for decryption software to run was the modern version of a watched pot, and if he sat around too much longer, his budding hangover was going to start the party.

Jenn ran her tongue across her teeth as she often did when considering her options. "We should wait here. This is pretty time sensitive."

Gibson fought back the urge to ask why. He didn't need another lesson in what a question was. "Okay, so why don't you go get some sleep. I'll wake you if we catch a break. You're looking pretty rough, Charles."

When Jenn didn't rise to the bait, Gibson knew that the danger was much closer than the *Topaz*. He just couldn't see it. Casually, he suggested calling Hendricks and asking him to bring breakfast.

"No, we can handle this. There's no need to get anyone else involved." She said it in her take-charge voice, but underneath lay a subdued, pleading note that only someone who knew Jenn well would pick out.

Gibson didn't argue, as he once would have done. Nor did he press her with the questions that were driving him crazy. Whatever was happening here, it was serious, and he would do his best to follow her lead. No matter how painful he found it.

In the end, they waited at the kitchen table all day while the combined power of his server cluster worked the problem. Jenn got up periodically to refill her coffee. Gibson drank his body weight in water, although it did little to stave off his blooming hangover. Otherwise, they sat in silence, somberly, as if waiting for a priest to eulogize the dearly departed.

Eventually, Jenn's eyes drifted closed, and she slept sitting up at the table, snoring lightly, chin on her chest. It made Gibson smile, but he soon followed suit, waking only when the sun hung low enough in the sky to shine through the kitchen window.

A quick look at the laptop told him that while they'd dozed, the cluster had stumbled upon the correct password. Gibson was stunned. In his wildest dreams, he wouldn't have dared hope to crack the password in a single day. Then he saw the password and understood. Instead of a complex password, the owner had repeated the same word twice. It was an incredibly foolish mistake and made no sense. Why go to the expense of top-shelf encryption only to undermine it with a bad password? Well, it only proved Gibson's first operating principle—never underestimate the stupidity of the average computer user.

A directory of the thumb drive now waited on his screen: three folders, all labeled in Cyrillic. That piqued his curiosity, but before going further, he booted a virtual machine within his laptop. A safe, hermetically sealed digital laboratory isolated from any of his personal data. If the thumb drive proved hostile, the virtual machine would prevent it from corrupting the rest of his computer.

Now what?

With Jenn asleep, he was sorely tempted to take a quick look. Purely to satisfy his curiosity. His cursor hovered over the first folder for what felt like an eternity. But then he reminded himself that this was her show, and while snooping might not technically qualify as a question, it did not honor the spirit of their agreement.

He reached across the table and shook her gently awake. Jenn's eyes snapped open, and she tried to act like she'd only been thinking, not sleeping. Gibson let her have it and looked away as she wiped her chin with the back of her thumb.

"What do we have?" she asked.

"We're in. Three folders."

"Did you open any?"

"Of course not," he said, far more offended than he had any right to be.

Jenn came around and looked over Gibson's shoulder while he scanned the decrypted directory for malware. It still came back clean. The three folders were labeled: "Klyuch," "Poleznaya Nagruzka," and "Dokumentatsiya."

"Any idea?" he asked. Jenn spoke more languages than Gibson knew words.

"It's Russian: 'Key,' 'Payload,' 'Documentation.'"

"Well, that sounds ominous. Know what it means?"

"No. Let's open them and take a look."

"Really?" Gibson hadn't expected that but wasn't about to pass up the opportunity. His curiosity was dialed up now.

"But don't copy anything. Am I clear?"

"Man, relax. No problem. Let's just take that look."

They started with the Poleznaya Nagruzka/Payload folder, which contained a single data file. Inside Klyuch, or "Key," were two executable program files, each a hair under two megabytes in size.

"What do you think those do?" she asked.

"Not a clue. Let's find out," Gibson replied and double-clicked on the first one before Jenn could stop him. A program window appeared with three buttons that Jenn translated as "Connect," "Read," "Write." "Read" and "Write" were grayed out, so Gibson clicked on "Connect."

An alert box from his virtual machine's firewall warned him that the program was attempting to connect to an IP address. The firewall asked if he wanted to allow it.

Hell no, he didn't. He recognized the location of the IP address and didn't like it. To be thorough, he tried the second executable program file and got the same alert box but with a slightly different IP address.

"What's happening?" Jenn asked.

"Both programs are trying to connect to computers," he said.

"Not the same one?"

"No, but the two IP addresses are closely related."

"Can you tell where the computers are located?"

"Only that both IP addresses are in the United States," Gibson said. "Other weird part, though? Both programs want to upload the 'Payload' data file."

"So, two programs, targeting two different computers with the same data file?"

"Correct."

"And that's weird?"

"It means something. Just don't know what."

Playing a hunch, he took the hash—a cryptographic fingerprint—of each of the programs and sent both to vLibrary, a subscription service that would check them against all known malware. If either program had been seen before, vLibrary would recognize it.

The results came back in less than a minute: "Unknown."

That made him nervous enough to decompile the programs so that he could look at the code. What he saw was incredibly complex and intricate. Whoever had written these programs knew their business. He was beginning to get a real bad feeling, but to be certain, he scanned them with malware and virus behavioral tools, looking for familiar malicious behaviors. He found none.

He sat back and stared at the screen while the implications of what he was looking at dawned on him.

"What is it?" Jenn asked.

"Well, this malware's brand new, never been seen before in the wild. No antivirus recognizes it, so no computer in the world would see it coming. Second, the coding is brilliant, dense and compact. It makes your run-of-the-mill software look like something out of the Stone Age."

"What does that mean?"

Gibson took a deep breath, unsure where to start. Especially with a layperson like Jenn. "Okay. So most malware is designed to infect as many machines as possible. They're indiscriminate, highly contagious, but as a result, their effects tend to be broad and generalized. But this baby right here? It was built with a very, very specific target in mind and has a very specific job to do."

"What's the job?"

"Don't know."

"Can't you tell from the code?"

Gibson did a double take to see if she was being serious. She was, which reminded him how ignorant even smart people were about how computers worked. "No, I can't. The programs would need to be reverse engineered, and something of this size and complexity would require a team working around the clock for months. All I can say is that someone put a lot of time and effort into this. Which leads me to assume that whatever the target is, it's high value."

They went through the last folder, hoping for anything that might point them in the right direction: Dokumentatsiya/Documentation. It held a raft of spreadsheets, PDF scans, and Word files. Most were written in Russian or German, so Jenn took over from Gibson and pored over them. The spreadsheets read like a nightmare. Broken down by month, they projected casualty figures across the United States over a two-year period. The numbers began relatively small, ticking slowly upward until a massive spike at month six catapulted the number into the tens of thousands. Over the subsequent eighteen months, the spreadsheets predicted half a million deaths. Indexes and sub-tables broke the numbers down further: by age, by gender, by race, by geographic region. All laid out antiseptically, devoid of any feeling or seeming comprehension of the monstrous loss it forecast.

The callousness of it chilled him; whatever its target and mission, this malware was pure malevolence.

What had his high-school history teacher called it? The banality of evil. A philosopher had used the term to describe the bureaucratic cruelty of Adolf Eichmann, who had overseen the logistics of transporting millions of Jews to concentration camps during the Second World War. These spreadsheets had a similar theoretical detachment. As if the author were counting widgets and not human lives.

Gibson wanted desperately to believe it was a hoax, an abstract academic exercise or war-game scenario, but given the labyrinthine code of the malware, he knew that wasn't true. He rubbed his temples; his head throbbed, though not from the hangover now.

"What's that?" Gibson asked, jabbing at the screen with one finger.

Jenn had opened a scan of an e-mail. In one corner was a handwritten note. She zoomed in. It was a name: "Liam Walsh," along with an address in Belfast, Northern Ireland. Encouraged by that success, Jenn went through the rest of the documents painstakingly but found nothing else.

It left them knowing only the outcome of the planned attack, not the target. Frustrating. And frightening.

"So now what?" Gibson asked.

"Now you leave."

Gibson didn't move. "What's going on? And I know that's a question."

"Please," she said, softening her tone. "Please go. I'll call you later."

"Jenn . . ."

Behind Gibson, the pantry door swung open with a low, stubborn groan. Gibson turned to look. A man stood inside, the gun in his hand pointed diplomatically to the floor. Gibson wondered how the man had gotten into the closet before realizing that he'd been in there all day. But how? The pantry was little more than a shallow closet; nowhere to sit; the man would have had to stand absolutely still for ten hours, and that simply wasn't possible.

"No!" Jenn said, voice rising. "We had a deal. We had a deal!"

Gibson's eyes drifted from the gun up to the man's face. He had the strangest feeling that they'd met, although he couldn't place where or when . . .

As he stared, his vision narrowed, growing dark and pixilated around the margins. Every muscle in his body clenched, and he broke out in a cold, malarial sweat. Where had he seen this man before? The question caused Gibson's stomach to twist, and he felt his feet leave the floor. The room swayed sickeningly. When he blinked, he was back in the basement of his childhood house in Charlottesville. A noose tightened around his neck, crushing his windpipe and tearing the skin from ear to ear. He kicked out, trying to find a toehold. A chair crashed on the floor. He was dying while the man who had killed his father stood there watching him, studying, like a cruel child with a magnifying glass kneeling over an anthill.

From a long way off, Jenn Charles yelled his name.

Jenn was coming. He felt relief at the sound of her voice. She would drive the man away. But still, Gibson couldn't breathe, and he hit the floor hard. Jenn must have cut him down. *Thank you, Jenn. Thank you for coming for me.*

She knelt beside him. "Gibson. Breathe."

It was good advice, but his chest felt like it was in a vise.

"Is he always like this?" the man interrupted in a gentle Southern accent. "So fragile?"

The hairs on Gibson's neck bristled. That voice. He knew that voice . . .

"You don't get to ask questions about him," Jenn spat back.

"Very well," the man said. "Return the thumb drive, and I will be going."

"Wait!" Jenn said. "Those spreadsheets. Are they real?"

"I don't see how that's any of my concern."

"Half a million deaths," she pleaded.

"Everyone dies. What does it matter when?" the man asked.

"It matters to them."

"Precisely," the man said, Southern accent evaporating. In its place was a hollow, affectless drone. A bleak approximation of human speech.

It *was* the man from the basement. The monster who'd killed his father. He'd returned. Gibson recognized the terrible danger they were in but couldn't rouse himself to act. It felt like he was watching the world from the bottom of a swimming pool, everything muffled and far away.

"Tell me where you got the thumb drive. I'll track them down myself," Jenn said.

"That is also not in my interests," the man replied.

"So, what? That's it?"

"You have kept your side of the bargain. I will keep mine."

Dan Hendricks appeared silently in the kitchen doorway. The man caught their eyes flicking toward the door and began to turn, but Hendricks took a step forward and pressed a gun to the side of the man's head.

"Don't," Hendricks said and took the man's gun out of his hand. His finger slipped inside the trigger guard and began to apply pressure. "I've got your ass now."

"Hendricks," said Jenn. "Don't!"

"What?" Hendricks demanded.

"Don't do it."

"What are you talking about? I've got him."

"Yes, Daniel," the man said conversationally. "Don't do it."

"No," Hendricks said, not taking his eyes off the man who had haunted his sleep ever since the two had fought to a standstill in an Atlanta motel room. "I *have* to do this. I say we buy that boat and go fishing. Use this motherfucker as chum."

"Dan, I swear to Christ, if you pull that trigger, you will regret it for the rest of your life," Jenn warned.

Hendricks looked uncertainly from Jenn to Gibson and back to the man. Who could blame him? thought Gibson. How many men got the opportunity to kill their nightmares?

"You want to give me one good reason?" he asked.

Jenn gave him half a million of them.

CHAPTER EIGHT

Gibson sat on the couch in Jenn's living room, nursing a Powerade. His body hurt; every muscle ached as if he'd run two marathons back to back. Jenn believed he'd suffered a post-traumatic-stress episode. Gibson had no idea what had happened; it was all very hazy in his memory. Mostly he felt angry and embarrassed that he'd reacted that way. Intellectually, he knew that it wasn't within his power to control, but that didn't stop him from feeling that he'd let everyone down.

"Are you up for this?" George asked, putting a hand on Gibson's shoulder. He'd only just arrived and was taking the temperature on everyone's state of mind.

"Yeah, I'm fine." That was anything but true, but Gibson needed people to stop asking him if he was all right. He didn't like feeling bubble wrapped. Was it too much to hope that Hendricks would say something cutting so he could stop feeling like the team mascot? Unfortunately, Hendricks was occupied at the moment.

At the far end of the room sat the man from Gibson's father's basement, restrained securely to a chair. Hendricks had tied the knots himself but kept his gun trained on the man as though he believed that, at any moment, the ropes might magically dissolve. Gibson understood the sentiment. Even though the man was bound and there were four of them and only one of him, Gibson couldn't outrun the feeling that they were the ones in danger.

His fingers felt under his beard for the scar that bisected his throat. He caught himself and pulled his hand away. It felt wrong to touch it in front of the man who had put it there. The man hadn't spoken a word since Hendricks had disarmed him, hadn't moved except when directed, and the only part of him that seemed alive were those pitiless black eyes. Eyes that never stopped watching and waiting. Gibson couldn't meet their gaze and had a hard time even looking at him. Was it weird that the man didn't look at all familiar? His hand drifted back to the scar.

"So, where are we?" George asked rhetorically when Jenn came downstairs from changing clothes. "Dan? Are you with us?"

"Yeah, I'm here," Hendricks said without moving his eyes or his gun from their prisoner.

"And what's your position on all this?"

"Put a bullet in him. Rent a boat. Feed him to the sharks."

The man from the basement had no reaction.

"So, an execution," George said.

"Call it whatever you like."

"Gibson?" George prompted.

"I'm with Hendricks on this. If he found us here, he can find us anywhere."

"What about the malware?" Jenn demanded, becoming impatient. "He's our only link to the thumb drive. Are we going to ignore what we found?"

"No one's saying that," Hendricks said. "We take what we have to the authorities. Let them deal with it."

"Deal with what?" Jenn said. "We don't know anything."

"Right, but at least they have the resources to investigate it," Gibson said. "We give it to them."

"Yeah, but they won't," she said.

"Of course they will," Hendricks said.

"No. They won't. Do you have any idea how many threat reports the United States receives each and every day?"

"Sure, but we're talking about a half-million lives here," Gibson said. "That's gotta move the needle, right? Jump us up the queue?"

"That's not how threat assessment works. This will go through the same vetting process as any other threat that's deemed credible. But how much credence do you think this will be given, coming from international fugitives?"

"So we report it anonymously."

"Same problem," Jenn said. "But let's say they overlook the source; again, we come back to my original question: What do we actually know for certain? Nothing actionable. We have a few spreadsheets and some malware that gives Gibson the willies. I'm telling you, if we go to them now with what we have, it will just wind up at the bottom of the pile on some analyst's desk at Langley."

"I'm afraid Jenn is right," George said. "No one will run this up the flagpole to senior leadership based on what we have now. And without that, no one will allocate the resources necessary to reverse engineer the malware on the thumb drive."

Jenn said, "Think about what we don't know. The target. The motive. The players."

"What are you talking about?" Hendricks said, gesturing to the man from the basement. "We have one of the players right here."

"The one you want to murder and dump in the Caribbean?"

Hendricks threw up his hands in frustration. "Fuck you, Jenn. Whatever. Let's say we turn *him* over along with the thumb drive. Does *that* get the attention of senior leadership?"

Gibson saw Jenn tense, on the brink of clapping back at Hendricks, before taking a deep breath to calm herself. "Even if he were cooperative, which I wouldn't bet on, he needed Gibson to break into the thumb drive. He had no more idea what was on it than we did."

"Maybe, but he's gotta know something. If he's not involved, why does he have it?"

"I was engaged to steal it," the man said. "The person I stole it from is still alive. Or was when I left their company."

The sound of the man's voice caused every hair on Gibson's body to prickle. His head became fuzzy again, as if he'd gotten a head rush from standing up too quickly. He took a sip of Powerade and focused on a spot on the floor until his vision cleared.

"Well, I'd highly recommend giving us the name, sunshine," Hendricks said. "You don't want to go in a room alone with her."

"Daniel, I am certain that Jennifer is a gifted interrogator and that the CIA trained her well, but I assure you, she could peel the meat from my bones, and I still would not give you the name. However, there may be another way."

"What other way?" Jenn said.

"An alliance," the man in the chair said.

Everyone looked at him, dumbfounded.

"No," Hendricks said. "No fucking way."

"What kind of an alliance?" Jenn said.

"I was hired to steal the thumb drive. My employer betrayed me and is hunting me even now."

"That's a real sad story," Hendricks said.

"I require his name. You require the name of the person I stole the thumb drive from. If you help arrange a face-to-face conversation for me, I will return the favor."

Hendricks laughed bitterly. "You want us to help save your life? You're even more bugshit-crazy than I thought."

"No, Daniel. I want to help you save half a million lives."

They all looked from one to the other, each attempting to reconcile what was right with what they needed. Jenn was the first to speak.

"Let's say I agreed."

"Jenn, no," Gibson said more loudly than he'd intended.

"I'm sorry, Gibson. Too many lives are at stake."

She was right, of course, but aligning herself with this monster who had murdered his father . . . ? How could she even consider it? Across the room, Hendricks was clearly struggling with similar thoughts.

"Let's say I agreed," Jenn began again. "Where would we start?"

"I have an aircraft at my disposal. We should pay a visit to Liam Walsh of Belfast."

"Agreed," Jenn said.

The man thought about it a long time. "And you won't interfere with what I need to do?"

"Not if you show me the same courtesy."

"Then we have an accord."

"Take me too," Gibson blurted, regretting it instantly but knowing he had no choice. Not if he wanted to live with himself.

Jenn shook her head. "I'm not asking you to do that."

"If you think I'm standing by while you go anywhere with him, you're out of your mind. Besides, this is computer related," he said, "and, I'm sorry, but Jenn is unqualified. Have you seen her laptop? It's a mess."

"Be that as it may," the man said, "I am not inclined to be outnumbered two to one."

"Three to one," Hendricks said. "Looks like this is a package deal."

"Absolutely unacceptable."

"Listen," Gibson told the man. "What if Liam Walsh is a dead end? What then? You're going to need a detective. We have a damn good one of those." He looked to Hendricks.

"The boy's right," Hendricks said. "Otherwise, we take you on that boat ride right now."

CHAPTER NINE

It was raining hard Russian rain, but Jurnjack hardly registered it. He'd been born wet, and chances were he'd die wet. What happened in between mattered less and less with each passing year. Out at the end of the runway, a plane launched itself into the evening sky over Saint Petersburg. From a distance, it was such a peaceful sight, silent as a falling coin.

He stood on the tarmac at the bottom of the airstairs, arms out to his sides, while a bodyguard scanned him with a handheld metal detector. Afterward, a second bodyguard conducted a physical search, patting him down crudely but thoroughly. A time-honored ritual that Jurnjack endured stoically. He had worked for Anatoly Skumin for more than fifty years, but the old Russian wouldn't be alone with him until Jurnjack had been searched and searched again. Some might call a personal security detail of twelve men paranoia; Jurnjack thought it wise. What he would give for even five minutes alone with Anatoly Skumin and a dull knife.

Fifty years. They weren't friends. They weren't partners.

What were they? Jurnjack worked for Skumin, but he wasn't an employee. That implied that he could retire or quit, but there was no walking away. Skumin referred to him as his Malinois—his Belgian attack dog—and that's exactly how he treated him. Like a dog. Skumin didn't trust him, didn't confide in him; there was never an explanation. Jurnjack had never been anything but a blunt tool to do Skumin's dirty work. When he had been a young man, Jurnjack had preferred that arrangement. So whose fault was it in the end for what he had become?

Skumin's limousine idled a short distance away. Jurnjack could feel him through the tinted glass, watching. Always watching, always evaluating. The man had a calculator where his heart should have been. They'd first met at a café in Antwerp in the spring of 1965 . . . how many lifetimes ago? Jurnjack remembered that first encounter well. His recruitment had already been underway for months, but it was the first time Jurnjack realized that he'd attracted powerful attention. Skumin had been all charm and oily smiles then. So cunning that Jurnjack hadn't realized he was KGB for another four years. By the time he did, it was far too late. Skumin was like a barbed arrow: the deeper into you he sunk, the more dangerous it became to pull free.

But Jurnjack had been a different man in those days. A sneering punk, no guile, all of seventeen, and already with a criminal record the length of his arm. Not including the two murders that the Belgium authorities had questioned him about. He had avoided a conviction in both cases, but that had been due to luck rather than careful planning. Skumin had offered to teach him how never to get caught again. He'd made many promises that day, but that was one of the few that he had kept.

Viktor Lebedev, Skumin's head of security, opened an umbrella and escorted Jurnjack across the tarmac to the waiting limousine. Jurnjack liked Viktor. He was a nice boy—honest, principled, and hardworking. Jurnjack himself had handpicked him to take responsibility for Skumin's day-to-day security.

"How is he?" Jurnjack asked in Russian, hoping for some sense of what he was walking into.

"Mr. Skumin is expecting you," Viktor replied, neutral as a Swiss mountain.

Smart. Always wise to know who buttered your bread and who stood to eat it. Viktor held open the door at the rear of the limousine. An umbrella emerged, followed by a young man of thirty. He wore an expensive suit and sniffed at the rain irritably. Lev Skumin, Anatoly's only son. Jurnjack thought he had grown up to be a good-looking boy, except for the angry scowl permanently etched into his face. It made Lev look old before his time, but what else could you expect of a boy who had grown up in the shadow of Anatoly Skumin's endless cruelty?

Especially since Skumin took such pleasure in tormenting his son. Deny a child affection and praise and warmth, replace it with scorn and criticism and malice, and you would end up with a young man like Lev Skumin. And that had been the point, Jurnjack supposed. Even though Sofia Skumin, Lev's mother, had been dead for more than twenty years, Skumin had still not forgiven her betrayal. She had fled to London with their son, attempted to establish residency, and filed for divorce. It had not been received well. So, when Lev had been brought home, Skumin had devoted himself to twisting the child in his own image—as venal, callous, and hollow as a shell casing—knowing full well that it would have broken his wife's heart. Death had never been enough for Skumin. Not for those he truly despised.

And, as is so often the case, the more disdain the father showed the son, the more the son worshiped the father. The harder Skumin berated and degraded him, the more Lev strove to earn his father's approval or any sign that his father held any affection for him at all. It had never come and would never come. After fifty years, Jurnjack knew firsthand the peril of betting on Skumin's humanity. How much worse would it be if Skumin learned that Lev was not his son at all?

Lev Skumin snapped his fingers imperiously at Jurnjack, who hurried over. The boy carried himself with the haughty, presumptuous confidence endemic to the children of the rich. Growing up on the shoulders of a powerful father, Lev expected obedience and loyalty. But it was never shown to him, only to the tyrant whose name he shared. Lev had never had to learn how to foster any of his own, and it made him a weak secondhand copy of his father. It always pained Jurnjack to see, and he kept his head down, ever wary of meeting the young man's eyes. Afraid that Anatoly Skumin would see his sadness and know why.

"Is it true? You lost the thumb drive?" Lev Skumin demanded.

"I don't know anything about a thumb drive," Jurnjack replied with a wince. Lev could stand to take a page from Viktor about discretion. His youthful arrogance often got him into trouble, and Anatoly would punish his son severely for disclosing the existence of the thumb drive. There was nothing Jurnjack could do to prevent it. "Perhaps it would be best if we not discuss it in the open?"

"That thumb drive represents five years of my work," Lev said. "Five years!"

At a young age, Lev had shown exceptional aptitude for computer programming. It was Lev who had convinced his father that cybercrime was the future and that he should let Lev start recruiting talent. In the early days, Lev's team had only tackled small-scale scams: ransomware attacks, identity theft, online fraud. Then they'd expanded their operations into election tampering and targeted social-media propaganda campaigns, both of which had proven lucrative revenue streams. Most recently, they'd added corporate espionage to their menu of services, contracting out to business interests seeking to gain a leg up on the competition.

The malware stored on the thumb drive represented the pinnacle of that work. A hack so complex that it would be studied for years to come. That is, if anyone realized that it had even happened, which, if it worked as well as Lev believed, no one would.

"Do you understand the consequences if it's not recovered?" Lev said.

Jurnjack shook his head that he did not, maintaining the deception that he knew nothing about the thumb drive. In truth, he understood far better than Lev the consequences because Lev still did not recognize the true nature of the monster that he had constructed. On that subject, Lev's father had left his son in the dark. Jurnjack had agonized over whether telling Lev the truth would have any effect. He feared the boy was too far gone and, even if he understood the lethality of his malware, that he would simply mimic his father and ignore the consequences until it was too late. So, in the end, Jurnjack had decided that he couldn't afford to take that risk and had stolen the thumb drive instead. Well, hired someone to steal it, but that someone had proven far more resourceful than expected.

"It would be catastrophic," Lev said. "Find it."

If Lev wanted someone to blame, he should look no further than his father. While the elder Skumin enjoyed the power and influence that his growing cyber operations afforded him, he barely comprehended it. The man was an eighty-year-old dinosaur who could barely operate his cell phone, let alone understand the intricacies of twenty-first-century cyber warfare. It was like explaining a stealth jet to a caveman.

It had been Skumin's brilliant idea, over Lev's strenuous objections, to store all the pieces on a single thumb drive and destroy all other copies. It had also been his decision to hide the thumb drive with Georgi Ivov, perhaps the only person in the organization who understood less about computers than Skumin himself. It was a tactic thirty years out of date, but the only kind that Skumin's analog brain understood. Supposedly, only three people had known its location: Skumin, Ivov, and Lev. That had given Jurnjack the sliver of plausible deniability necessary to exploit Skumin's colossal misstep. Had it been enough? Jurnjack would find out soon enough.

Lev went to get back into the limousine, but a voice from inside the vehicle stopped him.

"Wait outside. I will talk to our friend alone."

"Yes, Father." The affront in Lev's voice was palpable, but he didn't dare question the decision.

Jurnjack slipped out of the rain and into the back of the limousine. Skumin sat watching him through narrow, pinprick eyes set in a gaunt, bony face mottled with liver spots and streaked with broken blood vessels. His lustrous head of coal-black hair, meticulously dyed, only magnified his age and ill health like an ornate frame around an out-of-focus photograph. The limousine reeked of the old man, whose body lately had begun to stink like meat left out for too long on the kitchen counter. No amount of expensive cologne could cover it, although Lord knew, the old man tried.

Anatoly Skumin had traveled a long, inhospitable road—from a childhood on the ruined streets of Leningrad, clawing for survival among the feral orphans of the Nazi siege, to a distinguished military career that had led him to the KGB and leadership of the ruthless Thirteenth Department. Few alive knew the full extent of the fearsome campaign of assassination and intimidation that the Thirteenth had waged on Western Europe as their grip began to slip in the last decades of Soviet rule. Jurnjack had been one of Skumin's most reliable tools in those dark days and knew better than most where the bodies were buried.

One of the many reasons that it surprised Jurnjack to still be alive, but he knew that the day he ceased to be useful would be the day he joined the countless unmarked graves in Skumin's private cemetery. But for now, even though Skumin had long since retired from the KGB, Jurnjack's value had only increased. As it turned out, playing oligarch in the new Russia was not so terribly dissimilar to running a directorate in the KGB.

"Herr Skumin," Jurnjack said, noticing the bottle of nearly empty Moskovskaya Osobaya that sat on the console like a witness to an execution. Vodka had no discernable effect on Skumin, apart from whetting his legendary bloodlust; given the report that Jurnjack had flown here to deliver, it might as well have been pure gasoline in that bottle. Strangely, though, despite what had been lost on the thumb drive, Skumin seemed calmer than Jurnjack had dared to hope.

When Skumin replied, his voice was labored, a bronchial rumble, phlegmy and thick. "What news?"

"You've spoken to Herr Ivov?"

"Yes," Skumin replied. "He sounded stricken. Is what he says true? This man hid in his walls for a month?"

"Perhaps as long as six weeks."

"And you believe it?"

"His wife and eldest daughter *are* dead."

Skumin considered it. "Yes, that is compelling, I suppose. Could Ivov have the iron for such a deception?"

"No, Herr Skumin."

"No, I suppose not," Skumin agreed with only the faintest disappointment in his voice. "Are these deaths also his excuse for giving away my thumb drive?"

"They are. Do you want him dealt with?" Jurnjack ventured.

Skumin spun the vodka in the tumbler as if trying to separate it into its component parts. "No. He would be impossible to replace in time. Ivov was aware of how I would take his failure?"

"He is not a complete fool, Herr Skumin. He worries you will hold him responsible."

"Good. Let him go on thinking it," Skumin said, voice like a tunnel collapsing.

"Yes, Herr Skumin." Jurnjack knew then for certain that Georgi Ivov was a dead man; his children too. Skumin would wait until he had found a suitable replacement for Ivov's financial network, which laundered Skumin's rubles into euros. Any interruption would be intolerable to the old man. The money never stopped flowing. The singular rule by which Anatoly Skumin lived his life. Although why, Jurnjack couldn't comprehend. Skumin's health was failing. He had no passions or interests other than his business, no vision or agenda, no family other than a son he despised. The money had become an end in and of itself. Jurnjack had read once of a medical condition that caused a person to never feel full, no matter how much they consumed. If permitted, they would eat themselves to death, all the while convinced that they were starving. Anatoly Skumin had had that look in his eyes for half a century.

"So, what do we know about this vermin in the walls?" Skumin emptied the last of the vodka into a crystal tumbler and swirled it tidally. "Any idea who might have sent him?"

It was a dangerous question. Knowing it would come, Jurnjack had contemplated his answer for months before making his move. It was his job to know the answer, and from long experience, he knew the old man would not abide unanswered questions. On the other hand, if Jurnjack showed too much progress, Skumin would wonder how.

"I am looking into it, but so far I have nothing concrete. Is there anything you can tell me? May I ask what is on this thumb drive?"

Skumin's eyes narrowed. "How do you know about the thumb drive?"

"Lev just told me."

"That boy is an idiot."

"He was upset, Herr Skumin. He is young."

"I'm sure he will be grateful for your concern."

"Does it have anything to do with the malware?"

"What makes you say that?" Skumin snapped.

"Lev said it represented years of his work. I thought perhaps—"

Skumin stopped him with a gesture of his hand. "It's a little late in the day to be taking up new hobbies, don't you think?"

"Yes, Herr Skumin."

"The boy is very agitated. He's like a woman. Always talking."

"He only wants to please you," Jurnjack said, realizing immediately that he'd said too much.

"My son is none of your concern, dog. Do you understand me?"

Jurnjack lowered his eyes in a display of submission. "Yes, Herr Skumin. My apologies."

"Have you made any headway at all?"

"If you would share who knew of the thumb drive's existence . . . who knew it would be in Varna . . . If I had a clearer picture of the situation, I would not need to cast so wide a net."

"You are not my fisherman, Malinois. Put away your nets. I have begun my own inquiries. When I discover who is responsible, then you will know. In the meantime, you have several other matters requiring your attention, do you not?"

"Yes, Herr Skumin," Jurnjack said, doing his best to mask his surprise. When he'd first gotten into the limousine, he'd been so relieved at Skumin's outward calm that he hadn't asked himself why. The malware on the thumb drive represented potentially billions of euros and years of work. Skumin should have been apoplectic. Instead, he seemed irritated with Jurnjack for trying to do his job. Either Skumin was trying to conceal how much it mattered, which didn't strike Jurnjack as in character, or else it didn't matter to him nearly as much as it should.

"We have the French matter well in hand," Jurnjack said. "I do not think he will elude us for much longer. He is nothing but a hacker. Otherwise, we have tied off all remaining vulnerabilities."

"Would that include Ireland?"

"I am flying there from here to attend to it personally. What I do know is that the Irish contractor was eliminated. It was independently confirmed."

"Are you suggesting the dead are trying to hack us now?"

"No, Herr Skumin, of course not."

"If you have questions, speak to Lev. He's been tracking the attempted intrusion for several days now."

"I will, Herr Skumin," Jurnjack replied, although he had no intention of doing any such thing.

"And take Viktor with you."

The order dismayed Jurnjack. Not out of any personal animosity toward Viktor; he actually thought quite highly of the young man. It troubled Jurnjack because it meant two things: First, Skumin's doubts about Jurnjack were significant. And second, Jurnjack would likely have to kill Viktor Lebedev before it was all over. He would regret it if it came to that.

"Update me when you land," Skumin said, ending the conversation.

"Yes, Herr Skumin," Jurnjack repeated faithfully.

If there was one thing the old man enjoyed hearing, it was his own name along with the sound of compliance.

CHAPTER TEN

The pilot finished his visual inspection and boarded the aircraft to complete his preflight checklist. Stepping aside to let him go up the airstairs, Jenn ran her tongue across her front teeth and looked across the tarmac in the general direction of Gibson and Hendricks. In the shade of the hangar, Gibson sat staring off into space. He'd been doing that a lot in the twenty-four hours since they'd agreed to make the trip to Ireland. When he spoke, if he spoke at all, it was only to give curt answers to direct questions, as if he were paying by the monosyllable. She had no idea what was going on in his head.

Hendricks also hadn't had a lot to say, but at least his mood was easy to interpret: rage. He stood alone at the far end of the tarmac, furiously chain-smoking as though the cigarettes had insulted his mother. They had a nine-hour flight before them, and he was trying to get ahead of the nicotine curve. He had his back to her.

That was how they'd gone about the preparations for the trip—keeping their distance, keeping their own counsel. Their effortless camaraderie had been replaced by a tense, awkward silence. The reason, of course, was their new partner, who waited by the wingtip, in between Jenn and her colleagues. Sometimes life presented a metaphor so obvious even she couldn't miss it.

Jenn didn't doubt for a second that this was the right decision, but it didn't stop her from feeling guilty about it. She knew what this period of relative stability had meant to them, especially Gibson. Boarding the plane jeopardized all of that, but she found herself excited at the prospect. It meant the opportunity to do something meaningful again. She felt even guiltier because, despite their dread, Gibson and Hendricks hadn't hesitated to step up. Exactly as she'd known they would. It filled her with an odd sense of pride, despite the guilt. To have these people at her side. Maybe she'd made a few of the right choices along the way while making so many of the wrong ones. She realized how much she loved them.

Maybe try telling them that?

Well, now she was just talking crazy. If she started expressing her feelings, then the apocalypse couldn't be far behind.

The hardest part for her had been telling George that he couldn't come. It had broken her heart to do, but he wasn't physically up to a job like this. She'd done her best to let it appear to be his idea, despite being certain that George knew exactly what she was doing. Sparing his pride. He'd returned the favor, of course, and made it easy on her, suggesting that he remain behind to provide logistical support. Had she damaged that relationship irrevocably? She'd felt their roles changing for some time, gradually trading places. This might have been the final nail, though.

The pilot emerged and gave them permission to board the aircraft. Jenn put two fingers between her lips and whistled. Gibson climbed to his feet and walked toward her. Hendricks stamped out his last cigarette and followed behind. Their partner didn't move, waiting by the wing as if hewn from stone. His stillness unnerved her, and she prided herself on not being the unnerving type. They still didn't know his name. He hadn't offered it, and she hadn't asked. As if that much familiarity risked contaminating them with whatever was wrong with him. And there was most definitely something wrong with this man, no matter how

71

blandly ordinary he appeared. She'd been around him long enough now to realize that he never moved without purpose. He never scratched an itch, never shifted in his seat, never showed any expression when other people spoke. A spider waiting for something to catch in its web.

"You okay, there?" Jenn asked, elbowing Gibson in the side. She'd been keeping a watchful eye on him, and although he hadn't had a second PTSD episode, she worried about him. What kind of stress must he be under? Her father had been stationed in Beirut in 1983. One of the 220 Marines killed in the bombing on the twenty-third of October. She couldn't imagine being asked to work alongside the men who had planned the attack.

"It's nothing," he said. "It's just, the last time I got on one of these things, I disappeared for eighteen months."

"No, the last time one brought you home," she replied.

"That's a positive spin, coach," he said with a smile that didn't reach his eyes.

"I'm doing my best here."

"I know that," he said.

"You think *he's* going to make it?" She gestured with her chin toward Hendricks.

"I think the more important question is whether *we'll* make it. We're going to be trapped on this thing with him."

It was the first joke they'd shared in a while, and Jenn laughed in relief.

"This is going to be a long flight," Hendricks grumbled, walking up to join them.

"Here," Gibson said, holding out a pack of nicotine gum.

A surprised smile crossed Hendricks's face, which he quickly stowed. He snatched the gum from Gibson and climbed the airstairs.

"You're welcome . . . ," Gibson called out after him.

"Thank you," Hendricks said without turning around.

"You know what you are? Ungrateful," Gibson said, following him inside.

Jenn watched them disappear inside the aircraft, feeling strangely reassured that they could weather this thing together. When she turned back, their partner was standing in front of her. She flinched. On impulse, she asked, "What's your name? What do we call you?"

The man considered how to answer the question. "Fred Tinsley."

She hadn't known what to expect, but it certainly hadn't been that. For reasons she couldn't explain, it felt wildly insufficient. If an astronomer discovered an asteroid hurtling toward the earth, they didn't name it Petunia. And a ruthless assassin who had haunted the dreams of her two closest friends for years couldn't be named Fred Tinsley.

"Shall we?" he asked.

"Guess it's that time."

Jenn led him inside, where a steward welcomed her onboard. She sat across the aisle from Hendricks while Gibson had the seat facing them. Jenn whistled in appreciation—it was a gorgeous aircraft. Plush leather recliners. A wet bar. Two couches. No overhead compartments, so it felt less claustrophobic than a commercial aircraft. How much did it cost to charter a G5? Couldn't be cheap. Murder paid well.

"A man could get used to this," Hendricks said, making himself comfortable. He froze, looking past Gibson toward the front of the aircraft. "Oh, what the fuck now?"

Their partner stood in the door of the plane, studying the layout carefully. A minute passed, then another. The captain spoke over the intercom, requesting passengers take their seats. Reluctantly, the assassin chose the seat nearest the cockpit, facing back toward them.

"His name is Fred Tinsley," Jenn said. "I asked."

"Fred Tinsley? What kind of name is that?" Hendricks muttered.

Buckled up, Tinsley looked at each of them once, and then went to sleep. No, "sleep" wasn't the right word for it. To Jenn, he looked more like a lamp that had come unplugged, its light blinking out in an instant. Tinsley went limp, shoulders slumped, eyes falling heavily closed.

"Well, that's the creepiest thing I've ever seen," Gibson said.

Hendricks popped two pieces of gum into his mouth, grunted his agreement, and produced a deck of cards. "Anyone know any three-person card games? Because no way I'm sleeping."

"I'm in," Gibson said.

"Rummy?" Jenn suggested.

Hendricks shuffled and dealt.

CHAPTER ELEVEN

The original flight plan called for Tinsley's chartered aircraft to land at George Best Belfast City Airport, which was only a short drive from the home of Liam Walsh. But they all agreed that an international airport was too high profile, given their fugitive status. An hour out, the pilot filed an amended flight plan and diverted to a smaller airfield ninety minutes west of Belfast. Out of the way, but it meant fewer cameras, less scrutiny, and not as many hands in their pockets looking for a payoff.

While the pilot and Tinsley smoothed things over with the ground staff, Gibson and Hendricks stepped out to stretch their legs. The forecast had called for unseasonably cold weather, and the sky was slate gray from horizon to horizon. A fine misting rain fell like the kind that spritzed the vegetables at upscale grocery stores. After the long, sleepless flight, Gibson found it refreshing, although it quickly soaked through his T-shirt. After the balmy sunshine of the Caribbean, none of them was prepared for Northern Ireland.

"This is some San Francisco–type shit," Hendricks grumbled, rubbing his arms for warmth. He'd been raised in Oakland until his father had moved the family to Los Angeles. "It's May, man. Did they forget to pay the heating bill?"

"It's not that bad," Gibson said as a cold wind picked up, seeming somehow to blow from three directions simultaneously. *Point taken, wind,* he thought.

Tinsley's negotiations concluded, they were allowed to leave the airfield. Jenn emerged from the plane, and they walked out to the parking lot to find the car that George had arranged for them. It didn't take long, since there were only three vehicles in the entire lot: a Nissan, a Ford Fiesta, and a late-model minivan with tinted windows and enough cosmetic damage to suggest that its previous owner had struggled with lane integrity.

"A goddamn Citroën minivan . . . are you kidding me?" Hendricks said, freshly lit cigarette bouncing between his lips. He fished a magnetic key holder from under the wheel well. "Why does George hate me?"

Hendricks was their driver. A wizard behind the wheel who had begun his career as a patrolman. In the years since, he'd taught tactical and evasive driving courses after retiring from the LAPD. More than once, Gibson had witnessed the man coax a car into defying the basic laws of physics.

"Hey, at least it's not a Peugeot this time," Gibson said.

"True, but I drove the shit out of that hoopty."

Tinsley was circling the minivan like a critic preparing to render judgment on an unknown painter. "A good vehicle," he said upon completing his orbit. "Invisible. No one will pay it any attention."

"Glad you approve," Hendricks muttered.

"You're welcome, Daniel."

Hendricks spun toward Tinsley, fury and disgust making a jagged snarl of his face. "Hey, keep my name out of your mouth. Hear me?"

Tinsley stood there, unmoving and unmoved.

"You hear me?" Hendricks spat a second time and started toward him.

"Dan," Jenn said quietly and put a hand on his shoulder.

"Get something straight," Hendricks said. "We're not friends. We're not partners. You're nothing to me. So, don't be using my name like we know each other. We clear?"

Tinsley nodded, an expression of bemusement on his face, the way a tired parent might look at a child throwing a tantrum. At least that was how Gibson interpreted it, although he was less and less convinced that Tinsley's facial expressions corresponded to any known human emotion.

"Like talking to a damn alien," Hendricks said.

"Come on," said Jenn. "Let's get moving."

Hendricks relented, turning his back on Tinsley. He opened the back of the van, which contained three plastic storage bins labeled with their initials: "JC," "GV," "DH." Inside each was a set of clothes, an ID that would pass a cursory examination, a clean phone, and five hundred British pounds. Jenn changed in the minivan; the men got dressed in the rain. Everything fit perfectly.

Gibson stacked the bins and stowed their gear in back while Hendricks started the engine to let it warm up. The British drove on the left side of the road, so the steering wheel was on the right. Hendricks stared at the layout as if trying to make sense of a foreign language. He fished the owner's manual from the glove and read through it, familiarizing himself with every knob and button on the dashboard. It was his ritual in any unfamiliar car, and the ex-cop would not be hurried. Gibson had gotten used to it, but he watched Tinsley up in the passenger seat, expecting him to question the delay and spark another confrontation. Instead, Tinsley nodded approvingly, skill recognizing skill, and said nothing at all. When Hendricks was satisfied, he made three laps of the parking lot, testing the acceleration and the brakes, making sharp turns to feel how the minivan held the road. He pulled to a stop at the street and grunted.

"What's the verdict?" Jenn asked.

"Handles like a brick with high hopes. On the upside, we could probably outrun someone on foot."

They drove through towns with names like Enniskillen, Maguiresbridge, and Fivemiletown. Traffic was sparse at this hour, and what little there was meandered without seeming purpose. Much like the road itself, which followed a winding path that had been set down long before there had been automobiles. Out his window, Gibson watched the countryside roll by. He didn't know why the grass should be greener here than anywhere else, but it was achingly so, and he wished the sun would come out for a moment so he could see it in all its glory.

Without making a turn, Belfast Road became Colebrook Road, which itself became Ballagh Road as though designed purposefully to mislead outsiders. As they neared the village of Ballygawley, Tinsley broke the silence. "I have a stop to make in Armagh."

"That's twenty miles out of our way," Hendricks said, glancing at Jenn in the rearview mirror.

"What for?" Jenn asked.

"To collect a package."

"What kind of package?" She leaned forward between the two front seats.

"Not clothes," Tinsley said. "But I also need supplies."

"We're just going to talk to Liam Walsh," Jenn said. "That's it."

"Think of it as an icebreaker."

"We made a deal."

"Yes, we did. But I am not in the habit of traveling unarmed to places I do not know. Are you? But don't fret, I have something for you as well."

Gibson didn't think Tinsley had meant anything by it, but the way he phrased it—*I have something for you as well*—made all three of them flinch. It also elicited the first hint of emotion that he'd seen in Tinsley, who seemed pleased and possibly even amused by the effect his words had on them.

Jenn nodded to Hendricks, who hung a right instead of continuing straight, as though he'd driven these roads all his life. Gibson bet Hendricks could name every town between here and Belfast. He was part man, part atlas.

With a population of fewer than fifteen thousand, Armagh had nonetheless been labeled as a city. Perhaps that was due to the cathedral—twin spires soaring two hundred feet into the morning sky—that loomed on a rise overlooking the homes and shops below.

Tinsley directed Hendricks to the Armagh Observatory, which had probably been cutting edge when it had been built in 1789. Now it was a pretty, old building with copper domes turned green with age. They drove up to the observatory, passing the gardens that flanked the road. As they crested the hill, they saw a single car idling in the parking lot behind the main building. The other car's doors opened, and two hard men emerged, thick limbed, with wiry, asbestos beards that covered their faces like masks. They both wore matching black leather jackets as if their fashion sense came directly from seventies gangster movies. Hendricks slowed and made a gentle turn before rolling to a stop, facing back down the hill.

"Would you accompany me?" Tinsley asked, turning to face Gibson.

The request caught Gibson off guard, and he didn't reply immediately.

"This is not my traditional merchant," Tinsley explained, sensing Gibson's hesitation. "Since my network is compromised, I've had no alternative but to make other arrangements. But it means I have no relationship with these men. If I am alone, they might see that as a sign of weakness. It will be fine. I only need you to stand there."

"Why him?" Jenn asked.

"Because you're a woman, and because he is black," Tinsley said. "No offense is intended."

"No offense is taken."

"These kinds of men," Tinsley said, "they react poorly to the unexpected. You would provoke questions. He won't."

"It's fine," Gibson said, reaching for the door. "Let's just get it done."

They crossed the parking lot. When they were halfway, Tinsley paused and told Gibson to wait there.

"What for?"

"Appearances," Tinsley replied. "Try to look bored."

"Bored?"

Tinsley thought about it. "Aloof and disinterested."

"I could have done that from the car."

"Yes, but I need them to see you doing it," Tinsley explained, Gibson's joke leaving a neat part in his hair as it flew over his head.

Tinsley went to meet the two men. The rain and wind muffled their voices to the point that Gibson couldn't make out what they were saying, but he got the impression that he was the primary topic of conversation. One of the men didn't speak and never took his eyes off Tinsley, but the other one, older and clearly the boss, kept glancing his way. Gibson did his best to look disinterested, but it made him uneasy. Had Tinsley walked him into a setup? Gibson feared it would come eventually, but this would be sooner than he'd expected.

A thick envelope exchanged hands. The boss opened it and skimmed a thumb across the top of a stack of bills. He slipped the envelope into his breast pocket and rapped his young associate on the shoulder. The younger man trotted back to their car and fetched a hard-shell suitcase from the trunk. Returning, he set it on the ground at his feet, opened it, and spun it around to give Tinsley a better look.

Tinsley glanced back, gave Gibson a thumbs-up, and waited as if needing his permission to proceed.

Gibson saw it then—how he'd been set up. To preserve his anonymity, Tinsley had assumed the role of lackey, passing Gibson off as his boss. Irritated, Gibson considered blowing Tinsley's cover out of spite. But for what? It was no real skin off his back. Plus, this offered a little more insight into how Tinsley operated. Everything, no matter how small or seemingly insignificant, was part of a larger con. Nothing could be taken at face value. And knowing that was far more valuable right now than letting Tinsley know he knew. So, Gibson dutifully played along and gave Tinsley a curt nod. The boss pointed to the hedge that ran alongside the observatory. Tinsley walked over and dragged out a second hard-shell suitcase from beneath a bush. He knelt to open it and assess the contents.

The moment his back was turned, the younger man took out a phone and began scrolling through it. Whatever he was looking for, he found; Gibson saw it in his eyes. Subtly, the man tilted the screen so his boss could see it. The boss looked down, his face as still as a frozen lake. Except Gibson could see dark shapes swimming up from the depths, preparing to break through the ice. Funny thing was, if they hadn't tried to be slick, Gibson probably wouldn't have noticed—there was nothing inherently suspicious about looking at your phone. Secrets were like the small planets in distant solar systems that astronomers couldn't observe directly but knew had to be there by the way their gravity bent the light around them. Secrets had that same gravity and caused people holding them to behave strangely. Gibson didn't know what their secret was, but in trying to play it cool, the young associate had given himself away. Without moving his head, the boss looked over at Tinsley. That's when Gibson realized that they had a serious problem.

They knew Tinsley.

Well, they didn't know him, but they knew *of* him. Something on the phone had connected the dots. But what? The only explanation was that after Tinsley had gone to ground, his pursuers had hung a bounty on his head. Spread the word far and wide in the criminal underworld. Not a bad plan, and it looked like they had just scored a hit.

It was tempting to step away and let nature take its course. Leave the animals to devour each other. But they still might need Tinsley alive down the road. Maybe it was all a fantasy, but if Gibson let Tinsley die, and six months from now, Americans began to die . . . well, there would be no living with that knowledge. His need for vengeance would have to take a back seat. Sometimes, the greater good was such a pain in his ass.

Gibson took his hands out of his pockets, held them out at his side, and approached the men while Tinsley still remained at a distance. Up close, he saw that they were father and son. Despite the weathering of years, the resemblance was unmistakable. The son stepped between Gibson and his father, crossing his arms and spreading his legs.

"How much are they offering?" Gibson looked over the son's shoulder and asked his father.

"Don't know whatcha talking about, boy," the man said, his accent so thick and fluid that Gibson had trouble picking out where one word ended and the next began.

"It's not enough."

The man looked at Gibson for the first time, an amused twinkle in his eyes. "How can you say, not knowing how much it is?"

Gibson unwound the scarf around his neck. Unbuttoning his jacket, he pulled down the collar of his sweater and parted his beard to show them his throat.

"Nasty scar you got there. Cut yourself shaving, did you?"

His son snickered.

"That man over there? He hung me."

The son stopped laughing abruptly.

Over by the hedge, Tinsley was still crouched over the case inspecting his purchase, but Gibson could feel the searing heat of the killer's attention. The situation needed to be defused quickly or things were going to take an ugly turn right here, right now.

"He hung me from a beam in the basement of the house where I grew up. When I didn't answer his questions, he kicked the stool out from under my feet and watched me swing. The movies get that part wrong—you don't die right away. It can take twenty, even thirty, minutes. Whenever I came close to blacking out, he would put the stool back. Let me regain my strength before he dropped me again. Dragged it out. Enjoyed himself too."

"If all that's true, I'd think you'd be stepping aside, let us do what needs doing."

"I wish I could. Believe me. I'd enjoy nothing more in this world."

"So why don't you, then?"

"You're supposed to, what? Pass along where to find him?"

"For a finder's fee," the man said.

"A huge fucking finder's fee," the son piped up.

"What if they miss?" Gibson said.

"That's not our problem," the son said. "We'd have done our part."

"Oh, I'd say that would be exactly when it became your problem. Because if you let them know where to find him, your lives will depend on how good they are. And what do you really know about them anyway? My money would be on our man here. If you make that call and they miss, then he will kill you. Kill your son. Kill your families. Leave you all hanging from the end of ropes. I know he looks like a man, but he isn't one."

"You're being a wee bit dramatic now."

"Maybe I am. Maybe I'm trying to put the fear of God into you. Because fear can save your life. You really want to be looking over your shoulders for the rest of your life wondering if he's still out there? If he might be coming back. And for what? *A finder's fee?* You don't want to know the kind of nightmares that money will bring with it, trust me."

"So maybe we just take him ourselves," the younger man said.

"Then he'll kill you now," Gibson said without hesitation.

"And how's he going to do that, then? He's unarmed now, isn't he? He's got the guns, but we've got his ammo," the younger man said, kicking the first suitcase.

"That's true," Gibson said. "May I ask you a question?"

"If you like."

"What do you do for a living? Sell guns?"

"Among other things."

"Well, he doesn't sell guns. He buys them. You ask me how would he do it? Honestly, I have no damned idea—only that he already knows. He knew the moment he saw you. That's what he does. That's all he does: looks at a man and thinks of all the ways he can kill him."

"Ah, that's a bunch of shite," the younger man said, trying to puff himself up.

His father didn't look so sure, his enthusiasm for the plan waning. "So, what do you suggest?"

"Did he pay you well today?"

"He did at that."

"Then it was a good day. Keep it that way. Forget you ever saw him. Get in your car. Go kiss your wife."

The older man stood for a long time looking at the trees. "Let's go, Conor."

"Da. He's bluffing."

"I said let's go, boy. Don't make me tell you again."

He cuffed his son in the side of the head and pointed to their car. Reluctantly, his son backed away from Gibson and got into the car. When they were gone, Tinsley returned with the second suitcase.

"That was hardly necessary. I could have dealt with them."

"That's why it was necessary," Gibson said.

"Now it will be us who are looking over our shoulders. What makes them worth the risk?"

"Killing is not going to be our first, second, or third option. I don't care who it is."

Tinsley continued his thought as though he hadn't heard Gibson. "Is it because you're unable to protect your daughter and wife? Do you think that could be the reason? The fire that burned down their house must have been traumatic."

Gibson's hands balled into fists even as he tried to weigh his words carefully. Ever since his PTSD episode, he had known that he had a problem. In the years since the terrible night down in the basement of Gibson's childhood home—when Tinsley had hanged him, and Gibson had finally learned that his father's death was no suicide—Gibson had mythologized the assassin. Transformed Tinsley into something more than a man. Or perhaps less than one. Of course, to a point, fear was healthy and could keep you safe. But his fear had metastasized; like a malignant tumor, it had grown and grown until it had crowded out his rational mind. Either way, it would put him at a disadvantage until he stopped thinking about Tinsley as the bogeyman. And that meant not falling for Tinsley's mind games.

"Do I have you talking out your ass to look forward to for the entire trip, or is this a special occasion?"

"There is always the chance that they will be ungrateful for the charity you showed them."

"Then we probably shouldn't hang around," Gibson said and left Tinsley to carry the suitcases back to the minivan.

CHAPTER TWELVE

They exited the A12 motorway and drove into West Belfast along the peace wall that separated Catholic Falls Road from Protestant Shankill Road. Intended as provisional solutions to the outbreak of sectarian violence in 1969, the walls had proliferated across Belfast in the decades since, reinforced and expanded until the concrete and steel barriers loomed twenty feet overhead. Permanent fixtures in the lives of those who lived in their shadow, as testified to by the layer upon layer of graffiti that had accumulated over the years like silt settling to the bottom of a polluted pond.

The wall reminded Jenn of the dividers erected beside American highways to give residents of subdivisions the illusion that their dream home hadn't been built beside eight lanes of traffic. Except, in this case, the walls had been designed for both communities, Catholic and Protestant, to forget that their sworn enemy lived no more than a stone's throw away. Out of sight, out of mind, so that life could go on. Such as it was.

By most accounts, the walls had done exactly that. So much so that twenty years after the Good Friday Agreement, the two communities were wary of dismantling the barriers that separated them. *Sometimes people build their own prisons,* Jenn thought. How quickly people tuned out the bad in their worlds, internalizing and accepting it as a fact of life. She'd seen it in frontline soldiers who barely flinched at the sound of gunfire. In the way people who lived near noxious industrial plants stopped smelling anything at all. Who knew, maybe it was for the best. There was always going to be evil in the world, and she'd become too much of a cynic to believe most of it was solvable. Maybe the only solution was to build walls, either real or metaphoric, put your head down, and get on with your life as best you could.

If you believe that, then why did you drag these people here, you fool?

Jenn laughed out loud. She hadn't meant to, but out it came like a round she didn't know she'd chambered. Dan glanced over at her questioningly. She shook him off. If it got around that she was musing about the meaning of life, she'd never hear the end of it. Or worse, one of them would try to have a heart-to-heart with her. She loved them all, but that was a hard *no*, thank you very much. Jenn Charles had life all figured out. That was the impression she projected and the impression she wished them to have.

Hendricks turned into a neighborhood seemingly built entirely of red brick. At the first intersection, he paused to study the street signs, which were affixed to the sides of buildings in English and Gaelic. Having taken his bearings, Hendricks made a right, a left, and another left. He pulled up to the curb alongside a small redbrick row house, indistinguishable from any of its neighbors. A low redbrick wall, turned a mossy green in spots, ran the length of the block.

"Is this Liam Walsh's house?" Gibson asked.

"No," Hendricks said, pointing up the street to a cul-de-sac, square on three sides with only one way in and one way out. "It's down there, but we have a problem. No good way to case it without being made. Can't do a drive-by to get a good look at it."

"How about we pull up, act lost, take a quick look around, and then beat it?" Jenn said.

"Could do that. But that'll make coming back tricky. We'll have been seen."

"Seen by whom?" Tinsley asked doubtfully. "Do they have security?"

"Nah, they *are* the security. All the houses face out onto the courtyard. Neighborhood like this? Someone's always watching. People who've lived here their whole lives. No one drives in here by accident. Locals will know everyone who comes in and out. Know the faces. Know the cars. Know who they're visiting. Probably know why too."

"Hendricks . . . when was the last time you were in Belfast, exactly?" Gibson asked.

Hendricks shrugged. "Ghetto's a ghetto. Doesn't matter where you are."

"Do we care?" Jenn asked. "If we're seen, I mean."

They fell to arguing among themselves. Tinsley wanted to wait until nightfall and go in quietly. Hendricks wanted to stake out the cul-de-sac and tail Liam Walsh when he left the house. Jenn still thought they could get away with driving into the cul-de-sac for a brief reconnaissance. They went around in circles, making the same arguments, no one giving an inch. It made Jenn grateful for the tinted windows.

The problem was, she realized, that they had no way to break the deadlock. Tinsley didn't trust them, and that feeling was certainly mutual. It meant that no one stood clearly in charge. How were they supposed to function if they couldn't even reach a consensus about something this basic? It had been hard enough to knit them together into a functioning unit without Tinsley in the mix. Jenn was ostensibly the shot caller, but Hendricks and Gibson were strong personalities who took a lot of convincing. Even if she wanted to, she wouldn't know how to begin managing Tinsley. Did Myers-Briggs even have a personality type for what he was? The whole test would probably spontaneously combust.

Gibson, who had sat quietly in the back seat up until now, finally spoke up. "I think maybe we're overthinking this. We're just here to talk to him, right?" Gibson looked Tinsley in the eye. "Right? So, let's go talk to him."

"And if he doesn't want to talk to us?" Hendricks said.

"Then we sit back and tail him when he comes out of there. But at least then we'll know who to tail. We don't even know what he looks like right now."

Hendricks conceded the point. Scouring social media had turned up dozens of Liam Walshes, not exactly an uncommon name in Ireland.

"This plan is flawed," Tinsley said.

"Probably, but like hell you're sneaking in there at night. I know how that works out," Gibson said.

Tinsley bristled. "I do not take direction from you."

"Fine, do what you want, sneak in at night, but I'm going to go knock on his door."

"That will give away our—"

Gibson cut him off. "I don't take direction from you either."

The entrance to the cul-de-sac was flanked by two high brick walls missing only a gate to make the place feel like a fort. They drove through a scrum of pale boys kicking a ball, oblivious to the rain. Against the wall, one of the boys stood sullenly between the cardboard box and shoe that served as a makeshift goal. The others peppered shots at him, none of which he made any effort to stop. He simply waited like a man facing a firing squad. The boys paused as the minivan passed and watched it park before returning to their game. None was older than twelve, and all had no more than a half inch of hair on their heads. As if they'd all been inducted into the army that morning and been freshly shorn.

Hendricks chose a spot a few doors down from Liam Walsh's address. He was right, all the homes faced out onto the cul-de-sac. The windows were mostly dark, but Jenn couldn't escape the sense of being watched. Across the courtyard, three little girls rode bicycles in a tight circle, talking and laughing.

Hendricks and Jenn were nominated to ring the doorbell. Four strange faces at his door might come off as a little aggressive, and they didn't want to spook Liam Walsh. The rain was picking up again, so they huddled under the overhang, and Hendricks pressed the button lightly. It set off a cacophony of church bells inside the house as if high mass would be conducted in the Walsh kitchen this morning. After a minute, when they didn't hear any sounds of activity, Hendricks rang a second time. Not that anyone could have missed it the first time.

"Mister, they're not home."

The three girls had biked over to greet them. They sat side by side by side, studying Jenn and Hendricks over the handlebars of their bicycles like sheriffs come to see if the strangers to these parts meant to disturb the peace.

"Do you know where they are?" Jenn said.

"Ciara and her mummy are at the funeral," a second girl replied matter-of-factly. "Half the neighborhood is there."

Before Jenn could ask, the first girl said, "Poor Liam's funeral."

Hendricks caught Jenn's eye—Liam Walsh was dead. She nodded. Coincidences happened, happened all the time, but this felt wrong to both of them.

"Hit by a car, he was."

"Hit-and-run."

"Whack," the first girl said, slapping her hands together.

"Never saw it coming, so says me mum."

"That's because he was blocked," the first girl confided to her friend.

"He was always blocked," the second answered, and they both dissolved into giggles. The third girl frowned but said nothing.

"Blocked?" Jenn asked.

The girls looked at Jenn as if she'd come from another planet, which was how Jenn was beginning to feel.

"Blocked," said the first girl. "Like . . . blocked." As though that cleared up the matter.

"Fancied a pint, so he did," the second girl clarified.

"Fancied a dozen." More giggling.

"Shut yer bake," the third girl said, reaching the limits of her tolerance for her friends' disrespect. "It's not right the way youse are carrying on. Liam was an eejit, sure enough. But don't stand at his door and slag him. Not today."

The way the two girls fell silent and mumbled a chastened apology, Jenn knew who called their shots. Satisfied, the third girl turned her attention to Jenn and Hendricks. "So, where're you lot from, then?"

"America," Jenn said.

The girl was duly impressed. "Me aunt's been to America. Brought me a T-shirt from Orlando."

"Are you here for the funeral, then?" the first girl asked.

"Yes," Hendricks agreed. "We were supposed to arrive yesterday, but our flight got delayed."

This new information was met with a considered silence.

"So how does Liam know a black fella from America, then?"

"We're friends of the family," Hendricks said. "We didn't know Liam personally. Just here to lend our support."

This generosity and kinship was greeted with approval by the three girls. "That's very good of you. Proper like."

The back door of the minivan opened, and Gibson joined them outside Liam Walsh's home. The girls fell silent, gazing up at Gibson shyly like he was a movie star. It made Jenn reappraise her friend. With his blond beard framed by the collar of his navy peacoat, and those unwavering pale-green eyes that had struck her the first time she'd seen him, he looked the part. But it was more than that.

When she'd met Gibson, he'd been a very angry young man. Angry at everyone and everything, himself most of all. Then for a long time he'd been adrift, broken by guilt and by loss. So lost that Jenn doubted whether he'd ever find his way back. She realized now that he had found himself and that it had happened right under her nose. He'd learned how to hide his scars, but those scars had become a part of him too. Softened him. Smoothing the sharp edges that had made her so wary of him originally. He was still a pain in her ass, but when he smiled now, she no longer worried that he had thought of something cutting to say. When he smiled, it was because he was happy. That made all the difference. He looked healthy again for the first time in a long while. It surprised Jenn that it had taken three little girls swooning over him for her to notice, but she'd long since stopped looking at her friend, *really* looking at him.

Hendricks noticed it, too, and rolled his eyes.

"What's going on?" Gibson asked, looking more taken aback by the girls' reaction than anyone.

"We missed them," Hendricks said, catching Gibson up on the lie already in progress. "They're at the funeral. I told you we should have gone straight to the church."

Gibson picked up the narrative seamlessly and winced at the bad news. "Maybe. Yeah, you're right. That's my bad. I thought we'd have more time. But, look, we're here now. Let's get freshened up first. It was a long flight, and I don't want to go to the funeral looking like this."

Hendricks asked Jenn who they were supposed to pick up a spare key from. She started to answer and then stopped, pretending to be surprised not to remember the answer. She let a long moment pass while she struggled to remember a name she'd never known. Hendricks had set the table so that she would be the one who'd let everyone down. That would play well with the three girls, who were much more interested in Gibson.

"Didn't you write it down?" Gibson said with feigned exasperation. Jenn shrugged helplessly.

"The Thompsons have a key," the first girl volunteered.

"Thompson," Jenn exclaimed. "That's it."

The girls looked pleased that they'd been a help. Gibson gave them a grateful smile.

"They're at the funeral as well, but I know how to get it," the first girl said, eager to keep up her winning streak.

The trio's leader looked at her like she was the world's first fool. "Well, go fetch it, then. What're you waiting for?"

The girl pedaled away furiously, returning shortly with a single silver key on a long loop of string. She presented it like Excalibur to Gibson, who made a great show of unlocking the door and fussing over the girls. Jenn didn't know how she felt about conning three twelve-year-old girls. But it had gotten them inside and out of the rain. She was already over being wet all the time.

The front door opened directly into a small living room, where a dozen Mylar balloons bobbed against the ceiling. Ornate flower arrangements formed a neat semicircle around a coal-black fireplace. At the center was a framed photograph of a young man. It sat on a low wooden stool that had been fancied up with an ornate silk scarf. An impromptu altar for the recently deceased Liam Walsh.

In his school uniform and close-cropped hair, he looked all of seventeen. At most. Jenn hadn't expected him to be a kid. She didn't know why, though: cybercriminals often skewed young. Gibson Vaughn, case in point. He'd been even younger than Liam Walsh when the FBI had arrested him for hacking a senator's computer and turning the contents over to the *Washington Post*. Still, stealing documents from a computer was a long way from conspiring to murder tens of thousands of people. No matter how hard she looked, she couldn't see it in the boy's face. Neither in his portrait nor in any of the dozens of family photos that lined the living room walls.

In all of them, Liam sat on the living room couch beside his mother, a stout, middle-aged woman whose eyes sparkled and smiled despite the deep lines that a hard life had etched in her face. On her other side sat a girl who was the spitting image of her brother, apart from the long black hair and mouth full of braces.

Ciara Walsh, no doubt.

Jenn followed the line of photographs, tracing the family through the years. The earliest pictures showed Liam sitting between his mother and father. A little sister joined the family when Liam was still a toddler. When Liam was perhaps seven and the girl no older than four, a second sister appeared. Shortly thereafter, the father disappeared, never to return, and Jenn could sense the chip growing on Liam's shoulder with each subsequent photograph. From birth, the youngest child appeared horribly frail, skin mottled pink and white. She was only in the photographs for a few years, and Jenn didn't need to see the medical equipment to guess the tragic end of her story.

Off the small living room was an even smaller kitchen. A narrow flight of stairs led to the second floor. The house was cramped, yes, but Jenn liked it. It felt cozy. Warm and well loved. Even having lost her son, the mother had kept the house spotless. The couch was at least ten years old, but it had been maintained so carefully that it might last another hundred. All the art had a spiritual bent, and ceramic tchotchkes and figurines of angels decorated the shelves. In the kitchen, Jenn recognized a familiar poster—footprints in the sand to illustrate a poem about God. Her grandmother had kept a framed copy in her bedroom. It had hung alongside a copy of the Second Amendment, the other pillar of her grandmother's faith. Jenn knew the poem by heart, having been made to copy it over and over whenever she misbehaved, until her hand cramped. She despised its cloying sentimentality.

With Liam Walsh no longer among the living, Jenn knew they were back to square one. Unless the young man had left something behind to point them in the right direction . . .

Tinsley took up a post on the living room couch, among the balloons and flowers, to watch the front door in case someone came home unexpectedly. The thought didn't give Jenn much peace of mind, especially now that Tinsley was armed. But she reckoned the quicker they finished the search, the quicker they could get him out of there. She and Gibson followed Hendricks up the stairs and asked how they could be helpful.

"How about don't touch anything?" Hendricks suggested. "'Cause that would sure help."

"Guy spends twenty years in the LAPD, and it goes straight to his head," Gibson said and went to find the bathroom.

"Twenty-two," Hendricks corrected.

The logical starting point was Liam's bedroom. It was easy enough to pick out just from the combination of pheromones and body spray. Posters of Barcelona soccer stars decorated the walls, and a Lionel Messi jersey hung lovingly on the back of a chair. A soccer ball sat on the end of his bed as though Liam had set it down for a moment and would be right back for it. *No such luck,* thought Jenn, who stood in the doorway watching Hendricks. She didn't know the boy or his family, but the thought saddened her. She knew what it did to families when they contracted unnaturally. It had happened to her not once but twice.

Hendricks moved methodically through the room with the trained eye of an experienced investigator, looking in places that wouldn't have occurred to Jenn.

"Attack must be coming soon," he said, lifting the mattress to check if anything had been hidden on the box spring. "If they're eliminating their people."

It was a worrying development. Jenn wanted to believe that they had the only copy of the malware, but what if that was only wishful thinking? Had Liam been killed to tie up loose ends ahead of launching the malware? She thought about the spreadsheets and the trickle of deaths that would become a flood at the six-month mark. If they were already on a clock, how much time did this mean they had left?

"Can't say I blame them. Not if they're planning something like this. One slipup, and they'll never hear the drone strike hit them."

Hendricks sat on the bed and looked around for anything he might have missed. So far, he'd come up empty.

"Something's not right," Jenn said.

"Either that or someone already sanitized the room."

"Maybe he didn't work here?"

"Still, there'd be something, right?" Hendricks scratched his cheek and began testing the floorboards for irregularities. When that proved fruitless, he started on the electrical outlets and light fixtures, looking for any signs of wear that would suggest Liam had hidden something inside.

Jenn heard Gibson calling her name. She followed his voice back to the sister's room. It was the smallest of the three bedrooms, so narrow that from the twin bed you could reach out and pluck a book from one of the mismatched bookcases that lined the far wall. There were far more books than shelves, however, and stacked in precarious stalagmites were books of every description: N. K. Jemison novels, all the Harry Potters in hardcover, William Gibson, Neal Stephenson. History. Biology. Chemistry. Math. More math. Even more math. An entire bookshelf of nothing but computer-related books—everything from Python to Metasploit to network design. Jenn glanced up at the walls, which were decorated with academic awards and certificates.

What the hell . . . ?

Gibson sat at a small desk, really nothing more than a glorified end table. It was piled high with parts scavenged from computers. He nodded as Jenn reached the same conclusion.

"I think they killed the wrong Walsh," he said.

CHAPTER THIRTEEN

"She's only a kid," Hendricks said.

"A kid taking college-level math," Gibson replied, gesturing at the textbooks lining her bookcase.

They'd gathered in Ciara Walsh's bedroom while Gibson made his case that she was the Walsh they were after. It was a tight squeeze for four adults, so Hendricks stood in the hall, leaning against the doorframe. Tinsley sat on the end of her bed, which made Gibson mightily uncomfortable. As if Tinsley's mere presence would taint the room and invite in the monsters. *Already done that,* he thought. The monster was here, and Gibson had just given him her name.

"Then why was it his name in the documents?" Tinsley asked. "Why not hers?"

"I have not the first clue about that," Gibson admitted. "But look at the two bedrooms. You tell me which one belongs to a hacker."

"Did you find anything on her computer?" Jenn asked.

"It's not here." Gibson pointed to a bare rectangle amid the chaos on the small desk.

"She took her computer to the funeral?" Hendricks said.

"I would have. When you were a cop, did you go anywhere unarmed?"

Hendricks thought that one over.

"Where's the funeral?" asked Jenn. "Do we know?"

Hendricks produced a printed announcement from the pocket of his jacket. "Found this downstairs. Says they should still be at the cemetery, but it'll be wrapping up soon. The reception's at McElroy's, a local pub about a mile from here. Probably the place to catch up with her."

"But how do we do that without spooking her? Or her family?" Jenn asked rhetorically.

"Send in Gibson," Hendricks suggested. "Apparently, he's the teen whisperer."

"I agree," Tinsley said. "They are clearly drawn to him."

Hendricks frowned. "See, now you've gone and made it weird."

"That's probably the best plan," Jenn said. "If this girl really is our hacker, he'll speak her language."

They all looked at Gibson.

"Fine, I'll do it," he said, looking at Tinsley. "On one condition. You don't come within a hundred yards of her."

McElroy's occupied three floors at the corner of a busy intersection on Falls Road. Painted above the door in gold letters was a sign that read: "Est. 1814." The same year that the British had set fire to Washington, DC. Gibson thought it an inauspicious omen.

Hendricks circled the block twice, like a cat looking for a comfortable place for a nap, before squeezing the minivan into a spot behind a delivery truck. The rain had petered out for the moment, but the sun stayed resolutely behind the low-hanging clouds. They sat for a while, watching a steady trickle of mourners and well-wishers disappear inside the pub. For selfish reasons, Gibson hoped Liam Walsh was a popular guy and that his wake would be well attended. It would complicate things if it turned out to be only close family and friends.

Jenn passed Gibson a miniature two-way radio, a microphone, and an in-ear receiver, which was the size of a tuba and about as low profile as a neon sign.

"Are you kidding me with this?"

"What?" Jenn said.

"I thought RadioShack went out of business."

"Just put it on."

"Did it come with a sign to hang around my neck that reads 'undercover'?" But he threaded the mic down his sleeve to his wrist. When he got a good, clean signal, he gave her a sardonic thumbs-up and exited the minivan.

The rain began again on cue.

"Missed your window," Hendricks said, holding out an umbrella. Gibson waved it away. "I'd just lose it."

"Holler if you run into any problems," Jenn said.

"I think I can handle a kid," Gibson said and jogged up the block to McElroy's. At the door, he paused beneath the sunken overhang to shake off the rain. A lone smoker, cold and irritable, greeted him.

"Look what they got me doing," the smoker said with a half-hearted nod, holding out his half-smoked cigarette like it was exhibit A in a trial with a foregone verdict. "Like a trained bloody seal."

On an easel, a sign announced that McElroy's was closed for a private event. The front windows were a kaleidoscope of stained glass, making it impossible to estimate how many people were inside, but the warm murmur of voices and music beckoned invitingly. He had a vision of eight people standing around, wondering aloud what he was doing there. To be safe, he slipped off his earpiece and tucked it into his collar, out of sight. An older couple arrived. The man made a grand show of holding open the door for his wife. Gibson took the opportunity to slip inside after them.

He needn't have worried. The pub was mobbed, or maybe it was the low ceiling that made it seem so. Gibson, who was himself a hair under five ten, could have reached up and placed both palms on it without straightening his arms. Kids scurried everywhere underfoot, playing and laughing, but no one paid them any mind or scolded them to be more respectful. There was a sadness in the air, but it wasn't solemn. Gibson wasn't sure he would have known he was at a funeral reception if he hadn't had the announcement clasped in his hand.

In one corner, a group of musicians played in a loose circle around a crackling fireplace: two guitars, a handheld drum, an accordion, and a flute. Midsong, a young woman pulled up a chair and opened a violin case. With practiced fingers, she quickly tuned up, slipped the instrument under her chin, and joined in. He didn't recognize the tune, but it had that sweet, hopeful melancholy that Gibson associated with traditional Irish music. He realized that they weren't a regular band but neighborhood musicians who had come together spontaneously to play in honor of one of their own. When the song ended, the barroom applauded heartily. The musicians took a drink and stretched their legs before launching into the next song.

A man of perhaps sixty, with a few sickly stalks of gray hair to cover his bald pate, jaundiced eyes, and a nose that looked to have been caught in more than one door, blocked Gibson's way. *Busted.* That was fast. He braced himself for the bum's rush, but to Gibson's surprise, the man stuck out his hand. Gibson shook it.

"Thank ye fer coming. I'm Liam's uncle Bobby."

"Sad day."

"It's a fuckin' crime is what it is." The uncle's voice cracking under the weight of the injustice of it. He held a half-empty pint of something dark in one hand.

Gibson agreed that it was, and Bobby squeezed his shoulder gratefully. Even in the crowded pub, Gibson could smell the alcohol on him.

"Are ye from America, then? Did Liam's da send ye in his stead?" Bitterness creeping into his voice.

"No, just thought it was important to be here. I was in London when I heard. Wanted to come show my support."

"Were ye, now?" Bobby replied with just enough curiosity to make Gibson anxious to change the subject.

"Doesn't look like there's any shortage of that, though. Who is everyone?"

Bobby grinned, revealing a handful of blackened teeth poking up from his gums like the posts of a broken fence. "Need a bloody score-card to keep track of this lot, so you do." He pointed around the bar and began rattling off names. Far too fast for Gibson to follow, but the gist was that Liam had enough aunts and uncles to form a breakaway government, eleven on his mother's side alone. His father had six sisters, although only three were in attendance due to the bad blood between the families, what with Liam's da fucking off to America after little Penelope took sick. Gibson didn't ask what had become of Penelope, although he could imagine. This family had been through the wars.

Gibson offered to buy Uncle Bobby a round. Bobby thought that a splendid idea, clapped him on the back approvingly, and navigated Gibson to the bar, where the thirsty stood three deep waiting to order. It was clear that Bobby had no mind to wait his turn and risk his free drink wandering off. With the precision of a tunnel engineer, he burrowed his way between people, dragging Gibson along in his wake, until they emerged, belly up at the bar. General grumbling ensued up and down the bar, but Bobby hushed them with a wave of his hand. Gibson laid a twenty-pound note on the dark, pitted wood. How much blood and beer had soaked into it in the last two hundred years? Bobby ordered for the both of them while Gibson scanned the pub for anyone resembling Ciara Walsh. No one leapt out at him. Perhaps upstairs?

Bobby thrust a pint of Murphy's—a night-black stout rimmed with white—into his hand. They toasted to Liam's memory, and Gibson asked after Ciara and her mother.

"Haven't seen Ciara since the graveside. She's a strange girl," Bobby confided. "But she loved her Liam. Doted on him, so she did. Not taking it well."

Gibson thanked Bobby, put money on the bar for a second round, and left him holding court. Swimming against the tide, Gibson crossed the pub and climbed the main staircase, happy to be out of the throng. Upstairs, the restaurant was equally busy. Waiters in crimson vests and open-necked shirts navigated the crowd, holding enormous trays above their heads. From the steady stream of visitors who shuffled past the long table beneath the front windows, Gibson guessed the woman seated at it was Liam's mother, Ruth Walsh. Some said only a few words, others were offered a seat and stayed to lend moral support. Bobby was right, though: there was no sign of Ciara anywhere.

The third floor was a game room with snooker tables and dartboards. He thought about scouting it out when the hollow glow of a computer screen caught his eye. It came from beneath the tablecloth of an empty table in a back corner. He smiled at the familiarity of it; that's what he would have been doing at Ciara's age. Disappearing into his computer and online, sometimes for days at a time, had been appealing when his life felt out of control. Ciara Walsh had taken it a step further and made herself a cave to escape the death of her brother.

He sat down at the table. The typing stopped. He could feel her staring angrily at his offending shoes.

"Can ye no see this table's taken?" a chippy voice said from under the table. "Or are ye fuckin' blind?"

Gibson grinned. There was something about seething teenage resentment that made him feel at home. He crossed his feet at the ankles and stretched out his legs to let her know he wasn't going anywhere.

"I need to have a chat with you," he said.

"I've got a knife."

"No, you don't."

A surly silence followed.

"Whaddya want, then?"

"To talk."

"So talk."

"Can I come down there?"

The tablecloth lifted aside, and a surprisingly small, vulnerable face peered up at Gibson. All except her eyes; her eyes were defiant and hard. Bloodshot. The bags beneath them nearly black, telling a story of sleepless, tear-soaked nights since her brother's death. But despite that, her makeup was unblemished. She hadn't shed a tear today. Not one. She'd done her crying in private.

Gibson thought back to his father's funeral. For a day that had cast such a long shadow across his life, he had almost no distinct memories of it. Only that the overwhelming terror of seeing his dad in the open casket had stopped him from setting foot in the same room. And how ashamed he still felt for it.

"I'm sorry about your brother."

"Thank ye. You're very kind," she said and let the tablecloth fall back into place. When he didn't take the hint, she lifted the tablecloth again and gave him a longer look. She was sitting cross-legged on the floor with her knees tucked up under her black skirt. Resting between them was a laptop. When Gibson glanced at the screen, she angled it quickly away.

"Who are you? Are you here to give me advice about how I should be comforting my mum? Tell me how I'm not being a good daughter? 'Cause you can fuck right off with that shite."

"No. Nothing like that."

"Then what *do* ye want?"

"I'm here about whatever Liam was involved in."

The girl stiffened, emotions spilling across her face like someone fanning a deck of cards: fear, grief, anger, guilt. "Don't know what you're talkin' about, Mister."

Gibson admired her for keeping up the lie. She had a lousy poker face, but her toughness wasn't an act.

"He was working for some bad people."

"Are you a peeler, then?" she asked. When he looked blankly back, she explained. "Police. Are you from the police service?"

"Do I sound like I'm from the police?"

She shrugged. "You could be the FBI, like."

Gibson found it interesting that she thought it reasonable for the FBI to be questioning her at her brother's funeral. In Ireland. Jurisdictional issues aside, that was quite a leap. Any doubts that he'd harbored about Ciara Walsh being their hacker were gone now. She might look like a sad fifteen-year-old girl mourning the loss of her brother, but she was also wrapped up in a conspiracy to kill hundreds of thousands of Americans. *Keep that in mind,* he cautioned himself.

"I'm not with the FBI."

She looked relieved. She shouldn't. The FBI was her best-case scenario. What she ought to be doing was asking herself when her brother's killers would tip to her.

On cue, he saw her realize the same thing. Her eyes narrowed to slits. "Are you with the fuckers who killed Liam?"

"What makes you think he was killed?"

She went back to typing. "Are you always answering questions with questions? It's fuckin' irritating."

"Not always."

She paused her typing long enough to look him in the eye. "So? Are you?"

"No," Gibson said. "I had nothing to do with it."

"So, what's it to you?"

Much as he admired her bravado, he was running out of patience. He didn't have time to banter with a fifteen-year-old. He decided to force the issue. "Just curious."

"About what?"

Gibson leaned in, lowering his face to hers. "Why they killed him when it should have been you."

The color drained from the girl's face, and she lowered her head and sobbed, rocking back and forth like a sapling in a high wind. Sometimes all it took was some uncaring asshole asking the question you'd been punishing yourself over. Gibson felt like a heel and tried to picture the spreadsheets calculating casualty figures, hoping that would help justify picking on a kid at her brother's funeral. Hard to do while the child in question was crying at his feet. He passed her the napkins from the table and waited while she cried herself out.

"It wasn't my idea," she said, her voice as thin as the first frost. "Liam insisted."

"Insisted what?"

"On taking the credit, like. But I'm getting even."

Gibson didn't like the sound of that one bit. "What does that mean? What did you do?"

Ciara patted her laptop. "You wouldn't understand."

Gibson raised an eyebrow. "I'm not your uncle Bobby. I know how a computer works."

"Sure," she said with a patronizing half smile and gazed past him out to the restaurant.

He stopped himself from asking her if she knew who he was. "So, tell me what that means. What did you do?"

"We shouldn't talk here."

Gibson followed her eyes and scanned the crowd but didn't see anything that might have spooked her. She stowed her laptop in a backpack and emerged from under the table.

She pointed down the back stairs. "We can talk out back."

"Hold on," he said, taking a last gulp of his beer in order to look the part. But when he stood to follow her, she was gone and the door was swinging shut.

He hurried to catch up, taking the stairs five at a time, fearing that she'd made a break for it. He called after her. No answer. Down below, the hinges of the exit door complained as it opened. If he'd been hustled by a fifteen-year-old, Hendricks would never let him hear the end of it. Reaching the bottom of the stairwell, Gibson put his shoulder into the heavy fire door, calling for her to wait up.

He pulled up short at the feet of Uncle Bobby, who stood casually blocking the way, hands clasped in front of him like he was waiting for a bus.

"Bobby?" Gibson said in a tone suggesting that perhaps Bobby had a twin who liked to stand in the rain behind pubs.

In lieu of an answer, Bobby drilled him twice in the solar plexus, hard and fast. If it hadn't hurt so much, and if he weren't gasping for breath, he would have complimented Bobby on his precision. Instead, he doubled over, and his forehead made a rough introduction to Bobby's waiting knee.

A moment later, Gibson found himself sitting in a muddy puddle. He shook his head, trying to clear the cotton from his vision as strong hands seized him, rolling him onto his face to frisk him. They were looking for weapons so didn't find his communications gear, but took his money and phone. Fortunately, it wasn't a deep puddle.

Between Bobby's feet, Gibson saw Ciara leaning against an idling car. The trunk was open. He would just about fit. *Son of a bitch,* he thought. *She hustled me after all.*

Hendricks would be so pleased.

CHAPTER FOURTEEN

Ten minutes after Gibson walked into the pub, a white Mercedes sedan prowled past McElroy's. Jenn leaned across Hendricks to get a better look. Apart from the driver, she couldn't tell if anyone else was in the car because the back windows were heavily tinted. It felt wrong to her.

"Which of these things is not like the other," Hendricks asked rhetorically.

Such an expensive car looked out of place in a working-class neighborhood. Then again, what did they really know about car ownership in Belfast? Hendricks killed their engine as a precaution. An idling vehicle would draw more attention. They watched the Mercedes turn the corner and disappear from view. Maybe it was nothing; they would have to wait and see.

A few minutes later, Hendricks tapped her on the shoulder. "It's back."

The Mercedes had circled the block, coming up behind them and passing on the right. They sank down in their seats. The Mercedes pulled over across the street from the pub, where it idled by the curb.

She toggled her headset. "Gibson, we may have a situation out here."

No response.

She tried him twice more, but he still didn't answer.

"Two to one, he took his earpiece out," Hendricks said.

"I'm going to kill him."

"You may have to get in line."

A green Range Rover had pulled up directly in front of the pub. The doors opened. Three men stepped out. None went into McElroy's. One lingered by the pub's entrance while the other two fanned out. All three wore heavy coats, but from the way they compensated as they walked, Jenn could tell all three were righties and carrying. And not sidearms either; these boys had come to play.

"Who the hell is this, now?" Hendricks said.

"Maybe someone else figured out they got the wrong Walsh. Tinsley, are you seeing this?" Jenn asked, turning around in her seat as the side door of the minivan slid open.

"Where the hell are you going?" she called after him, but he gave no indication that he'd heard her. The door rolled shut emphatically behind him. She turned to Dan. "You can hear me, right? When I speak? You can hear me talking?"

"What?" he said.

"Funny."

She watched Tinsley walk briskly away down the street. When he turned the corner after one of the gunmen, she figured she had her answer. This situation was deteriorating rapidly. They had zero tactical coordination. Gibson wasn't answering, and Tinsley didn't have a headset, so he was in the wind.

She considered their options.

Gibson really ought to be warned, but that would mean going into the pub, which would risk giving themselves away. Maybe it wasn't necessary yet. Would Liam Walsh's killers chance hitting Ciara Walsh with so many witnesses? His murder had been staged to look like an accident, and she doubted they would change their MO now. Better to wait and watch. And if she proved to be wrong, well, Gibson could handle himself.

When she ran it all by Hendricks, he agreed except for one detail. "Tinsley."

Of course, Hendricks was right. Tinsley was a wild card. She couldn't begin to predict what he would or would not do. Hell, she couldn't even say for sure that they were on the same side.

Jurnjack blew on his tea and listened while Viktor Lebedev coordinated the operation by radio. Viktor kept glancing over for confirmation. It had become clear over the last forty-eight hours that whatever concerns Skumin might harbor about Jurnjack, they had not been shared with Viktor. If anything, the younger man viewed this assignment as a trial promotion and an indication of Skumin's esteem. Viktor's worry seemed to be that Jurnjack would resent his presence and freeze him out. To earn a little good will, Jurnjack had gone out of his way to include him, offering advice and taking him under his wing. He knew enough about Viktor's background to expect him to respond positively. Still, the intensity of Viktor's gratitude pained him. Jurnjack took a sip of his tea and sighed. If, later, he had to kill him, at least Viktor would die feeling accomplished.

Unless, of course, Jurnjack had that backward, and Viktor was here to kill him. That was also a distinct possibility, no matter how admiring and grateful the younger man appeared. It would be classic Skumin if Viktor didn't know that killing Jurnjack was his actual assignment. Skumin was miserly about two things: money and information. He preferred his operatives kept in the dark, often waiting until the last moment before ordering a hit. If Viktor seemed genuine, it was only because he was. It was easier to hide a guilty conscience when you didn't yet have one.

The question of Anatoly Skumin's inexplicable calm had been troubling Jurnjack ever since Saint Petersburg. How could Skumin be so nonchalant about the theft of the thumb drive when it represented five years of work and potentially tens of billions of euros in profit? Had Skumin kept a second copy of the malware? Had his ignorance of computers been a ruse all this time? It was certainly a gambit that Skumin had used to great effect in Department Thirteen—intentionally leaving himself vulnerable to draw out his enemies. It had often been Jurnjack who had been tasked with teaching those traitors their final lesson. Is that why Viktor had been sent along? Was he to be Jurnjack's tutor? If so, it was better than Jurnjack deserved.

Jurnjack and Viktor sat in an inconspicuous Ford Fiesta parked a block away from the pub where the reception following Liam Walsh's funeral was already underway. They'd been shadowing the family since last night, in an observational capacity only, but an hour ago, they'd received word from Skumin's son, Lev, that not only had the attacks on his servers resumed but were originating from inside the pub. That altered their timetable, although Jurnjack wasn't about to sanction a move on a crowded pub. Neither he nor Viktor had full confidence in the team that had been hastily contracted out of London. A little too blunt-force for an intrusion that would require considerable discretion. Discretion that the Englishmen's ridiculous white Mercedes indicated might be in extremely short supply. But to be ready if and when the target moved, Jurnjack had deployed the team to surveil the pub from all sides.

Whoever that target might prove to be.

Viktor had the preposterous notion that it was the fifteen-year-old sister of Liam Walsh, but Jurnjack had every confidence that it would turn out to be Bobby Byrne, Liam's uncle. They had even made a friendly wager on it. Time would tell.

From their vantage, they watched the Range Rover stop in front of the pub. Three men exited and spread out while the white Mercedes idled on the other side of the street like a neon billboard. Jurnjack had just about convinced himself that it didn't pose a risk—there was no reason that anyone would be watching—when across the street, the side door of an old minivan opened and a man got out.

Jurnjack's brow furrowed. It had to be the rain playing tricks on his eyes. The man had a common face, that was all. Jurnjack leaned forward in his seat, tea still pressed against his lips, trying to get a better look. It couldn't be him. Except he had no doubt that it was. The Origami Man was here in Belfast.

How had the assassin tracked Jurnjack down? How did he even know *who* to track down? But then the Origami Man turned away and walked toward the pub, and it occurred to Jurnjack that the Origami Man wasn't here for him. Not directly anyway. Somehow, the thumb drive had led the Origami Man to Liam Walsh. The assassin's resourcefulness, once an asset, was quickly becoming the bane of Jurnjack's existence.

"What is it?" Viktor asked, reacting to Jurnjack's expression. "What do you see?"

Jurnjack realized how foolish he must look and laughed to cover his embarrassment and his irritation. Viktor might be Skumin's unwitting pawn, but he was still Skumin's pawn. His presence limited Jurnjack's options, shackled him. Inconvenient, to say the least, because with the arrival of the Origami Man, Jurnjack had the opportunity to deal with two of his remaining problems in one decisive action. A lost opportunity with Viktor Lebedev looking over his shoulder. Something would have to be done.

"It's nothing," Jurnjack said. "Just worried that those fools in the Mercedes will give us away."

Viktor had been the one to hire them and, sensing an implicit criticism, protested that there hadn't been a better option on such short notice.

"There is always a better option," Jurnjack said curtly. Far from true, but he was pleased to put Viktor on the defensive. He settled back into his seat and set down his tea. What on earth was he going to do now? For the life of him, he couldn't see his next move.

Viktor's handheld radio broke the silence. There was activity in the alleyway behind the pub. A man was being assaulted. Hardly earth-shattering news after an Irish funeral. Jurnjack was fairly certain that one good fight was required by law.

"They just threw him in the trunk of a car," the radio said.

Interesting.

"Three men and a girl just got into the car. One is Bobby Byrne. Positive ID."

"How old is the girl?" Viktor asked.

"Sixteen? Hard to say for certain," the radio replied.

"Still think you're going to win our little wager?" Jurnjack asked Viktor.

"Double or nothing?" Viktor suggested.

Jurnjack nodded and they shook on it, although he was no longer confident that he was betting on the right horse.

Their headsets crackled to life. "Hey, Jenn? Hendricks? Are you guys there?"

"Gibson? Where the hell are you?" Hendricks answered.

"In the trunk of a car. I've been thinking about it, and we should go ahead and get that boat."

Jenn and Hendricks glanced at each other. They had a lot of questions, first and foremost: Why was he in the trunk of a car?

"What kind of car?" Jenn asked because it wasn't one of the two parked in front of the pub.

"I don't know."

"Color?"

"Jesus, Jenn, I got sucker punched and thrown in the trunk of a car by two burly dudes. I didn't have time to get all Sherlock Holmes about it. It's a small two-door car."

She rolled her eyes. He'd just described 90 percent of the cars in Belfast. "Where'd you get grabbed?"

"Alley behind McElroy's. Ciara Walsh's uncle jumped me."

That was a twist that they hadn't seen coming. Hendricks started the engine and pulled out into traffic. Tinsley would have to make his own way from here.

"Are you moving?" Hendricks asked.

"Yeah. For about a minute or so. Feels like a normal speed."

"Tell me if you stop." Jenn marked the time on the dashboard clock. It would at least give them a rough search radius.

"Roger that. We made a right and have been going straight since then."

Hendricks pulled up at the alleyway that ran behind McElroy's. At the far end, the alley opened onto another street, which meant that, depending on which way the car had been facing, a right turn could have taken Gibson in either direction.

"Gibson, do you remember which way the car was oriented in the alley? East or west?"

Gibson's garbled voice came back, but neither Jenn nor Hendricks could make it out. Whichever direction he was moving, it was quickly taking him out of the range of their headsets.

CHAPTER FIFTEEN

Wherever they drove him, it didn't take long to get there. But rattling around in the trunk like the last Altoid in the tin, Gibson could have sworn they'd aimed for every pothole along the way. If he got out of this, he would write a strongly worded e-mail to the city of Belfast.

The car screeched to a halt, throwing him forward roughly.

"We've stopped," Gibson reported, although he had to yank out his earpiece and hide it before getting any response.

The trunk opened, and the same iron hands bundled him out and into a nearby building before he could register his surroundings other than to note it was still raining. Behind him, a metal rollaway door slid closed with a clang. The rich aroma of leather and oil filled his nostrils. A comforting smell, the kind that took years, maybe decades, to work into a place. The lights crackled on. It was a small, claustrophobic work-shop. Shoes lined the walls in cubbyholes or hung from pegs. He was in a cobbler's and more than a little surprised to learn there still was such a thing as a cobbler.

The hands forced him down into a high-backed metal chair but didn't bother to tie him to the chair itself. Uncle Bobby was either cocky or stupid, but with his two goons standing guard, he probably figured he had a comfortable margin for error.

What kind of cobbler had goons anyway?

Bobby dropped heavily onto a tall stool and rolled it over to face Gibson. The smooth way he navigated the narrow spaces, Gibson guessed he'd spent a lifetime working here.

"You're a cobbler?" Gibson asked. "That's still a job?"

"That's right."

"And people still do that? Get their shoes fixed." It seemed such a bygone concept—repairing a broken thing instead of throwing it away.

"Some," Bobby allowed. "The young people not as much. They all wear crap trainers, so there's nothing to mend. Simpler to chuck them in the bin after they wear out and buy another pair. It was me da's shop, and his da's before him. How I learned the trade. Took over from him after I got paroled in '98." Bobby rolled up a sleeve and showed Gibson a tattoo that read "Long Kesh" intertwined with barbed wire and the Gaelic words *"Tiocfaidh ár lá."*

"What's that mean?" Gibson asked.

"'Our day will come.'"

"And has it?"

"Not as yet," Bobby said.

"I know the feeling."

"And who are you, exactly? I didn't catch yer last name earlier, and you have no identification on you."

"My name is Gibson Vaughn."

"That's a Welsh name, is it not?"

"I have no idea."

"And what is it you do, Mister Vaughn?"

"Computers."

Ciara's head bobbed up, but Gibson didn't look in her direction. Bobby did, though, thoughtfully, as if he'd been stuck on a crossword clue and Gibson had just given him a missing letter. He gave Ciara a look as if to say, *See? I told you.*

"And that pays the bills, does it?" Bobby asked.

"Better than cobbling, which doesn't pay shit by the look of things. This shop is just a cover for how you earn your real money, right?"

Bobby stood, and for a second, Gibson thought he was going to get used as a heavy bag again. But Bobby caught himself, let out a tired sigh, chuckled, and sat back down. "All right, lad. Well done, yes, but no call to be a snot about it."

"You coldcocked me. After I bought you two rounds. I think I'm entitled."

"That you did. But I was drinking for free today. Least I was until you showed up and took me away from me grieving." Bobby flashed his sewer grate of a smile. "So the way I'm seeing things is, you owe me about eight more pints."

"Then let's head back to McElroy's. Drinks are on me." Gibson started to stand, but the hands forced him back down.

"Ah, well, there's time for that yet. After we get a few things straight. Like why're you bothering wee Ciara. Because you don't know her da, and ye've no connection to this family." He picked up a sewing awl with a wicked point and flipped it end over end in his hand. "And if ye say otherwise, I'll sew yer mouth shut and make you write out the answers to me questions."

The glint in Bobby's eye told Gibson that it was no idle threat.

"I don't know her father. I've got no connection to your family."

Bobby put down the awl. "Smart boy."

"Can I ask you something?" Gibson said. "How did you make me so fast?"

"Ye didn't belong there," Bobby replied.

"Yeah, but how did you know?"

"Because ye said hello to no one, and no one said hello to you."

Gibson had to laugh. It was so simple, yet it would take someone perceptive and alert to pick up on it in a pub so crowded. Uncle Bobby might like to play the drunken buffoon, but there was more to him than met the eye.

"Are you really her uncle?"

"Oh, aye, her mum is me little sister. One of them anyway."

Ciara had skirted the edge of the room, giving Gibson and her uncle a wide berth. She was perched atop a worktable, legs crossed, engrossed in her laptop. Or so she wanted it to seem. Gibson could feel the attention of the odd girl, who, in her funeral dress, looked like something out of a Tim Burton movie.

"But this is more than just looking out for family, isn't it?" Gibson said.

"You're damn right it is. Christ, Liam's been dead less than a week, and already I've got you bastards sniffing around. Showing up on the day of the funeral. Have ye no decency?"

"It couldn't wait."

"Ye want to talk to her, ye talk to me first. Just because Liam's dead, that doesn't change."

Gibson was starting to see what was happening here. Ciara Walsh worked for her uncle. Liam too, more than likely. But where Liam had probably never been more than a foot soldier in Bobby's brigade, her uncle had recognized that little Ciara Walsh was a golden goose. Gibson hadn't been grabbed to protect her but to protect Bobby's financial interest in her.

"Does her mother know what you've got her mixed up in?"

Bobby smirked. "Don't get ideas, lad. My sister doesn't want to know, but she knows enough. How do you think she paid for wee Penelope's care after her da ran off to America? Me, that's how. So if you want to hire Ciara, then you go through me."

"Thing is, Bobby, I don't want to hire her. I just need to ask her some questions. You too."

Bobby clearly didn't like the sound of that. "About what?"

"Liam's murder."

"Liam was hit by a car."

"Yeah, but why?"

Bobby glanced back at his niece, who had stopped typing. "Ciara. Music."

Without acknowledging her uncle, Ciara fished around in her bag and retrieved an oversized pair of black headphones that she snapped over her ears. Bobby asked her another question, and when she didn't reply, he turned back to Gibson.

"It was an accident. He was blocked and weren't looking when he crossed the street. So don't go filling Ciara's head with that shite."

Behind Bobby, Ciara was staring daggers into the back of her uncle. She might be wearing headphones, but there was no music playing.

"I'd say her head was already full of it. Yours too. Why else are you so jumpy? You know Liam's death was no accident."

"So what if I do? What makes you think it had anything to do with Ciara? Belfast is a dangerous town."

"Because they're plugging leaks. Anyone who knows anything about their operation. Except they got the wrong Walsh. What I don't understand is why."

Bobby sighed. "Liam didn't want anyone to know Ciara was involved, so he stood in for her. Proxy like. Made me give his name so the clients thought it was his work, not hers. Wouldn't stand for it otherwise. Said it weren't safe. He was a stubborn bastard, was our Liam, I'll give him that."

"Looks like he was right."

"You really think one of these fuckers killed Liam over what she was doing for them?"

"Yeah, I do."

"Say you're right, she has a lot of clients. Where would I begin?"

"This one would be different. Something big. Something that got her excited. Focused like you'd never seen her before."

Bobby was nodding. "Yeah, most of the work bores that girl to tears, but there was one. We made more on that job than all the work she's ever done for us."

"What was it?"

"Like I would know. I'm the middleman, ye understand. She's the bloody prodigy. I grew up too busy fighting the British to learn computers. I can barely use me mobile. I just make the arrangements. After that, I'm not involved."

"So who was the client?"

Bobby shrugged. "Couldn't say. It was all anonymous like."

"How did you get paid?"

"Cash. On my doorstep. Bundles of new notes. It was brilliant."

Gibson nodded. Bobby was a dead end. "I need to talk to Ciara."

"And ye can, once we come to terms."

"These people killed her brother."

"And that's a damn tragedy. But Liam is dead. No changing that now. Liam wanted to protect Ciara, and he did it by taking her place. If these people are plugging leaks, like you say, well, then they must consider it plugged. I've got no cause to rock the boat. That'll only put Ciara in danger again."

That reminded Gibson of something that Ciara had said to him at McElroy's. How she was getting even. He had a sinking suspicion about what that meant. After all, it was the same thing he'd done after his father's death.

"Ciara, you've been trying to hack them, haven't you? The ones who killed Liam."

Bobby was on his feet, barking at her not to answer, but the look on her face told Gibson all he needed to know. Ciara Walsh had gone on the offensive, trying to hit back at her brother's murderers in the only way she knew how: through a computer. But hacking was all about patience, and Ciara didn't look like she was in a patient frame of mind.

What were the chances that, in her fury, she hadn't tipped them off that they had another Walsh to deal with?

Little to none.

Liam's sacrifice had been for nothing. Bobby's boat had already been rocked.

It was at that moment that the power went out.

CHAPTER SIXTEEN

When they lost contact with Gibson, Jenn and Hendricks made the decision to wait. Correction, Jenn talked Hendricks into waiting, though it didn't sit well with him. Didn't sit especially well with her either, but they didn't even know in which direction Gibson had been taken. It wasn't an ideal plan, but it beat driving aimlessly around Belfast. She figured that one of two things would happen—either Tinsley would return with news, or their party crashers would point them in the right direction. At least that's what she told herself, but it would be an easy decision to second-guess if Gibson got hurt. So when the Range Rover lurched away from the curb, made a right, and accelerated away, Jenn felt justifiably relieved. Something was happening somewhere. What were the odds it had nothing to do with Gibson?

Seconds later, the white Mercedes made a lazy U-turn and followed the Range Rover. Tinsley would have to make his own way. Hendricks joined the convoy but hung back at a safe distance. The Mercedes was an easy tail. It was making no effort to keep up with the Range Rover and stood out like it was radioactive. Jenn got back on the radio, hoping to raise Gibson, but either they were still out of range or else he couldn't respond.

"We're being followed," Hendricks said.

Jenn had been so focused on the Mercedes that she'd been oblivious to their six. "Which one?" she asked, looking in the side mirror.

"Dark-blue Ford Fiesta. Three back. It was parked down the block from McElroy's. Just popped up behind us."

She saw the car he meant, but it looked like half the cars in Belfast. "Are you sure it's the same one?"

"Same plates."

She had known Hendricks a long time now, but his ability to record every detail in his environment still amazed her.

"Are they following us or the Mercedes?" she asked.

"That's not an either-or."

He had a point. "What do you want to do?"

"Well, I can lose the Ford, but then we lose the Mercedes. Or we stick with the Mercedes and run the risk that they're on to us and it's a setup."

"I know our options, Dan. What do you want to do?" Her tone sharper than she'd intended, but if it bothered Hendricks, he didn't let on.

"Stick with the Mercedes."

"All right, then."

"All right."

The Mercedes made a left and then a right. Hendricks dropped back and then made up the distance on the turns. Behind them, the Ford didn't make any adjustments at all, riding up on their bumper at one point and then falling back when Hendricks accelerated. Almost as if the driver didn't care whether they knew. Hendricks clearly didn't know what to make of that and muttered to himself that he found it insultingly unprofessional.

After another mile, they came up on a quiet intersection. Despite having the light, the Range Rover and Mercedes were both stopped. Most likely deliberating their next steps. Hendricks leaned on the horn.

"What are you doing?" Jenn asked.

"It's a green light. It'd be weird not to honk."

The light blinked from yellow to red. Hendricks gave one final irritated honk and threw his hands up in disgust, putting on a show. The Ford came up behind, boxing them in. A young man was behind the wheel. In the passenger seat sat an older silver-haired man in oversized glasses that took up half his face. If this were a trap, now would be the time to spring it. Jenn and Hendricks braced themselves.

Nothing.

The light turned green again, and the Range Rover made a left. The Mercedes continued straight. Hendricks stayed with the Mercedes while the Range Rover made an immediate right and disappeared up an alley. A quarter of the way down the block, the Mercedes pulled to the curb. The quiet street was lined on both sides by small businesses—computer-repair shop, cobbler, tobacconist, candy shop, laundromat. At the end of the block, Hendricks made a left, pulled over, and killed the engine. Jenn hopped out and trotted back to the corner and radioed to Hendricks that the Ford had taken a spot up the block from the Mercedes.

"Maybe they weren't following us," Hendricks said.

"So who were they following?"

Jenn's money was on Ciara Walsh. Which, if true, also meant Gibson. Whoever it was, Jenn was getting the strong impression that Gibson must be in one of these shops. Why else would the Range Rover divert to the alley except to cover a rear entrance? But which one? And was Gibson inside? She tried raising him on the radio again but got no reply.

Around the corner, the driver of the Ford got out and walked to the Mercedes, leaving the old man alone in the small blue vehicle. Since he was in the trail car, far from the perceived danger, she reckoned that he must be in charge. She also assumed that these were the same people who had killed Liam Walsh, now returning for his sister. And if they wanted Ciara Walsh dead, then these men were responsible, or worked for those responsible, for the thumb drive. She had no proof of any of it, but nothing else made any sense.

She ran her theory by Hendricks, who grumbled that it was a lot of supposition wrapped in wishful thinking, but when she pressed him for an alternative interpretation, he couldn't give her one. She ran her tongue across her teeth. Maybe it was a reach, but if she was correct, then their answers sat in the passenger seat of the blue Ford Fiesta. What wouldn't she give for a private chat . . . It would jump them to the front of the line and let them be rid of Fred Tinsley that much sooner.

"I'm going," she said, drawing her weapon.

"I know."

"It's worth the risk."

"Yeah, all right."

"Quit being so agreeable."

"You're an idiot."

"Thank you."

She took a looping path to the Ford so she could approach from the driver's side. When she was a few car lengths away, she took a knee alongside a station wagon and raised her head to glance over the hood. The Ford was empty. The engine was still running, but no one was inside.

What the hell kind of abracadabra shit was this? Where had the old man gone?

CHAPTER SEVENTEEN

Tinsley listened to the confusion erupting inside the workshop. He had let himself into the cobbler's through the front door and located the circuit breaker. In his experience, abrupt darkness never failed to unnerve people. On the other side of the second door, someone crashed into a workbench, sending tools skittering across the floor. A voice bellowed for quiet. Must have been the boss, because it fell almost immediately silent. Someone named Charlie was ordered to check the "electric box." When the doorknob turned, Tinsley stepped back and out of sight.

A stout man—Charlie, evidently—came through the door holding his phone as a flashlight. Panning it back and forth, he turned right into Tinsley and dropped his phone in panic. It hit the ground only moments before Charlie did. Tinsley clubbed him once in the throat with the butt of his pistol, and then twice in the temple. It would have been simpler to shoot him, but he assumed that the white Mercedes and Range Rover couldn't be far behind. And those were only the vehicles that he knew of for certain, so Tinsley couldn't chance forcing their hand. Plus, there was the tiresome matter of Gibson Vaughn's naïve rules of engagement. Tinsley still needed his cooperation. Computers fatigued his mind, and he would need Gibson to translate Ciara Walsh into English. Still, this feeling of being hemmed in irritated him. There were limits.

Tinsley stepped into the workshop. The light from two phones and the glow of a laptop screen oriented him in the dark room. He counted three men. The girl must be Ciara Walsh. Gibson Vaughn sat on a metal chair. The boy did have a gift for being taken prisoner.

"Who the fuck are *you*, then?" the older man said, shining his phone on Tinsley.

Tinsley mimicked the man's thick Belfast accent. "I'll be needing the girl."

"Well, ye can't have her, can ye?"

To Tinsley's right, the younger man took a step toward him. He hadn't seen the gun, so Tinsley showed it to him helpfully. The man stopped.

"Down. On your face," Tinsley said.

The man did as he was told. It probably saved his life. Temporarily anyway.

A hollow pop punctured the tense silence like a hailstone ricocheting off a tin roof. A black loafer in a cubbyhole near Tinsley's head exploded into shredded leather. Through the rollaway door, a shaft of light shone into the workshop from a single jagged hole.

For an eternal second, all five looked from the door to the shoes, trying to reach the right answer in the limited time left to them. Gibson reacted first, throwing himself off the chair as the rollaway door began to buckle and shake. Holes erupted across it. *Tock, tock, tock.* The weapons were obviously suppressed because, aside from the impacts, it was an almost silent assault. A bullet struck the man in charge, driving him sideways like he'd been punched hard in the shoulder by an old friend. He stumbled, trying to keep his feet, but then his feet seemed to stop working, and he fell across a table and did not move again.

Tinsley ducked behind a heavy storage locker and put one knee on the prone guard to discourage him from getting up. Looking out through the door to the front of the shop, he realized the vulnerability of his position. When they came, it could be from either direction, or both; he would have his hands full then. Taking prisoners was a luxury he could no longer afford. Tinsley gazed down upon the man still lying dutifully at his feet. Pressing the barrel of his gun to the base of the man's neck, Tinsley pulled the trigger. Problem solved.

He glanced at Ciara Walsh. The girl hadn't moved. Frozen with fear, she sat like a statue as bullets tore the shop apart around her. Tinsley couldn't take his eyes off her, momentarily convinced that she couldn't be harmed. It was nonsense. Bullets had no sense of poetry. But watching her amid the carnage . . . well, he found the juxtaposition achingly beautiful for reasons he couldn't explain.

When he called her name and told her to get down, she only looked across to him, face blank, eyes glassy, as if immune to gunfire. He wasn't about to leave cover; from experience, he knew that he had no such immunity. Still, it felt anticlimactic to have come all this way only to watch her die. Picking up the dead man's phone, Tinsley threw it at her. Hard. It glanced off the girl's forehead, and she glared over at him, rubbing her face. Tinsley jabbed a finger in the direction of the floor; this time, she shut her laptop and slipped off the worktable onto the floor, still in no particular hurry, and wedged herself behind the workbench, clutching her laptop to her chest like a newborn.

The shooting paused. Gibson Vaughn took the opportunity to crawl over and put his back to the storage locker. "Is he dead?" he asked of the dead man.

"You're welcome to check."

Gibson gave him a queer look and beckoned for Ciara to come to them. She refused to budge. He called again, more forcefully, but she only shook her head petulantly as if he'd told her to finish her vegetables. Apparently, she had more sense than Tinsley had initially credited her.

"Are you in contact with Charles or Hendricks?" Tinsley asked.

Gibson slipped his earpiece back into place and tried but got no response. "Weren't they with you?" he asked, the distrust unmistakable in his voice.

"I got out of the van," Tinsley said, realizing now that it had been an error in judgment to do so without first making a plan. He had no facility for cooperation.

"Have another one of those?" Gibson asked, meaning the gun.

Tinsley hesitated, trying to recall if he'd ever willingly handed a weapon to anyone. Much less someone who meant him harm. He felt quite sure it would be something he would remember. For perhaps the thousandth time, he wondered if he was being manipulated by these people, or if that was the only lens through which he understood human interaction. In either case, he found the uncertainty unpleasant.

"Come on," Gibson said. "We don't have time for this."

Reluctantly, Tinsley handed Gibson his backup from an ankle holster. "We're not going to shoot our way out."

"What about out the front? Seems quiet enough."

"It's a trap," Tinsley said.

"How the hell do you know that?"

"Because it's what I would do. Small-arms fire to herd us to the front of the store where it appears safe. There will be an ambush waiting." To his surprise, Gibson didn't argue.

"Area denial."

"Precisely."

"So we wait for them to come to us?"

"Not if we want the girl to live."

On cue, the gunfire resumed, steady as Belfast rain.

"The basement!" Ciara yelled. "There's a basement." She pointed to a hinged steel door set into the floor and partially covered by crates.

"Where does it lead?" Gibson asked.

"The old coal cellar. Bobby had a tunnel dug so his mates could come and go without being seen from the roadway."

"Where does it go?"

"Across the alley to a wee park."

Gibson and Tinsley looked at each other, appraising their chances. Tinsley thought it might be the first time that they'd made eye contact since Jenn Charles's kitchen.

Gibson handed him back the gun. "Keep them off me. I'll get it open."

CHAPTER EIGHTEEN

Jurnjack watched the woman climb to her feet and put her back against the door of the nearby car. The gunfire from the rear of the cobbler's had driven her to the ground, but she'd gotten her bearings and realized that it wasn't meant for her. She hazarded a quick glance over the hood, saw that the Ford was empty, and grasped the terrible position she'd put herself in.

There weren't many advantages to getting old, but people's pathological underestimation of the elderly could serve as useful camouflage. Once he'd found it offensive, but he now understood its advantages and even cultivated the look. The thick eyeglasses were a helpful touch. A bit theatrical, but they added to the overall effect.

When Jurnjack had decided to wait behind in the car, Viktor had been wholly sympathetic. Poor, frail Jurnjack might catch his death of cold in the rain. The woman from the minivan had made the same misjudgment. From the way she moved and used cover, he could see she was a professional. Yet she'd taken a foolish, unnecessary risk because all she'd registered was a vulnerable old man.

As the gunfire resumed behind the cobbler's, Jurnjack stepped behind her and put his gun to her head. She was fortunate he did not intend to kill her. He saw from her face that she knew it too. *Good.*

While she recovered from her shock, he took the gun out of her hand. She'd been speaking to someone, most likely the driver of the minivan, but he left her comms in place. It would tell him more about her if she tried to use them.

"Do you speak English?" he asked.

She nodded.

"Good. You and I need to have a conversation." He could tell from her expression that she'd wanted the same, only that she'd expected to be the one holding the gun. Ah, the optimism of youth. "Get in the car. Hands on the steering wheel."

She did as she was told without a word. He found himself liking her instinctively—some people took any setback as defeat and leapt to bargaining for their lives. As if that had ever worked. But not this one. She was already assessing her options.

"I need to speak to your employer," he said.

"My employer?" Her accent was American.

"Don't waste time, young lady. We don't have long. I saw him leave your vehicle at the pub. The Origami Man."

He saw her trying to work out whom he meant. A look of realization mingled with disgust crossed her face. "Origami Man. You mean Tinsley? I don't work for him."

She was telling the truth, which genuinely surprised him. The Origami Man did not strike him as the type to have colleagues. "You are partners?"

"Temporarily," she said, underlining the word with her tone. "How do you know him?"

"I am the one who hired him and shot him."

"Oh. Well, word of warning, he's looking for you too. But it's not to talk."

"I see. And is it also your intention to kill me?"

"No, that's between you two. I'm only here about the thumb drive."

"You have it?"

"Yes, but you can't have it back," she said defiantly.

"Keep it. It's worthless to me now."

"Why?" she demanded. "What's it for?"

"Obviously you've seen what's on it."

"Yes, but what's it do?" she said, growing impatient.

"That, I do not know."

"Don't bullshit me."

"I have the gun. Why would I? I do not know how it works or its intended target. Only the devastation it would cause if released. That is why I hired him to steal it. To stop this before it began."

A look of profound relief came over her face. "To stop it? So, it's over."

"Unfortunately not."

Since their meeting in Saint Petersburg, Jurnjack had been ruminating on Anatoly Skumin's muted reaction to the theft of his malware. At first, he'd worried that there must be a second copy of the malware and that the version stolen from Georgi Ivov had been an elaborate charade to smoke out Skumin's enemies. If so, Jurnjack had blundered right into it. But if that were the case, why was he still drawing breath? That was when he'd had an epiphany. He realized that, after a half century of working for his old KGB handler, his near-superstitious dread of the old man had made him prone to imagining overly elaborate conspiracies where there were none. The explanation for Skumin's indifference was much simpler and far, far worse: Jurnjack was too late. He now had no doubt that the malware had already been launched. Released to complete its insidious task. Whatever that might be, it had already begun.

To her credit, the woman understood immediately. "How long ago? When did it start?"

He heard the rising fury in her voice. She was no mercenary. The Origami Man had made common cause with a patriot. She meant to save her countrymen. That filled in a lot of blanks. It also told him how to play her. This day was turning out to be full of surprises.

"How close are we to the sixth-month mark, you mean? I don't know that either."

"Well, who the hell does?"

"That is immaterial at this point. That person is untouchable. Trust me on that."

"Why should I?"

"Because if he weren't, I would have killed him many years ago."

"So, you work for him? The man responsible."

"I do."

"Tell me who he is, I'll do it," she said.

Jurnjack admired her confidence if not her lack of pragmatism. "You couldn't sneak up on one old man in a car. Forgive me for not being overwhelmed with confidence. No, the only way to prevent this calamity is to discover the malware's purpose."

"What's stopping you?"

"I had hoped that stealing the thumb drive would end this madness, but it has only succeeded in tying my hands. I am being watched and no longer have the freedom to act. I need an intermediary."

"I thought I was incompetent."

"That remains to be seen. In any event, you are my only candidate."

"I'm listening."

"How did you gain access to the thumb drive? Are you a hacker?"

"No, but I have one on my team."

"Do you think he could learn what it is for?"

"I've learned not to bet against him. We just need a place to start."

Jurnjack had an unpleasant thought. "Your hacker, he didn't happen to be in the trunk of a car earlier?"

She raised a single eyebrow. "Yes. Do you know where he is now?"

"Inside the cobbler's." He pointed back down the street toward the gunfire.

She paled. "Can you call them off?"

"I cannot. He will have to find his own way out. But if he does, then perhaps you and I can do business."

"And if he doesn't?" she asked, eyes drifting to the gun.

"Let's not dwell on such unpleasantness."

Behind them, the windows of the cobbler exploded outward, showering the street with broken glass. Fire licked up the exterior walls.

Jurnjack sighed and hoped the woman's hacker wasn't inside. He really was starting to like her.

CHAPTER NINETEEN

Gibson didn't know how the fire started exactly. But shoot enough rounds into a workshop, and something was bound to ignite. With a thrilling whoosh that sucked the air out of the room, flames raced across the walls, searching for fuel and engulfing the wooden shoe racks. In a matter of seconds, the old shop became a furnace of heat and noise and death. Thick, oily smoke swirled around the rafters like angry storm clouds. The only upside was that the shooting stopped. Easier to let them die of smoke inhalation than gunfire. Quieter too.

Lifting the steel hatch set into the floor, Gibson gazed down an ancient stone staircase, walls stained black from a century of coal dust. The spreading fire gave it an eerie amber glow. If it wasn't the way to hell, it looked to be a shortcut.

The fire was spreading too fast for second thoughts. Gibson went down first, hands on both walls to steady himself on the narrow steps that dared him not to fall. Had everyone had tiny feet in olden times?

By the time he got to the bottom and the door had clanked shut above them, he couldn't see his hand in front of his face. At least he could breathe. He found a light switch, but it must have been on the same circuit as the rest of the shop. They would have to find their way in the dark.

"Tinsley?" Gibson said.

"I'm here," came the reply out of the coiled black. "I have Ciara."

"Do you have a flashlight?"

"I do not have a flashlight."

"Ciara, where's the tunnel?" Gibson asked.

"I've no idea, do I?" she said at the absurdity of his question. "Never been down here before in me life."

"Then how do you know there is one?"

"Bobby told me so. Ask him."

Bobby lay dead upstairs. Even when he'd been alive, Gibson hadn't been sold on his reliability. In the dark, he breathed a lungful of smoke and coughed violently. Were they about to suffocate in this basement because a fifteen-year-old girl had taken her uncle's tall tale literally?

The two men each took a wall and worked their way around the coal cellar. Gibson felt his way with his toes and fingers, not certain what he was feeling for. He didn't have a fear of the dark, but this sure felt like a fine time to start cultivating one. Broken glass crunched beneath his shoes. It hurt to breathe. They were all coughing now.

In the far corner, the cold stone wall gave way to smooth wood. He'd found a door. Groping for the knob, Gibson turned it and yanked hard. It didn't budge. Not an inch. He dropped to one knee, trying to get beneath the thickening smoke. *What if the door's locked?* a voice laced with panic whispered. *What if Bobby has the key? What if Gibson should try pushing rather than pulling?* Hey, there was a thought. He tried that instead, and this time the door opened easily. Cool, damp air rushed in to greet him.

"Found it!" Gibson called out.

Ciara bumped into his hip. Guiding her through the door, he said he would meet her outside in the park. He called out to Tinsley but got no response. Gibson realized that he hadn't heard him coughing in the last minute. On hands and knees, he felt his way back through the cellar until he found Tinsley collapsed on the floor.

"No. No, no, no. Get the hell up." Gibson shook him violently, but Tinsley didn't stir. How far was the universe going to take this cruel joke? Just working alongside the freak made Gibson sick. Was he expected to save his life now as well? That was asking too much. It wasn't fair. This wasn't fair.

So, leave him.

It was a seductive thought. What more fitting way for this monster to die than alone in the dark? There would never be a better opportunity. All Gibson had to do was walk away. It was better than the man deserved; Tinsley had taken a normal life away from him. Taken everything. Memories that Gibson kept locked safely away were loose again. Stalking him. His father's face, purple and black and lifeless, swaying at the end of that rope. Walk away, and it would all be over. Finally.

But again, he came back to the same old question: Could he reconcile the deaths of half a million people with his need for revenge? Was that the kind of man he was? Gibson cursed, hating the answer. Seizing Tinsley by the armpits, he dragged him across the cellar and through the door. It led down a rough-hewn corridor with a floor of packed dirt. Gibson didn't know how long it was, maybe thirty feet, maybe a mile. It felt like it went on forever. He found the far end with the back of his head, which he cracked on a wood ladder set into the wall. He lost his footing and sat down hard. Rubbing his head, Gibson looked up at the most beautiful wet gray sky that he'd ever seen.

Ciara had made it.

"Come on, you bastard," Gibson said. Hoisting Tinsley over one shoulder, he began to climb. Once they got outside, though, Tinsley was on his own. Pulling him out of a burning building was one thing; Gibson drew the line at mouth to mouth.

At the top of the ladder, he heaved Tinsley up and out of the hole. He hauled himself out and rolled onto his back, dimly aware of the rain falling on his face. He took a deep, cleansing breath and dry heaved. A short distance away, Ciara Walsh sat crying in the wet grass. Her shock had given way to the enormity of what had happened.

"Where's Bobby?" she asked.

Gibson shook his head.

"Charlie? Tom?"

"I don't know."

Ciara lapsed into silence and stared forlornly at nothing at all. Gibson sat up. Although the trapdoor was well hidden, they weren't out of danger. Over the tall brick wall that separated the park from the alleyway, the sounds of men arguing were too close for comfort. The fire had spread to the two neighboring businesses and now threatened to engulf the entire block. In the distance, the rising wail of sirens filled the night. They needed to get moving.

Slipping his earpiece back in place, he tried to raise Hendricks and Jenn. No doubt they were out of range, but—

"Gibson. Where the hell you at?" Hendricks asked as if Gibson were running late for coffee.

Even under the circumstances, Gibson grinned. It was good to hear a friendly voice. "We're in a park. I don't know where exactly."

"Any chance you're near a burning building?" Hendricks asked.

"Yeah, wow, good guess. We were inside when it started. Got out through a tunnel. Now we're on the other side of the alley behind the fire."

"Yeah, I know where that is."

Gibson wanted to ask how that was possible but wasn't about to give Hendricks the satisfaction. "How far away are you?"

"Just around the corner. I'll come to you."

"You're a lifesaver."

"Are you ready to move?"

"We can be."

"Who is 'we'?"

"I've got Tinsley and Ciara Walsh with me. Where's Jenn?"

"Good question."

Jenn plucked out her earpiece and exhaled in relief. When she'd first seen the fire, she'd feared the worst, but Gibson was safe. And he had Ciara Walsh. Hendricks was on the way to pick them up. All in all, not bad for an operation that had been thrown together on the fly and only minutes earlier had looked poised to end in disaster.

The old man held out a hand. Jenn dropped her phone and comms into it, which he thrust deep into his jacket pocket, then shifted around in his seat to face her. The gun remained pointed at her chest, but his finger was no longer inside the trigger guard. The beginning of a beautiful friendship? Jenn wasn't expecting true love, but it was a step in the right direction.

"So what do you think?" she asked. "Going to give us that place to start?"

She saw him debating the question internally. Whatever his motives, they were far from pure. Anyone willing to kill a fifteen-year-old girl—or her brother, for that matter—wouldn't be trying to stop the malware out of a deeply held concern about the sanctity of life. No, his reasons were far more complex. Frankly, she didn't give a shit why. All that mattered was that he hadn't killed her outright and saw her as a potential ally.

The irony wasn't lost on her. She'd bemoaned working for the likes of Mirella Lima. So, what had she done instead? Made a pact with a monster like Tinsley and then aligned herself with another. It was for a good cause, though. When she died, her epitaph would read, "The ends justified the means." She hoped it would, at least.

The old man reached a decision. "Go to France. You must find a programmer. His name is Mahomet Rousseau. He is Parisian but is in hiding in Marseille."

"How do you know?"

"Because it is my job to hunt him down and kill him. We have killed everyone who had a hand in writing the malware except for him. He is the last. A contact found him in Marseille. So far, I've kept that information from my people."

"Besides Ciara Walsh?"

"Yes, but I believe he is much more important, which is why I have so far concealed his whereabouts. You see, none of the programmers knew what they were building. Like the blind men and the elephant, they only ever touched one small part of the whole. But Rousseau's piece was critical. He tested the finished malware."

"Which means he might know what it does."

"Yes. If he dies, then the only way to learn the malware's purpose will be to watch the news. But you will have to hurry. I can't feign ignorance much longer without being discovered. After I leave here, I will go to Marseille. If I locate him before you do, I will have no choice but to kill him. You must find him first."

"Where in Marseille?"

"I don't know," the old man admitted. "He was staying with a friend from university but slipped his tail yesterday and has not returned since. I would start with the friend."

The old man gave her the address, but Marseille was a city of one million people, and Jenn didn't like the odds of finding someone there who didn't want to be found. Still, what choice did she have? She'd seen the charts and believed the threat was real.

"How do I contact you if we need help?" she asked.

"You don't. If you need my help again, then I have misjudged you. We will not communicate after this. Not in such a congenial manner, at any rate. I have no further help to offer you."

"Let's say we figure it out. What then?"

"Take it to your government. Go public. Whatever it takes to stop this."

She glanced at his gun and the pocket where he'd stashed her comms. "So, now . . . ?"

"Now you should go," he said, turning the barrel of his pistol aside. "Please give my regards to our mutual friend."

"He won't stop looking for you."

"No, I don't imagine he will. Any suggestions?"

"Get your affairs in order."

"Young lady," he said. "What do you think I am trying to do?"

The resignation and certainty in his voice struck a chord. Jenn had come close to dying on this rain-swept Belfast street. Were her own affairs in order? A shape appeared at his window, interrupting her thoughts, and rapped on the glass. The old man lowered it, and a man with a mercenary's face, rugged and worn like an old Brillo pad at the bottom of a dirty sink, knelt to relay his report in a heavy Midlands accent: the fire in the cobbler's was raging out of control; a minivan had been spotted picking up three passengers; Lebedev was in pursuit now. As he talked, the mercenary kept glancing over at Jenn, trying to work out her role here. The old man ignored his evident curiosity.

"Remind me of your name?" the old man said.

"Grayson, sir."

"Grayson. Of course, thank you. Good work."

The mercenary nodded and turned away.

"Oh, Grayson, one more thing."

When the mercenary looked back, the old man shot him in the forehead.

Jenn was too shocked to move.

"What the hell?" she said instead, and when that did nothing to lessen the sick feeling in the pit of her stomach, she said it again.

"He saw us together. That would have raised questions I cannot afford."

"So, you killed him?"

"No," the old man said, handing back her gun. "You did."

So much for their beautiful friendship.

"These men all served together in Afghanistan. I don't recommend being captured alive," he said. "Well? What are you waiting for? Run."

CHAPTER TWENTY

The two holes that appeared, as if by magic, in the minivan's windshield were Gibson's first clue that they had not made a pristine getaway. His second knelt on one knee at the end of the block, calmly lacing the minivan with lead.

Hendricks looked at each hole, one on either side of his head, as if estimating how many inches separated living from dying. He had been showered with glass fragments, and his face bled from a dozen tiny cuts, but with deliberate calm, he wiped the blood from his eyes, punched the gas, and aimed them straight for the shooter, who held his ground while continuing to fire. The windshield buckled.

"I'd get down, I was you," Hendricks advised and ducked sideways in his seat. From that angle, he couldn't possibly see the road, but he managed somehow to steer using the buildings and trees as landmarks. At least that's how it looked to Gibson from the back, who had yanked Ciara down to the floor and was trying to shield her with his body. Tinsley, he left unconscious on the back seat. Gibson had had his fill of saving him today.

The minivan shuddered as it jumped the curb. One of the side windows shattered. Hendricks slammed on the brakes and cranked the wheel hard to the right. A hollow thud signaled the end of the shooting as the minivan hip-checked the shooter into a wall. Hendricks hit the gas again and straightened in his seat as they sped away into the night.

"How long was I in the LAPD?" Hendricks asked the occupants of the car rhetorically, although Gibson knew where this was going.

"Not now, man," Gibson said from the floor.

"How long?"

"Twenty-two years."

"Twenty-two years," Hendricks echoed. "And in those twenty-two years, how many times did I get shot at?"

"Zero," Gibson said, his lines well rehearsed.

"Zero. And how many times since I retired?"

"Twice."

"No, no. Oh, no, my friend. Three times. Three times. And what did all three have in common?"

"You were an asshole every time?"

Hendricks ignored the remark. "*You.* You were there. It's a peculiarity, you got to admit. Goddamn bullet magnet."

While they bickered—because, really, what else would you call it—Hendricks made a series of random-seeming turns. Gibson knew better. Nothing Hendricks did behind the wheel was ever random.

"What about Jenn?" Gibson asked.

"She's going to have to fend for herself. We got problems of our own."

As if to underscore the point, a Range Rover peeled around the corner and rode up on their bumper. For the next few miles, every time Hendricks turned, the Range Rover did the same.

"I think they're upset you used their guy as a Ping-Pong ball."

"Yeah . . . well," Hendricks replied, too busy to think of anything pithy.

As the neighborhood turned over, the buildings grew in size and architectural grandeur. Traffic became denser, and the sidewalks thronged with pedestrians.

"Where are we?" Gibson asked.

"Downtown. City Centre."

"Why? What's here?"

"A shit ton of security cameras. Brits are obsessed with the damn things. Less chance of these boys getting trigger happy."

Tinsley chose that moment to sit up sharply as if defibrillated back to consciousness. He took one deep breath and looked around, taking his bearings. There was no acknowledgment that he'd been unconscious or any curiosity about how he'd gotten back to the minivan. He simply moved on to the matter at hand. It was infuriating.

"What have I missed?" he asked, drawing his gun.

"What have you missed? Well, for starters, youngblood there dragged your psycho ass out of a burning building. So, you're welcome. Then we got shot to hell while you played Sleeping Beauty."

"Is Jenn Charles dead?"

Hendricks locked eyes with him in the rearview mirror. "What? Why would you say that shit?"

"Because she's not here. And, in my experience, you don't leave your people behind."

"We're being tailed. She's on her own until we figure out how to lose them."

"In this?" Tinsley asked skeptically.

"Exactly," Hendricks said and pulled the minivan over to the curb. He did not put it in park, ready to go at a moment's notice. The Range Rover followed suit. Gibson counted four heads, but they weren't shooting and they weren't getting out either. The vehicles idled while, around them, Belfast got on with its evening. A temporary cease-fire appeared to have been called, but Gibson had doubts that it would hold. This was Northern Ireland, after all.

"So what's the plan now?" Gibson said. "Parley?"

"I think we're past the point of negotiating," Hendricks replied.

"What does the girl know?" Tinsley asked. "Was that discussed in my absence?"

"Absence? You mean when you were passed out like a bitch?" Hendricks asked. "And how is that relevant to our current situation?"

"It's her they want. If she can't help us, this would be the time to find that out."

Ciara shrunk down in her seat.

"What in the hell is wrong with you?" Gibson snapped.

"Belfast is no longer safe for us. We should return to the aircraft. If the girl can help us, we take her with us. If not, I see no reason to protect her further," Tinsley said and looked down at Ciara. "What do you think, child?"

Simultaneously, Gibson and Hendricks tore into Tinsley for suggesting that they abandon a child to trained killers. Tinsley made no effort to refute their arguments; he merely weathered them like a lighthouse in a storm.

"What is it you want to know, then?" Ciara asked.

Gibson shook his head. "Don't. We're not giving you to them. No matter what he says. Do you understand?"

But Ciara wasn't listening. She was staring defiantly up at Tinsley. "Well?" she asked.

"I want to know who hired you," Tinsley said.

"Don't know, do I? None of us did."

"None of who?" Gibson asked.

Ciara grimaced. "The other programmers. I only came on board last year, but Mahomet thinks there were probably fifty of us over the last four years. Hired to do pieces of it."

Given the malware's level of sophistication, it didn't surprise Gibson to hear how long it had taken to design. Or how many programmers had been involved. Programmers were specialists, and no one programmer had the breadth of knowledge to write the software he'd seen on their own. It would be the equivalent of a musician playing every instrument in an orchestra. No, this had been a team effort. Still, Gibson had no doubt that there was a conductor who had overseen things.

"What was your piece?" Gibson asked.

"To hijack a server that could be used to launch the attack."

"Where?" he asked, although he expected the answer.

"In America."

Exactly what he feared. American cyber defenses were geared heavily toward protecting the US against attacks coming from abroad. Seizing control of a domestic server as a base of operations would make an attack more difficult to detect.

"Are you really Gibson Vaughn?" she asked.

"You know who I am?" Gibson said. It surprised him but might speed things along.

"Course I do. Ye told Bobby your name like an eejit, didn't you? I Googled ye back at the shop."

"Oh." He had forgotten he'd done that.

"What? Ye thought I just knew yer rep? Mister, you're a thousand years old to me."

Hendricks's eyes got wide, but he said nothing. Small favors.

"You're a bad fella, ye know that? Your government is offering a reward."

"That's true. And I still risked coming here to find you. Maybe that tells you how dangerous this malware is."

"Why? What's it do anyway?" Ciara asked, unable to contain her curiosity.

The question caught Gibson by surprise. "You're saying you really don't know?"

She blew out her lips. "Had our suspicions, but none of us knew what it did. Compartmentalized, so we were. Like proper spies."

Gibson told her, and he didn't pull any punches either. By the time he finished, Ciara looked stricken, eyes wide and wet.

In a voice as quiet as a sparrow's wing, she said, "I didn't know. I swear. Thought we were stealing industrial secrets or the like."

"You think that's an excuse?" Hendricks said, chiming in angrily. "You didn't know? That shit don't fly, little sister. Are you going to help us stop this or not? They killed your brother."

"And your uncle," Gibson added.

"I know! Why you think I've been trying to hack them back? It's me what let this happen." Ciara was crying now. "Mo tried to warn me. Said that the programmers before us had all been murdered. I just thought he was being paranoid. I'm so stupid." She hit herself in the side of her head with a closed fist over and over until Gibson grabbed her by the wrist to stop her. She twisted free. "You mean to stop them?"

"We do."

"And you'll take me with you?"

Gibson looked up at Hendricks, who nodded reluctantly. Neither was crazy about the idea. The less time she spent around Tinsley, the better, but leaving her in Belfast amounted to a death sentence. Ciara was a minor, so it looked like they were adding kidnapping to their list of crimes.

"What about your mother? She'll be worried sick," Gibson asked.

"It'll be fine," Ciara said. "Trust me, she's used to it."

"You can come with us until we get this sorted out."

"Then you'll be wanting to talk to Mo, I reckon."

"Who the hell is Mo?" Hendricks asked.

"Mo ran the final tests. Wouldn't tell me what it was for, but he talked like it was mega."

"Is Mo a friend of yours?" Gibson asked.

"Not exactly a friend. Well, yeah, sorta. We became mates working on this. They didn't know we knew each other." She shrugged. "He's in love with me."

"Is he here in Belfast too?" Tinsley asked.

"Don't be daft. Never met him, have I? He's French. Lives in Paris, like, but I don't think he's there anymore."

"Why not?"

"Reckoned they'd kill him, too, once he'd finished his piece, so he's been moving around. Like a proper spy."

"Do you have any way to reach him?" Gibson asked.

"Course I do," she said defensively. "But . . . I haven't heard from him in a day or two."

"This had better not be a ruse," Tinsley said, leaning forward, "to save your own neck. Because if that is the case, I assure you that you would be better off here."

"That's enough," Gibson warned.

Ciara swallowed hard and shook her head. "Mister, it's the truth. Cross my heart and hope to die."

The minivan shuddered.

The Range Rover had apparently run out of patience. It had given the minivan a love tap. The driver was pointing a finger at them as if to say, *Let's finish this.* Hendricks threw the minivan into reverse, meaning to return the favor with interest.

"No," Gibson said. "Don't."

"Well, what's the plan, then? Because if he bumps me again, I'm going to put his shit in the shop."

Tinsley drew his weapon and fitted a suppressor to it. "Circle the block. Slowly."

Happy to be in motion again, Hendricks made an easy lap while Tinsley studied the surroundings carefully, getting the lay of the land. It was much quieter on the other side of the block. The Range Rover followed. It reminded Gibson of a racetrack under caution, pace car keeping things in check, no one allowed to pass or jockey for position, with that sense that at any moment the caution would be lifted and the race would be on again.

"Now what?" Hendricks said as they arrived back where they'd begun.

"Again," Tinsley said, moving up to the front seat and unlocking the door. "This should do, but a little faster this time."

Around they went again—lap two—the Range Rover slightly more impatient this time, slowing and then accelerating onto their bumper like a dog straining at the leash, anxious for the chase to begin.

"Again," Tinsley said. "Faster."

Lap three.

At the second corner, Tinsley said, "I will meet you exactly here. Make another lap, but like the first time."

"Okay," Hendricks said. "Are you getting out?"

"Yes, but do not slow down." Tinsley cracked the door an inch.

At the third corner, two delivery trucks idled at the curb. As the minivan turned and they momentarily lost sight of the Range Rover, Tinsley walked out of the moving vehicle, took two awkward steps, and fell forward, rolling painfully into the curb. When he didn't move, Gibson thought maybe he'd knocked himself senseless. What the hell was he thinking? But then the Range Rover passed, and Tinsley rose silently to his feet and walked around the corner.

"Was that all bullshit?" Hendricks asked. "Did we just get ditched?"

It wasn't out of the question, but there was only one way to know for sure. They went around again.

Lap four. At a crawl.

Gibson watched for Tinsley. He didn't see him. But neither did the Range Rover. All Gibson saw was the strobe of a muzzle flash from between the two delivery trucks and heard the sound of breaking glass. The minivan made the turn at the corner, but the Range Rover rolled straight through the intersection and struck a parked car. Hendricks didn't wait to see what happened next, instead speeding away.

Tinsley was waiting for them right where he said he would, one finger raised as if hailing a taxi. He got in beside Hendricks looking calm and relaxed—light, even. Nothing to suggest he'd just killed a man, maybe more.

"Shall we go to the airfield?" he suggested.

Looking in Tinsley's eyes reminded Gibson that there was nothing in there, nothing but a broad, unending sea filled with sharks. No dry land. Nowhere that something might have crawled ashore and become a man.

CHAPTER TWENTY-ONE

Halfway to the airfield, Hendricks had worked himself up into a righteous fury. He had tried Jenn's phone a half dozen times, growing more and more agitated each time it went to voice mail. As he drove, he struck up an argument with the road ahead.

"What the hell were you thinking, going after that old man alone? It was amateur, Jenn. Got to be smarter than that. Swear to God, you turn up dead, I'm not going to the damn funeral. Hell with that. I don't pay no last respects to stupid." Hendricks hammered the steering wheel with a fist, accentuating his points, building to a crescendo and then lapsing into brooding silence.

Gibson stayed out of it, leaving him to work it out. Sometimes it took a good fight with the phantoms in your head to ensure you never had the fight for real.

When Jenn finally called, Hendricks handed his phone to Gibson, relieved but still too agitated to speak to her.

"Hey, stranger," Gibson said. "You had us worried."

"Gibson? Yeah, I'm fine."

Gibson caught Hendricks's eyes in the mirror and nodded that she was safe. Hendricks's shoulders slumped, and his head dropped as if all the air had rushed out of him. Then he took a deep breath and got back to driving.

"You're both okay?" she asked.

"Well, we're in one piece anyway. Hendricks says hi. Ciara Walsh is with us."

"Tinsley?"

"Yeah, him too."

He briefly sketched out their escape from the cobbler's.

"Where are you now?"

"On the way back to the airfield," he answered guiltily. "There was too much heat in town."

"That was the right call."

"Where are you? We'll come get you."

Hendricks nodded emphatic agreement.

"No," she said. "Still too many eyes out on the streets right now to risk it. I'm on foot, holed up in some pub on their phone, but I almost got caught three different times. Don't come back. Get the girl out of Ireland, and I'll find my way to you. Any idea where that might be? Did she give you anything useful?"

"A name but not much else. Some French hacker who worked on the malware with her. Sounds like he was a central player. Ciara says she has a way to reach him. When we get to Paris, we'll try to make contact."

"Paris?" Jenn's voice perked up. "What's the hacker's name?"

"Mahomet. At least that's the one he gave her. But hackers aren't notorious for handing out their real names."

"That could be Mahomet Rousseau," she said. "But he's not in Paris anymore. Possible he's in Marseille. Or was as of yesterday." She gave him the address.

"How the hell do you know all this?"

Jenn described her meeting with the old man and their unexpected marriage of convenience. Gibson gritted his teeth at the news that the malware had already been deployed. They'd all held out hope that it could be stopped before it began, so it hurt like hell knowing that they were too late. That people were already dying. He didn't need to look at the spreadsheets—he knew the projected casualties by heart. The only question now was how close they were to the six-month mark—the red line between tragic and catastrophic.

"Why do you think he's helping us?" Gibson asked.

"I think he works for whoever bankrolled the malware. I think he's had a change of heart—don't ask me why, but it's not because he's turned white knight. What is certain is he is too chickenshit to move against his boss openly. He's hoping we'll do his dirty work for him. Oh, and fun fact, he's the one who hired Tinsley to steal the malware in the first place. And then tried to kill him for it."

"Got it," Gibson said, careful to keep his voice level. He glanced over at Tinsley, who, in the darkness, appeared to be dozing. But then headlights from an oncoming car splashed through the windshield, and he saw Tinsley watching him. The eyes of a predator, hunched low at the property line, waiting for the last light to dim in the big house.

"Tinsley right there?" Jenn asked.

"Oh, yeah."

"Okay, so this is your and Dan's call, since you've got to deal with him, but my vote is to hold off telling Tinsley we found his guy. I know that was our deal, but I think this guy's on the level. I don't see how feeding him to Tinsley is in our interests. Yet. Let's wait until we see if Mahomet Rousseau has anything useful to say."

"Agreed."

"Anyway, run it by Dan and see what he thinks."

"Will do. It's a hell of a situation," Gibson said.

"Yeah, we need to start associating with a better class of sociopaths."

"Next time."

"Yeah, next time." She laughed humorlessly.

Gibson hung up, not liking the risk Jenn had taken—on that, he and Hendricks were in total agreement—but her new lead presented them with options. And not being beholden to Tinsley held an undeniable appeal. Too much was at stake to depend on him to hold up his end. Better first to track down Mahomet Rousseau, shake his tree hard, and see what fell out. But eventually, Tinsley would have to be dealt with. One way or another.

"Jenn thinks Ciara's 'Mo' may be hiding in Marseille," Gibson told the others in the van. "I have an address."

He could feel Tinsley's eyes crawling over him.

"And how does she know this?"

"She snatched one of the guys. After they wrap up in Belfast, they're headed there next."

"And he simply volunteered this information."

"She can be pretty damn persuasive," Hendricks chimed in.

"We have a head start, but not much of one," Gibson said, encouraging Tinsley to focus on the urgency of the information rather than its source.

Tinsley would not be hurried, however, and fell silent for a long time before responding. Gibson couldn't decide whether Tinsley was really thinking or merely waiting to see if Gibson would blink first.

"Marseille, then," Tinsley said at last, but Gibson knew that the subject was far from closed.

When they arrived at the airfield, Hendricks parked the minivan in its original spot. A little the worse for wear, but it had taken good care of them. Hendricks patted the dashboard affectionately.

One hell of a day, but at least it had finally stopped raining. Hendricks took advantage of the break in the weather to walk to the chain-link fence and smoke.

When he returned, he pulled Gibson aside. "I'm going back for Jenn."

Gibson had been expecting it, but he had concerns. "In that?" He gestured at the minivan. "Shape it's in, you're pushing your luck. Only reason we didn't get pulled over is because it's too dark to see bullet holes."

"I called George. He's arranging another car."

"Saint George provides."

"Better than Oprah," Hendricks deadpanned.

"We'll wait here for you."

"No, you go on ahead. I'll pick up Jenn and meet you in Marseille."

"Hendricks, Marseille's in France. This car George is arranging, it come with fins?"

"No one likes a smart-ass," Hendricks said. "So what's the story with Marseille?"

Gibson told him how Jenn had really come by her information.

"I don't like it," Hendricks said.

"You disagree?"

"No, I just don't like it. Listen. You keep your eyes open, hear me? Don't be sleeping on this motherfucker. We got a scorpion on our back. Remember that. Don't make no difference how high the water gets, only a matter of time before he figures it out and gets to stinging."

"One hell of a trip, huh?" Gibson said, meaning the day now behind them, but realizing even as he said it that he meant something much more. How long could they expect to live like this? Over the past few years, they'd shown a callous disregard for the odds. Sooner or later, the odds would show a callous disregard for them too. That was just life. Especially if they kept taking foolish risks like the ones they'd taken today. Nothing like a rain-swept runway in Ireland to bring on a bout of aimless philosophy.

"Easy there, chief," Hendricks said. "Race ain't run yet."

"When is it ever?" Gibson said, and looked to the waiting aircraft. "Want to trade?"

"Nah, you're a terrible driver," Hendricks said and embraced him with one arm. To Gibson's knowledge, it was the first time Hendricks had ever touched him on purpose. Ireland was full of surprises.

"See you in Marseille."

"Tomorrow, day after, at the outside," Hendricks said. "Oh, there's something I've been wanting to ask you."

From the look on Hendricks's face, Gibson knew there was no way this was going to end well for him. "What?"

"The girl led you into that ambush behind McElroy's, didn't she?"

Gibson hesitated.

"Come on. Tell your old pal Hendricks. It'll keep me warm on the long drive back to Belfast."

"Played me like a fiddle."

Hendricks showed him his teeth, every last one of them. Gibson thought he might sprain something if he kept grinning that way.

"See? Doesn't it feel good to admit the truth?" Hendricks asked.

"That I got suckered by a teenager? Feels great."

"Well, keep her out of harm's way anyway. She's just a kid, and it's not her fault that you've got no sense."

"You're an asshole."

Hendricks didn't argue the point. Happy to have that settled, Gibson hustled out to the runway, afraid that Tinsley might double-cross them and leave with the girl. He found them both standing at the bottom of the airstairs.

"What is it?" Gibson asked.

"Never been on a plane before," she said.

"Are you afraid?"

She shot him a pained look. "Don't be a prick. Just savoring the moment, aren't I?" She put a foot on the first stair, wiggling her ankle back and forth as if testing whether the stairs would support her weight.

"One small step for a girl, one giant leap for—"

"Jaysus, yer old," she said, her jaw setting determinedly.

Gibson recognized the expression. It was a look born of doing things because you'd been told all your life that you couldn't or you shouldn't. Ciara began to climb the steps. One tough kid.

If Tinsley found the exchange amusing, he gave no indication, and stood there doing his impression of a dry-erase board.

"Where is Daniel Hendricks?" Tinsley asked once Ciara was onboard.

"Gone back for Jenn. They'll meet us in Marseille."

"So it's to be the two of us in Marseille."

It felt like there ought to be a second half to that thought, but Tinsley said nothing else and boarded the plane. Gibson scratched his throat, feeling the scar beneath his beard, and followed Tinsley up the stairs.

Once they were safely airborne, Ciara fell asleep immediately, her fear of aircraft proving no match for her utter exhaustion. She'd buried her brother, lost her uncle, survived a shooting, a fire, and a car chase. That was more than most experienced in a lifetime; she'd done it all since breakfast. One tough kid. Gibson found a blanket and spread it over her. She didn't need it, but it made him feel better.

"The hat." Tinsley gestured to the red Phillies baseball cap on Gibson's head. "It belonged to Suzanne Lombard."

"Still does." Suzanne Lombard—Bear, as Gibson had called her when they'd been kids—had been dead going on twenty years now, but days that he didn't think about her were few and far between.

"Then why do you wear it? There are better hats."

"I like this one."

Tinsley nodded as if Gibson had answered a different question entirely. "You wear it to remember her. Honor her memory."

Gibson had nothing to say to that. "She's dead."

"I am well aware," Tinsley said. "You blame yourself."

Gibson was afraid if Tinsley didn't stop talking, he would try to kill him. "We're not talking about this."

"You were only a child at the time," Tinsley said. "There was nothing you could have done. I know. I was there."

Tinsley had been the hired assassin of Calista Dauplaise. He had done all her dirty work in her mad quest to place Suzanne's father, Benjamin Lombard, in the Oval Office. Suzanne had been an important piece of that plan, and doubtless Tinsley knew where all the bodies were buried.

"So what's it to you? You trying to offer me absolution?"

"No, you simply puzzle me. What happened to Suzanne Lombard had nothing to do with you. You were a boy when she ran away. And yet, when the chance arrived, you went to extraordinary lengths, sacrificed so much of yourself, to find her."

"She was my friend. How would you possibly understand?"

"You believe that you failed her."

"Yeah, fine, I failed her. Is that what you want to hear? Now will you please shut your goddamn mouth?"

Tinsley nodded and looked past him to the front of the plane. They sat in silence. Minutes passed. Gibson listened to his pulse pounding in his ears as it slowly returned to something approximating normal.

"I didn't say that you failed her. I said that you believe you did. This is what I don't understand about you. You didn't fail Suzanne Lombard. Far from it. You were her champion."

"How the hell do you figure that?"

"Why do you think Suzanne ran away in the first place?"

"To get away from her father."

"To protect her unborn child. That was all she cared about. When Ms. Dauplaise found her at the lake house in Pennsylvania, Suzanne spoke of nothing else. She knew she was dying; it was already too late by the time we arrived."

"You could have taken her to a hospital."

"She refused. It would have meant involving her father."

"She was fourteen."

"If you believe we could have made Suzanne Lombard go to a hospital against her will, then you don't know her as well as you think you did. She was willing to die to keep her daughter safe from him."

"So how exactly was I her champion?"

"Her father is dead. Ms. Dauplaise is dead. Suzanne's daughter is growing up safe in the care of her grandmother. Do you not see all the ways that Suzanne sowed the seeds of that victory? All she lacked was a champion to see it through after she was gone."

"Give me a fucking break," Gibson said.

"As I said, I was there, and still I do not understand you."

"Honestly, that's a relief."

"She's sleeping now," Tinsley said.

"She's dead, you freak."

"No." Tinsley pointed to Ciara. "She's sleeping."

"Oh. Yeah."

"She does not like you at all," Tinsley observed. "The harder you try, the worse it gets. Have you noticed?"

Gibson couldn't argue with that and fell silent. He thought about failure. About loss. The daughter he no longer knew except in the photographs his ex-wife shared. In his mind, Ellie was still only a child of six, but she was now eleven. What must she think of him? Did she think of him at all? Cruelly, he missed her more, not less, with each passing day. It was far from the first time he'd entertained such thoughts—they had been his constant companion for years, now—but to hear his failure enunciated in Tinsley's dead voice made the pain brand new.

CHAPTER TWENTY-TWO

Mahomet Rousseau shifted around, trying to get comfortable in the crate. It was wasted energy. After twenty-four hours, he'd worn out what little comfort an unventilated wooden box had to offer. He'd pissed himself so many times that he didn't even smell it anymore. It was just part of the ambiance of crate life.

It hadn't been his best couple of days.

Looking back, Mahomet knew he never should have taken the job in the first place. But they'd doubled his asking price, and then doubled it again. And if he was being totally honest, his initial asking price had been three times higher than normal. Who could say no to that kind of money? Certainly not a poor French Algerian kid from Ménilmontant, which had probably been the point all along.

In hindsight, it was all so painfully obvious. The trick, he supposed, was to have hindsight ahead of time. That was the kind of cheap wisdom to be gained after a day inside a four-by-four-by-four-foot shipping crate. If he ever got out of this, maybe he'd start a crate cult. Grow a beard, talk cryptically, and charge rich people ten thousand euros for a cleansing night in a crate. The opportunity to gain just a little of the clarity that Mahomet had attained in the last day had to be worth at least ten thousand, right? He'd have paid twice that to go back to the time before he'd agreed to work for that crazy Russian.

It had been monumentally stupid, when he got right down to it. And the thing was, he had been breaking the law since he was eleven years old, so he should have known better. He wasn't a criminal; he only broke the law for money. Crucial difference. And part of that difference, as Mahomet saw it, was that the people who hired him only ever knew him by one of his online personas. Anonymity had always been his armor. It had kept him safe for twelve years. No names. No faces. Just the cool, immaculate distance of a computer screen. So, of course, the Russian had insisted on a face-to-face and kept doubling his offer until Mahomet had caved.

That had been two years ago, and he still remembered the meeting vividly. By any known metric, Mahomet was not a stupid man. But it hadn't taken long to realize that he was vastly out of his depth. The Russian had grilled him relentlessly, stumping him over and over again with hypotheticals for which Mahomet simply had no solutions. It had all been incredibly dispiriting. When they'd parted ways, Mahomet had been convinced that he'd lost the job. So when he received the first payment, he'd been overjoyed. Now, he wished he'd been right the first time.

For the first six months, life had been good. The money had made a huge difference. But then an old-timer who went by "Aegis" had vanished and stopped responding to Mahomet's messages. It had given him a bad, bad feeling. Aegis was well respected, knew his trade, and had been hinting about some big job. More money than he'd ever seen. It had made Mahomet wonder if maybe they were both working on the same project. He'd meant to ask Aegis about the crazy Russian, but before he could, Aegis wasn't around to answer.

And Aegis hadn't been the only one. Over the following twelve months, one after another, a series of the top European talent went offline for good. Rumors circulated on the forums where Mahomet traded tips and code. Vague talk of some big job, but everyone was far too cautious to say more than that.

Mahomet had tried to tell himself that he was just being paranoid. Still, he'd started looking over his shoulder, missing his armor, his anonymity. And then, this thing with C. She was an Irish hacker, working on a big job too. They'd become friends. Maybe more than friends, he wasn't sure. He'd never been good with girls, but he definitely liked her a lot, even if, judging by her picture, she was way out of his league. Anyway, C told him about having met the crazy Russian. Only, it hadn't been C, it had been her older brother, who had insisted on taking her place. And five days ago, her brother had been killed in a hit-and-run.

That was when Mahomet realized that if he didn't get out of Paris, he would be next. He had university friends in Marseille. No one would think to look for him there.

Except, of course, they had.

What Mahomet couldn't work out was how. He'd been careful, told no one where he was going, taken an indirect route, paid cash. He'd left his phone behind and switched to an untraceable prepaid. And despite all that, they'd found him within thirty-six hours. So far, the crate had no wisdom to offer on the subject. If they ever let him out, he'd be sure to ask.

CHAPTER TWENTY-THREE

It was only a two-hour flight from Ireland, but the south of France might as well have been on the other side of the world. When they stepped off the plane, it was well into the seventies, and by midday, it was north of ninety. It took them that long to make it to Marseille from the out-of-the-way airfield they were forced to use for discretion's sake. They shed their Belfast layers, but it made little difference; the sun was open for business, and the cloudless blue sky offered no respite. Every so often, a teasing breeze kicked up off the Mediterranean, hinting at the possibility of a perfect world. It never lasted.

Neither Tinsley nor Gibson spoke French. Gibson had taken it in high school—at least until the FBI had handcuffed him during chemistry class—but to call him rusty would be generous. All he remembered was *bonjour, au revoir*, and how to conjugate the verb "to be." Oh, and the expression *faire l'andouille*, which meant literally "to make the sausage." At fourteen, Gibson had found the phrase hilarious, but how far were they going to get on that?

As luck would have it, Ciara was taking French in school. Gibson wasn't crazy about the idea of relying on her as translator. First off, he wasn't entirely convinced that they could trust her, although he would be the first to admit that might just be his bruised ego talking. More important, it didn't exactly pass Hendricks's "out of harm's way" test. But if they stashed the girl in a hotel, what were the chances that she'd stay put? No, better to have her where they could keep an eye on her. Besides, Ciara seemed eager to be helpful, which she demonstrated by reading factoids from a tourist pamphlet.

"Marseille was founded twenty-six hundred years ago by the Greeks. It is currently the second largest city in France, although most of the population died during the Great Plague of 1720. Marseille is—"

Tinsley snatched the pamphlet out of her hands and put it in his pocket.

"What'd you do that for?"

"We're here," said Tinsley.

Jenn's address had led them to a building in Malpassé, a poor arrondissement in the northeast of the city. Somewhere in this squat low-rise apartment complex were Mahomet Rousseau's university friends and, hopefully, a clue to finding him. Gibson had to hand it to the architect; the complex was brutally ugly in its no-frills utilitarianism. Beauty was for the middle class, apparently. Every unit did have a narrow balcony, but it was little more than a glorified ledge, not even wide enough for a single chair.

Most residents used their railings either as clotheslines or precarious mounts for oversized satellite dishes. Directly overhead, a man in a PSG soccer jersey several sizes too small watched them while smoking a cigarette dispassionately. Clearly, whatever pleasure he'd once found in tobacco had long since faded, and now he smoked because that was what he did. As they pushed into the lobby, the man leaned over his railing for a closer look. The neighborhood was predominantly North African, so two white men and a teenage girl must have looked a peculiar sight.

There was no elevator, so they walked the five flights of concrete stairs. No air-conditioning either, so it was stifling. By the time they reached the top, Gibson was soaked through and longing for a little

Belfast rain. That and a bite to eat. Dinnertime was not far off, and the hall was heavy with the rich aromas of cumin and ginger. One of the guys in his unit had been from Morocco, and it reminded him of the huge spreads he would put on.

They paused outside the apartment. Gibson wanted to lay down some kind of ground rules with Tinsley. Basic rules of engagement. *Don't shoot everyone in the head.* That sort of thing. But before he could think of how to phrase it so he didn't traumatize the girl, Ciara reached out and banged on the door with a fist. Both Tinsley and Gibson glared down at her, but their irritation had no discernable effect.

From inside the apartment, they heard men arguing, then the heavy footsteps of someone running toward the door. Gibson braced himself. Tinsley stepped back and turned in profile, hand drifting inside his jacket.

The dead bolt turned. The door opened, but no more than an inch, and then hung there like an unanswered question. The footsteps retreated back the way they had come. Gibson heard what he thought might be distant explosions. They all stared at the door, waiting for something to happen. Ciara reached out for it, but this time Tinsley was ready and took her by the collar, lifting her off her feet, and deposited her safely behind him. For once, she didn't complain but just stood there rubbing the back of her neck.

Pressing himself to the wall, Gibson gave the door a gentle push and let it swing open. Nothing happened. Glancing around the corner, he saw no one, just a short, cluttered hallway. The explosions were coming from the other end of it. A man's voice yelled something in French, provoking peals of laughter. Tinsley looked at Gibson, brow furrowed, as it dawned on Gibson what was happening.

"Come on," he said, stepping inside. "They're not expecting us."

At the end of the hall, four men sat hunched forward in front of the largest television Gibson had ever seen. Or maybe it just seemed enormous because of the way it dwarfed the rest of the room. The screen was so large that, from their perches on the edge of a threadbare couch, the men had to crane their necks up as if watching an IMAX movie from the front row. They all clutched video-game controllers as they gleefully slaughtered each other. The empty beers and take-out containers suggested the war had been underway for some time, and an eye-watering haze of body odor and pot hung over the room like male smog. It reminded Gibson of being in the service. The only thing Marines liked more than war was killing their buddies in video games and the bragging rights that came with it.

They were so engrossed in battle that it took them a minute to notice that Gibson wasn't whichever of their friends they had unlocked the door for before scampering back to their game. The one nearest Gibson, a young, thin man with a beard so precisely sculpted it looked painted on, hit pause on his controller. It provoked a chorus of disgruntled complaining, but when they saw Gibson standing there, they fell silent.

"*Bonjour,*" Gibson said with an awkward wave, exhausting a third of his French.

They took that in for a moment before leaping to their feet and exploding in a mixture of Arabic and French. Demanding, Gibson assumed, to know who the hell he was and what he was doing in their living room. Both fair questions, neither of which he had a good answer for in English, much less their native languages. He asked if any of them spoke English. Either they didn't, or they found the question offensive, because they yelled back twice as loud.

Gibson showed them his palms, hoping to signal that he came in peace. To his surprise, the room fell spontaneously still. They weren't looking at him, though. Gibson turned, following their eyes. Tinsley stood behind him, gun in hand, using it to make the international sign for *Sit your asses down*. All four men sat in unison. Ciara drifted into the room, pulling anxiously at her earlobe.

"Tell them we're not here to hurt anyone?" Gibson suggested.

Whatever Ciara said did little to reassure the men. The problem with pointing a gun at people while claiming they were perfectly safe was that actions most definitely spoke louder than words. But at least she had their undivided attention. She explained that they were friends of Mahomet Rousseau and that it was important that they find him. The men talked among themselves heatedly. A heavyset man with an Afro that would have made Angela Davis proud was nominated to act as group spokesperson.

Ciara translated as best she could. "He says that Mahomet was staying here, but that he left a couple of days ago and never came back. They figured he went back to Paris."

"He just left? Without saying anything?" Gibson asked. "So all his stuff is gone?"

Ciara relayed the question. The men nodded, except for Mr. Sharp Beard, who looked at his feet. When she pressed him, Sharp Beard admitted that Mahomet's clothes and laptop were still in his bottom drawer.

Maybe, possibly, Gibson could imagine Mahomet Rousseau going home without his clothes, but there was no way he would leave his computer behind. Not a chance in hell. The three other men thought the same thing and fell to arguing among themselves despite Tinsley's gun.

Gibson saw piled in a corner of the room the long, flat box that the gigantic television had come in. Curious, he wandered over and pushed shredded packing material around with his foot to reveal an empty PlayStation box. The television, the games—they were all brand new. And the television wasn't some bargain model. It was a top-of-the-line eighty-five-inch 4K Sony that ran around five thousand, American. Someone had come into a little money and splurged.

"Ask them when they bought the TV," Gibson said.

Last night, it turned out. They'd all called in sick to work and had been playing around the clock for the last eighteen hours. That explained the man smog.

Gibson pointed a finger at the Beard. "This is all his, isn't it?"

Ciara translated, but this time all four men shook their heads. Gibson had guessed wrong. Who, then?

The spokesperson hooked a thumb toward the back hallway that led off the kitchen. "It's Sami's. A rich uncle left him some money."

Even as the spokesperson said it, Gibson could see him realizing how far-fetched it sounded. Gibson didn't blame him or his friends. Who didn't want a new television and gaming console?

Whoever this Sami was, he'd bought the fancy electronics to make his friends complicit in whatever he'd done to pay for it all. Keep them from wondering about his sudden good fortune or why this was their first time hearing about this mythic, rich uncle. Gibson had to hand it to him, this Sami was a shrewd customer. But his roommates were now tipping to what had actually earned Sami his newfound wealth. And, judging by their rapidly growing ire, it would take a lot more than a new television to win them back.

Gibson signaled for Ciara to follow him back to the bedroom. They needed to have a little conversation with Sami while Tinsley supervised his agitated flock.

"Don't kill anyone," Gibson warned before leaving the room.

"Why would I?"

Gibson didn't have time for deep philosophical questions. "Just don't."

He found Sami fast asleep in his bed. Out cold might be closer to the mark. When Gibson couldn't rouse him, he resorted to slapping him but still got no response. Coma victims were more responsive. From the smell, Sami had been on a Vegas-size bender. Guilt could do that to a man. The newly flush Sami had rolled himself up into his blanket like a burrito and lay there dead to the world. His sandaled feet jutted out from one end of his cocoon. Gibson didn't have time for pleasantries. He straddled Sami—the blanket burrito made a surprisingly effective restraint—pinched his nose, covered his mouth, and waited for Sami's brain to register the lack of oxygen. Sami's eyes flew open, and his body tried to buck Gibson off.

Score one for the autonomous nervous system.

Once Sami collected his wits and accepted that cursing Gibson in Arabic wasn't getting him out of this, he calmed down. To an extent. The truth came tumbling out with almost no prompting at all. In English, which Gibson also appreciated. He told Ciara to go wait in the living room. She didn't budge.

Turned out betraying a friend was harder than Sami had anticipated. Ten thousand euros had sounded like a lot of money. It wasn't. He'd spent the last two days doing his best to get rid of every last cent, giving half to an ex-girlfriend in nursing school and using the rest to buy the television and gaming console.

Gibson didn't care.

"I can't even watch it," Sami cried.

Gibson cared even less.

"He said they only wanted to talk to him."

Still no sympathy from Gibson. Sami had known perfectly well that no one pays ten thousand euros for a conversation.

"Who?" Gibson demanded.

Sami shook his head vehemently. Apparently, his need to confess had its limits.

"Let me ask you a question, Sami."

"What?"

Gibson looked around curiously. "Is there another way out of this bedroom that I'm not seeing? Besides the window, I mean? It's only five stories."

"Just the front door."

"Yeah, no, I know. That's how *I'll* be leaving. I'm just wondering how you think *you're* getting out of here. Because your friends out there are pretty pissed off already. How do you think they're going to take the news that you gave up Mahomet for a PlayStation?"

Sami paled. "If I give you his name, you will take me out with you?"

"Make me believe, Sami."

Sami's story was straightforward. He played soccer in a local rec league. The goalie on his team was a hard case named Khalil. He sidelined as a mechanic at a garage in Malpassé, but his real job was muscle for a local crew that ran drugs and dabbled in extortion. Small-time independents with delusions of grandeur who were always doing crazy shit to make a name for themselves, hoping to catch the eye of the organizations that ran Marseille. All they'd accomplished was earning a reputation as violent hotheads who couldn't perform even the simplest tasks without drawing unnecessary attention from the police. But rather than learn their lesson, Khalil's crew kept doubling down, escalating their reckless violence. None of the serious players in Marseille wanted anything to do with them.

"How do you know all this?" Gibson asked.

"Because Khalil talks too much. After games, the team gets a drink or two. But Khalil, he gets drunk and complains how his crew doesn't get the respect it deserves. Then he picks a fight and spends the night with the police. But this week after the game, he drank water only. He said that the word was out for an Algerian hacker from Paris who might be hiding in Marseille. There was a bounty offered, and Khalil thought this was their big opportunity to prove themselves."

"And you realized the hacker they wanted was sleeping on your couch." Gibson climbed off Sami, who was still wrapped in his blanket.

"Yes."

Ciara, who hadn't taken her eyes off Sami, crossed over to him and stuck a finger in his face. "You're a bad man."

"Let's go," Gibson said, eager to get out of here as soon as they had Mahomet Rousseau's laptop.

"A very bad man," she repeated.

CHAPTER TWENTY-FOUR

Jurnjack sipped his tea and waited for the aircraft to taxi to the gate. Beside him, Viktor Lebedev stirred and sat forward, yawning. Viktor possessed a child's gift for sleeping soundly at any time, in any position. For Jurnjack, sleep, when it came at all, was fitful and as ill-fitting as a borrowed jacket. It was probably just as well. What little time he had left could not be squandered on something so frivolous as sleep.

All in all, it had not been a pleasant twenty-four hours. Absolutely nothing had broken his way, but at least he was out of Ireland. Never again. Really, he shouldn't have been surprised, given his history with that wretched little island. For one brief moment yesterday, Jurnjack had dared hope that Ireland and fate had smiled on him, the fire in the cobbler's providing the perfect cover for Ciara Walsh's escape. But then one of the English mercenaries had spotted the girl climbing into the minivan and the initiative had been lost. That merc had been fortunate. With only a concussion, a cracked sternum, and a broken ankle for his troubles, he would live to fight another day. But when he regained consciousness, he would learn that half his team had not been nearly so lucky. Jurnjack did not envy the person sent to deliver that news.

The only upside was that the chaos on the streets had muddied the picture and helped, at least in the short term, to hide the fact that Jurnjack had executed one of the mercenaries. But not entirely. Jurnjack could feel Viktor's attention on him now. Before, it had been admiring and respectful, but it had changed in the night to something harder and more cautious. Not suspicion, not yet, and initially Viktor had accepted his version of events. But he'd asked one too many questions about it, signaling to Jurnjack that doubt had begun to fester. And doubt, like certain cancers, could never completely be eradicated without killing the patient.

Without doubt, killing the mercenary had made Jurnjack's already tenuous position that much more complex. He wouldn't describe himself as an impulsive man. What, then, to make of his decision to throw in with the American woman? He knew next to nothing about her, not even her name. Only what instinct told him—that she was smart, resourceful, and capable. And judging by the short work made of the English mercenaries, so were her people. What Jurnjack couldn't decide was whether that made him feel better or worse. Had he committed the blunder of combating a threat by unleashing something far worse? Was this what desperation felt like?

And when he thought things couldn't get any worse, Viktor had received word through intermediaries that Mahomet Rousseau had been captured in Marseille. Given the vastness of Anatoly Skumin's network, it had been an inevitability. But Jurnjack was still surprised by how quickly Rousseau had been found. It didn't leave his new American partners much time. Jurnjack looked out the window at the Marseille Provence Airport.

No, not much time at all.

Viktor's phone rang. They both knew who it would be, and to say that Jurnjack had been dreading it would be to put it mildly. Skumin would have questions for which he had no answers. At least none he could offer that wouldn't end in a slow death. Viktor plucked the phone from the breast pocket of his jacket with two fingers, as if it were radio-active. Glancing at the display, he held it out to Jurnjack.

"It's him."

With a heavy sigh, Jurnjack set down his tea and took the phone, briefly entertaining the suicidal impulse to let it go to voice mail. But there were simpler and far less painful ways to end one's life. He could sense Skumin's fury even before he answered.

Viktor was watching him. No, Viktor was studying him.

Jurnjack felt the net closing.

Few who knew him would list patience among Khalil Basher's virtues. Khalil himself recognized that it wasn't his strong suit but thought patience was an invention of cowards too afraid to act. *Impetuous,* his mother had called him at seven when he'd run across three lanes of heavy traffic after a football. *Passionate,* she'd said at twelve when he'd been suspended from school for dislocating another boy's shoulder. *Menace,* the director of his school had called him almost every step along the way. Damn right he was a menace. Especially if you came talking that anti-Algerian shit around him. A dislocated shoulder was getting off easy.

While he closed up the garage for the day, Khalil entertained thoughts of tracking down that boy from school to teach him another lesson. In his experience, racist scum always needed refresher courses in not being racist scum. It helped lighten Khalil's mood—as thoughts of righteous violence often did. In truth, it wasn't that racist *connard* who had Khalil in such a nasty frame of mind. No, he was angry that he'd stayed late for an American *fils de pute* who'd come by the garage earlier about needing his car repaired.

The American had asked for Khalil by name, which had been deeply satisfying because Timothée, the smug *branleur* who believed himself to be the best mechanic in the garage, had expected to get the job. The look on his face had been priceless. Khalil had fawned over the American for Timothée's benefit—in English, since Timothée barely spoke a word. Of course, Khalil was delighted to stay open late so that the American could tow his sports car to the shop. Of course, Khalil would take care of everything personally. Of course, Timothée could eat shit.

But the American hadn't come back, and now Khalil was late. Tonight, of all nights, for the handoff of Mahomet Rousseau. It would look bad to miss it, but the thought of showing up Timothée had been too tempting to resist. *Impetuous . . . passionate . . . menace,* the voices of his past whispered accusingly. He needed to start using his head. Think through the consequences of his actions. It was the same resolution he made every time he screwed up. And he always meant it at the time, but when push came to shove, Khalil always chose shove. *Hard.*

He finished locking up and hurried up the street. No doubt Timothée would find some small way to rub Khalil's failure in his face. Some offhanded remark that would stay with Khalil for days, burrowing into his skin. The kind Khalil hated because he wasn't clever with words. *Let him say something,* Khalil thought. See how clever he was after Khalil beat him with a wrench. And even if the American showed up tomorrow and apologized, Khalil would send him away. If a man said he would do something, he did it. That's what Khalil believed. Stay open late when he had somewhere to be? Khalil had said he would, so he had. A man of his word. Something that American *putain* clearly knew nothing about.

Like that deadbeat grocer who had refused to pay for protection on principle. No one in the crew had wanted to harm him because he was a sweet old man who was nice to them when they were children. So what? Business was business. The crew couldn't afford to hand out free passes simply because a person had lived in the neighborhood for a long time. That kind of sentimentality was as small-time as it got. No, it needed doing, so Khalil had volunteered to do it. And had he? Damn right he had. Sure, he might have gone overboard and broken all ten of the grocer's fingers when he'd only been told to break two, but Khalil knew the value of sending clear messages. Sometimes, people were a little hard of hearing. One sharp message was worth a thousand gentle reminders.

That little incident had landed Khalil on the boss's bad side, and Khalil had taken his punishment like a good soldier. That was only fair. But if the boss gave him any attitude for being late tonight . . . well, it might be time to discuss who should be running things. After all, who had delivered Mahomet Rousseau? Khalil had. The biggest opportunity their crew had ever had, and they owed it all to him. He still couldn't believe his good luck.

When word had come down that the big gang was looking for Mahomet Rousseau, the boss had insisted on getting the message out in the neighborhood. Khalil had done it like a good soldier, sure that it would be a waste of time. Even after Sami from the rec league had told Khalil about Mahomet Rousseau, Khalil had remained skeptical. Anyone with that big a price on his head wouldn't hide out in Malpassé. And if he did, he definitely wouldn't be sleeping on Sami Radwan's couch. It offended Khalil's sense of scale.

He strode out into the street against traffic, causing a car to slam on its brakes. Khalil gave the driver a look to let him know that *he* was the lucky one. This was Khalil's neighborhood. The first of many. And people would learn to stop when they saw him coming.

Mahomet Rousseau sat in a shipping crate awaiting delivery. Things were about to change for Khalil and for the crew.

They operated out of a small warehouse that the boss used to make deliveries to local businesses. That made the gang sound bigger than it really was—the boss only had two actual clients—but the warehouse made an ideal front and the perfect spot to stash stolen goods or, in this case, human cargo. It was also extremely difficult to sneak up on. It sat on the corner of a quiet block. Every face was immediately recognizable, and if you didn't have business, then you had no reason to be there.

Khalil went around to the side door, banged on the doorbell with the side of his fist, then stepped away to let the security camera see his face.

"Excuse me," a voice said in English as the door buzzed open with an audible click.

Turning around, Khalil saw a small man with narrow, judgmental eyes that reminded him of the teachers who had busted his balls in school. How had this white fool come up behind him so quietly, and in his own neighborhood? Khalil suddenly had a hollow feeling in the pit of his stomach. The kind that only came after he'd been arrested and knew he was going back inside. But he shook it off.

"Get lost, little man," he said with a dismissive wave of his hand.

But to his surprise, the little man didn't get lost. The man set his feet, stood his ground, and gave Khalil the weirdest smile he'd ever seen. *Hungry*, if that was a word that could be applied to smiles. The hollow feeling returned, and that made Khalil angry all over again. Had he noticed that the little man was standing just outside the range of the security camera, or that one hand was palming the haft of a knife, blade up and out of sight, he might have given the hollow feeling more credence. As it was, Khalil had been the subject of too much disrespect already today. He took an aggressive step forward and shoved the man hard. The man fell back, but not far enough for Khalil's liking. Stronger than he looked.

Never mind that. Khalil was stronger than he looked too.

Both men were now out of sight of the security camera.

"Pussy," the little man said and smiled that crazy smile.

Khalil couldn't believe his ears. He'd tried to give this fool an easy way out. Time for a reminder of whose neighborhood this was. Lunging forward, Khalil swung a fist at the little man's head. But by the time the fist arrived, the little man's head was gone. He'd moved forward with frightening speed.

That's when Khalil saw the knife.

It was a long, delicate blade. Khalil was deathly afraid of knives, much more than he was of guns. But he'd thrown his punch, and now all he could do was watch events unfold like a passenger in a skidding car. The man let Khalil's momentum bring him to the blade. It disappeared into his side between two ribs. The pain was scalding, as if someone had made an incision and poured boiling oil into him. But the heat faded almost immediately, replaced by a radiating coldness. His instinct was to yank himself free, but then he felt the knife begin to turn, and he froze in place.

"Good boy," the little man said. "The knife has ruptured your vernacular artery. If I remove it, you will bleed out in less than a minute. No one will save you in time. Do you understand?"

"Yes," Khalil said in a small, shaky voice that he hated. He had seen this in movies—how knives left in a wound could act as temporary bandages. But he would need to get to a hospital soon.

"Do you still have Mahomet Rousseau? When is the exchange?"

"Yes, we have him. Tonight."

"Then let's go inside," the little man said, stepping behind Khalil and using the knife like a joystick to steer him toward the door.

Through the door was a narrow hallway that led to the warehouse floor. But first, to the right, came a small office.

"Où diable avez-vous été?" Jean demanded from inside.

The little man whispered in his ear. "Tell him the truth, that you were delayed at the garage. Find out how many are here. If he comes out of the office, you will live just long enough to see him die."

The knife guided him to the doorway. Khalil leaned his head inside and told Jean about the American and his sports car. Jean agreed that that sucked but warned the boss was pissed.

Despite his current predicament, Khalil felt his temper begin to rise. But then a strange thing happened: he thought about the consequences of his anger. Could he afford to elevate his blood pressure? He willed himself to calm down, even feeling momentarily proud of himself. Apparently, all it took to learn profound life lessons was a potentially fatal knife wound.

"Are you okay?" Jean asked. "You don't look so good."

"I ran all the way here from the garage." Khalil, who wasn't usually quick on his feet, felt pleased by the plausibility of his lie. "Is everyone here?"

"You're the last," Jean confirmed.

"When do we leave for the meet?"

"We don't. The boss doubled the price, so they're coming to us. Should be here soon."

"No kidding?" Khalil said, impressed. It seemed the boss had finally grown a pair.

"Go kiss a little ass," Jean suggested. "He's in a good mood."

"Yeah, sounds like a plan."

"Really?" Jean said, surprised to hear Khalil take his advice so readily. "You sure you're okay?"

The knife in his side suddenly woke and drove Khalil forward into the cramped room. The man put a gun to the bridge of Jean's nose.

"Tell me about the cameras," the man asked, gesturing with his head to the bank of black-and-white monitors. "Are they recording?"

"Hell no," Jean said. "We don't keep records. What are we, stupid?"

"No," the man said and pulled the trigger. "Not anymore."

At the same instant, the man yanked the knife free. Khalil screamed and fell to the floor, clutching his side, frantic to stanch the flow of blood. Keeping pressure on the wound, he cast about for anything that he could use as a makeshift bandage. There wasn't going to be time.

"There's no such thing as a vernacular artery," the man said, gazing down on him.

Khalil heard him, but it took several moments to process what he was saying. Gradually, his mind cleared. He wasn't bleeding nearly as much as he'd feared.

"There's not?"

"No."

"So I'm not going to die?"

The man smiled that hungry smile. "Well, that all depends on how useful you intend to be."

CHAPTER TWENTY-FIVE

Jurnjack and Viktor had come directly from the airport, but it looked like they were too late. Careful to hide his pleasure, Jurnjack stepped over the dead man blocking the doorway and into the warehouse. He stopped there to survey the carnage, bodies strewn everywhere. He had staged enough crime scenes in his time that he could see the precise point where the battle had begun and trace a path through the warehouse to the place where the last man had fallen. Most of the dead had never drawn their weapon or fired a shot. This had been one-way traffic, start to finish.

"Fucking massacre," Viktor said with a whistle. "How many do you think it took?"

"This was one man," Jurnjack said, feeling quite certain that he knew the one. The Origami Man had been a busy, busy boy.

"What? No way, be serious." Viktor saw that the older man wasn't joking and looked again. "Only one? How?"

Jurnjack didn't know how. Or how the American woman had gotten her team here ahead of him, but he was feeling better and better about his decision to take a chance on her. Hopefully, they were wise enough to be far away from here, because if they were caught in Marseille after this . . . well, they wouldn't die nearly so fast. Two days ago, Mahomet Rousseau had been picked up by a local crew. Strictly street level. They'd been scheduled to sell the hacker up the food chain to Farid Zia, a business associate of Skumin and leader of one of the organizations competing for control of Marseille. But, apparently, the local crew, sensing what they had stumbled onto, had doubled its ask at the last moment, forestalling the handoff.

When Farid had greeted Jurnjack and Viktor at the airport, he had been extremely apologetic that Mahomet Rousseau was not already in hand. Farid might be a player in Marseille, but he knew what disappointing Skumin could cost. He'd sworn that those responsible for the delay would be taught a severe lesson, but looking around the warehouse, it was clear that someone had clearly beaten Farid to school. To put it mildly, Farid was not happy about it.

Farid ordered the warehouse searched and stood to one side, making calls. The search was a pointless exercise, and they all knew it. All it confirmed was that Mahomet Rousseau was indeed gone and that the local crew had all died in anger. Well, not all. One survivor was found behind a stack of boxes in a pool of his own blood. They dragged him to Farid and dropped the man unceremoniously at his feet.

"What is your name?" Farid asked.

"Khalil Basher."

"I am Farid Zia. You know me?"

Khalil nodded, fear in his eyes.

"Good. That is good," Farid said. "Who did this?"

"A man. I don't know who he is."

"A man? One man did this?" Farid said, disbelieving.

Viktor glanced admiringly in the direction of Jurnjack, who pretended not to notice.

"Can you describe him?" Farid said.

"There is nothing to describe. White. Thin."

"Young? Old?" Farid demanded.

"Both?" A shrug. "He's nothing to look at, but . . ." Khalil trailed off at the memory. The man looked on the verge of tears.

"And this man who is nothing to look at took Mahomet Rousseau?"

"Yes. Others arrived and loaded the crate onto a pickup truck."

"The manufacturer? Model? Color?"

"Nissan Frontier. The 2015. Red."

"Don't lie. How do you know all that for certain?"

"I work in a garage, Monsieur Zia. I know cars."

Farid accepted the explanation and snapped his fingers at two of his men, who began making calls, spreading the word across Marseille. More questions followed, but Khalil had nothing else useful to share.

A call came in. A red Nissan pickup carrying a crate had been spotted across town.

Farid squatted beside Khalil and put a gun to his head. "If I bring you along, can you identify the man who did this? If you see him again?"

Khalil turned pale at the thought.

"Or you can stay here with your friends," Farid said.

"I can identify him," Khalil said, his survival instinct, for the moment, stronger than his fear of the man who'd done this. But it was a close call. A very close call.

Jurnjack did not blame him.

––––––––––––––

For a few glorious minutes, Gibson convinced himself that they'd managed to get away clean with Mahomet Rousseau. They were on their way to meet Jenn and Hendricks, who had finally arrived in Marseille. Gibson was looking forward to giving Hendricks some well-deserved crap. He hadn't settled on a topic yet but felt confident something would occur to him when they saw each other. At some point, Gibson intended to stop and let Mahomet Rousseau out of his crate, but there hadn't been time back at the warehouse. For the time being, Gibson figured it was the safest place for him.

And then he saw that yellow car again. It was the same one that had been behind them earlier. He was pretty sure anyway. He tried to talk himself out of it. That it was nighttime. That he didn't know the city. That it was only a coincidence. But then he remembered what Hendricks had preached back in the Caymans about evasive driving: if you get a bad feeling, trust that bad feeling. Coincidences were for people on golf courses in Florida, not fugitives in hostile cities. Well, Gibson sure had a bad feeling now.

To be certain, he made a series of turns at random. He kept his speed constant, not trying to get away. The yellow car dropped back but stayed with them. So much for getting away clean. Gibson sighed. He'd been a fool to think otherwise. Being chased around Europe by organized crime appeared to be one of his specialties. Why would Marseille be any different?

Gibson caught Tinsley's eye. Silently, they agreed that they needed to get off the streets and out of sight. This wasn't their town, and the people to whom it belonged would have eyes everywhere. How far were they going to get in a red pickup truck carrying a crate?

"What do you say we find somewhere quiet and let your friend out of the crate? I think we're safe now," Gibson said to Ciara.

The girl looked jittery and pale. She was plenty tough, but the warehouse had been too much. Hell, it had been too much for him. Tinsley had swept through the warehouse like a butcher, leaving a grisly trail of bodies in his wake. How would she hold up if she knew they were being followed? He couldn't afford to find out.

Gibson's driving had improved markedly under Hendricks's tutelage, but this was his first time in the field, and a hysterical kid had not been one of the situations that they'd covered in the Caymans. Spotting a small gap in traffic, Gibson accelerated, making a sharp turn that left the yellow car to choose between slamming on its brakes or getting pancaked by a bus. Pulling in front of a truck, Gibson used it as a blocker to camouflage his turn into an aboveground parking garage. With any luck, between the bus and the truck, he hadn't been seen.

After taking the spiral ramp up four flights to the open-air top level, he backed into a spot offering unobstructed views of both the ramp and the stairwell. Tinsley hopped out and took up a position that let him watch the street below. Nothing to do now but wait and hope that they'd lost their tail. Assuming, of course, that the yellow car had been alone, and there hadn't been a lead car that Gibson had missed. He called Jenn to check on their status.

"Question—what are you guys driving? Any chance it can hold six?"

"Panel van, not a problem. What's up?"

Gibson gave her the rundown and their current location.

"All right," Jenn said. "Sit tight. Dan says we're about ten minutes out."

In the background, Gibson could hear Hendricks yelling, "Cavalry's on the way, boy."

Despite the precariousness of their situation, Gibson chuckled. "I feel safer already." Hanging up, he nudged Ciara with his elbow. "Ready to go say hello?"

Ciara looked less than enthused at the idea. If Gibson had to name the emotion he was seeing, he would call it guilt. But what did she have to feel guilty about?

"What's going on?" he asked.

"Can't I just wait here? He speaks English well enough."

"I need your help. He's probably terrified and doesn't know me. A friendly face would go a long way right about now."

Ciara winced. "Well, yeah, that's the problem, isn't it?"

"I thought you'd talked to him."

"We had some voice chats like, but that's all."

"So he doesn't know what you look like?"

"Sort of, he does."

"What's sort of?"

Reluctantly, Ciara showed Gibson a picture of a woman with delicate, lovely features and gorgeous red hair that spun in perfect ringlets down her back.

"Who's that?"

"Girl on Instagram, from Dublin."

"And he thinks that's you?"

"Yeah, he's pretty much in love with me," Ciara admitted.

"He's twenty-three."

"Yeah, well . . ."

"How old does he think you are?"

Ciara looked at her feet. "Twenty-six."

"You catfished him."

"What?" Ciara said, offended. "No. I'm a girl."

"Yeah, a fifteen-year-old girl."

"Still a girl."

Gibson sighed and rubbed his tired eyes. "Fine. Good luck explaining that to him."

"No," Ciara moaned. "Please—"

"Listen to me," Gibson said, cutting her short. "I have to let him out. If he's really your friend, prove it. Get your butt out of this truck and be the first face that he sees."

With that, Gibson went around and dropped the tailgate. He climbed up into the bed and pried open one side of the crate. When he looked up, Ciara was standing at the back of the pickup dejectedly.

"Are you ready?" Gibson asked, feeling unexpectedly proud of her.

"Whatever. Yeah."

So much for a bonding moment. Levering the tip of the crowbar in farther, Gibson heard the nails groan and give way. The side of the crate clattered into the truck bed.

Inside, Mahomet Rousseau crouched, pressing himself against the back of the crate like a cornered animal. The rank stink of fear and urine was overpowering. Mahomet began talking a mile a minute, gesturing angrily to stay back. Gibson might not speak French, but he understood threats in any language. Weak as he looked, the hacker sounded determined to fight for his life. Gibson had some experience with solitary confinement and admired Mahomet for his nerve. Not that he wanted to get into a wrestling match with that smell. Gibson glanced back at Ciara for help.

Swallowing hard, the young girl stepped forward. "Mo, it's all right. You're safe. It's me, C. From Belfast."

Mahomet fell silent, trying to reconcile Ciara's voice coming out of a teenager.

"It's me. I swear."

"Is this a trick?" Mahomet asked.

Ciara reddened. "It's no trick, you ganch. It's me. How many times did I save your ass in *Fortnite*? And how many times would the storm have got you if I hadn't been there?"

Gibson knew *Fortnite* was a video game, but otherwise he had no idea what she was talking about. Mahomet's eyes widened with recognition. "C? It's really you?"

"Yeah, it's me. How about you get your wee ass out of that crate? These are friends. I brought them to save you."

She had? That was news to Gibson, but he was willing to let it slide since it appeared to have done the trick. Mahomet crawled forward out of the crate and shaded his eyes even though the sun had already set.

"Who is this?" Mahomet asked Ciara.

"Gibson Vaughn. He hacked something once."

"Thank you." Mahomet put out his hand.

"You're welcome," Gibson said, putting a bottle of water in the hand. "Look. There will be time for introductions later. We need to get moving."

Together, Gibson and Ciara helped Mahomet down from the truck. He walked in looping figure eights, getting some circulation back into his unused legs. The dazed grin on his face was a mile wide.

"Has he gone mental?" Ciara said. "Cracked like?"

"Nah, we call that 'happy to be alive.' He'll be fine."

"Think he'll be cross with me?"

"He's entitled. Try and keep that in mind."

Ciara nodded and went over to Mahomet. They talked quietly for a minute before he suddenly threw his arms around her, lifting her off her feet and giving her an enormous hug. Looked like he wasn't the type to hold a grudge. Saving someone's life had a way of putting everything else in proper perspective.

The phone rang. It was Jenn. "We're on our way up. Big white van. Don't let Tinsley shoot us."

Gibson hung up and relayed the message to Tinsley, who walked back to the pickup.

"See anything down there?" Gibson asked.

"No," Tinsley replied. "Nothing."

"Doesn't mean anything, though, does it?"

"It means one of two things. Either they aren't there, or they are competent."

"Or both," Gibson said.

"Or both."

CHAPTER TWENTY-SIX

The reunion was brief. Jenn gave Gibson a one-armed hug, while Hendricks offered little more than a perfunctory grunt. Heartfelt greetings would have to wait. While Jenn helped Gibson get Ciara and Mahomet situated in the van, Hendricks sat behind the wheel in silent contemplation. If you didn't know Dan, it would be tempting to accuse him of being unhelpful, but Jenn knew his human GPS of a brain was calculating the safest route out of Marseille. A much, much better use of his time as far as she was concerned. They needed to put miles between themselves and this city.

Loaded up, Jenn rode shotgun beside Dan; Tinsley took the far back seat to keep an eye on the road behind them while Gibson sat in the middle to keep Ciara and Mahomet calm in the event there was trouble.

Jenn told herself she was being paranoid. They hadn't been followed. No one was looking for a white van. Why would they be? So why was she trying so hard to convince herself? She noticed she was tapping her gun against her thigh and forced herself to stop. If they played it cool, they shouldn't have a problem.

They took the spiral ramp down to street level. As they came off the ramp, a car pulling out of a spot forced Dan to stop. Jenn tensed. But then the car's reverse lights blinked off, and it drove away. She exhaled, anxious to be out on the street. Dan gave the other car a cushion and followed behind. Forty feet from the exit, the car slowed as though the driver had forgotten something. Maybe the parking ticket. Dan slowed also, being patient, but when the car stopped short, Jenn could feel her paranoia tapping her on the shoulder with an *I told you so* smile on its face.

"I don't like this," she said to no one and everyone.

"Yeah," Hendricks agreed and threw the van in reverse.

Immediately behind them, a second car pulled out of a spot and stopped on their bumper. The lead car had teed them up perfectly. They were boxed in.

"Contact right," she called out.

"I have movement on our nine," Gibson added.

Armed men emerged from the shadows like dancers from the wings of a theater. The trap was sprung, and it was a good one. Jenn started to count heads but stopped after five—they were outmanned and outgunned. The van would offer little in the way of protection; those rifles would cut right through it. And them.

In the haze of adrenaline, it took Jenn a moment to grasp one crucial fact. They weren't shooting.

"They want us alive," Hendricks said. "If they wanted us dead, we'd be dead."

"Yeah, but how far are we willing to test their commitment to that principle?" Jenn said, looking out the window at the firepower arrayed against them.

"Do we negotiate?"

From the back, Tinsley said, "They want us alive to question us. Once they have their answers, we will die."

It was the undisputable truth.

A voice began barking orders for them to exit the vehicle with empty hands held high.

"Well, I'm open to suggestions," Jenn said.

None were forthcoming.

"I think we have to surrender. Roll the dice that they're reasonable men," Hendricks said.

"They are not," Tinsley replied from the back.

"Then we're going to die."

"You're already dead," Tinsley replied. "You just haven't gotten there yet."

Ciara began to cry. Jenn knew exactly how she felt. She caught Gibson's eye, her patron saint of bad ideas.

"I got nothing," he said.

"Me either," she replied.

Then the damnedest thing happened. The men backed away from the van. The cars pulled away and disappeared from sight. After a minute, they were alone in the garage.

"What the hell just happened?" Jenn demanded.

No one had an answer. They were all too busy savoring being alive.

"Should we go?" Ciara piped up.

"Yeah," Dan said, clearly spooked. "Let's do that." He put the van back into drive and inched forward, as if anticipating a second ambush. Something. Anything. None of this made a bit of sense. They'd been got. You didn't get any more got than that. So why were they still breathing free air?

———

"You're a dead man," Farid Zia snarled, the blood and brains of his driver dripping from the windshield of his car.

Jurnjack didn't doubt that to be true. But not today. Or at least not for the next thirty minutes. Not until the white van was safely gone from Marseille.

They were in Farid's car in an alley two blocks from the parking garage that the pickup truck had been seen entering. It had become clear that, for all of his posturing, Farid Zia preferred to coordinate his men from a distance that could charitably be called abundantly cautious. But being so removed from the action had cursed Farid with an unreasonable sense of security. One driver-slash-bodyguard had seemed more than sufficient. Say what you would about Anatoly Skumin, but it was not a mistake he would have made.

Jurnjack would have liked to be able to say that he'd thought through this decision. That it had been part of a plan. But in truth, he'd seen no alternative. Not that he gave this—whatever this was—much hope of succeeding, but some hope felt leagues better than none at all. Even if it did mean his race was over. Regardless of what Jurnjack did from here onward, Skumin would learn of his betrayal. It made no difference whether Jurnjack killed Farid and Viktor in the back of this car, not even if he were skilled enough to make it look like anything other than what it would be: an execution.

Viktor shifted in his seat, trying to disguise the fact that he had been easing his hand ever closer to the holster beneath his jacket. It was a good way to get himself killed. Jurnjack wanted to admonish the boy against such foolish risks, but he doubted that it would be taken in the spirit in which it was intended. Besides, having just signed his own death warrant, who was he to lecture anyone on foolish risks? Instead, Jurnjack made the point clear by turning the gun on Viktor and clearing his throat disapprovingly.

Viktor stopped.

Good boy.

Meanwhile, Farid hadn't ceased threatening grievous bodily harm. It really was a virtuoso performance, bordering on the operatic. "I will feed you your own fingertips."

"There will be time for dinner later," Jurnjack said. "First, tell your men that the van is not to be followed. Make it convincing or I will put a bullet through your throat."

"What are you doing?" Viktor said. "Are you mad?"

"For longer than I can remember," Jurnjack admitted.

With eyes like setting suns, Farid relayed the instruction to his men. It was not a bad performance; opera was not his only talent.

"Now what?" Farid demanded.

Jurnjack shot him in the forehead, then watched the body carefully to confirm that Farid was truly dead. Skulls were funny things, and sometimes bullets took the scenic route instead of doing their work. But there didn't appear to be anything worth seeing in Farid's head. Satisfied, Jurnjack turned to Viktor, who had let loose with a string of Russian profanity that would have made Khrushchev blush.

"Why?" Viktor asked at last.

"I didn't care for his tone," Jurnjack said, although that wasn't really it. He certainly didn't care to be threatened, but that was not why he had killed Farid. What better way to sow confusion into the Marseille outfit than by decapitating it? By the time it figured out what had happened, the white panel van could be halfway to Afghanistan for all they knew.

"I don't understand," Viktor said. "So, what now?"

"I doubt they will take kindly to any of this. We should go."

"*We?*" Viktor said, somewhat surprised to be included, extremely surprised not to be dead. "Where are we going?"

"Why, to see the boss, of course."

"But he'll kill you for what you've done. Then he'll probably kill me for seeing you do it." .

Jurnjack smiled. He really did like the boy. "Not if it's you who brings me in."

"That's not how that works," Viktor said, gesturing to the gun pointed at his chest.

A reasonable observation. Jurnjack held his gun out to Viktor. "Take it. I will tell him that you disarmed me heroically."

Viktor took the gun and sat there deep in thought. It was under-standable. There was a lot to take in.

Jurnjack looked at the two dead men in the front seat. "I don't mean to overstep my place as your prisoner, but we really ought to be going."

"Where to now? We need somewhere to hole up," Gibson said.

"Don't care as long as it's not in France," Hendricks said, pushing the van to the speed limit. "Come morning, there's gonna be a bounty on our heads behind this."

"Are you sure we're not being followed?"

"Unless they have air support, we're not being followed," Hendricks said.

How did that make any sense? Not that Gibson was complaining, but he'd really like to know why, since he was still struggling to believe that they hadn't died back in the garage. They all were. This was the first time any of them had spoken. It had felt like bad luck to break the silence, lest the universe notice them and send someone to correct the oversight.

"So where to?" Jenn asked.

"Portugal?" Gibson suggested, although his first choice was the International Space Station.

"Don't be smart."

"Well, in what countries haven't we pissed off the local mob?" Gibson asked rhetorically. The number was dwindling rapidly.

"There's always Augsburg," Hendricks said.

"Germany's not France," Gibson agreed.

"No," Jenn said emphatically. "Absolutely not."

Hendricks nodded. "Yeah, bad idea. Sorry. I'll get on the horn with George. See if he can't hustle up someplace for us to lie low. Could take a while, though."

"Don't play me, Dan," Jenn warned.

Gibson and Hendricks both fell silent to let Jenn debate herself.

"What's in Augsburg?" Ciara asked with a teenager's gift for terrible timing.

It was less of a what than a who.

"Fuck," Jenn said and then said it twice more.

"We can figure something else out," Gibson said.

"Shut up and give me the phone," Jenn replied. "I'll call him. But I hate both of you."

CHAPTER TWENTY-SEVEN

Jurnjack allowed himself to be led across the wide marble lobby of the hotel. It was regarded as one of the finest in Europe, and Skumin never stayed anywhere else when in Monaco, always taking the same corner suite for its breathtaking view of the Mediterranean. Jurnjack had always loved the sea. With a little luck, when it happened, that would be the last thing he saw. He would look away toward the horizon and find out for himself if what he had been telling his many victims was true—that there was no pain.

How many men had Jurnjack escorted across hotel lobbies such as this? Shown the same deferential, gentlemanly treatment? How many had left in one piece? And Jurnjack meant that quite literally. Sheep to the slaughter, one and all, allowing themselves to be lulled into a false sense of security by the beauty and opulence of their surroundings. For reasons that eluded him, people mistakenly equated money with civilization, while any history book showed that to find the worst humanity had to offer, one had to look no further than the most gilded palaces. And what were the palaces of the twenty-first century but luxury five-star hotels that catered to the new ruling class?

Viktor called for the elevator and stepped back alongside Jurnjack. At no point during the trip from Marseille to Monaco had Jurnjack been restrained. After a point, Viktor had lost interest in keeping a gun on him. There was simply no need. Jurnjack was long past the point of running. Even if he wanted to make a break for it, he knew that just out of sight lurked a safety net of men waiting for him to be that stupid.

Riding up in the elevator, Viktor began to look a little green. Jurnjack recognized the symptoms. His young colleague was thinking about what was to come, and his part in it. Remarkable, given Viktor's decorated military service, that he could feel squeamish, but there was a vast difference between killing in battle and escorting a man to his death. Jurnjack found his obvious discomfort endearing.

"It will be fine," Jurnjack said. "This is just how life is sometimes."

"Why?" Viktor asked, breaking his silence. He had not spoken since leaving Marseille, and Jurnjack had been afraid that he would never speak to him again. "Why did you do it? Why didn't you run?"

Jurnjack smiled at the thought. How did you explain such things to a thirty-year-old? How different the view when you were still on your way up the hill? When your back was strong and everything seemed possible? Jurnjack had been making his way cautiously down the other side of the hill for a long while now. He was nearly at the bottom, where the air was cooler and the temptation to sit a spell grew stronger each day. "You wouldn't understand. But ask me again in forty years."

The suite was as breathtaking as Jurnjack remembered. The morning sun warmed the room and the doors to the balcony stood open, letting a light breeze heavy with sea salt fill the living room. Jurnjack marked the location of Skumin's bodyguards. He tallied six, not including the two in the dining room to the left. Not that it would make any difference, but he was too old to start cutting corners.

In the center of the room, Skumin sat alone on a broad sofa like an old, well-fed spider. To his right, in a nearby armchair, sat Lev. It surprised Jurnjack to see Skumin's son here. Father and son never traveled together, so why now? Searching for an answer to that question, Jurnjack took the armchair to Skumin's left and, facing

Lev, completed their twisted little triangle. Lev crossed his arms and scowled across at him.

Good to see you too, son.

On the coffee table separating them sat an unopened bottle of Moskovskaya Osobaya. Although there were three of them, there were only two glasses. Viktor stood behind Jurnjack, one hand resting on the armchair as a reminder not to try anything foolish.

"It has been an extremely disappointing few days," Skumin said after a considerable and dramatic pause.

"I've always liked this hotel. The view," Jurnjack replied, gesturing toward the balcony. "You have good taste."

Skumin seemed disappointed by the response. He had been rehearsing this conversation the way an actor prepared for a scene, and clearly Jurnjack had gone and flubbed his lines.

Undeterred, Skumin tried again. "You can understand why, though? After all we've been through together. Did you imagine it ending this way?"

Jurnjack doubted Skumin would enjoy hearing all the ways that he had imagined it ending. "Do you remember our first meeting?"

"Antwerp."

"We drank vodka that day too."

"Did we?" Skumin's eyes went dark at the memory. "Those were very different days. Different times."

"Yes, they were." How often had Jurnjack relived that fateful meeting, urging his younger self to get up and walk away. To live a different kind of life. But, of course, Jurnjack could no more walk away in 1965 than he could today. There was nothing for it but to play out the string.

Skumin said to Lev, "If you had any idea how deadly this old bastard was in his day . . . You can't imagine. How could you? You've lived your entire life safe in the womb of the security he provides."

Jurnjack cast a wary eye toward Lev. Gone was the scowl, replaced with an expression of curiosity. As if Lev were seeing him for the first time. Perhaps he was. This was likely the first compliment Lev had ever heard his father pay anyone in his life, and the old man wasn't finished singing Jurnjack's praises.

"Everything you see, everything I have built, would have been impossible without him." Skumin turned now to Jurnjack. "Does it surprise you to hear me say that? Well, it's true. Perhaps if I had admitted it before, we would not be here now."

"That's not why we're here," Jurnjack said.

"No," Skumin agreed, cracking the seal on the vodka and filling two glasses. "That's not why we're here."

Lev continued to study Jurnjack across the table. What was it that Jurnjack saw in his eyes? Respect? He had dreamed of such a look for thirty years but was still embarrassed at the rush of emotion it brought. It felt good, though, at least until he remembered why his son was looking at him with admiration. The good feeling turned to ash. Skumin saw the change and took the opportunity to tighten the screw.

"Come. A story. From the old days. To give Lev an appreciation for your abilities."

Jurnjack eyed the glass of vodka, suddenly thirsty.

"Look, he's modest," Skumin said. "Never been one to take the credit. Isn't that so, old friend? Well, in that case, allow me. The year was 1994. A hotel not so dissimilar from this one."

Jurnjack went cold, knowing which story Skumin meant to tell. He tried to change the subject, but Skumin would not hear of it.

"Don't be rude. I'm telling the story now, so no more interruptions. You've had your chance," Skumin said, his voice cheerful and good-humored but with a threat swimming just beneath the surface. Skumin looked Lev in the eye. "Where was I? Yes, the spring of 1994. Your bitch whore of a mother had fled to London. I know, I know, it's unkind to speak ill of the dead, but believe me, she was always so high strung. Dramatic. You were five, I think. She meant to divorce me in British court. Using you as leverage. She had no interest in you or motherhood. Nothing but a gold-digging whore, believe me."

None of that was remotely true, and Skumin knew it. This was cruelty for cruelty's sake. Even after all these years, Skumin wasn't finished punishing the boy for the supposed sins of the mother.

"Obviously, I couldn't have that," Skumin said. "But she refused to be reasonable. So I sent our friend here to bring you home." Skumin paused for dramatic effect, long enough for the blood to drain from Lev's face. "Have I never told you? How careless of me. It was sad. I hated that it had to be done. She was a beautiful woman, but when a dog can't be taught to heel, then it must be put down. You're old enough now to know the truth."

"She jumped," Lev said quietly. "You always said that she jumped. That she got drunk and jumped and that the police found me asleep alone in the hotel. That's what you always said."

"Yes, that's what the London police concluded, thanks to the ingenuity of our friend here. I thought it best that you only hear that version of events."

"But that's not what happened."

"No, far from it," Skumin said. "I'm afraid she didn't jump."

Except she did. Jurnjack closed his eyes. To make it easy on him, she had stepped off the ledge and into the London night. Sofia by the window. Her blonde hair around her shoulders. Only the second time he had ever seen it down . . . painful in her beauty. Most people in her position cried and begged for their lives. Sofia did neither. Her marriage had long ago taught her that begging only ever made things worse.

"I'm glad that he sent you," she had said.

"Why?"

"Because if it were someone else, then it would mean you were already dead."

"I wish I were," Jurnjack said because he did, ever the coward.

"No, one of us has to survive. All that matters now is Lev," she said and looked to the door that led to their son asleep in the next room. "He can't go back. Please. Promise me that. That you won't take him back to that bastard."

And he had promised her. He'd even meant it for a moment. But by the time the elevator doors opened down in the lobby, and he took the sleepy boy's hand, Jurnjack had known he would take Lev back to Russia. Because, unlike Sofia, he was a dog who had been taught to heel and knew no other way. If he took the boy and ran, Skumin would find them. Of that, there was no doubt. Then Jurnjack would die, and the boy would be left alone with a monster. Better to take him home and stay close so he could look out for the boy. Surely that would be better.

Jurnjack opened his eyes.

Skumin was watching him with the seriousness of a man cutting into a steak to see if it had been cooked to his liking. Lev was standing, screaming at Jurnjack, his face a mask of rage and pain. But it was as if the volume had been turned down on the world. The only sound Jurnjack heard was the beating of his own heart. The heart of a coward and a fool. His son had grown up with a monster, and Jurnjack had allowed it to happen. Sofia would never forgive him.

Skumin snapped his fingers at Lev, and two of the bodyguards took him by the arms and dragged him out of the suite. When they were alone, or as alone as Skumin dared let them be, the older man pushed one of the glasses of vodka toward Jurnjack.

"How long have you known?" Jurnjack asked, lifting his own glass.

"Only a few days. You and Sofia covered your tracks well. I am not easily fooled, so credit where it's due."

"How?"

"Your concern for Lev at the airport in Saint Petersburg. It raised my curiosity. I suppose it had always been there to see, I simply chose not to see. So, how many times did you fuck my wife?"

"Once."

A stunned silence, and then Skumin guffawed. "Once? And you got her pregnant? Someone is a marksman in more ways than one."

Jurnjack reddened. "It was an accident."

"Was it?" Skumin said. "Perhaps she thought a child would encourage you to kill me on her behalf."

"I wish I had."

Skumin lifted his glass to him. "Yes, I know."

They touched rims, tapped the glasses on the table, and threw back the vodka.

"Tell me, why now?" Skumin asked. "After all these years, why did you wait until now to betray me?"

Jurnjack shrugged. "Money. I thought it might be nice to retire a wealthy man."

"Is that all? I admit that I'd hoped for something a little more exotic."

"That is ironic coming from you."

Skumin chuckled. "I suppose it is. Did you ever learn what it does? Were you able to sniff out the target, or did I conceal it well enough?"

"An American industry. Beyond that, I wasn't able to discover. I hoped the thumb drive would tell me."

"Which is why you've been protecting the two hackers."

"Yes," Jurnjack agreed, more than willing to let Skumin write his own false narrative.

"Your tragedy has always been that while you are effective at gathering information, you have never known what to do with it. Do you want to hear something amusing?" Skumin asked, enjoying the opportunity to toy with Jurnjack. "I worried that, in my eagerness to get the operation underway, I had been too hasty in covering my tracks. That someone clever would see the pattern I had tried so hard to disguise. You have no idea how hard she tried to persuade me to kill you all. Wipe the slate clean of anyone with even a tangential knowledge of the operation. In the end, I decided there was no one clever enough to pose a threat. I suppose, in retrospect, I somewhat underestimated you."

She? Only one woman's name came to mind. An old business partner who had crossed Skumin. The fallout had been ugly, and both sides had incurred heavy losses—Jurnjack knew the name of every man who had died. Was it possible the entire feud had been staged? That Skumin had sacrificed four of his men to camouflage his intentions? Jurnjack knew the answer to that question. He counted back—one, two, three, four, five, six, seven years ago. There was no question.

"So what now?" Jurnjack asked, hoping that he'd kept his epiphany hidden. Not that it made a difference now.

"How will I kill you? Perhaps you're hoping to step off the balcony and follow our lovely Sofia down?"

"It would save cleaning up a mess."

"Perhaps, but I'm not going to kill you today. In fact, you're going to walk out that door with Viktor. You're going to do the job I sent you to do in Saint Petersburg. Get my thumb drive and eliminate the two hackers. And no more pretending you don't know exactly who they are and how to find them."

"And then?" Jurnjack asked, grinning inwardly.

"And then I will hand you over to the Marseille syndicate to smooth things over. You've made quite a mess there."

"I understand." Jurnjack rose to follow Viktor, who despite his stone-faced resolve could not hide his dismay. Knowing the truth about Lev's parentage would not be a good career move.

"There is one caveat. If it's not done in seventy-two hours, I will butcher your son in front of you. Do you believe me?"

Jurnjack did. Of course he did.

CHAPTER TWENTY-EIGHT

It should have been a ten-hour drive from Marseille to Augsburg, but Hendricks estimated it would take closer to fourteen. Ciara Walsh kept having panic attacks, forcing them to pull over so she could walk around in the fresh air. Since escaping Marseille, the girl had been attached to Jenn at the hip, finding comfort in her presence. It was sweet in its way, although Jenn mostly found it irritating as hell. The voice of her grandmother speaking through her: *Girl, just 'cause you messed up and feel bad, don't think you can come around me expecting a cookie.* Jenn had never seen eye to eye with her grandmother, but the older she got, the more she realized that she lived her life by Gammie Charles's rules. Despite Jenn's best efforts, the old bitch's philosophy had sunk into her groundwater, and now when Jenn turned the tap, that's what poured out. She would hate to say anything so cruel to the girl, but if Ciara kept doe-eying her, eventually the faucet was going to open of its own accord.

Mahomet Rousseau, on the other hand, Jenn didn't have any kind of read on. He'd slept the entire way from Marseille. Even when they'd stopped for a meal. For a while, she'd suspected maybe he was possuming to avoid facing what he'd done, but that wasn't it. He'd spent the last forty-eight hours in a crate, expecting to die. The man was exhausted.

Fine, let him sleep; there was nothing they could do now anyway. But when they arrived in Augsburg, he had better be ready to sing or else Jenn would be happy to help warm up his vocal cords. She offered deep discounts to mass murderers, even accidental ones.

They'd driven the northern edge of Switzerland through Geneva and along the shores of Lac Léman, Bern to Zurich, and into Austria and Germany at last. Hendricks behind the wheel from start to finish, the years and the pain flaking off like a bad paint job as he drove new roads and saw new places. Gibson rode shotgun, swapping stories and laughing at old jokes. The sense of relief was palpable. That giddy feeling that came when you stuck your hand into the blender and came out with all your fingers. And the people you loved had theirs too.

They weren't out of it yet. The blender was still waiting, daring them to roll the dice one more time. And they would, too, if that's what it took, but for now they were all together again, safe and sound, and that felt pretty good. So long as she didn't think about Tinsley alone in the back like a suitcase they'd picked up off the carousel by mistake. Or where exactly they were headed and who would be waiting when they arrived. That, she wanted to think about least of all. She did a fair job of it too. At least until she saw the signs for Augsburg. Then her stomach started doing an interpretive dance. Never had she wanted a drink so badly.

Hendricks pulled up outside the house. It was large but not nearly as flashy as Jenn had expected. When they took their gear from the trunk, she had to pause to steady herself.

"You all right there?" Hendricks asked.

"This is a bad idea," Jenn said.

"We're here, and he's expecting us. You really going to bail now and leave him hanging?"

"That's not what I'm saying. I'm saying it's a bad idea."

On their way up the front walk to the house, the door opened, and Sebastião Coval stepped out into the sunshine. He looked great, tan and fit. Handsome in a pair of chinos and a polo shirt. Jenn's mind went places it had no business going.

Sebastião looked at them all in surprise. "There are more of you than I remember."

An awkward silence followed, everyone waiting for Jenn to say something. She knew she should be the one to greet him but couldn't find her voice. The urge to duck behind Hendricks and hope Sebastião hadn't seen her was nearly overwhelming. What was she? Thirteen?

Ciara came to everyone's rescue, blurting out: "You're Sebastião fucking Coval, aren't you?"

She and Mahomet both stared in wide-eyed awe. Anyone who followed football knew Sebastião Coval. An imperious and gifted Portuguese midfielder, he had begun and ended his career with Benfica, spending the middle five years with the English club Arsenal. A chronic knee injury had cut short his last years, but rather than continue to play at a diminished level, he had retired to become a manager in the German Bundesliga. At least that was the official story. Jenn knew intimately that the truth was more complex than that.

"I am the same," Sebastião said with characteristic charm. He shook Ciara's hand with a flourish. "And who might you be?"

"Ciara Walsh. Very pleased to meet you, I'm sure," she said, more formally than Jenn thought her capable.

"Welcome to my home, Ciara. It is my honor to have you here."

That exceeded Ciara's capacity for coherence, and she giggled instead of answering. Mahomet's dazed expression suggested he wasn't entirely convinced he wasn't still asleep in the van or, worse, nailed up inside that crate. After that, introductions and greetings were exchanged quickly. Gibson and then Hendricks stuck out their hands.

"Good to see you, Sebastião. Thank you for this," Hendricks said. "I know it's a big ask."

"It's nothing, my friend. You're most welcome."

Sebastião hugged Jenn warmly and kissed her cheek, his familiar stubble raising goose bumps on her shoulders. When she stepped back, part of her wished that he would hold on to her for a moment longer, but like a damn gentleman, he let her go.

"It is so wonderful to see you."

"I'm sorry," she said.

"No more apologies," he said and smiled that smile that had always given her knees a run for their money. "Come, everyone, let me show you around."

Jenn liked to joke that if you broke into Sebastião's home in Portugal, it would take less than a minute to identify the owner. His name and face literally hung on every wall: framed jerseys, trophies, and about a thousand photographs of him with actors and musicians and celebrities of all stripes. Sebastião had grown up desperately poor, and the house served as a reminder to visitors—or maybe to reassure Sebastião himself—that those days were behind him. A monument to his ego and success. Why else would a bachelor need a bathroom with three sinks? Jenn had found his excesses endearing when they weren't driving her crazy.

By contrast, Sebastião's new house bordered on modest. It was still a beautiful, spacious home, no question of that, but on the tour, she saw not a single photograph of Sebastião anywhere. Nothing with Sebastião's name on it apart from a framed newspaper story announcing his appointment as the new manager of Augsburg. And that was tucked away in the downstairs bathroom. It seemed so unlike him, but what did she really know about him now, apart from what she'd read in the media? She hadn't seen him since that night eighteen months ago when she had fled Portugal in a fishing boat with Gibson and Hendricks and George.

The house was large enough that if Hendricks and Gibson bunked together, everyone could have their own room. None of them had taken a shower or seen a bed in days. Mahomet, in particular, needed both.

They agreed to reconvene at dinnertime and map out their next steps. Jenn tried to lie down but felt restless. She got up and found Sebastião in the garden drinking wine and reading scouting reports. He put them aside when he saw her and invited her to sit.

"I'm sorry about all this," she said but remained standing. "We were desperate. It wasn't my idea."

"I am sorry to hear that," Sebastião said with a wink.

Jenn winced. "No, that's not what I mean. Of course, it's good to see you, but I know you're busy."

"It's the off-season," he said. "A perfect time to catch up with old friends."

"Is that what we are now?"

"What do you think of Augsburg?" Sebastião asked, not taking the bait. "I know it's not Salzburg, but they already had a manager, so . . ."

He'd asked her once where she would live if money and circumstances were no obstacle. Much to her own surprise, she'd answered Salzburg because she'd spent a few days there once, a lifetime ago. Sebastião had suggested that they go together. He'd seemed earnest, but she had never known whether it'd been a serious suggestion or only wishful thinking.

"Have you been yet?" she asked, finally taking a seat.

He nodded shyly, like he'd been caught at something shameful. "I see why you loved it. I thought of you the entire trip. *Did Jenn go here? Did she go there?*"

"It's beautiful here," she said, her turn to change the subject. "Your team did well last season."

"You saw us play?" he said.

"No, they don't show Bundesliga games where we are, but I read all the articles I could find. Saw some highlights online."

Sebastião blushed, and Jenn didn't think she'd ever seen anything more adorable than him trying to hide his evident happiness and pride. "We are still learning each other. Our link-up play is shit. It takes time.

I need a defensive midfielder who can boss the line. Perhaps in this transfer window. But they are good boys. They play hard for each other. This is the important thing."

"Do you like coaching?"

He laughed. "It is an adjustment. Is that the right word? Adjustment. A change, yes? I feel powerless sometimes, sitting on my ass watching the game instead of playing. I was never patient on the bench. A bit of an asshole. Perhaps I should apologize to my old managers. I see now why they all looked so old."

"You look good, though," she said and regretted it immediately.

"Where are my manners? Would you like a glass of wine?"

"No, thank you." Her reply surprised Sebastião, so she felt compelled to explain. "I quit drinking."

"Bom," Sebastião said in Portuguese. "Is this true?"

"I was in a bad place in Portugal."

"Is that what I was? A bad place?" Sebastião said, then: "Sorry. It is a bad joke. Forgive me. I have missed you."

"Oh, I'm sure you were just pining away. Women have lost all interest in you. Food has no taste anymore."

Sebastião chuckled. "I wouldn't go so far."

"Ha! I knew it."

"I love you, Jenn, but I am not a fool. I've done my best to get over you."

"Did it work?"

"Are you over me?" Sebastião replied.

"I was never under you."

Sebastião nodded as if she'd said something profound, then sat back, lost in thought. "I did not think I would ever see you again."

"We shouldn't have come. It was selfish."

"Was I ever anything to you?" he asked. "Or was I just someone to share your bad place?"

It was the least Sebastião question that she'd ever heard, vulnerable in a way that she didn't associate with him. The kind of question that normally she'd deflect and get safely away from. Her feelings weren't anything that she ever spoke honestly about. But she found she couldn't lie to him, much as she would have liked. She chalked it up to the fact that she wouldn't be staying long. There was no real risk, nothing at stake, and perhaps she owed him the truth.

"I didn't think we were anything to each other. Like I said, I was in a bad place when you knew me, but you weren't the bad place. I just thought we were partying, you know? Just fucking."

"We were," Sebastião agreed. "At the beginning."

Jenn nodded. "I don't think I noticed things had changed until . . ."

"Until I asked you to marry me?"

"Yeah. I'm the worst."

"You're not alone. I did notice. But I have no experience with such things. I thought it would pass. Like a cold. And then it was too late. I had waited too long."

"No, you didn't," she said and put her hand to his cheek, feeling the soft scruff of his permanent five-o'clock shadow.

"When will you go?"

"Soon. A day or two. If that's all right."

"It is not," he said. "But you can make it up to me."

"How?"

"Come back," he said, taking her hand and kissing her knuckles.

Then he gathered up his things and went into the house. She was grateful to him for taking the wine away.

CHAPTER TWENTY-NINE

Bernadette Autry served the tea and pastries from a tray, setting them down on the small oval table noiselessly. Viktor had not wanted anything, but Jurnjack had insisted that he at least taste an éclair. Zola's was among the finest pâtisseries in all of France, and Jurnjack always made a point to stop in when in Monaco. It would be a shame to miss out simply because Viktor was angry with him. Since leaving Skumin's hotel, the two men had barely spoken a word.

Zola's had been in Bernadette's family since before the war. She was the third-generation owner, and Jurnjack was pleased to say that the quality had not slipped one iota since her father had passed. He remembered that first visit vividly. Bernadette had been a real looker in those days, but time and pastries had done their work well. To be fair, though, neither of them had aged gracefully. Was there even such a thing?

"*Merci*, Bernadette," Jurnjack said and squeezed her wrist affectionately. "This is my friend Viktor Lebedev. Viktor, this is Bernadette Autry."

Viktor and Bernadette nodded politely in the manner of two people who had no great desire to meet. Jurnjack found it charming.

"*Bon appétit,*" said Bernadette and went on to her next table.

"Some people would say you're a very loyal man," Jurnjack said.

"Thank you," Viktor replied, stirring cream into his coffee.

"That wasn't a compliment."

Viktor stared out the shop window at the busy street beyond, unwilling to be goaded into an argument. Jurnjack could see that the boy was offended and felt that he had been treated unjustly. That was fair; still, Jurnjack hoped Viktor might forgive him.

"Don't be upset with me."

"You treated me like a fool."

Jurnjack sighed. "I lied to you. I did not treat you like a fool. There is a difference."

"You are making my head hurt," Viktor said, rubbing a spot between his eyebrows with his index finger.

"Yes, I've felt that way for several days myself." Jurnjack took a bottle of pills from his coat pocket and gave it a shake. Popping the lid, he tapped three tablets out into his palm, stopped to consider, and added one more. "For a man your size, four is best." He pushed them across the table.

"A headache will be the least of your troubles in three days."

"True, but in four days all my troubles will be over."

Viktor crossed himself. "The Lord protect me if I ever become as addled as you." He scooped up the pills. "What are these anyway?"

"Diazepam," Jurnjack said, holding up the bottle so Viktor could read the label.

"Is that like aspirin?" Viktor asked, dry swallowing the pills.

"Perhaps a little stronger. Now, at least try your éclair. It's out of this world."

"Seventy-two hours. Are you certain that you wish to spend them touring French bakeries and irritating me?" Viktor asked, taking a big bite. "This is actually very good."

"Oh, it won't take seventy-two hours."

"So, you *do* know where they are," Viktor said, making eye contact at last.

"Of course."

Viktor set down his éclair and brushed his fingertips together. "Then why are we here?"

"I like éclairs. This bakery, in particular, is exquisite. I discovered it in 1989. October third to be precise."

"The Berlin Wall," Viktor said.

"You know your history, I'm impressed. I came here to celebrate, quietly, by myself. The dawn of a new era, or so I thought at the time. An éclair and tea, just as now."

"There will be no walls falling today," Viktor said.

"During the war, the Resistance used this bakery to hide escaped prisoners of war until they could be shepherded across the border into Spain. Bernadette's grandfather was a legend. He opened it in 1937. Such a long time."

"Yes, I read that on the shop window on the way in," Viktor said and abruptly changed the subject, finally getting to what had been on his mind since the hotel. "Lev Skumin doesn't give a shit about you, believe me."

"I know."

"Then why? Because he's your blood? Is that it?"

"You have a son, yes?"

"Be careful now," Viktor said.

"Three years old? Starting to take an interest in the world?"

"He loves trains." Viktor shrugged. "It is a mystery. On YouTube, there are compilations. Fifteen minutes of trains passing. One after another after another. You can't imagine how dull it is. But he's transfixed. He would sit in my lap all day if I let him, naming every train— diesel, electric, passenger, double-decker."

"You're a lucky man," Jurnjack said, and leaned forward. "Now imagine you had handed him over to Anatoly Skumin to raise."

"I would never do something so stupid."

"And here I thought you were a loyal man."

"The reason I am loyal to him is the same reason I wouldn't let him raise my son," Viktor said.

"Well, you are wiser than I was at your age. Where were you when I needed you?"

"I was three. So why are you telling me all this? Is that the real reason you brought us here? To make common cause? Two fathers working for the same cruel bastard?"

Viktor put his elbow on the table so he could rest his heavy head on his hand.

"No, but I'll be leaving in a few minutes, and I wanted you to understand."

"Don't be an idiot. I'm sure you were something in your day, but even if you get past me, I have men in front and back."

"But I won't be going out the front or the back. Did I mention that the Resistance used this bakery during the war?"

Viktor yawned so widely that Jurnjack thought he caught sight of the éclair on the way down.

"I don't feel right," Viktor said.

"That's because I drugged you."

"That wasn't aspirin."

"No, it was diazepam. I told you that."

"Which is what?"

"Valium."

"See?" Viktor said, rubbing his face vainly to rouse himself. "You do treat me like a fool."

This time Jurnjack had no choice but to agree, but there had been no alternative. Skumin, in his zeal for taunting him, had put the final pieces together. Jurnjack still didn't know the malware's precise target, but he suspected that he knew who did. It gave him hope, although he would need to do a little detective work to be certain. Viktor would not have understood.

Jurnjack finished his tea and waited patiently until Viktor was snoring gently.

Bernadette returned.

"Is it time?" she asked.

"Yes," he said and handed her an envelope. "Will you give this to the boy when he wakes?"

"But of course," she replied, gesturing to the staircase that led to the second floor. "You remember the way?"

"But of course," Jurnjack responded in kind and kissed both her cheeks. "*Au revoir*, Bernadette."

"*Au revoir*, Peter."

Peter—the name he had told her in 1989. Not expecting to be asked, he hadn't had a name ready to give her. *Peter*, he'd blurted. To this day, he had not the first idea why. It wasn't as if he had ever known a Peter.

Truth be told, neither had Bernadette.

CHAPTER THIRTY

By nightfall, everyone had slept and showered. Sebastião ordered enough pizza to feed an army, then set it out in the kitchen along with soda and beer and wine. Since leaving the Cayman Islands, they'd been snatching sleep and food where they could, so to Jenn, pizza and a Coke sounded like the promised land. Spirits were generally higher than they had been in a while. She couldn't say specifically why, though; it wasn't as if they knew any more than they had when this had all started. It all came down to whether Mahomet Rousseau could be persuaded to talk, and if, when he did, he had anything useful to tell them.

After two days in a crate, Mahomet's soiled clothes were good only for kindling, so Sebastião had lent him a football jersey and sweatpants. Mahomet was delighted with his rapid change in fortune. He seemed like a genuinely sweet guy, all things considered, waiting until everyone else had taken pizza before having any himself. He'd handled learning Ciara's true age surprisingly well and was doing a tactful job of ignoring the way she mooned over him while not quite ignoring the young woman herself. Ciara might play at being made of stone, but everyone could see that, in this case, the catfish had gone and gotten herself good and hooked.

They ate in the dining room because it had the largest table in the house. Ciara and Mahomet sat on one side; Dan and Gibson and Jenn sat opposite. Tinsley stood off to the side, separate from the group as always. Sebastião made himself scarce, remembering an urgent errand in town. When everyone had eaten and guards were down, Dan slapped down a printout of casualty figures.

"Since we saved your lives, it's time we talked about all the people you've helped kill."

And talk Dan did, laying out exactly what the two young hackers had been hired to do. He wasn't gentle about it either, coming in hot, not shy about letting his anger show. Ciara had heard the broad strokes in Belfast, but her eyes went wide as Dan hit her with the specifics. The blood drained from Mahomet's face like a thermometer in a polar vortex. From long experience, Jenn knew what it was like to be on the receiving end of Dan's fury. He had one of the highest clearance rates in LAPD history, and watching him work, Jenn wondered how many thousands of times Dan Hendricks had gone into an interrogation room and walked out with a signed confession.

Neither Jenn nor Gibson said a word. Their job was to gauge Ciara's and Mahomet's reactions. Watch for signs that either was being disingenuous or knew the true nature of the project. Jenn drew Mahomet, who looked genuinely horrified: his pupils were dilated, and despite the air-conditioning, he broke out in a beaded sweat. A person could be taught to lie that convincingly, but it took time and years of practice. If she had to bet on it, Mahomet Rousseau had been an unwitting pawn in the design of the two programs.

Gibson was already convinced that Ciara didn't know, but he grudgingly agreed to put her through the wringer anyway. They had to be certain. Too many lives were at stake to find out later that Ciara and Mahomet had been playing them. As Dan reached the finale of his indictment, Jenn caught Gibson's eye. He nodded that Ciara was on the level.

All right, then, Jenn thought. *First hurdle cleared.*

"So, you're telling us this because you believe it can be prevented? There is still a chance?" Mahomet asked hopefully; his lilting Parisian accent was thick, but his English was solid.

"Too late for that," Dan said. "It's already started."

Mahomet and Ciara took that news badly. In the corner, Tinsley straightened, clearly wondering how Dan could possibly know that.

"How long ago?" Mahomet asked. "How long since the malware was deployed?"

"That we don't know."

"But it's not been six months yet, has it?" Ciara said.

"No," Mahomet said reassuringly. "Otherwise, it would be every-where in the media."

"That's what we think," Dan said, then corrected himself. "That's what we hope."

"So there's still time, yeah?" Ciara asked, looking hopefully around the table. "It can still be stopped?"

"Well, that's the problem," Gibson said. "We only know its ulti-mate effect. A lot of people are going to die. What we don't know is how. We don't know the target."

"So what do you say, Mahomet?" Dan said with a wink, suddenly his best friend in the world. "Want to do some good?"

Mahomet looked back at him blankly. "You think that I know this?"

"Don't play it that way, kid," Dan warned. "Trust me, I'm the nice one. I'm your door number one. Remember that. You don't want to be going through door number two and get our friend here involved." Dan hooked a thumb at Jenn. "Want to know what she did for the CIA?"

"We know you tested the malware," Gibson interrupted before Dan could unleash the other three horsemen of the apocalypse. "That's what you told Ciara. So cut the bullshit."

In the wake of Dan's description of her, Jenn felt Tinsley watching, dead eyes gleaming as if he'd just met his long-lost sister. *In your dreams.* That is, if the strange man dreamed at all.

"Yeah, I did," Mahomet said.

"So what did you test?"

"I was given the specifications to a specific line of mainframes. Very common. Used all over the world in a variety of manufacturing plants. I built two replicas, one for each of the programs. We tested the malware on them. To make sure it worked perfectly, we kept the replicas patched with all current security updates."

"And the program worked anyway?" Gibson asked.

"Every time."

"So it's exploiting a zero day."

"Without question. Whatever vulnerability the program is attacking, the mainframe's manufacturer has no idea it exists."

"What's your best guess about the target?" Dan asked.

"A factory in the United States."

"We know it's in the United States. What kind of factory?" Jenn asked as calmly as she could. In the last few minutes, the temperature in the room felt as if it had gone up twenty degrees.

"I have no idea. I swear. Like I said, they're common mainframes. I thought it was straight corporate sabotage, one big company pissing in the soup of another. He never said anything about killing people."

"He?" Dan asked.

"The Russian who hired me. A real bastard. Crazy, you could see it in his eyes. Scared me so bad, I almost walked away. Wish that I had, but he kept doubling his offer until I said yes. We met once in Paris before the work started. He insisted. Grilled me for hours on every angle. I know my shit, man, but the Russian? He ran circles around me. So I asked why he didn't do it himself since he knew it so much better than me. He said he should but there wasn't time, so he'd just have to fix all my code." Mahomet swore in French at the memory. "I thought he was just showing off, but a few times he didn't like my work. I would get it back with an angry note. He'd take my code and expand on it like I'd played three notes on a piano, and he'd turned them into a symphony. It was depressing. We must have run thousands of simulations. He was never satisfied. I learned so much from him. He's a bastard, but he's also a genius."

"Why two replicas?" Jenn asked.

Gibson jumped in to explain. "Because, to compromise a factory, it's necessary to target two separate networks—production and quality control. See, manufacturing is all automated now. One computer tells the factory what to make, provides instructions—that's the production server. Then at the other end, a separate computer tests the end product against the same instructions to make certain that they are the same— that's the quality-control server. And, as a precaution, there's no connection between those two servers so that they do not communicate in any manner." Gibson paused to be certain everyone was keeping up. "So to make changes to one, you had to make changes to both. Otherwise, the product would have been flagged by quality control and never left the warehouse."

"How long has this been in the works?" Jenn asked, trying to grasp its scope.

"I don't know. Not exactly. I've been on it for two years, and it had already been going on for a while. My guess is at least four," Mahomet said.

"Four years?" Jenn said. "Excuse my ignorance, but that seems like a long time for one hack."

"Not if you want to get away with it. Really get away with it, I mean to say. Penetrating a computer is the easy part. The challenge is leaving no trace that you were there. Any fool can walk across the beach, but only a genius leaves no footprints. That is why what we built was like Stuxnet, only several steps more complicated," Mahomet said, referring to the malware that destroyed one-fifth of Iranian nuclear centrifuges.

"Why more complex?" Hendricks asked.

"Because times, they have changed. Stuxnet was, like, ten years ago. It's harder to get away with such things in the United States. Your country is very bad at stopping attacks, but they are very good when an attack has been discovered."

Gibson was nodding now. "The idea is to make it look like an industrial accident, not hacking."

"So he's going to kill half a million people, and the US will think it was human error?" Hendricks said, disbelief in his voice.

"Yeah," Gibson said. "The manufacturer would take all the responsibility."

They sat somberly digesting the fact that they'd come up short. No more leads to run down, no more hunches to play. They still lacked enough information about the target to credibly go public. Even if they did, thought Jenn, what would the response be? That every factory in the continental United States would be shut down on the word of a couple of international fugitives peddling a crackpot conspiracy theory. Yeah, that sounded likely.

"So that's it? All these people are just going to die?" Ciara said quietly. "And all we can do is wait and watch?"

"Mahomet was our last shot," Gibson said. "Unless someone knows something I don't, I think we're at a dead end."

"I am so sorry," Mahomet said.

"Excuse me for interrupting," a voice said from the doorway. "But I may be able to help with that."

Everyone swiveled in its direction. Jenn recognized the gun in the old man's hand. She never forgot a face and never forgot a gun that had been pointed at her. It wasn't pointed at her now, though. That honor was reserved for Tinsley.

"You," Tinsley said in a voice that expressed no surprise, no curiosity, no alarm. A simple statement of fact.

"Yes," the old man replied.

"I have been looking for you."

"And here I am."

"And here you are."

"I have a proposition for you."

"I have one for you as well," Tinsley replied.

Jenn saw the blade of a cruel tactical knife in Tinsley's fist. She had no idea where it had been hidden.

"Yes, I can imagine," the old man said. "I have a feeling they might complement one another."

"Tell me more," Tinsley droned. He had been in motion the entire time, not hurrying but flowing steadily across the crowded dining room like water running downhill. He'd already closed more than half the distance between himself and the old man.

The old man fired two shots into the wall next to the assassin. Even with the suppressor, it sent everyone diving to the floor, scrambling for cover. All except for Tinsley, who simply came to a precipitous halt, his face vacant as he weighed his options.

"That's quite far enough," the old man warned. "Don't count on my sloppiness in Varna. It was out of character, I assure you. Kick the knife to me and sit cross-legged on the floor. Do it now."

Tinsley kicked the knife to the old man and sat cross-legged on the floor.

"Hello, young lady," the old man said to Jenn, where she'd crouched behind her chair. "You've done remarkably well getting this far. I questioned my sanity involving you, but you and your people have exceeded my every expectation."

"Thanks?" She'd take a compliment over a bullet any day, but she wasn't yet convinced it wasn't a package deal.

"You can relax," the old man said. "I am alone. If I'd wanted you dead, I would have let them kill you in the parking garage in Marseille."

"That was you? You stopped that?" Jenn asked.

"Well, it wasn't in the spirit of brotherhood."

Tinsley's head swung toward Jenn. "You know this man?"

"Yes," the man said. "We met in Belfast."

"I see," Tinsley said as something behind his eyes snapped shut.

"So, what now?" Jenn asked.

"Now I would like you and your associate to take a walk out to my car," the old man said, referring to Tinsley.

Dan and Gibson voiced their displeasure with that idea in different but equally colorful terms. Jenn quieted them.

"Where are we going?"

"No great distance, I assure you. There is something we need to discuss."

"And it will tell us the malware's target?"

"Yes, if I'm correct, it will solve your problem."

"Well, let's go, then," Jenn said, rising. She turned to Dan and Gibson. "Why don't you see if you can get George on the horn. I'll be back as soon as I can."

CHAPTER THIRTY-ONE

From the back seat, Jurnjack could keep his gun on both the woman and the Origami Man. The latter's wrists and ankles were bound securely, but Jurnjack did not let his guard down for an instant. The usual assumptions would not suffice.

Jurnjack directed Jenn to drive to Gögginger Park. The park was closed at night, which would grant them privacy to conduct their business. But it also made Jurnjack a little melancholy. He was fond of its pond and would have liked to sit on one of the benches and feed the ducks. One last time. He frowned at his whimsy. It was remarkable, as the end drew near, how the list of things he wanted to do—one last time—grew and grew. Silly, trivial things like feeding ducks by a pond in the warm German sunshine. For the first time, he understood that the look on his victims' faces had not been fear but regret.

After they had parked, Jurnjack passed the woman a manila folder. He wished that it were thicker, and judging by her face, she wished the same. By the dome light, she read the contents, cover to cover. When she was finished, she switched off the light and thought it all through. Another quality he admired in her. She didn't speak until she had something to say. In the passenger seat, the Origami Man sat so unnaturally still that you might be excused for forgetting he was even there.

"Is this all you have?" she asked. There was no accusation in her voice, but it felt that way to Jurnjack.

"I had hoped with what you knew from the thumb drive, it would be enough."

"It fills in some of the blanks, but not all of them," she said. "And there's one really big one left."

"I know. Find the woman."

"Who is she?" Jenn asked, holding up the photograph of a heavyset white female. "What's her connection to all this?"

"Gerda König. She is the last piece of the puzzle," Jurnjack said and explained everything that he had pieced together since his last meeting with Anatoly Skumin. It sounded much thinner when he said it aloud, but it was all he had.

"She works for Anatoly Skumin as well?"

"They were partners."

"And if she doesn't know?"

"She must. But don't let her appearance fool you; she is a snake and won't be charmed easily."

"You know her?"

"Yes, although I have not seen her in many years. I believed their business relationship had ended, but I realize now that their falling-out was a deception."

"And you're sure she still is working with him?"

"I am betting my life on it."

The woman turned in her seat to look back at him. There must have been something in his eyes that he had meant to keep hidden.

She said, "You're paying a heavy price to give me this, aren't you?"

"We all pay the same price eventually. I've come to realize that all that matters is that we have something to show for it."

She nodded. "I've started thinking the same thing lately."

"May I offer you some advice?"

She stared at him for a long moment. "You understand why I don't want advice from you?"

"I do. It's the comedy of life—the people best equipped to give advice are the very ones no one will take it from. Well, don't forget to feed the ducks before you do whatever it is you decide to do," he said, then waved the remark away when she didn't understand. "May I ask your name?"

"Jenn Charles."

"Mathias Sacha Jurnjack," he said and offered his hand.

After a moment's consideration, she shook it. "So, will I not be seeing you again?"

He chuckled. "No, I'm afraid this really will be our last meeting. Although it has been my pleasure."

"Can't say the same."

"I know. I've never made a good impression."

"So what now?"

"You take the car and go. Your colleague and I—"

"He's not my colleague," she cut in.

"—have unfinished business."

The Origami Man's head turned slowly to her. "We had an arrangement."

"Yeah?" she said. "Well, you wanted to meet the man who tried to kill you. Wasn't my job to make sure you were holding the gun when you did."

When the car's headlights had disappeared around the bend, Jurnjack tried the park gate. No luck. It was locked up tight. That was a shame.

"Is that where you intend to do it?" the Origami Man asked, gesturing toward the park with both fists. Jurnjack had cut free the Origami Man's ankles, but his wrists remained bound. "Will you tell me to get on my knees? That's how you old-timers like it done, isn't it? Back of the head."

"There's a little pond . . ."

"Drowning? That's not very practical."

"Don't tell me my business," Jurnjack snapped. "And no, I just wanted to . . . Never mind, it's not important."

"So you have some experience?"

"Since before you were born."

"And yet you are such a terrible shot," the Origami Man said and took a small step forward.

"Yes, well. Skills fade with time, but I still have enough wits about me to drop you now, so that's close enough."

"As you wish. So where to?"

"I was thinking Monaco."

A look of surprise from the Origami Man, or what passed for surprise on that inscrutably blank face. "Monaco? If you think I will permit you to transport me to Monaco in order to kill me, you misunderstand me."

"Ah, no, it is you who misunderstands me. I didn't come to kill you; I came to hire you."

The Origami Man gazed at him evenly. If the proposal surprised him, he gave no indication. "You think I forgive or forget? I already know what your money buys."

"I'm not offering money. In truth, I don't have enough left. I spent the better part of my life savings to hire you the first time."

"Then how would you propose to pay me?" the Origami Man said, clearly humoring him and stalling for time.

"With my life."

For the first time, Jurnjack saw a ripple of curiosity from his prisoner.

"Go on."

"For my betrayal in Varna, you mean to kill me. And were circumstances different, you would have done so already. But as Ms. Charles so eloquently put it, I hold the gun and you do not. So I am offering you a choice. I can kill you now, or you can agree to my offer. Kill one man for me, and once I know that he is dead, my life is forfeit."

Anyone else would have been taken aback by such a dramatic proposition, but the Origami Man took it in stride. "And you believe that I would abide by the terms of that contract. That I wouldn't turn on you at the first opportunity? You are living in a romantic fairy tale if you think I possess honor."

"Well, I might not use that word, but, in your way, I think you do. Otherwise, you would have already taken my deal instead of trying to argue me out of it."

"I suppose that was unwise of me. But there is one other problem."

"What's that?"

"You might trust me, but you are counting on me to trust you. I do not."

Jurnjack turned the gun in his hand. "True. There is always the possibility that, after I do my job, I will double-cross you."

"Again."

"I could always kill you now."

"I would prefer that to the alternative."

"Look me in the eye," Jurnjack said, wearying of their dance. "I am tired. My race is run. When this is over, so am I. Come to Monaco. I will offer no resistance."

The Origami Man stood there for a long time before smiling a strange, cancerous smile that had no humor in it. "I accept your offer."

And that was all there was to it. The two men did not shake hands, no contracts were signed, but it felt binding and unbreakable. Jurnjack holstered his weapon and freed the Origami Man's wrists with his own knife. After a moment's hesitation, Jurnjack returned the knife and turned away to look at the park. If he had misread the Origami Man, then he would rather die here than in Monaco.

"So . . . ," the Origami Man said. "Why is this man so difficult to kill that you would trade your life for his death?"

Jurnjack turned back. The knife was gone; the Origami Man's hands were empty. So far, so good.

"It's a long story. I'll tell you on the way."

CHAPTER THIRTY-TWO

"Hello, Gibson," George Abe said. "Good to see you."

Gibson had set up a video call at one end of the dining room table so that George could see everyone. They had big decisions to make tonight, an all-hands-on-deck situation. Gibson started to say something about how it had been a while, but they'd been together at the beginning of the week. It only felt like a lifetime.

Jenn had returned from her drive. Alone. When Gibson had asked where Tinsley was, she'd hugged him and said, "He's gone."

He wasn't sure if she'd meant what he thought she meant. Wishful thinking was one hell of a drug. "Gone as in gone? Gone gone?"

She described what had transpired between Jurnjack and Tinsley, dodging Gibson's question and clearly unwilling to say the words that Gibson wanted to hear. Gibson wanted to believe that Fred Tinsley was dead—he wouldn't hurt anyone else now—but beyond that, he felt little one way or another. No joy. No sense of resolution. While Tinsley might have been connected to much of the misery in Gibson's life, he was also distinct from it. A mere tool. And Gibson didn't hate the gun, he hated the hand that pulled the trigger: Calista Dauplaise, who had been dead for nearly three years. How much closure had that brought him? Honestly, he thought closure might be a myth, like the cure for cancer or fair and open elections.

Hendricks appeared, grinning like a fool. Actually grinning. Apparently one of them still believed in closure. Hendricks looked like he'd OD'd on the stuff. "Did you hear? Dead."

"Amen," Gibson replied.

Jenn gave them both a pained look. "I didn't say he was dead. I said he was gone." When she saw they weren't listening, she excused herself and went to reassure Sebastião, who had understandable concerns about the two bullet holes in his dining room wall.

Hendricks slapped Gibson on the back. "Ding dong, the mother-fucker's dead."

"Hello, Daniel," George said from the monitor.

Hendricks straightened up like he'd been caught sneaking in after curfew. "Hey, boss, didn't see you there."

"So who is it who is no longer among us? Or can I guess?"

While they waited for the class to assemble, Gibson and Hendricks brought George up to speed on their warm reception in Marseille, subsequent cross-continent exodus to Germany, and the excitement of the last hour.

"Wait," George said. "Where are you now?"

"Augsburg."

"Oh, dear. How is she?"

"You're asking us?" Hendricks said.

"Point taken. And how is Sebastião?"

"Looks like he got hit by the crosstown bus."

"You boys about done gossiping?" Jenn asked from the doorway.

Gibson had a fair bit of experience being embarrassed, but it was the first time he'd ever seen George flustered.

"Jennifer. You're looking well," George said.

"Did you remember to water my plants?" she asked, slipping into the seat at the far end of the table.

"Your plants?" George said, sounding alarmed. "Uh, no. Did you—"

"I don't have any plants, sir," Jenn said and smiled a *gotcha* smile.

"I see," George said, locating a speck of lint on his lapel and removing it. "Well, now that everyone is here, shall we get started? Daniel and Gibson were just bringing me up to speed."

"Mm-hmm," Jenn said.

"They told me that you've been speaking with your contact."

"Yeah, tell me you got something good," Hendricks said.

"Well, I wouldn't say we hit the mother lode, but we're mother lode adjacent," Jenn said.

"Define 'adjacent,'" Gibson said.

Jenn opened a manila folder on the table and flipped through the pages inside. "We know the industry now. The malware on the thumb drive is targeting a US pharmaceutical company."

"But not which one?" George asked. "There are at least ten major firms in the United States, and myriad midsize ones. Not to mention the biotech sector and various hybrid startups. It's a long list. Your source was unable to narrow it down further?"

"No, but if you factor in the casualty figures on those spreadsheets, it has to be a major one. Right?"

"Possibly. Jennifer—how is your contact in possession of this information?"

"If what he says is true, and my instincts say it is, he's the longtime triggerman for a Russian oligarch by the name of Anatoly Skumin. Skumin is a former KGB boss who grabbed his piece of the pie when the old Soviet Union fell."

"Yes," George said. "I'm familiar with Anatoly Skumin and his methods. He is more than capable of such a thing."

"Why, though?" Hendricks asked. "Is it terrorism? Kill some Americans, is that it?"

Jenn shook her head. "Money. A lot of money."

"How does killing five hundred thousand people make you rich?"

"Not to play the cynic, Daniel, but when has killing five hundred thousand people not made someone rich?" George replied. "And at this stage, I don't know that it matters why. It only matters how it can be stopped."

"Yeah, did your guy happen to mention anything about that?" Gibson asked.

Jenn shook her head grimly. She took a photo of a woman out of her folder and held it up. "No, but he gave me a name—Gerda König."

"Sounds like an IKEA bookshelf," Gibson said.

"So who is Gerda König and how can she serve the cause?" asked Hendricks.

"Gerda König is a German pharmaceutical engineer. Former, I should say. Sounds like she was a rising star back in the nineties but got busted for cutting serious ethical corners. People died."

"Did she serve time?" Jenn asked.

"No, it all got swept under the rug by her employer. Bad for business. But Gerda König became persona non grata in the industry. A little bitter about it, too, by the sound of it. She's been working the other side ever since. Apparently, she was known as the Queen of MDMA before moving on to synthetic opioids and cannabinoids."

"She sounds like a hit at parties," Hendricks said.

"And that's how she and Skumin know each other?" George said. "They were in the drug business together?"

"Correct. My contact had been under the impression that they severed their working relationship seven years ago. That appears now to have been a diversionary tactic. What happened instead was Skumin and König moved on to a new project, one so risky that Skumin masked its true scope even from his own people—corrupting the supply chain of an American pharmaceutical company."

Even though they knew most of this already, hearing Jenn lay it all out stunned the room into silence. Sometimes you had to let the sheer monstrousness of human behavior sink in anew. It was Hendricks who spoke first.

"Any good news in that folder about the six-month mark? How close are we?"

"Actually, yes. We have fifty-five days, a little less than two months," Jenn said. "It's not ideal, but it means we have a little wiggle room."

The room perked up at the news. At least until George rained on their parade. "I'm afraid not, Jenn."

"Why is that, sir?"

"Because the target is a pharmaceutical company. Our assumptions have been wrong."

Everyone leaned in to listen carefully.

"When we first discovered the six-month mark, we assumed that there would be a major event associated with it," George said. "Some kind of trigger that would cause the escalation in casualties. But that's not what's happening. These monsters have corrupted the entire supply chain. Turning medications to poison. And in targeting the sick, they've given doctors a plausible explanation to discount any early fatalities. Until the six-month mark comes and goes, by which time it will be too late."

"Oh my God," Jenn said, articulating everyone's reaction.

"Every day we wait," George said, painting the picture, "people, children, will go on taking their medicine, trusting it to keep them alive, while poison builds up in their bloodstream. Slowly killing them."

"So what do we do?" Jenn asked.

The room appeared out of answers. Gibson had an idea, but he didn't think anyone was going to like it much.

"We fix it," he said quietly.

"Fix what, Gibson?" George asked, seemingly the only one who had heard him.

"We fix the factory."

Hendricks shot him a look that suggested strongly that Gibson had sprouted a second and possibly third head. But Hendricks wasn't telling him that he was an idiot either, so Gibson figured he had a chance here.

"Fix it how?" George asked.

"Look at who's sitting in this room. We have three very skilled hackers. Two who worked on the original malware. We also have an experienced LAPD detective, and a former CIA officer. I say we leverage that talent. Jenn and Hendricks go after Gerda König. She knows the target, and more importantly, I guarantee she has the original pharmaceutical formulas."

"What do we need the original formulas for?"

"Well, the malware corrupted the manufacturing server and the quality-control server at this company, right? So, me and Ciara and Mahomet here, we load the original formulas back into the malware and use them to reset only the quality-control server."

Jenn was smiling now, and even Hendricks wasn't looking at him like he was entirely certifiable.

"And that will set off the alarms," George said.

"When the poison being manufactured doesn't match what quality control is looking for, it'll be game over. Fastest way I see to stopping all this. Afterward, we can take it to the proper authorities so they can make sure that Anatoly Skumin meets the business end of a drone strike. But right now, in this moment, mission one is to repurpose the malware to halt the distribution of the corrupted medicine."

"Then I guess you'll be needing this," Jenn said, reaching into a pocket. Her expression froze as she checked the rest of her pockets.

"What is it?" Hendricks asked, but Jenn was up and out of the room.

"Oh, no," Hendricks said with a terrible realization. "The thumb drive."

Jenn returned and stood in the doorway, hand-combing angry furrows into her hair. "Tinsley took the thumb drive."

"Yeah, about that," Gibson said, unable to keep the guilt out of his voice.

"What?" Jenn asked.

"I made a copy."

"You made a copy? When?"

"In your kitchen," Gibson confessed.

"My kitchen? You've had a copy since the Caymans? I explicitly told you not to make a copy."

"Yeah," Gibson agreed. "Wait, you meant that?"

"Yeah, I meant it. But you went and did anyway because . . . of course you did."

"Come on. You were acting all janky, and I was curious. Anyway, maybe you should focus on the fact that we *have* a copy and not *why* we have a copy. Just a thought."

CHAPTER THIRTY-THREE

Jenn eased the bedroom door closed. It was after three a.m., but she'd had to pry the laptop out of Ciara's hands to get her even to contemplate sleep. Jenn admired the young woman's dedication, especially given what she'd gone through in the last week. Many adults didn't possess the capacity to own their mistakes, but not only had Ciara not shied away from responsibility, she meant to atone. Mahomet as well. Jenn knew a little about atonement and considered it a good sign. But Ciara was still only fifteen, and she could start atoning in the morning when she was fresh.

Jenn stowed the laptop on a shelf until morning, sparking memories from her own childhood. The way her mother would put things up out of reach if Jenn misbehaved. "The High Shelf," her mom had called it— *Don't make me put that on the High Shelf.* Jenn had dreaded that punishment, because the High Shelf was in their living room. So although Jenn could see the confiscated item, she couldn't touch it until her mother decided that the lesson had been taught. Of course, that had been before her dad had died in Beirut. After that, her mom had lost interest in teaching her daughter lessons, lost interest in most everything but vodka.

When Jenn knocked on their door, Dan and Gibson were getting ready for bed as well.

"Lights out now, boys. Don't be up all night talking."

"Yes, Mom," Gibson said midyawn. "What time are you guys out of here?"

"Too damn early" was Jenn's answer. "Dan, you want me to wake you up?"

Gerda König wasn't exactly keeping a low profile. Using real-estate records, Gibson had tracked her to a small town in Switzerland. There was no guaranteeing she would be there, but at least it gave them a place to start. Jenn intended to early-bird the situation.

"Yeah, that would be good," Hendricks said, his enthusiasm dialed to a one. "This whole situation is messing with my REM. I'm afraid I'd sleep through the big one at this point."

"Question," Gibson said.

"Uh-oh," said Hendricks.

"Assuming we pull this thing off," Gibson said, "we're going to need a way out of Europe. Don't think we should be hanging around after kicking the hornet's nest. And we can't exactly fly commercial. So, any ideas on how we're going to afford that?"

It was a good question, but with all that was going on, one that hadn't even crossed Jenn's mind. And it was definitely going to be an issue, given George's discouraging news. They were all but broke. Turned out all the logistical support George had been providing them had added up. Their little tour of Europe had burned through 90 percent of their operating capital for the year. If it went on much longer, they would need to dip into their rainy-day fund—the money they kept in reserve in case they had to go back on the run. Despite that, the vote had been unanimous—see this thing through, regardless. There had never been any doubt in her mind.

"I don't know," she said, her brain too tired to tackle even one more issue tonight. "Would you query George and see if he has any bright ideas?"

"Sure thing. You okay?"

"Just beat, you know? I'll be fine."

Jenn really was running on fumes, but she had one thing left to do. She found Sebastião alone in his office, watching game footage on his enormous television and taking notes on a laptop. When she'd known him in Portugal, he'd still been a player, but he'd shown the same relentless work ethic while rehabbing his damaged knee. She was ashamed to admit that she'd written him off as a bit of a meathead jock, pretty but shallow. Nothing but a good time with washboard abs. In retrospect, she realized that she hadn't wanted depth so had avoided seeing it in him. When you were that far down in the bottle, depth wasn't something you could afford. Not if you wanted the endless party to keep on a-rolling.

She rapped her knuckles on the doorframe lightly. "Hey, didn't anyone tell you it was the off-season?"

Sebastião smiled up at her. "I was waiting for you."

"Sorry, we had a lot of logistics to go over."

"When do you leave?"

"First light."

"First light," Sebastião repeated. "It sounds so romantic. So much better than 'dawn.'"

"George is working on a place for Gibson and the other two to use. So they should be out of your hair by noon."

Sebastião made an uncomprehending face. "What is 'out of my hair'?"

"Gone. Leaving your house."

His face turned offended. "No, absolutely not. They will stay here. In my home."

"No, I appreciate it, that's very generous, but it's too dangerous. You remember what happened last time I got you involved in my shit."

"I remember very well, Jennifer. But you did not get me involved, and it was my shit long before it was ever yours," Sebastião said. "How old is that girl?"

"Fifteen."

"Fifteen! Is it not too dangerous for her as well? And you would have me put this girl out on the street. They will stay here. I will not hear another word about it or I will become very angry."

"All right, fine. Thank you. You're sure about this? You and Gibson here? Together? With no adult supervision? That ought to be interesting."

Sebastião arched a single eyebrow in her direction.

"Would you quit with that?" Jenn said. "We work together, that's it."

"Well, he is very jealous and does not seem to like me very much. And I have to wonder why that is."

"Not everyone likes you, you know."

"That is simply not true," Sebastião said with a grin.

"Come on, you were always kind of an asshole to him."

"He was always kind of an asshole to me."

"Oh, no doubt," Jenn agreed. "I think he thought he was looking out for me."

"Was I such a bad influence?"

"No," Jenn said. "I was the bad influence."

"So what was I?"

"A man I underestimated."

"Oh. That is a very good answer," Sebastião said. "Come, sit. You look tired."

She meant to say that she needed to get to bed, that she was only there to say good night, but her Benedict Arnold feet carried her to the couch before she could form the words. To no one's surprise, it was the world's most comfortable couch. She slipped off her shoes and put her feet up. On the TV, a highlight reel played of a young man with shoulder-length hair in full flight. He danced by one defender and then another, the ball attached to his feet like a magnet.

"Who's the kid?" she asked.

"Attacking midfielder. A true *trequartista* in the Italian style."

"A what now?"

Sebastião grinned. "*Trequartista*. A withdrawn forward. A creator." Sebastião rewound the tape. "See here how he anticipates where his teammate will be, and moves the defender aside with his feet to open up the pass? He is a conductor. It is very beautiful."

"Can't be taught, huh?" she said and pushed his leg teasingly with her foot.

Sebastião took hold of her foot in his hand and pressed his thumb into the arch of her foot. Jenn made a sound in her throat that she didn't appreciate her throat making and covered it badly with a cough. If Sebastião noticed, he was far too smooth to let on.

"Everything can be taught, not everything can be learned. This boy learns like few I've seen. Jimmy Hirsh, an American. I wish to sign him. I have much I would teach him."

"He would be very lucky."

He stared wistfully up at the television. "Only nineteen years old and already he can play like this. Can you imagine? Nineteen and the world in his hand."

"Would you do it all again? If you could?"

"Yes," he said without hesitation. "Why not? Being so young and simple is a blessing. Look at him, he cares about nothing but the ball."

"Is there anything else you would do over?"

He studied her carefully before answering. "No, I think not. Not knowing life as I do now. It would feel like a failure to go backward. A disrespect. Can I say this? A disrespect? Yes. A disrespect to all I have learned. This is my life, and I would not erase one day of it. I would rather be here on this couch with you."

"Would you really want me to come back?" She had been thinking about it since this afternoon but hadn't meant to ask the question. First her feet, now her mouth . . . she was starting to wonder if she was in charge of a damned thing. Unable to look Sebastião in the eye, she watched the boy with the black hair dance with the ball.

"I do not say things just to say them," Sebastião said.

"I know."

"Would you?"

"If I can find a way. But it may take some time. Years."

"Years . . ." He searched her eyes until she looked away. "You intend to turn yourself in."

She wiped her eye before it shed a tear. "I'm so tired of running. Quitting drinking was good for me, but it made everything else so much harder to ignore. After this is over, I'm going to surrender myself. Do my time. Start my life again, whenever that is."

"Do they know?"

She shrugged. "Dan suspects, I think. George always knows what I'm thinking before I do."

"But not Gibson?"

She shook her head. "I don't think so."

"Would he go with you? Turn himself in also? He would follow you anywhere. Maybe all he needs is a push."

Jenn thought of the eighteen months that Gibson had spent in solitary confinement at a CIA black-site prison. It had broken him utterly, and he had only recently finished reassembling the pieces. He would never get back in a cage. Not willingly. And she would never let him. She loved him too much.

"No, if I went, it would be alone."

"You are the bravest person that I know. And I have known some bulls in my time," he said with a grave smile.

"I don't know about all that, but that's my plan. And when I get out, if I'm not too old . . ." Her voice hitched painfully in her throat, and her chin began to tremble. She blew out all the air that had been accumulating like fire in her chest. It didn't help a bit. *Show some fucking dignity,* she commanded in her grandmother's voice. She began again, aiming to prove to herself that she could, indeed, say it out loud.

"When I get out, if I'm not too old, and if you're still—" She was blinking back tears, but there were too many to stop.

"I will be here," Sebastião said.

"Don't say that. You don't have to say that. It's a long time. No one is asking you to say that."

He took her hand and held it to his heart. "I will always be here."

Jennifer Auden Charles wept.

CHAPTER THIRTY-FOUR

When morning came, Gibson walked Jenn and Hendricks out to the van to help them load up. The good-byes were brief and perfunctory. No grand send-offs—a pat on the arm, a nod of the head, and Dan and Jenn would be on their way. As if they were running to the supermarket for groceries. Acknowledging that Gerda König might be dangerous would only invite that danger. Not that they were superstitious, but they all knew better than to tempt fate. All right, maybe they were superstitious. A little. Still, Gibson thought, if keeping their good-byes low-key gave them confidence that they'd all come out okay, then where was the harm? The illusion of control went a long, long way in situations like this.

"Did you get any sleep at all?" he asked Jenn.

"What do you mean?" she asked sharply.

"I mean . . . we went to bed late and got up early. Did you get any sleep?" he said cautiously, unclear how his question had led him into this minefield.

Hendricks took that opportunity to make himself scarce and went to start the van.

Jenn checked her tone. "No, not so much. Too much going on to sleep. Just want to get my hands on this bitch, dangle her off the side of a mountain."

"Oorah," Gibson said. Jenn might not be a Marine, but sometimes she thought like one. Her dad had been in the Corps, so he reckoned she came by it honestly. "We'll be ready when you do."

Hendricks rolled down the window and beckoned Gibson over. "You're an idiot."

"What did I do?" Gibson asked. He'd been awake for all of twenty minutes, so if everyone could kindly get off his back, that would be great.

Hendricks seemed disinclined to elaborate. "We'll see you in a couple days."

That was unusually optimistic of Hendricks. Truth was, they had no concrete sense of how long this might take. Everything hinged on the reliability of Jurnjack's information, which remained a big question mark. Gibson hoped Hendricks was right. Staying behind where it was safe felt cowardly, and he wished that he were going with them. But Gibson knew he could do the most good with Ciara and Mahomet, so, echoing Hendricks's sentiment, he slapped the side of the van and stepped back to watch them pull out of the driveway.

The major revelation of the morning was that Sebastião had offered to let them stay on at the house even after Jenn departed. Unexpected, since Sebastião hadn't even bothered to get out of bed to see her off. It appeared that relationship had well and truly run its course. Not that Gibson would pretend he wasn't good with that. In Portugal, Sebastião had pulled Jenn into his orbit and spun her around like a top. All the way around, it had been a bad scene, and she was better off without him. Jenn could call Gibson a patronizing jerk all she liked, but he could see she knew he was right.

Still, Gibson appreciated Sebastião's generosity. He'd gotten up this morning prepared to relocate; now they'd be able to save time and get straight to work. Time to blow the work whistle. He went back inside the house, fully expecting to have to drag Ciara and Mahomet out of bed, but found them already in the dining room, plugging in laptops and getting settled in for the long haul. Ciara had a huge mug of coffee, and Gibson wracked his brain wondering whether fifteen-year-olds should be drinking coffee. Didn't it stunt kids' growth or something? And sure, he'd drunk coffee at that age, but that didn't mean it was a good idea. Ellie might still only be eleven, but there was no way in hell she'd be drinking coffee at fifteen.

"Did you really do all of this?" Mahomet said, turning his laptop around. His browser was open to AmericanJudas.com, a conspiracy website that had been fixated on Gibson since Vice President Benjamin Lombard's suicide nearly five years ago. AmericanJudas saw Gibson as some kind of cyber Lee Harvey Oswald, a pawn in a vague global conspiracy. It was all nonsense, but like any good conspiracy, the theory hewed closely to the factual events of Gibson's life but wove them together into an absurd narrative that cast him as some kind of radicalized extremist. And, yes, he freely admitted that breaking into Dulles International Airport and hijacking an aircraft had not helped his cause, but that had been Jenn's idea, not his.

"It's complicated," Gibson replied. "Yes but no."

"You killed the vice president of America?"

"No, definitely not. No. Like I said, it's complicated," Gibson said, casting an uncomfortable eye toward Ciara. "I was in Atlanta, but, no, I didn't kill him."

"But, you know who did . . . ?"

"Look, can we not talk about this?"

Mahomet looked to Ciara. "You didn't tell me he was such a badass."

Ciara shrugged. "I said he was a hacker."

"You said that he hacked something once, you did not say that he was an international man of mystery."

Oh, for God's sake.

"Well, why don't you marry him, then, if you fancy him?" Ciara suggested, eyes narrow behind her mug.

"What's your problem?" Mahomet asked.

"Did you get to the part where he burned his wife's house down?"

"Hey!" Gibson snapped. "I did *not* do that."

Ciara pursed her lips, narrowed her eyes even further, and nodded in sarcastic disbelief. "If you say so. And I'm supposing you don't know nothing about their disappearances neither, do you?"

"They're both somewhere safe, I promise."

"How do you know? You're here, aren't you? How can she be safe if you're here?" The anger in her voice white hot, Ciara shoved back her chair and stalked out of the room.

Gibson realized now what Ciara saw when she looked at him. Why she'd been hostile to him from the outset. What was he to her but one more coward who had run out on his family? And here Gibson had thought that he could bond with her over hacking. She wanted nothing to do with him, and he couldn't say that he blamed her.

What would happen when Ellie reached Ciara's age? Would she see him any differently? If the day ever came that he got to beg her forgiveness, would his daughter find his rationalizations any less hollow? That he'd stayed away to keep her safe? Did he really believe that the money he'd put aside for her would buy his redemption?

Mahomet, who had busied himself on his laptop, cleared his throat apologetically. "We may have an idea."

Gibson blinked and looked up while Mahomet explained what he had been working on. Gibson's mind was still on Ellie, and he was only half listening. It took a minute before the implications hit him.

"Hold on, back up a sec. What do you mean, 'we may have an idea'? Have you been working on . . . did you open the programs?"

Mahomet made an apologetic face. "I know you said to wait, but I couldn't sleep. So I got up and made an early start. Ciara was the same."

"Were you online when you opened it?"

"*Oui*, but it's not so bad. I—"

Gibson cut him short. "Mahomet. Stop. I told you to wait for a reason. You've never done any white-hat work; I have. This malware needs to be in a sandbox. You know what that means? Isolated. So it has *no* chance of getting out in the wild."

Mahomet stiffened. "It did not get out. I am not stupid."

"Good. Great. But you had no idea of how it would behave. You got lucky. There's a reason that doctors don't research deadly diseases on a crowded train. They take steps to minimize the possibility of infections. We have to do the same. Got it?"

For a moment, Mahomet struggled with whether to dig in his heels, but he relented. "Okay, I'm sorry. I will be more cautious."

"Thank you. Look, I know you meant well. We just need to be airtight. We're after the same thing here."

"Yes, I know. So, what now?"

"I'm going to go find Ciara. Then you're going to tell me about your idea. Deal?"

Mahomet smiled shyly. "Deal."

Gibson went into the kitchen and swore audibly. This is why he avoided working with other hackers. However many you had, that was how many thought they were the smartest person in the room. Was this how crazy he made Jenn? If so, it was a wonder she hadn't put a bullet in his head five times over.

CHAPTER THIRTY-FIVE

Jurnjack waited for Viktor Lebedev in the shade of a handsome sycamore. A short distance away, three cows stood watching him like wise men curious about this disruption to their daily routine. He had been born on a farm, and the smells made him nostalgic. His father had been a terrible farmer, a miserable bastard, and a mean drunk. One night after a particularly bad beating, Jurnjack had looked at his swollen face in the mirror and decided enough was enough. He'd been twelve, but even today he wondered whether he'd been brave or a coward for running away. Would he have made a good farmer?

"Thank you for coming," Jurnjack said as Viktor trudged across the field. "It's good to see you."

"Stop," Viktor said, inspecting the mud splattered on his shoes and trousers. "I'm done with this game. Place your hands on the tree or I will break an arm. There are two snipers observing us. If you try anything, you won't get three feet."

"Game?" Jurnjack asked but did as instructed as a show of good faith. He was pleased with Viktor's precautions. They still weren't sufficient, but the boy was learning.

"You know exactly what I mean. Don't play innocent." Viktor put on a pair of latex gloves before thoroughly searching Jurnjack from head to toes.

"You're angry because of our last conversation."

"I can't remember our last conversation."

"That's a shame. Would you like me to catch you up?"

Viktor finished his search and stepped back. "No, let me catch you up. Skumin threatened my life and the lives of my family for allowing you to escape."

Jurnjack nodded sadly. "That is why I never had a family."

"You did have a family."

"Yes, I suppose you're right. And see where that has gotten me?"

"Well, I'm not a fuckup like you."

"Viktor, I didn't used to be a fuckup like me either. It makes no difference how well you do your work. You will live in fear of that man for the rest of your life."

"Perhaps, but it will still be longer than yours, old man," Viktor said.

"You say that like it's an accomplishment. Did you at least read my letter?"

Viktor took out an envelope and slapped it against Jurnjack's chest. "I didn't read your pathetic letter."

Jurnjack turned the envelope over in his hands. It was unopened. Of course. This was like some hellish Greek myth: all his life's wisdom, ready to share, but no one would listen. Jurnjack had always been a loner, private and reclusive, but for the first time in his life, he felt alone. So desperately alone. This was why people had families, he realized. So that on their deathbed they didn't have to lie and stare at the walls, waiting for the end. So when the complete arc of one's life finally revealed itself and they understood, as Jurnjack now understood, all the ways that it had been squandered, they had someone to tell. Otherwise, what was the point of it all?

"Will you take it? Please?" Jurnjack held the letter out.

"No," Viktor said, happy to be able to deny him something. A little revenge for Jurnjack's betrayal at the pâtisserie. "I don't give a damn what you have to say."

"I'm sorry." Unable to throw it away, Jurnjack folded the letter in half.

"I don't care about that either," Viktor said defiantly, but the apology threw him momentarily off his game. He hesitated as if trying to decide what to say next, then settled on a threat. "Skumin said to tell you that his offer still stands. Take me to the thumb drive, clean up your mess, or watch Lev die painfully."

Jurnjack held out a fist, then opened it to reveal the thumb drive. "As you see, that won't be necessary."

Viktor took it. "All this trouble over something so small. How do I know it's authentic?"

"Well, you can take my word for it, but there has to be a way to authenticate it."

"And the two hackers?"

"Germany. Alive, but I can provide their precise location."

"No need. They won't be for long. We already know where they are."

Jurnjack couldn't hide his surprise. "You do?"

"We do." Viktor threw a canvas bag at his feet. Inside were light-blue coveralls and a pair of canvas shoes. "Take off everything you're wearing. Put that on."

"Out here in the open? That's not very dignified. You've already searched me."

To his credit, Viktor wasn't interested in Jurnjack's wheedling. The boy really was learning. So, before God, snipers, and three dispassionate cows, Jurnjack stripped naked. He didn't care for his body in the daylight. He knew what he looked like without his clothes—a frail, tired old man. Viktor didn't take the opportunity to mock him for it.

A reminder that Viktor wasn't a needlessly cruel man and that there was still a chance for him. Jurnjack knelt and folded his clothes neatly into the bag. Not that he would ever wear them again, but old habits died harder than hope. The rudimentary pockets of his new coveralls had been sewn shut, so he put the letter in the sole of his shoe for safekeeping. Perhaps Viktor would take pity on him.

The drive into Monaco was scenic but uneventful. Viktor was a taciturn statue, and Jurnjack didn't bother trying to engage him in conversation. The only question was which of Skumin's innate urges would win out—his bottomless need to drape himself in luxury, or the paranoia that fed on the rotting corpse of his peace of mind. Had caution gotten the best of Skumin, compelling him to move to another hotel, or would he still be staying in the same corner penthouse suite overlooking the Mediterranean? So much hinged on it, and Jurnjack had bet everything that he knew Skumin better than the old criminal knew himself.

When the car turned onto Avenue d'Ostende, fronting the harbor, Jurnjack knew that he had guessed correctly. Apparently, he was enough of a bogeyman to necessitate a change of clothes, but not one worth sacrificing a good view. Twenty years ago, if Jurnjack had gone rogue, Skumin would have cowered in a Swiss vault. But one could only coast on a reputation for so long before people called the bluff. Well, his body might no longer be a temple, but Jurnjack's mind remained a fortress.

At the curb, a stately bellhop held open the door and welcomed Jurnjack to the hotel. If Jurnjack's odd appearance was a concern, the bellhop did not let on, probably assuming that Jurnjack was some rich eccentric who collected his piss in glass jars. Inside the lobby, they crossed to the bank of elevators, where a group of men waited. Viktor kept a light hand on Jurnjack's arm. Not even the illusion of civilization this time. One of the men detached himself from the group and rang for the elevator so that it was opening as they arrived. Jurnjack recognized him, Gregor, a vicious thug with a temper like shifting sand. Gregor,

Viktor, and Jurnjack boarded the elevator together. As soon as the door closed, Gregor shoved Jurnjack face-first against the wall.

"I have already been searched capably," said Jurnjack. "These aren't even my clothes. Is this really necessary?"

Gregor replied with a flurry of kidney punches that took Jurnjack's breath away and his legs out from under him. Slumping to the floor, he felt hands roughly search him.

"What's this? What the hell is this?" Gregor said, holding up the letter.

Jurnjack was impressed that Gregor had discovered it.

"It's nothing," Viktor said. "Give it here."

"Like hell," Gregor said and pocketed the letter. "It's contraband. The boss is right, you've lost it."

A week ago, none of Skumin's men would have dared talk to Viktor that way. A week ago, Viktor would have knocked Gregor's teeth out for his insolence. Now, he simply sighed and watched the floors tick by.

"Help me get the old bastard up," Gregor said.

"You knocked him down. You get him up."

Gregor swore and hauled Jurnjack roughly to his feet as the elevator arrived at the top floor. They had arrived.

With effort that cost additional pain, Jurnjack reached up and finger-combed his hair back into place. It was time to see if he could perform one last magic trick before the curtain closed for good.

CHAPTER THIRTY-SIX

The address Gibson had found for Gerda König was in Glion, a small Swiss village nestled in the mountains above Lac Léman. They parked the van and rode the funicular up the mountain. Out the windows of the cable car, the town of Montreux spread out beneath them. The lake glittered in the sun, and on the far shore, mountains rose up to frame the lake like a painting. Jenn could only imagine how beautiful it must look in the winter, but in the summer it was lush and verdant and perfect.

"When this is over, we need to talk," Dan said.

"Yeah? What's up?"

"I think I'm ready to go home."

That caught Jenn by surprise, and it was so close to her own thinking that she wondered if Dan had been talking to Sebastião. "Home to California?"

"I don't know if I'll go back to California. But home. Somewhere of my choosing, you know what I'm saying? Ever since Atlanta, I've been in hiding, one way or another. I've had my fill."

"Well, I know you're not asking permission, but do what you need to do. What you've already done for us? For me? It's above and beyond."

Hendricks shrugged, looking unconvinced that he'd done nearly enough.

"What I don't get," she said, "is why you've stayed this long. I've always wondered."

"If you wondered, why didn't you ask?"

Jenn laughed. "Afraid if I asked, you'd realize you didn't need us and get the hell out of Dodge. Couldn't imagine doing all this without you."

"Guess I hated the thought of leaving you and youngblood in the lurch. But I'm not getting any younger, and getting shot at has a way of focusing the mind, you know?" Dan sounded miserable at the prospect. They sat in silence, side by side, looking out over the lake. "Plus, I'd have missed all this damn scenery."

"Can you imagine living anywhere so beautiful?"

"Too many stairs," Dan said. "My knees couldn't take it."

"But the fresh air."

"What is with white people and fresh air?"

The funicular arrived at its destination, shuddering to a halt. When the doors opened, they disembarked and went up the stairs to a little train station where Jenn asked directions in French. The woman at the ticket window gave her an odd look but told them how to get into town. Back out on the train platform, they tried to get their bearings.

"So, that's the Hotel Victoria," Jenn said, pointing to the white building off to the right that the woman had used as a landmark. Enormous gold letters on its roof spelled "Victoria."

"You think? You should have been a detective."

"Shut up. Lady said to keep the Victoria to our right, so we should go up that way."

Dan didn't disagree, so up that way they went. They walked through the center of the village, a series of houses, shops, and small buildings. Dan wasn't wrong about the stairs. Every step they took was uphill.

"Remind me why we didn't drive?" he said.

Jenn didn't know. It had seemed like a good idea to walk, reasoning that an unfamiliar vehicle would draw unwanted attention. But she hadn't considered how small Glion would be, or how much Dan would stick out here. People kept giving him double takes as they passed.

"Not sure they get a lot of brothers up here," Dan said. "Feeling that stranger-in-the-village vibe."

"They've just never seen anyone so good-looking."

"Let's just get this done so I can stop feeling like a wart on the back of someone's hand."

They passed through the village and walked out along a road running parallel to the lake. As the road curved around the mountain, the houses became progressively grander. Jenn's thoughts turned to Sebastião and waking up beside him every morning to these views. Or maybe it was the peace and quiet that she coveted. Either way, it was a nice pipe dream. One best saved for the long nights in the six-by-eight cell she'd have waiting for her.

When they neared the end of the road, Jenn realized why the woman back at the ticket window had given her such a peculiar look—Gerda König's address was a vacant lot. Well, not vacant, a foundation had been laid, and workmen were beginning to frame out a new house. Judging by the size of the foundation's footprint, it would absolutely dwarf its neighbors, but it would be at least a year before anyone moved in.

When they finally tracked down the foreman, he couldn't shed any light on the situation. He said he had never met Madam König and had been contracted directly by the architect. Jenn asked if she could speak to the architect, but the best the foreman could do was give her a business card for a firm located in Geneva. Jenn flicked it with her thumbnail. It wasn't much, but it was better than nothing.

"Are you looking for Gerda?" a voice asked in French from behind the next-door neighbor's fence. A woman in her sixties stood up from where she had been weeding her flower beds. Her gray hair was held back perfectly by a yellow handkerchief, and she looked like she had stepped straight out of a fashion spread. Who got dressed up to garden? And she had on more makeup than Jenn would wear to a wedding, much less to dig around in the dirt. But what else did wealthy retirees have to do but get dressed to the nines for a day of gardening?

Must be nice.

"Yes, we are." Approaching the fence, Jenn asked, "Do you speak English by any chance?"

"No, I'm so sorry," the woman said, removing her gloves and dabbing her forehead with the back of her wrist.

"That's okay," Jenn replied in French. "Do you know where we might find Madam König?"

"Sadly, you only missed her by a few days. She left in quite a bit of a hurry."

"Did she say where she was going?"

"Well, she's never actually lived in the old house, you must understand. So we're acquaintances at best, and, between us, she's not the warmest of women. Quite cold, actually. Look at all the mess," she said, shaking her hand at the construction. "The disruption. The noise. And did she once offer her sincere regrets or acknowledge the inconvenience?"

Jenn could guess the answer. That Gerda König, a woman who'd conspired to kill hundreds of thousands of people, wasn't a considerate neighbor didn't qualify as earth-shattering news. It also didn't answer Jenn's question. She wished Dan spoke French so he could talk to the woman; Jenn had never had much talent for voluntary interviews. Meanwhile, the neighbor was still pontificating on all things Gerda König. Apparently, she'd been itching for an opportunity to unburden herself, but Jenn didn't have the time or temperament to play therapist.

"Did she mention where she was going?" Jenn asked a second time, doing her best to get a word in edgewise. "It's very important."

"Oh?" The woman leaned across the fence eagerly. "Does it have anything to do with her business in America? I heard her discussing it on her mobile. She seems so animated about it."

"Yes, in fact, it does. It's an urgent matter."

"All I can tell you is that her mother has taken ill. She retired to Italy. Naples. Gerda went to be with her."

"Nothing more specific than that? An address? A telephone number? Anything at all would be an enormous help."

"I'm afraid not. I wish I could be of more assistance."

Jenn shook her head at Dan. This looked to be a dead end. "I think the architect in Geneva's our best bet," she told him in English.

"One moment," the woman said, something jogging her memory. "I believe her mother is a patient at one of the lesser hospitals in Naples. I remember Gerda worrying that it wouldn't be sufficient for her mother's care."

That was something to consider. Jenn thanked her for her help but lingered by the fence in case the woman remembered anything else useful. When it became clear that the well had run dry, Jenn extricated herself politely and made her escape before the neighbor could catch her breath for another rant. On their way back to the village, Jenn briefed Dan on what she'd learned. Dan was starving, and Jenn could stand to eat, so they stopped at a café before riding the funicular back to Montreux.

"So, Naples or Geneva?" Jenn asked after they'd ordered.

"My vote is the architect. We have an actual address. A name. Plus, it's only two hours away. Naples is a good twelve and a half hours from here."

"Seriously, Dan, how do you know that?"

Dan shrugged. "I say we pay a visit to the architect, and if that's a nonstarter, then we start searching 'lesser' hospitals in the greater Naples area."

It was a good suggestion, but Jenn couldn't see what an architect would know about a client's sick mother. With construction on König's new house underway, it wasn't as if architect and client would be in regular communication. Wouldn't it be better to get to Naples as soon as possible in case König decided to relocate her mother? Dan saw her point but still leaned toward Geneva. Problem was, there was no clear-cut right answer. At least not until they picked one. It was a coin toss at best. The food came, and they took a break to eat, hoping maybe a next step would leap out at them.

"That neighbor was some piece of work," Dan said in between bites. "Who gardens in high heels?"

"She was wearing heels?"

"Pantsuit and heels. And not a speck of dirt on her. You didn't notice?"

"I was a little busy getting my ear talked off. And getting blinded by her perfect mascara."

They laughed at the absurdity of it and went back to eating, but Jenn could tell he was chewing over more than his meal.

"What?" she asked.

"You have that picture of Gerda König on you?"

Jenn fished the manila folder out of her bag and slid it across the table.

Dan studied it while he ate. He turned the picture around and slid it back. "When would you say this picture was taken?"

Jenn hadn't given it any thought, but now that Dan mentioned it, the fashion and hairstyle did look dated.

"Late nineties?" she said, hazarding a guess.

"Not bad," Dan said and flipped it over. Printed across the back in red lettering, it read: "FEB95 001 0111 NNNN." The picture was more than twenty years old. Dan was smiling now; he flipped the picture over once more.

"What do you think she looks like now?"

Suddenly she understood where he was going with this. She tapped the photo, playing devil's advocate. "That woman was at least forty pounds lighter than König is here."

"So she got a Jane Fonda tape in the last twenty-five years. Look at her eyes. Eyes don't change."

Jenn looked again. More carefully this time. Well, she'd be damned, he was right—the eyes were the same.

"Naples is a lot farther away than Geneva," Dan said. "Gives her a bigger head start if we went there first on a wild-goose chase."

"Son of a bitch," Jenn said. They'd had her, *had* her, and let her go. It was a slick move, renting the house next door to keep an eye on the construction. Clearly, König hadn't told the foreman that she was living next door. She was a crafty bitch; Jenn would give her that. How many more people would die now because Jenn had allowed herself to be fooled? König would slip off the mountain, and they would never find her in time. Not now that she knew someone was pursuing her.

Dan had his phone out.

"Who are you calling?" Jenn asked.

"Gibson," Dan replied, sounding far too calm for Jenn's liking. "Want to let him know to be ready for us."

"Ready for what? We let her go."

"Well, unless König is planning on going all *Sound of Music* on us, she lives on a dead-end street. She has to come to us."

Jenn grinned. Throwing money on the table for lunch, she headed quickly for the door. Now that König knew she wasn't safe in Glion, she'd be prepping to move. But so long as they moved fast, they'd have her penned in. With a little luck, she might even be overconfident and take her time, believing that she'd fooled the gullible Americans. There was still a chance.

At a table near the door, two men were watching her. They'd come in a few minutes after Dan and her. Casually dressed, polite, nothing about them had set off any alarms. Well, the alarms were going off now. One of the men stood to bar the way. Big fellow too. Jenn wondered how good his knees were. His buddy was reaching for his phone. Looked like Gerda König was keeping tabs on them until she fled Glion, which meant she was definitely still here. Buoyed by the thought, Jenn plucked a pepper mill off a table and closed her fist around it. It was heavy, solid construction. She smiled sweetly at the man blocking her path and kept coming.

CHAPTER THIRTY-SEVEN

Gibson was so deep into coding that he didn't immediately register the phone ringing.

Once Ciara had been coaxed back to the dining room, they'd had a productive morning. Mahomet and Ciara knew the malware's design well enough that they'd been able to extract the payload with relative ease. The next phase, however, had had a much steeper learning curve, as the three hackers attempted to comprehend how Gerda König's counterfeit drug formulas had been coded into the payload. If they could understand that, then they would be able to reproduce the work quickly if Jenn and Hendricks got lucky. It was complex, mentally taxing work, but between the three of them, working the problem from three different angles, they were beginning to wrap their heads around it.

A crumpled piece of paper bounced off Gibson's face. Across the table, Mahomet was pointing at Gibson's ringing phone. It was Hendricks.

He said they'd located Gerda König in Glion and wanted to know if Gibson was ready.

"We're making progress," Gibson said vaguely. "You have her now?"

"Not exactly," Hendricks said, seeing Gibson's vagueness and raising him.

"What's not exactly?"

"All I can tell you is the lady lost a lot of weight."

"What? What does that even mean?"

"Shit, man, gotta go!" Hendricks said, and the line went dead.

Gibson stared at his phone. He could have sworn he'd heard the sounds of fighting in the background and then a man screaming in pain. When he called back, there was no answer.

"What's going on, then?" Ciara wanted to know.

"They found Gerda König."

"Have they, now? Already?" Ciara sounded duly impressed.

"Hypothetical for both of you—assuming König has what we need. How soon can we be ready?"

Ciara guessed two days, Mahomet three. Both were being optimistic. Under ordinary circumstances, Gibson would have said a week. At minimum. To be absolutely certain and test the newly configured malware thoroughly. But every day they delayed sentenced more people to die, so Gibson appreciated their desire to tighten the timeline. If they worked around the clock and cut a few corners and were half as smart as they thought they were, maybe it could be done in two.

Sebastião appeared at the doorway in a tracksuit. He'd been at his club's training facilities all morning for meetings. He looked panicked and beckoned Gibson out into the hall.

"What's going on?" Gibson asked.

"You have to leave. You have to leave right now. There are men in cars parked on the street."

"Are you sure they're not paparazzi?"

"Paparazzi carry cameras, not guns."

Sebastião had a solid point there.

"Is there a back way out of here?" Gibson asked.

"On foot, yes. But how far would you get with a child?"

Gibson ran through their limited options. The Marine in him said stand and fight. The rest of him cleared its throat and pointed out that with only one pistol and two magazines, staying meant dying. What else could they do? Make a run for it on foot, likely die. Make a run for it in the little car Jenn had brought back from meeting Jurnjack, get to the end of the block, and die. All bad options that all ended the same bad way.

"Gather them, bring everything. Meet me in the garage," Sebastião said.

Apparently, there was a fourth option that Gibson wasn't seeing. He went back into the dining room, where Mahomet and Ciara were waiting in tense silence. They knew something was up from the look on his face, so he decided not to varnish the situation.

"No questions," Gibson said curtly as Ciara started to speak. "You can hate me later, but right now I need you both to listen to me. Am I clear?"

To his surprise, both nodded.

"Good. There are men on the street. They are not our friends. We have to go now. Bring everything we need—laptops, notes, anything to do with the malware. We leave in two minutes."

Ciara raised a tentative hand.

"What?"

"I need to pee like a monster," she said apologetically.

Despite everything, Gibson smiled. "Okay, and everyone pee. That's a solid idea."

———————

Sebastião had three cars in his garage. The first was the same electric-blue Audi R8 Spyder that he'd owned in Portugal. It was a sleek sports car, but the only way four people could fit would be to strap two of them to the hood. The middle vehicle was a surprisingly middle-of-the-road SUV that Gibson couldn't see Sebastião driving in a million years. On the plus side, everyone would fit inside, but he could already hear

Hendricks complaining about its shoddy giddyup. The last vehicle was a burnt-orange 2019 Bentley Mulsanne. The sedan would fit four in style, but it was not exactly subtle. Sebastião had the keys to the Bentley in his hand.

"Is it fast?"

"Five hundred and thirty horsepower."

From the way Sebastião said it, Gibson assumed that was a good number. The two cars Gibson had owned in his life included his dad's station wagon and a Honda Accord, which Gibson was fairly sure had shared a single horse between them. He held out his hands for the keys, but Sebastião shook his head.

"Get in. I will drive."

"Sebastião. I can't let you do that. It's not safe. Jenn'll kill me if I get you involved."

"These men are outside my house. I am already involved. Jenn is not here, and no one drives this car but me. Besides, how well do you know German roads?"

Not one bit. *Who was he, Dan Hendricks?* Gibson got in the passenger side. The interior of the Bentley smelled how Gibson imagined a library would smell in a wealthy man's house. At the touch of a button, the engine throbbed to life with a throaty, self-satisfied rumble. Sebastião slipped on his sunglasses and shifted into drive.

"I suggest everyone put on their seat belts."

Gibson put a hand on top of Sebastião's. "Why don't we try something else first?"

"What do you have in mind?" Sebastião asked.

Gibson bent as low as he could in the seat. "Ciara, Mahomet, get down below the windows."

Sebastião was smiling. "Like a Trojan horse. No . . . Trojan Bentley. Yes, I like this," he said, putting down the windows and turning up the stereo. Portuguese pop filled the garage. "Now, let us see if we are clever or not."

Sebastião opened the garage door and nosed the Bentley down the driveway. From his crouch, Gibson could only chart their progress by the expression on Sebastião's face. When the car made a right turn out of the driveway, Sebastião's lips pursed. Gibson prayed that Sebastião could hold his nerve a little while longer. As if to answer, Sebastião began to sing loudly in Portuguese, keeping time on the steering wheel like a man without a care in the world.

"How are we looking?" Gibson asked.

"Good, I think that we . . ." Sebastião trailed off, watching in the mirror. "*Merda.* One of the cars is following us."

"And the other?" Gibson said, inching up in his seat so he could see the car in the rearview mirror.

"It pulled into my driveway. They are going inside, I think."

Gibson reckoned that leaving had forced these men to act. They would need to know if their targets were still in the house or in the car.

Sebastião continued straight, speed steady, time ticking by.

"I have a small problem," he said.

"How small?"

"We are almost out of petrol."

How did that qualify as a small problem, Gibson wanted to know.

"I'm sorry," Sebastião said. "I meant to fill the tank yesterday, but then Jenn called, and I forgot. We have maybe enough petrol for twenty more kilometers, and then *pfff.*"

Twenty kilometers? What alternative did they have but to stop? Running out of gas amounted to a death sentence. Gibson's only advice was to find a busy gas station with as many eyes and cameras as possible. Perhaps that would deter their pursuers from doing anything aggressive. Sebastião said he knew just such a place and drove with urgent efficiency on a whiplash tour of Augsburg. After blowing through two red lights, he braked abruptly and swung into a half-block-wide gas station with his credit card already between his teeth. The moment the Bentley stopped at the pump, he leapt out and got to work.

"The car," he said through the open window. "They are here."

Gibson, still in a crouch, drew his gun. "Where?"

"Right behind us. Four men. They are all looking at me. I don't like this."

"Come on, I thought you'd be used to hostile crowds," Gibson said, trying to keep Sebastião calm with a bad joke.

"Not this hostile. What do you want me to do?"

"Nothing. Finish pumping the gas. Stay close to the car."

Being surrounded by gasoline pumps didn't guarantee that the men chasing them would keep the peace, but it would give them something to think about.

"Are they still in the car?"

"Yes," Sebastião said, and then almost immediately: "No, one of the men just got out."

"What's he doing?"

"Standing there. Smiling at me."

"Anything in his hands?"

"The one I see is empty. The other is behind his back."

Gibson had had about all of this he could take. Cracking his door, he took a deep, steadying breath and stepped out of the car. As Sebastião had described, a man stood behind the open door of the car behind them, empty hand resting on the doorframe. Taking long strides, Gibson closed the distance between himself and the other man, quickly enough that by the time the man decided how to react, it was too late.

"Hi," Gibson said cheerfu'ly, fitting the gun through the gap between the car and door, and jabbing it into the man's gut. The tinted window and the man's back concealed the gun from the customers around them as they went about their business. At the next pump, a sunburned man in a Mickey Mouse T-shirt washing his windshield offered a friendly wave.

"How are you doing? Do you speak English?" Gibson asked the startled man.

The man stared down at the gun. "Yes."

"Good. Quick ground rules. Any of your friends move, best case, you shit into a bag for the rest of your life. If any of them are heavy on the trigger, maybe remind them that gas stations react very poorly to gunfire."

The man looked around, recognizing where they were and the risks. He paled.

"Well, go on, then, tell them," Gibson said, nudging him with the gun. "We don't have all day."

The man translated into whatever language they all spoke. Gibson really didn't care at this point.

"What do you want?" the man asked.

"I could ask you the same question."

"The girl and the Frenchman. Give them to us, there will be no problems for you."

"Right, well, that's not happening. Drop your gun, kick it under the car."

To his credit, the man took Gibson's threat seriously. The gun clattered to the ground and disappeared under the car. "Now you will die with them," he said.

"What makes you think that?"

The man looked over Gibson's shoulder, the outline of a smirk forming on his lips. A second vehicle had backed up to the fender of the Bentley, boxing them in. Having found Sebastião's house empty, they'd joined the party. That was not awesome.

"How are we coming, Sebastião?" Gibson called out.

"Done. Be there in a moment."

"Good. Okay. Wait . . . *what?*"

The Bentley backed up a foot, locking bumpers with the car behind it and giving it a love tap. *Oh,* he thought. *That's what Sebastião meant.* This didn't look to be a fair fight.

Gibson winked at the man. "Hold tight."

The Bentley's oversized engine roared, and the luxury vehicle plowed the smaller car backward like it was shoveling an inch of snow. The man put one hand on the car door and the other on the roof and danced backward, trying to get his feet into his car before getting dragged under. He succeeded as the car spun sideways. The Bentley stopped so Gibson could throw himself in.

"Five hundred and thirty horsepower, huh?" Gibson said.

Sebastião gave Gibson a serious look and shifted back into drive. "Five hundred and thirty horsepower."

The Bentley turned sharply and screeched out of the gas station, the two cars close behind. Sebastião took a ramp onto the highway.

"Can you keep them off us?" Gibson asked.

"Off us? I'd like to see them catch us," Sebastião said and accelerated to one hundred miles an hour. One ten. One twenty. One thirty . . .

"Try not to get us pulled over," Gibson suggested.

Sebastião shrugged and gunned the engine. "For what? This is the autobahn."

Gibson glanced back to make sure everyone was ready. "Ciara, put on your seat belt."

"Put on your own," she said but did as she was told.

Outside, the world was a blur. Gibson wondered what would happen when they broke the sound barrier.

CHAPTER THIRTY-EIGHT

"You all right?"

"That bad? How do I look?" Jenn asked.

"Like you've been in a fight," said Hendricks.

"Yeah, you too."

"Jenn. Stop." He put a hand on her shoulder.

She shook loose but turned to face him. "What?" It came out angry, and she was, but not at him. The fight in the café had been desperate. Jenn's attackers each had had fifty pounds on her, Dan nearly as much. She could only see out of one eye. Her hands looked like raw meat. And her right hip felt like someone had tried to use it to make a wish. Dan didn't look much better. Fingernails had left deep claw marks down the left side of his face, and he kept one arm folded tight against his chest like a broken wing. The walk back to Gerda König's property had been agony. She didn't dare stop, though, even for a moment, afraid that the urge to lie down and curl up into a ball would overwhelm her. But it wasn't time to rest, not yet; she had an appointment to keep at the end of the road.

"We go in there, I want us to be on the same page," Dan said.

"We're on the same page, Dan."

"Are we? 'Cause I'm getting a bad feeling like my book didn't even come with the page you're on right now."

"I'm fine," Jenn said, taking a deep breath to show him how fucking fine she was. "We're going back to that house, and she's going to tell me what I need to know."

"And if she doesn't want to tell you?"

"Oh, she's going to want to tell me."

"See? This is not us on the same page," Dan said.

"Then wait here," she suggested unkindly and limped up the road, knowing, without having to look, that Dan would be right behind her. She felt bad about that. It wasn't the first time that she'd put him in this position—his principles versus her methods. But Jenn wasn't going to pretend, given a choice between five hundred thousand lives and Gerda König's civil rights, that there were any lines she wouldn't cross. It was Gerda König's choice how badly this went. Jenn had already made hers.

Assuming that König was still up at the house . . . Jenn felt confident she was. Dan had seen to that. He'd had the presence of mind to take the men's phones before leaving the café, one of which had been unlocked. A chain of text messages with König charted their walk from the garden fence to the café, right down to their lunch orders. Posing as König's bodyguard, Dan relayed the good news that the two Americans had finished their lunch, boarded the funicular, and were on their way down the mountain to Montreux. König had been delighted at the news and ordered them back to the house.

When they arrived, the garage was wide open, and a large black Mercedes protruded into the driveway. The trunk was open. Someone was packing for a trip. Jenn and Dan crept into the garage on either side of the SUV. A man in a charcoal suit came out carrying two floral-print suitcases. Jenn let him load them into the trunk before introducing herself with the barrel of her gun. She ordered him to his knees, where Dan disarmed and then bound him with twine scrounged from a corner of the garage.

"You're hired security, right? This is just a paycheck to you?" Jenn asked.

The man nodded.

"Good, because we're not here for you. So be helpful, and this will be nothing but a bad day at the office. How many inside?"

"Only Madam König."

She pressed the gun harder into his temple. "You fucking lying to me? I don't like being lied to."

"Jenn . . . ," Dan said.

"She sent two into the village to follow you," the bodyguard said. "I stayed behind."

"Three-man detail, huh? All right, this is what's going to happen now. You're staying right here. If there's anyone else in the house beside Gerda König, when I get back, I kill you," Jenn said and found she meant it. "So, once more with feeling: How many in the house?"

"Madam König and one other," the man admitted.

"See? Doesn't it feel good to tell the truth?"

───────────────

It was cool in the house when they slipped inside. Thick carpet muffled their feet. Jenn had expected some sort of Swedish minimalist décor to match the arid portrait of Gerda König that had formed in her mind, but the house was warm and cozy. Everywhere Jenn looked, pictures of König with family, nieces, nephews, cousins, uncles displayed wide smiles and happy memories. Not the home of a monster. At least not if you needed your monsters to be one-dimensional. But the real monsters could plant pretty flowers in their garden all afternoon and still commit atrocities come nightfall.

An ancient dachshund opened one milky eye to watch them cross the living room but otherwise hardly stirred from the couch where it sunned itself. Dan reached down with his good arm to scratch the dog behind the ear as they passed. The sound of voices drew them up to the second floor.

At the top of the stairs, the corridor forked left and right. To the right, it was dark and quiet. To the left, at the end of the hall, light spilled from a half-open door, and the sound of television news filled the hallway. Dan gestured in that direction, and Jenn nodded her agreement. Together, they worked their way down the hall, pausing outside the door. Dan pointed to the door and then at himself to indicate that he'd take point. He held up three fingers, counting down silently.

At two, Gerda König called out in German, "Gunther, bring me the external hard drive as well."

Jenn spoke German; Dan did not. In the time it took Dan to finish his countdown, Jenn had a series of thoughts:

Who is König talking to, and why so loudly?

Whoever it is, he's not in the room with her.

Someone's behind me.

The last thought came too late. As Dan burst through the door, Jenn felt an arm slip around her neck and the barrel of a gun press to her temple. She dropped her gun and allowed herself to be herded into the bedroom where Dan was ordering Gerda König to the ground.

Shouting.

Threats.

Dan pivoted so he could see the entire room, but his gun never wavered from Gerda König's forehead.

"Drop your weapon," König demanded in English, her claim to the contrary only another part of her ruse. A triumphant smile curled her lips.

"Not happening," Dan answered.

"Drop the weapon or Gunther will kill your partner."

Dan glanced in Jenn's direction. The look in his eyes told Jenn that he had crossed a threshold from which there was no coming back. No more than she deserved for strong-arming him into doing things her way.

"So kill her."

"I am not bluffing," König said.

"It look like I am?" Dan spat back. "Listen, bitch, I am too tired and too sore to go messing around with being taken alive. Gunther here kills my partner, you die. He may kill me after, but let me be real clear on one thing. There's no scenario where you don't get dead."

Gunther tightened his grip around Jenn's neck and demanded instructions. König silenced him with a raised palm.

"Men are on the way," König said.

"No, they aren't. You're packing to run. You may have more men, but, sister, they ain't coming here."

"Are you Skumin's?" König asked, her confidence flickering off and on like a porchlight in a storm.

"Afraid of your own partner?"

König gave him a look like he'd asked an idiot's question.

"No," Dan said. "We don't work for that psychopath."

"So what is it you want from me?"

"A conversation."

"And if you get it?"

"Tell us what we need to know, you get to finish packing for your little trip. Maybe even get to go on it."

"Will you put down the gun so we can talk like civilized people?"

"If I thought you *were* one," Dan shot back.

"Half a million casualties," Jenn added.

"Yeah, our people have your projections," Dan said. "We know exactly what you've done. Just 'cause you buy all your shit at Pottery Barn doesn't make you civilized."

"'We'? Your government knows?"

"Why else would we be here?" Jenn said, playing the bluff handed her. If König thought they represented the US government, it could only increase their leverage.

"Well, I cannot think with that thing pointed at me," König said.

"Tough."

"Please," König said, her voice turning shrill.

"Easier killing people from a distance, ain't it?" Dan replied. "Now get to talking or get to shooting, your call."

There was a weightless pause. The kind that fell between slamming on the brakes and learning whether the car would stop in time. Jenn held her breath, hoping Dan hadn't overplayed his hand. König looked on the edge of a panic that would get them all killed. With a curse, König told her bodyguard to release Jenn and put down his gun. The bodyguard complied and seemed deeply relieved when Jenn ordered him to kneel in a corner.

König frowned at them both. "So, if your people know everything, why are you here?"

"We know the target is an American pharmaceutical company. Not which one."

"Ah," König said, weighing her options. "The target is Senigen. Not a familiar name, I'm sure, but a growing powerhouse."

"Why?" Jenn asked. "What was the point?"

"Really? It's not complicated. Can you imagine what a loss of confidence in the pharmaceutical sector would do to the stock market? A person who knew that a market correction was coming and was correctly positioned would stand to make billions."

Jenn stared at her. "So this really is just about money?"

"What?" König asked impatiently. "You would feel better if it was for God or politics?"

"But why specifically Senigen?" Dan asked.

"Ah, for that you would have to ask Skumin. I simply created formulae from the list of drugs that he provided."

"We'll be needing that list," Dan said.

"I can do better than that. I have the coded formulas themselves. But you will tell them that I cooperated."

Jenn and Dan exchanged a look. That was more than they'd dared hope.

"If it's valuable, that will be taken into consideration," Jenn said.

"And then you go," König said.

"And then we go," Dan said and held out a thumb drive. "Now fill me up, Gerda."

Under Dan's watchful eye, König unpacked her laptop and loaded the contents of a folder onto the thumb drive. Given the time it took, Jenn guessed it must be a lot of data.

"Now, you will get out of my house?" König said, handing Dan the thumb drive.

"Just one more thing."

"What now?" she demanded.

They left König and her bodyguard tied to chairs; Jenn figured it would take the bodyguard about an hour to work his way free. Enough time to get safely away. She found her gun in the hallway, and, together, she and Dan backed their way down the corridor.

On the way out, Dan paused to search the bodyguard they'd left trussed up in the garage.

"What are you doing?"

He held up a set of car keys. "I don't feel like watching your narrow ass limp down that road again."

"Next time, we drive," Jenn admitted.

"Mm-hmm."

CHAPTER THIRTY-NINE

Viktor and Gregor stopped Jurnjack a few steps inside the suite and waited for their presence to be acknowledged. Something Anatoly Skumin seemed in no hurry to do. He sat alone at the far end of the long dining table, picking over the carcass of a roasted chicken. He looked to be in rare good humor, although Jurnjack knew better than to interpret it as forgiveness. No, before the execution would come the ritual taunting and lording his victory over the vanquished. As far as Jurnjack could tell, that was the only thing that Skumin took pleasure in anymore.

At the near end of the table, his back to the door, sat Lev Skumin, hunched over his laptop. His son didn't turn around, but Jurnjack could feel his anger like a clenched fist. He regretted all the things he had never said and now would never have the opportunity to say. There were a lot of clichés about seizing the day, and every last one of them was true.

In addition to Viktor and Gregor, Jurnjack counted four body-guards already in the room. Good, competent men. It would take a miracle to get to Skumin in such circumstances. Jurnjack hoped the Origami Man hadn't used his last one up in Varna.

Sitting back, Skumin mopped at his chin with a cloth napkin, probing his teeth with his tongue for bits of meat. He nodded to Viktor, who patted down Jurnjack, never mind that he had been searched twice already: standard operating procedure necessitated a body search under Skumin's direct supervision. Only then did Gregor maneuver Jurnjack to the table and firmly place him between Lev and Anatoly. Viktor handed the thumb drive to Skumin and bent to whisper in his ear. For once, the balcony doors were closed, but Jurnjack focused on the horizon through the narrow panes. He'd had enough of looking at Anatoly Skumin for one lifetime.

"You have made this far more complicated than it needed to be," Skumin said, reaching for the bottle of vodka to top off his glass. "What did you hope to accomplish?"

"You would understand if you'd ever had any children of your own."

Lev's hands froze in the air above his keyboard, the muscles around his mouth working as though an animal were trying to force its way out from between his lips.

Skumin set down the bottle and let out a braying laugh. "Had I known you were this funny fifty years ago, we might have become friends."

Neither man believed that, but Jurnjack didn't dare correct him. Skumin had vowed to deliver Jurnjack to the Marseille syndicate for killing Farid Zia; he hadn't promised how many pieces that delivery would include.

"Viktor informs me that you've located the two hackers," Jurnjack said.

"Yes, we will have them shortly. My people are in pursuit on the autobahn as we speak."

"How did you find them?" Jurnjack asked, certain that he had not been followed to Germany.

Lev Skumin spoke for the first time. "The idiots opened my malware. I designed it to alert me if anyone tampered with it."

"Which means this is worthless," Skumin said, holding up the thumb drive. "It hardly matters now, but what do they hope to accomplish?"

"To put a stop to your madness."

"So, the truth comes out at last. It was never about the money for you."

"Lev doesn't know you the way I do. He doesn't understand how far you have taken this. When he finds out what he's done, it will destroy him. Which I know is the point. Punishing him for Sofia. But inside, he's a good boy. He shouldn't be a part of this evil."

"Ah, I see." Skumin shook a fist in the air, mocking Jurnjack's nobility. "You mean to save your son's soul, is that it? Be a real father."

"As I said, you would not understand."

"Boy," Skumin said, snapping his finger twice.

Lev looked up.

"Tell our friend here what your malware does."

"It was designed to poison the production supply of Senigen, the American pharmaceutical company. Estimated casualties after two years in excess of five hundred thousand," Lev said flatly, as if reciting scores from the sports page.

"And what effect will that have?"

"A crisis of confidence that will depress the stock market. Anyone with the foresight to short the pharmaceutical sector will make billions," Lev replied.

"You knew? All this time, you knew?" Jurnjack asked, his heart breaking. It had all been for nothing. He had refused to believe it, but his son had known all along. All these years, Jurnjack had viewed Lev as an impressionable boy who might still be saved. But he wasn't a boy anymore; Lev was a grown man and an evil one. After a brief life of breathing Anatoly Skumin's toxic atmosphere, he was beyond redemption. Jurnjack's flesh and blood was as poisonous as anything in the

Senigen warehouse. He was too late; he had always been too late. Lev was a Skumin, now and forever.

"Of course I knew," Lev said, never once glancing in Jurnjack's direction, only looking past him down the table for Skumin's approval. "Do you think I could have designed something so complex without understanding every aspect?"

Approval he did not get. How long could a dog be beaten before it finally turned on its master? A stupid question, of course, when Jurnjack knew the answer to be fifty years.

Skumin, for his part, wore the delighted look of a man who had come into an unexpected windfall. He took a gulp of vodka, savoring Jurnjack's defeat. Viktor approached apologetically and whispered in Skumin's ear.

"Very well, show him in," Skumin said, clearly disappointed to be interrupted during his playtime, then turned his attention back to Jurnjack. "I am afraid that duty calls. Marseille has arrived to collect its trophy."

And so the moment of truth had arrived.

The door opened, and a man was admitted to the suite. Out of the corner of his eye, Jurnjack watched Viktor search the man. The urge to turn his head was nearly overpowering, but Jurnjack willed himself to keep his eyes down, afraid that Skumin would see through his curiosity. Skumin switched from Russian to French, welcoming his guest and apologizing for the inconvenience.

The guest said nothing, enduring the search stoically.

Say something, damn you. The suspense was unbearable.

Viktor found a pair of goggles in the man's jacket pocket and held them up for inspection.

"You're a swimmer?" Skumin asked the man.

"Every morning," a hard-edged voice replied in a heavy Marseille accent.

Jurnjack sagged in his seat. He didn't recognize that voice. How fitting that his final gambit should end in betrayal.

"Give the man back his goggles."

"Yes, sir," Viktor said.

"So they sent only one of you?" Skumin said, stabbing a morsel of dark meat with his fork.

"For an old man? We should have sent an army?"

"I suppose not," Skumin said, aiming his fork at Jurnjack. "But keep an eye on him, he's a sly one."

"This is the one? The one who shot Zia?"

"In the flesh," Skumin assured him.

The man took Jurnjack by the back of the neck and twisted his head up to snap his picture with a cell phone. "A photograph for my boss. He has much in store for you. The end of your life, but not the beginning of your death. Not for a long time, now."

Jurnjack blinked, trying to make sense of what he was seeing. The eyes glaring down at him belonged to the Origami Man. Other than that, Jurnjack did not recognize the man. Skin deeply tanned, hair thicker and darker, he looked twenty pounds heavier and ten years younger. And the voice—his accent was flawless, the authentic French growl of the Marseille streets. It was less a transformation than a metamorphosis.

"Please convey my regrets again for this unforgivable treachery," Skumin said. "Our business is far too important and our relationship too strong to be jeopardized by the independent actions of one man."

"Mokrani feels the same. After seventeen years, such a thing cannot be allowed to disrupt our business."

David Mokrani was the head of the Marseille syndicate. On the drive from Augsburg, Jurnjack had drilled into the Origami Man every aspect of their operation and organizational hierarchy. By the time they had arrived in Monaco, the killer could regurgitate thirty years of Marseille history from memory.

"I am still surprised that Mokrani sent only one man. That is not like him," Skumin said. "You must be very good."

"I have earned his confidence."

"Tell him that, as a sign of my appreciation, I will adjust Marseille's cut by three points to eleven percent."

Jurnjack held his breath, seeing the trap.

"You're very generous, but . . . ," the Origami Man began.

"Yes? Is there a problem? Do you intend to haggle?"

"No, however, Mokrani's cut is currently nine percent."

"Is it?" Skumin said, feigning surprise. It was a bluff, of course. Skumin did not make mistakes where money was concerned and knew every number to two decimal points. "Yes, yes, you are correct. That should be twelve percent, not eleven."

Skumin switched back to Russian for one last parting shot at Jurnjack. "Consider yourself lucky, dog. Whatever they do to you, it would have been infinitely worse for you here."

"I know."

"And your hackers will stop nothing. They'll be dead within the next thirty minutes."

"Half a million. Even for you, it's barbaric."

"Yes, well, the irony is that's not what we were hired to do."

That news genuinely surprised Jurnjack. He had assumed the hack was the brainchild of Skumin and Gerda König. "Hired? Who?"

"Ambricel Pharmaceuticals. An American company. Rival of Senigen."

"Americans hired you to kill Americans?"

"Well, let's say that we've . . . amplified the desired results for our own purposes. Sickening a few thousand, as Ambricel requested, would not push the needle the way a half million dead will. Ambricel's leadership won't like it, but what can they do? Go to the authorities? They'd spend the rest of their lives in prison."

"You should have died in Leningrad with your parents."

It was the only open disrespect Jurnjack had ever shown, and Skumin's expression darkened, the corners of his mouth twitching. Leningrad was not a subject that anyone ever broached. It felt like a small victory until Skumin composed himself and even chuckled at Jurnjack's audacity.

"Still some fight in you, dog?"

"A little."

"Lev, do you wish to say good-bye?"

Lev paused momentarily from his work, then resumed typing without uttering a word.

"I guess there will be no tearful farewells today," Skumin said and switched back to French. "Well, take him. He is yours."

As if to punctuate the moment—the culmination of fifty years of unspoken animosity and mistrust—an explosion ripped through the suite. It hadn't originated inside the room—too muffled for that—but the blast threw everyone back. Jurnjack fell sideways and rolled under the dining table as chunks of debris rained down. Dust and smoke followed, billowing across the suite like an approaching storm and causing Jurnjack's eyes to water. The sounds of coughing and yelling came from every direction. Despite everything, he couldn't help but feel relief that Lev had been smart enough to put his back in a corner and keep his head down.

To Jurnjack's left, Viktor and Gregor knelt beside the dining table, guns drawn. The ceiling by the suite's entrance had caved in, burying two of Skumin's bodyguards, and Viktor was trying to organize the remaining men to repel whatever might come through the door. His efforts were being complicated by Anatoly Skumin himself, who was bellowing at the top of his voice for protection.

No sign of the Origami Man, who had somehow disappeared in the tumult. A gurgling cry from the back of the room told Jurnjack where to look. A single gunshot. A scream. That brought the room momentarily to a standstill before Gregor began firing blindly into the smoke.

The Origami Man appeared from the haze, low to the ground, like a jungle cat prowling through the tall grass. With the swimming goggles and thin dust mask fitted over his nose and mouth, he looked like an alien being.

Jurnjack now realized that when the Origami Man had taken his photograph with the cell phone, it had started the timer on the explosives. Itself a diversion to draw everyone's attention to a fictitious assault on the hotel suite while the Origami Man cleared the room from the back. He had one of the dead bodyguard's guns in his hand. Jurnjack admired the plan's simple brilliance and audacity.

Ironically, Skumin's cry for protection had the opposite effect, guiding the Origami Man to him. From beneath the dining table, Jurnjack watched him circle behind Skumin, take a fistful of lustrous black hair, and haul him unceremoniously to his feet. Then, using Skumin as a shield, the Origami Man edged around the table. Gregor died without ever seeing him coming.

As Viktor raised his gun, the Origami Man shot him, spinning him back the way he had come. Viktor stumbled to his knees, using his gun like a cane to balance himself on the carpet. Remarkably, he tried to raise his weapon again.

"Viktor, no!" Jurnjack said. "Put it down. He won't hurt you. You have my word."

"You," Skumin said, seeming to forget the gun pressed to his head. "You are behind this."

"You trained me well, Herr Skumin."

"Kill him! Kill them both!"

Viktor was even more obedient than Jurnjack feared. His gun began to rise, instinctively. The Origami Man shot him again, and this time Viktor lost his balance for good and toppled to the ground. Jurnjack crawled out from under the table to take Viktor by the hand.

"That was not part of our arrangement," Jurnjack told the Origami Man. "He was to live."

"He should have listened to you instead of pointing a gun at me," the Origami Man said without rancor.

"Why didn't you read my letter?" Jurnjack asked, as though Viktor were in any condition to answer.

The Origami Man took Skumin's legs out, driving him to his knees, and looked to Jurnjack. "May I proceed?"

"Yes," Jurnjack replied. Prolonging the end would accomplish nothing. Jurnjack had no dramatic final words prepared. He was tired, his throat raw from the dust, and he simply wanted it over.

"Wait. Wait. I have more—"

A single bullet ended Anatoly Skumin's existence, worthless by any measure other than his bank account.

A flood of emotions washed through Jurnjack, carrying him away like a small town at the foot of an ancient dam that had finally given way. He deemed Skumin's life worthless, but what did that say about his own? He'd worked for this meaningless monster for fifty years. Killing. Done it for no other reason than that it was a talent. What was more meaningless than that?

Jurnjack looked at Lev, huddled in the corner, and thought of the letter still in Gregor's pocket. It had been written to Viktor, but given the shock of what had just happened, it might be a bridge to his son. His unreachable son, who had never had a chance to be other than he was.

Jurnjack looked up at the Origami Man and pleaded quietly. "May I have a moment with my—"

The bullet cut short the question. Jurnjack slumped back onto the floor at Skumin's feet, the old dog come to die with its master. Pain and blood spread across his chest. He looked toward the sea, but the doors were closed.

"That was not part of our arrangement," the Origami Man said.

Tinsley moved swiftly around the room, confirming that everyone who should be dead was no longer among the living. Satisfied that he had control of the room, he returned to Jurnjack and removed his shoes, placing them side by side at an angle from the body. Contented in a way that he could not articulate, he went to Jurnjack's son, who had curled into a fetal ball against the wall.

"Are you going to kill me?" Lev Skumin asked without raising his head.

"That was not my arrangement with your father."

"Then what do you want?"

"There are cars chasing the hackers on the autobahn?"

"Yes."

"Are you in communication with them?"

"Ah . . . I can be, yes."

"Then I wish to make a new arrangement. One with you," Tinsley said.

"What kind of arrangement?"

CHAPTER FORTY

The way Sebastião described the autobahn, Gibson had envisioned wide lanes of orderly German traffic that would part like the Dead Sea, making outrunning their pursuers a simple matter of 530 horsepower. It turned out that the myth of the open road was as much a fantasy in Germany as it was in American car commercials. The reality was that the autobahn was the congested highway system for a densely populated nation. One thing became clear quickly: Sebastião was out of his mind if he thought he was losing anyone in a bright-orange Bentley.

It didn't help that in stretches the autobahn dropped to only two lanes. That was when things got really hairy. The right lane, reserved for slower traffic, became a ninety-mile-an-hour wall of semis while the cars in the left lane made the semis look like they were standing still. Switching lanes required lunatic changes of speed and not an inconsiderable amount of luck. Gibson wasn't sure he'd have felt safe with Hendricks behind the wheel, much less a retired athlete with a dangerously unshakeable faith in his own abilities. There was the expectation in America that being in a high-speed chase meant that you would be the fastest thing on the road. Gibson found it disconcerting, therefore, to be running for their lives while being tailgated by angry drivers wanting to pass them.

"Swonger would love this," Gibson muttered.

"What?" Sebastião asked, both hands on the wheel.

"Friend of mine back home."

"Invite him next time."

In the back seat of the Bentley, Ciara and Mahomet had discovered power outlets and foldout tray tables like on an airplane. They remained hard at work, oblivious to the game of chicken the Bentley was playing with the laws of physics. Gibson felt jealous of their ability to tune it all out. A side effect of youth that he'd lost somewhere along the line. All of his brushes with death hadn't made Gibson feel invincible so much as convinced him that he was overdue. Every time a car flashed in his peripheral vision, his head would jerk up from his laptop, and he would forget what it was he was supposed to be doing. So when his phone rang, he was grateful for the distraction.

"Where are you?" Jenn asked.

Gibson didn't want to answer that one. "Germany."

"Gibson . . ."

"We had company at the house. We're on the autobahn."

There was a pause like the hammer on a pistol being pulled slowly back. "Who is 'we'?"

"Come on, Jenn."

"Gibson, I swear to God."

"Sebastião knows the roads. And his car is just a little faster than ours. Anyway, we couldn't leave him behind with gunmen entering his house. Be reasonable."

"Is that Jenn?" Sebastião said. "Let me speak to her."

Given how fast they were going, Gibson didn't think that was such a good idea.

"How bad is it?" Jenn asked. "No bullshit."

"It's not awesome, but we're holding our own. How is Switzerland? Any progress on Gerda König?"

"We talked to her."

"No shit? How did that go?"

"We held our own too."

"But did you get the formulas?" Gibson asked. The suspense was killing him, and he wanted an answer before Sebastião turned the Bentley into a can of tomato paste.

"Oh, yeah, and then some."

Gibson listened to Jenn outline their encounter with Gerda König, a smile widening on his face. If König had told the truth about Senigen, this really was the mother lode.

"Send the files this way," Gibson said. "We're on it."

"Already en route. Call us when it's done and let us know you're safe."

"How is she?" Sebastião asked after Gibson hung up.

"In one piece, by the sound of it. They did it. How are we looking?"

"No change. We are here. They are there." By "there," Sebastião meant that their pursuers were three cars back and holding steady. There simply wasn't enough open road for the Bentley to escape, but neither could their pursuers stop them. It was a standoff at 120 miles an hour.

"There has to be some way to lose them. We need to find somewhere safe to work. Somewhere with Wi-Fi. Jenn's sending files that we need, and once we finish assembling the new data file, we'll need connectivity to send it to the target."

Sebastião shook his head dismissively. "Why? The Bentley has a Wi-Fi hotspot. You just need to log in."

"That's wicked," Ciara said. "I would live in this car."

"What is the password?" Mahomet asked.

"SEBCOV#10. All in capital letters," Sebastião said.

Gibson rolled his eyes. Of course it was. Sebastião probably dreamed in all-caps. But Gibson reminded himself that Sebastião was putting his life at risk to protect them. The guy might have an ego that would affect the tides, but this was above and beyond, so maybe cut him a little slack.

The three hackers dug into everything Jenn and Hendricks had plundered from Gerda König. It became immediately clear that they'd struck it rich. Not only did it include the original pharmaceutical formulas, but those formulas were already formatted as a data file. It shortened their timetable from days to less than an hour. Working as a team, they prepped the new data file for upload. While Mahomet and Ciara tested the finished product, Gibson glanced up at Sebastião for the first time in a long while. He didn't look so great.

"How are you holding up?" Gibson asked. The concentration and energy required to drive at these speeds, under these conditions, was profound and draining. Sebastião's fatigue showed on his face, his eyes blinking rapidly as if struggling to focus while his hands maintained their death grip on the steering wheel.

"It is nothing," Sebastião said stoically.

Gibson looked around them. The heavy traffic had conspired against them, slowing their progress and allowing the two pursuit cars to close the distance. One aggressively rode the Bentley's bumper while the second hemmed them in to the left. Out Sebastião's window, Gibson's friend from the gas station gave him an unfriendly smile. Gibson got the impression that they were getting ready to make their move.

Gibson didn't want it to end like this, and maybe they would find a way out, but he didn't love their odds. That made it vital to stop the Senigen hack now. Any thoughts of escape had to come second. If they died before delivering the reconfigured data file, then Senigen's factory would keep pumping out its poison long after the six-month mark had come and gone.

It was a hell of a thing to ask of the people in the car, one of them still a child, which was why Gibson decided not to ask them. What point was there? Four lives against half a million—this was simply how it had to be. Besides, telling them would only stress them out when he needed them calm. To some people, that would make him a good leader, to others a monster. The irony wasn't lost on him.

"How much longer?" Gibson asked, keeping his voice level and calm.

"Twenty minutes?" Mahomet said without a great deal of confidence.

"No," Gibson said. "Unacceptable. How long?"

Ciara and Mahomet looked at each other, mentally cutting corners and steps to come up with a number that Gibson would accept.

"Ten minutes," Ciara said. "We can do it in ten."

"Good. Get it done," Gibson said and turned back to Sebastião. "I need you to keep them off us for ten minutes. No matter what. Do you understand?"

"*Sim,*" Sebastião said with a grim nod. "I understand."

"Can we put on some music?" Ciara piped up. "I can't bloody think in all this quiet."

Sebastião looked at Gibson questioningly.

"Hey, it's your car," Gibson said.

Sebastião reached out and snapped on his satellite radio. The display read: "'Just Like Heaven'—The Cure." Gibson didn't recognize the band or the song, but Ciara's head seemed to approve, bobbing to the music as she got back to work. Sebastião saw a narrow opening in the traffic and accelerated into it. For a moment, Gibson thought they had caught a break, but the two pursuit cars zipped in behind them before the gap closed.

No joy.

Were the last minutes of his life really going to be scored to this music? Gibson supposed there were worse ways to go.

The minutes ticked by, and Sebastião slowed to a paltry eighty miles an hour before rocketing back to a hundred and thirty, slaloming between lanes.

"Done!" Mahomet shouted. "Done! It works."

Ciara agreed and forwarded the data file to Gibson's laptop. Gibson double-checked their work, then did it again. His ten-minute deadline had come and gone, but now he hesitated, aware that they might not get another chance.

"Hey," Ciara said. "It works, yeah?"

It did. Gibson said a silent prayer and launched the data file with a single click. As with most everything to do with a computer, it was profoundly anticlimactic. Nothing to do but wait to see how Senigen responded in the coming days. Assuming they lived that long.

Gibson turned off the radio. "Okay, now that we're done, listen up. Put away your laptops. Anything that might turn into debris during an accident goes away now."

"Are we going to crash?" Ciara said.

"No," Sebastião said. "But it is better to be safe."

Gibson turned around in his seat. "I want to say that you guys are incredible. I was in the United States Marines, and you're as brave as anyone I ever served with."

"Brave as Jenn?" Ciara asked.

"Every bit. She'd say the same if she were here. I mean that. You should be very proud."

Tears filled Ciara's eyes, but she did not cry. Mahomet took her hand and held it tightly.

"Something is happening," Sebastião said.

"What?" Gibson said, drawing his gun.

"They are leaving."

Out the rear window, Gibson saw the two pursuit cars decelerate and move into the exit lane. At the next exit, both vehicles pulled off the highway. The back seat let out a whoop and cheered riotously, while, dumbfounded, Gibson watched the cars disappear from sight.

"What just happened?" he said to himself.

"Was it the data file?" Sebastião asked. "Did it work? Did they give up because they know we beat them?"

"No," Gibson said. "There's no way they could know."

"Then what?"

Gibson had no damn idea.

CHAPTER FORTY-ONE

Gibson and Hendricks rented a hotel room, though they had no intention of spending even one night there. They were in Manosque, a pretty French town some two hours north of the Mediterranean coast. But they weren't here to sightsee. They had a job to do.

While Gibson set up at a little desk in the corner, Hendricks took one last look out the window and closed the curtains on the bright morning sunshine. Making himself comfortable on the bed, the ex-cop eased his legs up one at a time, eyes closed in concentration. He had taken a real beating in Switzerland—one arm was in a sling under his jacket, and try as he might, he couldn't hide the limp. Gibson had offered to make this trip alone. That suggestion had not been received well, to put it mildly.

It had been three days since Gibson had inserted the correct formulas into Senigen's quality-control server. Three days and not a word about it in the media. Nada. That was troubling on many levels and suggested that either the "good" malware had failed or Senigen was engaging in a cover-up. The idea of their going public had been proposed again and dropped again. Gibson had suggested an alternative. No one liked it, least of all him, but it would get the job done.

Rather than risk the hotel Wi-Fi, Gibson set up an encrypted cellular Wi-Fi hotspot. He checked his laptop configuration for the tenth time. The plan was to spoof his number and route the call through multiple switches, hopefully masking their location. Gibson didn't hold out a lot of hope that he could keep the CIA at bay for long; he didn't have the equipment to pull that off. Hence the two-hour drive. A minimum safe distance in the likely event that things took a turn.

The phone by the bed rang. Hendricks answered, but it was only the front desk letting them know they were sending up a porter. A knock came at the door a moment later, giving them insufficient time to question why a porter would be coming to their door.

"Man, that was fast," Gibson said, hurrying over so Hendricks wouldn't try to get up. "What's up?" he asked, opening the door.

A gun came through the crack in the door, unerringly finding the bridge of Gibson's nose and forcing him backward. Tinsley followed, closing the door behind him. Something acidic and viscous climbed Gibson's throat; when he tried to swallow, it spread like lit gasoline through his chest. Closing the door behind him, Tinsley guided Gibson into the room. When Hendricks saw who it was, he didn't even bother to get up, only let out a defeated groan and sank back into the mattress.

"Sit," Tinsley said, forcing Gibson into the chair by the desk.

"Should have known it was too good to be true," Hendricks said.

"How did you find us?" Gibson asked.

"There is nowhere you can hide that I won't find you."

"So why are you here?" Gibson asked.

"To honor my arrangement with Jennifer Charles."

"Yeah, well," Hendricks said, "she's not here, so why don't you just fuck off."

"Honor it how?" Gibson said.

"She promised to help me meet my employer and not to interfere when I did."

"Way I heard it, she did just that," Hendricks said.

"Precisely," Tinsley said. "It took me time to appreciate that she had, in fact, met the terms of our accord. She is very clever."

"So, if you're satisfied, what do you want?"

"Appreciative, not satisfied. For that, I will need to return the favor."

"I must have been unconscious for the part where killing us was part of your arrangement," Gibson said.

"I'm not here to kill you. You continue to labor under the misapprehension that you matter to me," Tinsley said.

"You killed my father."

"Which is why I matter to you. Do you have any idea how many fathers I've killed?"

That stunned Gibson into silence.

"So, what, then?" Hendricks said.

"Anatoly Skumin was behind the malware that attacked Senigen."

"Yeah, we know. He'll get his."

"He already did," said Tinsley.

Gibson and Hendricks exchanged a look.

"But Senigen was not his idea."

"Yeah, Gerda König. We know about her too."

"Skumin had an American partner. Ambricel Pharmaceuticals, one of Senigen's rivals. Both have a diabetes treatment in phase three of human trials. My understanding is that it will radically change the lives of the more than half a billion people worldwide living with the disease. I'll leave you to calculate how much potential revenue that would represent."

"So Ambricel sabotaged Senigen's trials?"

"Of course not, that would have made Ambricel a prime suspect. No, Ambricel was far craftier than that. It hired Anatoly Skumin to corrupt eleven Senigen drugs. Drugs for which Ambricel did not directly compete. The plan was to leave Senigen discredited and financially insolvent before the diabetes drug came to market."

"Can you prove any of that?" Gibson asked.

"I could, yes," Tinsley said. "But I will not. As part of our arrangement, I agreed to point Jennifer Charles toward those responsible. So I am pointing. But that is as far as I will ever go. I will never give her the evidence. The wealthy men and women responsible will never face justice. Tell Jennifer Charles that. Tell her this is the price she pays for being clever."

"You petty motherfucker," Hendricks said.

"That concludes our business. Do not follow me or try and find me, and I will feel no need to follow or find you. Am I understood?"

"Yes," Gibson said.

Tinsley looked sternly at Hendricks.

"Yeah," Hendricks growled.

Tinsley tossed a thumb drive to Gibson, who caught it and turned it over in his hand questioningly. It was old. Maybe twenty years out of date and a fraction of the capacity of the one that had held the malware.

"What's this?" Gibson asked.

"A parting gift," Tinsley said. "Your father's diary."

Gibson looked at the thumb drive again, this time in a state of near shock. During the search for Suzanne Lombard, he had found this thumb drive hidden in the pedestal of a bust of James Madison that had belonged to his father. Tinsley had taken it before Gibson had had a chance to read it through. He'd assumed that any insights into his father's life had been lost forever.

"You think this buys you anything with me?"

"No," Tinsley replied. "The question is whether it will buy you anything with yourself."

"What does that even mean?"

"I was hired to kill your father. I did. I was hired to kill you. I tried and failed. That is the truth of the matter. Will you continue to live in that past, trying to balance scales that don't even exist, or will you move on to something that might possibly make a difference now?" Tinsley was at the door and opened it without taking his eyes off Gibson. "What will it be?"

"I don't know," Gibson admitted.

"Then I will await your reply," Tinsley said and let the door swing shut behind him.

When the latch clicked, Gibson rushed over and turned the lock. Then he went back and sat on the end of the bed until his hands stopped shaking. He needed to pull himself together; they still had a call to make.

———————

The phone rang seven, eight, nine times. Gibson was ready to hang up when a familiar voice finally came on the line.

"Who's this?"

"Hi, Damon."

There was no reply, but Gibson could hear the mental gears turning at the other end of the line.

"Gibson Vaughn. Long time," Damon Ogden said, his voice level but wary.

"Get the recorder started, okay?"

"You bet."

"Good. I was afraid you didn't recognize me for a second there."

"Oh, you're not so easy to forget as that. Gotta say, though, I wasn't expecting to hear from you. I thought we had us an understanding."

"Something's come up."

"Why don't I like the sound of that?"

"Are you near a computer?" Gibson asked.

"And I really don't like the sound of *that*."

"You have mail."

"And you think I'd open it? I'm offended."

"I'm not spear-phishing you," Gibson said but recognized it as a legitimate suspicion given their history. "Fine, after we get off the phone, have one of your IT people verify my e-mail's safe. You're going to want to see what's in it."

"This have something to do with why you and your crew left the Caymans?"

It was Gibson's turn to be struck dumb. "You know about the Caymans?"

"You kidding me? You kidnapped me and held me hostage in an abandoned power plant. I don't go to sleep at night until I know your precise coordinates. So, yeah, I know you left the Caymans and that you've been a busy boy the last few days. Facial recognition picked you up in Belfast. You've also been tied to a bunch of dead Algerians in Marseille. Between you and me, after what went down in Portugal eighteen months ago? I figured you'd have learned to keep a lower profile."

Gibson let Ogden say his piece. Calling him out of the blue like this had obviously rattled him. Ogden couldn't like knowing that Gibson had his phone number. He needed to reassert dominance, reminding Gibson who exactly was in control. It was only fair. And, Gibson reasoned, it would make it easier for Ogden to hear what he had to tell him.

Damon came to his big finish. "Pro tip? You're an international fugitive, so maybe don't pull guns at German gas stations and don't go on high-speed chases on the autobahn in half-million-dollar automobiles. Just a suggestion. Put it in the background and see what you think."

"Like I said, something came up."

"Well, don't keep me in suspense. Let's hear the bait."

"Senigen."

Even long distance, Gibson heard Ogden's breath catch. A long, weighty silence followed, and when Ogden spoke again, all of the gamesmanship had dropped from his voice.

"How the hell do you know about that? That's not been made public."

"It wasn't a production-line error. Senigen was hacked."

"All right, you've got my undivided. What makes you say that?"

"Because I hacked it."

Gibson spent the next hour walking Ogden through the events of the previous week and a half. Laying out the purpose of his hack and all it had been intended to expose.

"Well, you've never done things the easy way. You consider letting us know sooner?"

"And you'd have snapped into action, right?"

"Yes, I would have," Ogden said without conviction. "So, you're saying the *original* hack was four months ago?"

"Yes. And that factory's been pumping out poison ever since. You need to pull everything off the shelves like yesterday. People have likely already begun dying but in small enough numbers that it hasn't been noticed."

"How is that possible?" Damon asked.

"The thing about killing sick people is they're already sick."

Ogden chewed that over. "Damn. And the proof of this is in this e-mail?"

"Yes. There's a written summary of our findings along with all the information we acquired. Copies of both pieces of malware as well as DAT files with the changes to the original drug formulas."

"And you are laying this all at the feet of Anatoly Skumin, close personal friend of the Russian president?"

"Too big a fish for you?"

Ogden chuckled. "No, but you understand that's not an accusation to be made lightly. Especially with you as the source."

"So, check it out. There's no big rush now anyway."

"And why's that?"

"Anatoly Skumin is dead."

"What?" Ogden sounded generally startled, which Gibson would be lying if he said he didn't enjoy. "Since when?"

"I guess the CIA doesn't know everything after all."

"Have you been a bad boy, Gibson?"

"Not this time. He got taken out by his own people, but you're going to want to have a long conversation with his son, Lev Skumin, and a Swiss pharma engineer named Gerda König. Oh, and the folks at Ambricel Pharmaceuticals." Gibson outlined the corporate-espionage angle that Tinsley had provided.

"But the only proof of that is a dead Russian oligarch?"

"Afraid so. Didn't want to make you feel irrelevant."

"Thoughtful. Why bring it to me? Why not go public?"

"Well, like you said, who would believe someone like me?"

"But you think I will."

"I figure you know what I think of you and that I wouldn't risk calling if it wasn't this important."

"What is it you want?"

"For you to do your job."

"That's all? Nothing for yourself?"

"Well, there is one thing."

"Here it comes. I knew it."

"Jenn Charles."

In the corner, Hendricks sat forward, head cocked to one side.

"What about her?" Ogden asked.

"Clean the slate."

"She hijacked a plane from an international airport, Gibson."

"I know Dulles was a red line for you guys, but it also stopped a massive national security breach. She saved your asses. And she just did it again. Hundreds of thousands would have died if not for her. All I'm saying is she was one of you once. She's a hero, not a criminal. Let her come home."

"You done?"

"Yeah."

"That was quite a speech. Look, I'm not making any promises, but if what you're saying pans out . . . if your e-mail's legit, I'll see what I can do."

"Thank you."

"You'll be in the Caymans?"

"You tell me."

"Cute. All right, then, I think we're done here. You've done good." Ogden cleared his throat. "One more thing. I'll see what I can do for Charles, but this isn't a package deal. There's no get-out-of-jail for you. The only thing waiting for you here is a cell."

The line went dead, but Gibson kept the phone to his ear, pretending to listen to a voice on the other end. He couldn't breathe and needed a minute to swallow the bile building in his throat. When he finally put away the phone, Hendricks spoke up.

"How did you know about Jenn?"

"Sebastião. After the autobahn, he was feeling talkative. Wanted to know what I thought about her plans. How about you?"

"She told me in Switzerland," Hendricks said. "That's a hell of a thing you did there. Did he say anything about you?"

"Yeah," Gibson said, forcing a laugh. "Sounds like it'll be a package deal."

If Hendricks knew Gibson was lying, he didn't let on. Instead, Hendricks stood and cracked his back. "What do you say we get packed up and you let me buy you lunch. Maybe a beer or two as well."

"Yeah, that sounds good. That sounds real good."

The trick, Gibson knew, would be stopping at two.

CHAPTER FORTY-TWO

Gibson and Hendricks made it back by dusk. The traffic around Cannes was an unholy mess, so they ditched the van on the outskirts of the city. Hendricks insisted on wiping down the interior and giving the van a once-over for any identifying trace evidence they might have missed. Gibson didn't see the point—Damon Ogden knew where they had been and where they were headed—but it made Hendricks happy to be thorough, so Gibson got down on the floor and reached around under the seats. All he came up with was a candy-bar wrapper.

"Think CSI could pull prints off this?"

Hendricks snatched it out of his hand, folded it up neatly, and slipped it into a pocket as if it were a vital clue. "Don't be smart."

Gibson didn't think there was any danger of that. Not with the memory of Tinsley forcing his way into the hotel room replaying endlessly in his head like a high-resolution GIF. *There is nowhere you can hide that I won't find you,* Tinsley had said. Why, if Gibson believed him, which he most certainly did, was he having so much trouble believing the other part? The part where Tinsley wouldn't come looking.

It took an hour to hail a cab and another hour to make the drive downtown to Le Vieux Port—"the Old Port"—the beating heart of Cannes. Traffic was bumper to bumper on Boulevard Carnot, the city grinding to a standstill for the celebrations surrounding opening night of the film festival. When they finally saw the golden lights of the harbor, they paid the fare and strolled the rest of the way, mixing in with the slow-moving crowd.

There was no particular hurry. They wouldn't be leaving France until after the festival. On the thorny question of how to get back to the Cayman Islands, George had worked some heavy-duty magic, brokering an arrangement with Mirella Lima. While it felt like a hundred years since that night off the coast of Grand Cayman, in actuality, it had been a little over a week. The *Topaz* had arrived in Cannes only the day before, completing its transatlantic voyage. In exchange for three months of complimentary security work, Lima had been delighted to give them safe passage back to the Caymans once the festival was over. All they had to do in the meantime was keep a low profile and enjoy their host's hospitality.

"So that Ogden thing," Hendricks said. "Let's keep it between us for now."

"How come?"

"You tell me. Does Ogden strike you as predisposed to doing you favors?"

"Not especially," Gibson admitted. "But we did the country a pretty huge solid."

"Yeah. Did. As in, done. As in, what have we done for him lately?"

"Still, it's got to be worth something."

"In my experience, criminals sign cooperation agreements before they cooperate. So maybe you caught him all magnanimous, but I'd say it's a long shot. Meantime, let's not get her hopes up. You hear?"

"Yeah, I hear you."

They walked on a while, each lost in their own thoughts. The idea of Jenn moving on made Gibson happy—she deserved that chance—but it was also hard to imagine life without her. She was the glue that held the four of them together. With Tinsley out of the picture, what would keep Hendricks from going home now? George too. They hadn't hung around for two years for Gibson. That much he knew. Everything had felt so solid two weeks ago, and now the landscape was shifting under his feet once more. He'd been foolish to think their life on the run was sustainable. It had been an illusion that he'd let himself believe. He saw that now. George and Hendricks had every right to get on with their lives. Well, he would just have to figure it out.

"So, what kind of boat should we get?" Hendricks asked out of the blue.

"Huh?"

"When we get back to the Caymans. I think we should go for it. Buy a used boat. Run fishing and diving charters like we've been talking about."

"Really?" Gibson said, unable to keep the surprise out of his voice. He'd always thought Hendricks was just passing time with that kind of talk.

"Why not?"

Gibson grinned at the prospect. "So, like . . . partners?"

"I'd imagine," Hendricks said, ducking into a café for a cup of coffee.

"Will you let me drive sometimes?" Gibson asked while they waited at the counter.

"Is that what it's called? Driving? Do you drive a boat?"

"There's a steering wheel, isn't there?"

"To your question, no. No driving. You'll be on suntan-lotion and night-crawler patrol. And icing down the beer."

"Come on, now!" Gibson cried at the injustice of it. "If we're partners, then I get to drive sometimes."

"No deal."

"Fine, but I get to name her." He already had four or five boat names in mind that Hendricks would hate.

Crossing Promenade de la Pantiero, they worked their way through the crowd to the main gate. Le Vieux Port was at capacity. Row after row of gleaming yachts, each seemingly grander and more luxurious than the last, filled every available berth in the harbor. They were all lit up, the deck lights a mix of spectral purples, reds, blues. Music from a dozen different parties carried across the water.

Due to the wealth and stature of the assembled guests, security around the docks was airtight. That meant that, despite their guest passes, Gibson and Hendricks still had to wait while calls were made to the *Topaz* to confirm that they were actually on the list.

While they waited, a portly, middle-aged man in a white-on-black tuxedo waddled out through the gate. He held a champagne flute in one hand, a vape pen in the other. The master of ceremonies of his own private carnival of sycophants, bodyguards, and a stunning coterie of women in sheath dresses who followed behind him. The women were barely half the man's age, talking and laughing among themselves. They also held champagne flutes, which were being aggressively topped off by two servants who trailed behind with bottles chilling in ice buckets.

"Is that some kind of actor?" Gibson asked as he watched the entire entourage disappear inside an impossibly long limousine.

"Producer," Hendricks said. "Does those movies with the aliens."

That didn't narrow things down any for Gibson. "So they're with him for his charming personality."

"Hey. They're doing what they have to do to survive. Same as us."

"Yeah, but—"

"Boy, I appreciate you were raised by the Marines, but sometimes you're a little third century for me. If you're born with brains, you use them. Born athletic, you use that. Born with beauty, well, that's what you got to get you from here to there. I got no patience for anyone saying one way's noble and the other's a sin."

"Is that like your credo?"

"One of many."

"So, what if you're born with none of the above?"

"Don't ask me, that's your area of expertise," Hendricks said.

Security waved them through, and they went down the pier to the *Topaz*. Hendricks lit a last cigarette before they stepped aboard. Gibson feared for their future safety after Hendricks had been at sea for a week without a smoke. There wasn't enough nicotine gum in the world for that.

Mirella Lima had already departed for a party in town, but a crew member welcomed them onboard and led them up to the sundeck. They found Jenn sitting down to dinner with Mahomet and Ciara. Mahomet had a train ticket back to Paris in the morning, and Ciara's mother was flying in tomorrow afternoon to pick her up. As Ciara predicted, her mother had taken her disappearance remarkably well. A little too well, as far as Gibson was concerned, but he kept the thought to himself. His glass house was not safety rated for stones that size.

"Went well with Ogden, I take it," Jenn said, pointing to a television behind them. On-screen, a newscaster was reporting on a massive emergency recall underway in the United States for all Senigen products. "News broke about an hour ago."

"Guess we got his attention," Gibson said.

They stood watching for a few minutes, but having lived through it, their interest waned quickly. Half of the reporting was inaccurate anyway, and the breakthrough was already being credited to the swift work of American intelligence assets.

"Hey, look. We're assets," Gibson said.

The crew set two more places at the table. Taking their seats, they asked for a beer and were offered a choice of ten.

"I could get used to this," Hendricks said.

"Sure beats the last time," Jenn said.

Eighteen months ago, they'd fled Europe on an old Portuguese fishing boat. The *Topaz* was an upgrade in every conceivable way except for the owner. Gibson had genuinely liked the young man who had delivered them to North Africa.

He tried hard not to notice the bottle of wine or the glass in Jenn's hand. Hendricks saw it too, but neither said a word. None of the words were theirs to say. If Jenn was off the wagon, it was up to her whether it would be a fall or a gentle step. All they could do was wait, watch, and be there when she needed their help. It made his heart hurt for her, but given the stress they'd been under, Gibson wasn't that surprised. Sometimes falling back on bad habits and comforting addictions was the only way to confront surviving a thing like this.

Jenn splashed a sip of wine into an empty glass and pushed it across the table to Ciara. Ciara took the glass solemnly. The girl had grown up a lot in the last few days. Either that, or she was still too shell-shocked to be her usual caustic self.

"A toast," Jenn said.

Everyone lifted their glasses and waited expectantly for Jenn to go on, but she looked at a loss for words. Hendricks cleared his throat, and all eyes turned to him.

"Half a million, boys and girls. Think on that. Won't never know our names, but half a million lives go on because of what we did here. Children too. I was a cop for twenty years—"

"Twenty-two," Jenn and Gibson corrected in unison.

"Twenty-two," Hendricks amended. "I'm fifty-three years old now, and I can't tell you much for a fact, but I can tell you this—aren't too many days like this one. Aren't too many wins this pure. Where you can say you did some good and don't have to tarnish it with a 'but.' Where you can say, 'I changed the world,' and mean it. So, Ciara, Mahomet . . . take that with you tomorrow when you go home. It's a hard life, but you show this memory the respect it deserves, and it'll sustain you when the shit comes down again. Which it most certainly will. That I can tell you for a fact as well." He looked around the table.

"I'm proud to know all of you. I . . ." Hendricks paused and looked over to Gibson. "Hell, I'm just rambling now. Got anything to add?"

"No, I think you said it all," Gibson said and clapped Hendricks gratefully on the arm.

"All right, then, I guess that does it," Hendricks said. "Cheers."

"Cheers," they all answered in chorus, reaching into the center to touch glasses.